Copyright

All rights reserved

The characters and events portrayed in this book are fictitious. Any similarity to real persons, living or dead, is coincidental and not intended by the author.

Hayes Davenport and Georgiana Crawford are the intellectual property of Daria M. Loshlin and used with permission.

No part of this book may be reproduced, or stored in a retrieval system, or transmitted in any form or by any means, electronic, mechanical, photocopying, recording, or otherwise, without express written permission of the publisher or author.

Edited by: Dangerous Trinity Designs

Cover Art: Nola Marie/Daria Loshlin

Photographs: Adobe photo stock

Printed in the United States

CONTENTS

Bastian-The storm is on it's way — 7
Maddox-There's a distant call — 16
Quinn-Without you, I'll never be the same — 22
Quinn-Much yet to prove — 26
Quinn-A trail of tears — 36
Quinn-I must reveal I'm falling — 42
Maddox-Knowing none of this is real — 53
Quinn-Blindsided — 57
Quinn-Keep strong — 70
Quinn-Battered, worn, and so afraid — 77
Quinn-Don't forget we're here to stay — 89
Bastian-How many lies? — 97
Quinn-Never turn away — 104
Maddox-I don't wanna die — 116
Maddox-Only you can make it right — 125
Quinn-Cast away regrets — 136
Maddox-The fault is mine — 145
Maddox-To every fool with an opinion — 150
Quinn-We're here to stay — 159
Maddox-Left in the Silence — 170
Maddox-I'm selfish — 175
Quinn-One must decide — 193
Quinn-Stand up and fight — 199
Maddox-A cutting anguish — 209
Maddox-Let it go — 215
Quinn-Just look to the morning — 224
Maddox-What it is that's killing me — 234
Quinn-Like a song was sung — 240
Quinn-Just pay no mind at all — 249
Maddox-Light the spark within — 254
Maddox-Cast your sorrows in the wind — 264
Quinn-As we escape disorder 271

Maddox-Hope is not gone	279
Maddox-Touch the light	288
Quinn-Through the suffering	299
Quinn-How many lies	310
Maddox-Into the fire	320
Maddox-Breathe again	327
Quinn-We will make a brand new start	332
Maddox-This is our destiny	340

River City Series

Violent Life
A friends to lovers romance

Violent Night
A second chance, secret baby romance

Violent Truth
An enemies to lovers romance

Violent Victory
A sister's best friend romance

Sons of Sin

Goodbye is a Second Chance
A second chance romance

Bed of Nails
A friends to lovers romance

Shooting Star in the Rain
A best friend's little sister romance, single dad romance

Break Me Down

A second chance, secret baby romance

Shed My Skin

A soul mates/accidental pregnancy romance

AUTHOR'S NOTE

Maddox Masters has been a hell of a journey. He was a character that was never supposed to have a story. I should've known he'd flip the script. Of course, only Maddox would be the small side character that made every book I've written be the prologue to his story.

I've struggled with his story. At first, it was fear of writing someone so tragic. Then it was because he and I didn't see eye to eye on the storyline. (He won, by the way). But perhaps the biggest struggle, and the reason it has taken me so long to finish, is because I wasn't ready to let go. I wasn't ready to say the end on this character that has lived in my mind for years. The Maddox withdrawals are real.

But he deserves to be happy. I only hope I did him justice. And I hope all of you love him as much as I do.

XOXO,

Nola Marie

DEDICATION

To my Maddox. I hope someday you will see yourself as I do and overcome your demons. Until then, you always have me.

PLAYLIST

CLOSER TO YOU – ADAM LAMBER
ALIVE – ADELITAS WAY
ONE MORE I LOVE YOU – ALEX WARREN
WHAT IF I WAS NOTHING – ALL THAT REMAINS
GHOSTS OF DAYS GONE BY – ALTER BRIDGE
CROWS ON A WIRE – ALTER BRIDGE
MAKE IT RIGHT = ALTER BRIDGE
WONDERFUL LIFE = ALTER BRIDGE
I KNOW IT HURTS -ALTER BRIDGE
WONDERFUL LIFE – ALTER BRIDGE
I KNOW IT HURTS – ALTER BRIDGE
BREATHE AGAIN – ALTER BRIDGE
LIFE MUST GO ON – ALTER BRIDGE
COME TO LIFE = ALTER BRIDGE
BEFORE TOMORROW COMES – ALTER BRIDGE
CRY OF ACHILLES – ALTER BRIDGE
ALL ENDS WELL – ALTER BRIDGE
FIND THE REAL – ALTER BRIDGE
OPEN YOUR EYES – ALTER BRIDGE
IN LOVING MEMORY – ALTER BRIDGE
WOULDN'T YOU RATHER – ALTER BRIDGE
GODSPEED – ALTER BRIDGE
THE ENEMY – ANDREW BELLE
CALL ON ME – ANGELS FALL
DUST AND GOLD – ARROWS TO ATHENS
JUST TO SEE YOU SMILE – ART OF DYING

BEST I CAN – ART OF DYING

END OF ME – ASHES REMAIN

MOVING ON = ASKING ALEXANDRIA

KEEP HOLDING ON – AVRIL LAVIGNE

PLEASE DON'T GO – BARCELONA

WHEN THEY CALL MY NAME – BLACK VEIL BRIDES

FEAR – BLUE OCTOBER

THE FAMOUS FINAL SCENE – BOB SEGAR

TWO IS BETTER THAN ONE – BOYS LIKE GIRLS/TAYLOR SWIFT

ASHES OF EDEN – BREAKING BENJAMIN

ANGELS FALL – BREAKING BENJAMIN

YOU ARE THE REASON – CALUM SCOTT/LEONA LEWIS

EVERGONE – CHRISTIANA PERRI

RUNAWAY (FROM MYSELF) – CITIZEN SOLDIER

FLY – CORVYX

KINGS IN THE NORTH – LIVE

HEAVY IS THE CROWN – DAUGHTRY

HURRICANE – DAYSEEKER

IRIS – DIAMANTE, BREAKING BENJAMIN

HOLD ON TO THE MEMORIES – DISTURBED

A REASON TO FIGHT – DISTURBED

IT'S OVER WHEN IT'S OVER – FALLING IN REVERSE

LOST WITHIN – FIVEFOLD

I WILL FOLLOW YOU INTO THE DARK – FUTURE SUNSETS/JACLYN GLENN/DAVID MICHAEL

WE ARE – HOLLYWOOD UNDEAD

THE REASON – HOOBASTANK

SHADOW – ICON FOR HIRE

BONES – IMAGINE DRAGONS

LET ME BE SAD – I PREVAIL

SELFLESS – IT'S ALIVE

FOUND – JACOB BANKS

GIVE ME THE REASON – JAMES BAY

TRAIN WRECK – JAMES BAY

BROKEN – JONAH KAGEN

OPEN ARMS – JOURNEY

FAITHFULLY – JOURNEY

UNSTABLE – JUSTIN BIEBER, THE KID LAROI

LOVER OF MINE – LOUYAH

I'LL NEVER NOT LOVE YOU – MICHAEL BUBLE

WITHOUT YOU – MY DARKEST DAYS

ANGELS AND DEMONS – NATHAN WAGNER

DON'T FORGET ME – NATHAN WAGNER

SICK OF YOUR OPINIONS – NATHAN WAGNER

MOUTAIN TO MOVE – NICK MULVEY

FADE IN/FADE OUT – NOTHING MORE

MAYBE I'M AMAZED – PAUL MCCARTNEY

FRONTLINE – PILLAR

MY ESCAPE – RAVENSCODE

BREATHE INTO ME – RED

BURIED BENEATH – RED

NOT ALONE – RED

BLUE BAYOU – ROY ORBISON

GHOST OF YOU – SAD HEROES

YOU WILL BE FOUND – SAM SMITH/SUMMER WALKER

I NEED YOU – SAVING ABEL

HERE'S MY HEART – SAYWWECANFLY

BROKEN – SEETHER

WITH A LITTLE HELP FROM MY FRIENDS – SHINEDOWN

FIRE MEET GASOLINE – SIA

HERE WITH YOU – SICK PUPPIES

LIFE IS BEAUTFIUL – SIXX:A.M.

SKIN – SIXX:A.M.

MAYBE IT'S TIME – SIXX: A.M./COREY TAYLOR/JOE ELLIOT/BRANTLEY GILBERT/IVAN MOODY/AWOLNATION/SLASH/ TOMMY VEXT

ANCHOR – SKILLET

GOODBYE- SLIPKNOT

UNTIL I FOUND YOU – STEPHEN SANCHEZ

PRICE OF FAME – SUBMERSED

WORLD WAR ME – THEORY OF A DEADMAN

THE MOUTAIN – THREE DAYS GRACE

BREATHE – THROUGH THE FIRE

WITH YOU 'TIL THE END – TOMMEE PROFITT/SAM TINNESZ

MAY I – TRADING YESTERDAY

LEARNING TO SURVIVE – WE CAME AS ROMANS

FOREVER AND ALWAYS – WRITTEN BY WOLVES

LOVE SONG - YUNGBLUD

BASTIAN

the storm is on its way

We pull up to the house, and panic rushes into me at the sight of the ambulance lights. My heart thrashes in my chest, and my lungs seize with every inch we travel through the gated property, up the driveway that leads to the house directly behind Maddox's father's house. Bile rises in my throat as we watch EMTs running to get inside.

The entire ride here, I've suffered the glares and outbursts. I've tolerated the accusations thrown at me. In part because I know they're angry and worried and scared. The other reason is that I know I should've done more.

How did I not know? How is it possible that I missed this? I try to think if there were signs I missed. I knew he had problems with depression. Fuck knows; he had a right. The shit he's gone through was more than anyone should have to handle. The weight he carried, trying to be strong for everyone, to hide his demons, was insurmountable. I knew he'd tried to hurt himself in the past. Shouldn't I have seen this coming?

We jump out of the SUV, running to the house. Police sirens sound in the distance, no doubt coming this way, and I'm already dreading the media circus. They don't care about our feelings. They only want their story. Usually, I would circumvent them, but I don't have time.

When we step into the house, my knees nearly give out. Paper litters every surface of the large, dusty living room that was once the home of Maddox's grandparents. Furniture has been broken. Glass is shattered across the space. The walls look like they've had a hammer taken to them.

"Give us room to work," one of the paramedics says as he waves his arms to keep us away. Their orders don't mean shit to me.

I keep walking until I'm standing right over them—one of the few times in my life, the sight of blood curls my stomach.

"Twenty-nine-year-old male. Gunshot wound to the chest," the paramedic answers the questions of the cops who just entered the scene. My eyes jump to Chris standing in the far corner, trying not to be seen. His behavior seems off.

But it's a small gasp sounding behind me that has my attention. My eyes close, knowing exactly what I will find when I turn around.

Quinn stands there with tears in her eyes that make me weak because they remind me so much of my wife's. *She* reminds me of my wife. They're so similar yet so different.

She begins to sway on her feet. I start for her, but Ryder gets there first. "Hold on, sweetheart," he tells her as he wraps an arm around her. "Don't give up on him."

I grip the back of my neck as I watch them load him onto a gurney and rush out of the house. "I'm going with them," Ryder tells them.

"Me too," I hear Quinn reply.

"I'm sorry," the paramedic tells them. "We need the room to work. You'll have to follow us."

"No one is leaving until we ask a few questions," one of the officers commands. "And I'm going to need you to put that down." He nods to Dane and Hayes, who are standing there with confusion and pain in their eyes as they hold several sheets of paper.

I look over to the officer. He must be new because I don't recognize him. I turn my attention to his partner. "You don't have any questions to ask because nothing happened here, right?"

Officer Jackson swallows hard with a nod. "Yes, sir, Mr. Delrie. Nothing to report."

"But—" his partner starts.

"*Nothing* to report," he repeats with a warning. Better his than mine.

The man nods, clearly confused, but seems to get the message. "What do they say?" I ask as I nod to the sheets in their hands.

"Mostly nothing," Hayes says. "Just a bunch of gibberish. Except these."

I take the papers from him. My black heart bleeds at the words written on the papers, and I wonder how I missed the signs for the second time. I should've been more vigilant. Kept a closer watch on him. This is my fault.

"He was saying goodbye," Dane whispers as he holds the broken neck of an antique guitar in his hands. "I don't understand. I knew he dealt with some dark emotions, but why?"

"There's a lot you don't know," I tell him.

"And you do?" he challenges.

I expected this reaction from Ryder, not Dane. But as I look him over, I realize Ryder knows more than he's told them. Or, at the very least, he suspects.

"Not everything," I finally admit. "Or this wouldn't have happened."

"Then tell us what you do know."

It's Maddox's story to tell. It should be his decision to share it. But he lost that right. Now it's on me to fill in the blanks.

I toss Ryder the keys to my Suburban with a jerk of my head. "You guys take the truck and follow. I'll follow on my bike. I'll tell you what I know when we get there."

MADDOX

There's a distant call

Jasmine and wisteria wrap around the oversized pergola, providing fragrant shade from the sun. I look around, attempting to get my bearings. Trying to figure out where I am.

There's a familiarity to this place. Something I can't quite put my finger on. But it's not bringing feelings of comfort or peace.

My stomach tightens the more I realize…

This is not real. I don't know if it's a dream or if… If I'm hallucinating again. Something isn't right.

A hand lands on my shoulder. My entire body goes taut as a chill runs down my spine. I refuse to turn around. I recognize that hand before he utters the first word. "I'm proud of you, son." Five words I waited a lifetime to hear. Five words that meant more than anything he ever said to me. They will also haunt me forever because right now, they're a reminder of time cut short.

And more proof that this is all the machinations of my mind.

My eyes squeeze tightly, and I grip my hair, desperate to pull myself out of whatever this is. This perfectly orchestrated façade of peace and contentment. I try to remember what I was doing before this—whatever this is.

I can't remember. I can't remember anything beyond the phone call that sent me on my latest mental spiral.

I prepared for that phone call for weeks. Knew it was coming. Yet the moment my sister spoke the words, my mind shut down.

Maybe that's what this is. My mind has finally cracked. I'm locked away *from the world in the recesses of my mind. In the place that my subconscious has decided is safe.*

If that's the case, then even my mind doesn't know me. Because this unknown—this strange place of existence is making me itch. I don't want to be here.

I want to move. Go somewhere else, but my feet feel heavy. As if some invisible force weighs them down.

My heart races in my chest, pounding to the rhythm of my erratic breathing. Pain—so much pain rips through me as my mind begins to race.

"Fucking wonderful," I wheeze for no one to hear. "I'm having a goddamn panic attack in my head."

I bend at the waist, palms on my thighs, and focus on my breathing. I close my eyes, trying to shut out the chaos that threatens to form. Hoping I wake up from this nightmare soon because I've decided that's what this is. A nightmare.

A gentle breeze begins to blow, cooling my heated skin and filling my lungs with much-needed air. The fragrant aroma of the vines swirls around me, igniting a memory. A sweet sound fills the space around me, calming my mind and slowing my heart.

I search, looking for the source of the sound. For the raspy, melodic voice that calls to my soul. That speaks to my spirit.

As if summoned by my desperate need, an ethereal vision appears. Her golden curls, illuminated by the sun, flow around her like a halo. Those deep amber eyes, the color of the smoothest whiskey and enhanced by the sunshine-colored dress that falls gracefully down her lithe body, shine back at me with a warmth that I feel in my marrow.

My chest tightens as my heart begins to gallop. The breath her sweet symphony returned only moments ago has been stolen by the sight of an angel in the flesh. Nearly painful to behold, but if this is how I die, then it's worth it to simply stand in her presence.

She walks slowly toward me, her brilliant smile as bright as the most perfect diamond. Excitement and nervous anticipation dance in her expression, matching my own feverish elation. The urge to go to her—run to her—is strong, but my feet are still firmly cemented into the ground below me.

A growl of impatience and irritation tumbles from my chest the longer it takes her to reach me.

Her head falls back with a giddy laugh at my obvious enthusiasm. I toss a smirk her way that promises she will answer for her indiscretion. Her cheeks flush brightly. My threats mean little when she enjoys my form of punishment.

"Canary," the only word I whisper when I pull her to me.

Another sweet giggle escapes her as she throws her arms around me.

I lose myself in the endlessness of her burnished pools. Get lost in the emotions radiating from her.

"I love you, Maddox," she tells me. And I believe it without question.

Threading my fingers through her thick mass of craziness, I tug her head back slightly. I open my mouth, ready to declare my feelings for her—to let her know I love her more than anything—when shadows fall over us.

My brows tug low as I look around us. The sky has grown dark, and ominous shades of green and gray fill it, replacing the clear blue. Wind picks up speed and force, roaring all around us.

Fear settles deep in my gut, turning violently as I look into the face of the reason my heart beats. Her dazzling smile does little to ease the tension, and when lightning strikes the ground with a deafening crash, my arms tighten around her.

"We need to go," I tell her, willing my feet to move. The need to get her to safety—to protect her is consuming.

Her tiny hand cups my jaw, and those beautiful eyes smile back at me. "I love you, Maddox," she says again as if I never said a word. As if death and destruction don't swirl around us.

I grip her tightly, staring down at her with an angry, frustrated glare. "We need to get out of here," I demand. "It's not safe."

"I will always love you," she tells me.

Dread pools and anxiety grows. I hear her words. I can see the truth in her eyes. But this doesn't feel right.

The storm builds. Thunder roars, and lightning strikes like fire in the sky. The wind blows at gale-force speeds.

The sweet scent of the woody vines covering the pergola has been replaced with the promise of death and destruction. The wooden structure of the pergola has begun to crumble. Purple and yellow blossoms fly around us as they are ripped from their stems.

Everything is wrong.

"Until my last breath. Until my heart stops beating."

"Stop it," I demand. "We need to leave. Don't you see what's happening?"

She pushes up on her tiptoes, gently brushing her lips over mine. I want to shake her—or throw her over my shoulder. I don't understand why she doesn't see what's happening around us.

I also don't understand why I can't move. Why my feet won't cooperate.

A powerful gust rips through the air. Her feet fly out until she is floating in the air.

I grasp hold of her, trying desperately to keep her safe. To keep her with me.

"In this life and the next, my heart is always yours." She smiles brightly, and my anger boils over.

"Stop," I yell. "Just stop. You can tell me this later."

She begins to slip from my grasp. Terror washes over me at the thought of losing her. "Hang on to me," I order. "Don't let go."

She slides through my fingers some more, and my hammering heart drops. "Don't. Let. Go. Don't leave me," I yell.

Another forceful blast sweeps through, pulling her from my grip. I watch helplessly as my whiskey eyes is torn from me.

Despair takes me to my knees. My fingers twist in my hair. Pain and anguish grip me like a vice. It feels as if my heart has been ripped from my chest.

"Quinn!" I cry out, begging for whatever power to bring her back.

"Quinn!"

Thunder crashes and lightning strikes.

My eyes open as searing pain slices through my chest. Burning, squeezing agony courses through me as if tearing me in two.

I hear voices calling out around me, tossing out medical terms, confusing me further than I already am.

I look around, realizing I'm in an ambulance, but with no idea why. I glance at unfamiliar faces in search of one face. One pair of eyes. One golden halo of curls.

"Quinn," I gasp with a ragged breath

"Mr. Maddox, you're going to be okay, sir. We're doing everything we can to help you, but we need you to calm down, sir."

I thrash and jerk, needing desperately to get to her, but restraints hold me down. I swear and curse hysterically, demanding answers, but all they do is tell me to calm down.

I can't calm down. Don't they understand?

I can see the storm raging outside. Did they find her? Is she okay?

"2 cc's Ativan," I hear someone call out.

No. No, no, no.

I need to know she's okay. "I need to... Quinn." I plead with one woman.

Her eyes soften sympathetically. "We are going to help you, Mr. Masters."

I try to refuse them. To tell them no, but my mouth goes dry, and my tongue feels thick. I continue to struggle, but eventually, weightless oblivion settles over me, and darkness takes over.

QUINN

Without you, I'll never be the same

Tears stream down my cheeks in hot rivulets of heartbreak and terror. I keep my attention out the window of the moving vehicle, watching as the buildings and lights pass by in a liquid haze as flashing red and blue lights tint the world in a dizzying effect.

I cling to the door of the moving SUV, trying to make myself as small as possible—as invisible as possible, not wanting the attention of the men I'm surrounded by on me. Dread and loneliness settle deep. I am an outsider in this situation. They don't know me. Have no clue who I am except for the minuscule amount of information they got before they took off in search of Maddox.

Desperation and isolation settle deep—bone-deep, creating a physical ache. My heart feels like it's being ripped from my chest with every mile we go as we make our way to the hospital. Realizing that I have no one to call and no one to lean on is more agonizing.

It may seem selfish and self-centered for me to think this way right now, but I feel alone. Not because I'm an outsider surrounded by the friends and family of the man I love. But because the man I love isn't here with me.

I'm an intruder, listening to the conversations of virtual strangers as they place calls to their loved ones. Eavesdropping is not my intention, but it cannot be helped, so I further my attempts to be as unobtrusive as possible.

"There's nothing you can do right now. Just get here when you can," Dane tells someone through his Bluetooth earpiece. I watch his reflection through the window, noticing his white-knuckled grip on the steering wheel.

From behind me, the other two men speak softly into their phones.

"It's Mads, Sunshine." I hear Hayes say solemnly. "We're on our way to the hospital now. By what I saw, it doesn't bode well for him."

"I need you, Pixie," Ryder says roughly with a crack in his voice as he desperately tries to control his emotions. "No, no. I do need you, but you should stay there."

Their grief and concern fill the confines of the vehicle. With each passing breath, the space feels like it grows smaller. Each call to their loved ones shows how much Maddox means to them. He's their friend and their brother.

The irony is that a man who felt so incredibly lonely has many people concerned for him. So many people that love him. That love Maddox Masters. Not the public persona but the man.

It's obvious these people would fight for him to the last breath. I can only hope he's fighting too.

"Please be fighting, Maddox," I whisper to myself. "I need you. We need you." I subtly rub my stomach.

I press my hot face against the cool glass of the blacked-out SUV as more droplets escape down my face. I close my eyes to stop the onslaught of emotions, but they continue to spill over as his face fills my mind.

My beautifully broken man with so much pain behind those shimmering blue eyes, carrying the weight and burden of his past, unable to let go of his mistakes. It seemed like his heart broke a little more every day, but he never let his smile falter, always determined to heal the mangled spirits of those around him.

That's what he did for me. That smile healed the cracks in my heart, and with a breath, he stole it. Completely, wholly, irrevocably, my heart became his.

There is nothing he could say or do to make me run away from him, but he tried to break me. Tried to push me away with words fueled by fear, but beyond the angst, I could still see his love. Felt it as strongly as I feel my own for him. I could see his determination to protect me from himself because he never realized I didn't want or need protection from him.

I know him.

Or at least, I thought I did. I could see his pain and the demons he fought so hard to hide. Buried deep, afraid someone would notice. I could feel his torment like a tangible force strangling him. It's why I knew what he was doing when he said what he did.

And I wish I hadn't left him on the balcony to cry in my room. He didn't know I was only giving him space. Space that I thought he needed because he was hell-bent on pushing me away and believed he had succeeded.

And I'm the fool. I'm the fool that never saw what was right in front of me. This man I claim to see beyond what he shows to the world—the man I claimed to love was falling apart before my eyes, and I missed it.

I missed that the demons didn't just torment his heart but were also at war with his mind. I didn't recognize the signs that were in front of me. If I had looked a little deeper, a little harder...

No one knew. I try to remind myself of that. Not one of his friends or family realized his mental health was damaged more than the depression, even though I think we saw *something* else.

Maddox carried the burden alone. He heaved the weight of everyone on his overloaded shoulders while refusing to share any of the albatross tied around his neck.

His selflessness knows no end. His heart holds more love than I think it could bear. His worries were always for those around him. His concerns were that his affliction would hinder and harm his loved ones. With every conversation we had, that much was abundantly clear. He thought it was his job to shield everyone from himself.

But one thing I know for sure because he showed me even when he couldn't say it. He loves me.

He loves me with an all-consuming fire that threatens to scorch us both. That's why he couldn't say it. He was afraid saying it would throw gasoline on that fire.

And I love him so much that it hurts. I didn't know it was possible to feel this way about another person. To feel like my next breath is dependent on his. That the beat of my heart is solely for him. I don't understand how anyone could know Maddox Masters and not love him with everything they are. It seems impossible.

I was a moth to his flame destined to burn. Like Icarus to the sun, knowing that I would fall to the depths and drown. He was dangerous to behold but irresistible to deny.

"He will be okay, Ry," Dane says, looking through the review mirror.

Another sob escapes me. And another. I grip the cross around my neck, sending up prayers, begging God not to take him from me. Not when I've only just found him. Not when I've experienced a taste of life with him.

I'll never be the same without him.

And I don't want to be.

QUINN

Much yet to prove

My eyes flutter open when the vehicle begins to slow and we turn into the hospital entrance. I've never been a fan of hospitals or doctors, especially after the last few years I've had, but this one seems particularly ominous. Maybe it's the sense that Heaven and Hell are at war as lightning pierces the sky in a fiery rage and thunder vibrates the city. Rain falls in sheets around us as if God himself weeps at the raging battle.

The battle for his soul.

"The vultures have descended," Hayes remarks dryly as we drive by the front entrance.

"Bloody hell," Ryder hisses behind me. Without looking, I know his teeth are clenched. I can practically hear his molars grinding into dust.

The urge to vomit is nearly unbearable as I take in the horde of people. Dozens circling the door with flashing lights of cameras and phones. A few news vans are parked in the fire lanes. Even with the windows up and the motor running, I can hear the chattering and murmurings of the mob. Maddox's name filters through the vehicle.

I'm appalled at the lack of respect they seem to have. The uncaring nature of these people makes my spirit ache. They are callous and insensitive, to say the least. Their pictures and stories fuel them, driven by the almighty dollar. They want to fill their tabloid trash with the fall of an icon. The playboy-heir-turned-rockstar's fall from glory. Forget that he is a man, a fellow human being first.

My stomach turns, and my head spins. Maddox isn't a story. They have ayed such a massive part in his problems. He learned long ago to smile for the camera. Learned to wear the mask for the crowd. He's been performing his entire life. He's never felt safe letting anyone see into the depths of his soul.

They don't know the beautiful heart he has. Or the pain in his eyes. Pain he's only given to me in glimpses because of his need to protect me from his demons. They don't know the weight of the burden of guilt and responsibility he carries. Shame that doesn't belong to him and the responsibility to make sure everyone he cares for is safe and happy.

Cruel. That's what they are. Vultures, as Hayes said, swooping down to devour the damaged and the dead. Nothing more than scavengers. Bottom feeders.

We circle the parking lot before pulling into a dimly lit covered garage. The entrance to the hospital is still visible, but under cover of the storm, the slew of people won't be able to see anything. They should be safe from the masses for the moment.

We park next to another SUV with out-of-state plates and the decals of the rental company on the windows. On the other side of that vehicle, I recognize Tristan's Mercedes.

Everyone climbs out of the cars. I move slowly, letting them out ahead of me so I can stay out of their way. They gather between the two SUVs and discuss how they will get through the mob.

Feeling like an intruder and needing to get to Maddox, I turn around and walk toward the entrance. I'm petite and quiet. Very adept at making myself unseen, so it's not surprising when they don't notice.

When I turn the corner of the SUV, I bump into a tall, dark figure wearing a suit and expensive shoes. His large hands wrap around my elbows after I'm knocked off balance from our encounter.

Hazel eyes bore into mine, cold and emotionless yet intimidating all the same. A chill runs down my spine at his frosty demeanor. "Going somewhere?" His baritone timbre reverberates through me just as forcefully as his eyes.

I swallow hard as I stand toe-to-toe with Rory's imposing frame.

Sebastian and Rory made me nervous when I first arrived for very different reasons. Both are very intense men with glares that cause the most powerful men to shrink away, yet very different. Bastian always exudes strength and fear. The feeling of standing too close to a fire that would love nothing more than to melt flesh from bone. But a passion for protecting those he loves lies beyond power and intimidation.

Rory is his polar opposite. Controlled. Always. Almost as if he doesn't have emotions. That coolness he exudes feels like it might give you frostbite. The world could collapse around him, and he'd never crack or break. But I have also seen that frosty façade waver and thaw when his girlfriend and children walk into the room.

I meet his eyes, trying hard not to flinch from the harshness of his glare. "I was going inside," I say softly.

"I don't think so." My head snaps back. I am quiet and non-confrontational, but I won't let them keep me from Maddox.

I open my mouth to argue, but he cuts me off. "That kid has busted his ass trying to protect you from that trash." He jerks his head in the direction of the growing crowd, and I swear I see a flicker of annoyance in his eyes. "You are not undoing that by walking into the lion's den."

My brows pull down as I gnaw on my lip. I shake my head, unable to understand what he means. "Why would they care about me?"

His cool gaze searches my face. I can see him wondering about the seriousness of my question. "Sweetheart," his tone and icy façade thaw minutely, "the world knows exactly who you are. Maddox has had others, along with himself, pull every photo that appears on the web as quickly as possible. They may not stay up long, but it only takes a minute for everyone to see. Especially when you're with someone like him. If you were anywhere but River City, you wouldn't be able to walk down the street."

Gripping my elbow a bit tighter, he turns me back in the direction of the men. I absently follow as my mind runs rampant. More hot tears spill from my lashes as I mentally chastise myself for my naivete and foolishness. My lungs seize as the realization hits hard.

How I thought I could go out in public with Maddox Masters and go unnoticed is absurd. And in his hometown, no less. Of course, we were seen! Everyone knows him. They all want a piece of him.

"Did you lose something?" Rory asks them as we step into their circle.

Their eyes all snap to us. Heat races up my neck, heating my cheeks from their stares. My head drops, and I quickly swipe at the tears in an effort to conceal them.

"Shit," Ryder hisses. "I forgot about her." He turns his attention to me, offering an almost apologetic look.

"Why is *she* here?" a man with long hair pulled back into a low ponytail and tattoos traveling both arms scans me with distrust and disdain.

"She's Mads' girlfriend, Liam." Ryder roughly scrubs a hand over his face. "Or she was."

"The fuck!" Liam bellows out. "The stripper is his girlfriend? Has he—"

"Shut up, Liam!" Ryder orders. "None of that matters, right? Understand? I don't care about anything but getting in there to Maddox."

"I agree, but I don't think the chick he fucked in an alley has any part of that."

My already flushed face grows hotter. Nausea fills my belly, and bile rises in my throat. "Oh God," I breathe as humiliation floods me that they know. Not that they know, but *how* they know. Because the only way—

I spin on my heels, barely making a few steps before heaving onto the concrete. Nothing more than a bit of acid falls from my lips, but the heaving doesn't stop.

A pair of hands pull my hair back. "I get you're upset," Rory says in my ear, "but you will have to get a backbone and speak up if you want to be noticed because those guys will walk all over you if you don't."

I turn slightly, meeting his eyes as I clutch my rolling stomach. "What do you mean?"

He gestures to me. "This. Getting sick when they say something upsetting? You can't do that."

"Easier said than done. I am upset and scared I'm about to lose the man I love and the father to my child so forgive me for having a weak moment. And I didn't get sick because of what they said. I got sick because that meant some weirdo was standing in the shadows taking pictures of us."

"Ah. So you're not this little timid thing I always thought you were. I love Verity, but her personality was never going to work with Maddox or his friends," he smirks, then tilts his head as he examines me. "And you're pregnant? That's an interesting turn of events."

"I'm not timid. I'm quiet. There's a difference. And I don't like attention on me. I don't *want them* to notice me. I just want Maddox."

He jerks his head in their direction. "Then you *need* them to notice you. They are who you have to go through. Right now, they have tunnel vision. Maddox is the only thing they care about. You're the outsider to them, and they don't like outsiders. Something I understand. You must speak up because no one will do it for you. And if they do, you won't be taken seriously when they're not around. Assert yourself. Now."

I nod in understanding, following him back to the men standing around. I do my best to appear confident and self-assured, though, to be honest, my confidence has been shaky at best in recent years. At least until Maddox. And for him, I will do anything.

I fight the flush their harsh stares elicit as Rory begins talking again. "You the bodyguard?" He nods to the other man whose name I haven't heard. "Why the hell do you have only one?"

"I'm not here as the bodyguard," the man answers as he rolls his head, irritation whirling off him.

"We've never been surrounded by bodyguards. We're not starting now," Dane stands a little taller as his chin raises slightly.

"Seems like I read somewhere that John Lennon had a similar idea. You guys are musicians. I assume you know how well that turned out for him." I cringe at the insensitive statement.

The tension in the air is thick. Emotions are high with grief, panic, fear, and frustration. Ryder is practically growling when he steps up to Rory. "Why are you here?"

"To get you," he waves a finger between them, "in there. The bodyguard and Christian will take you through the employee entrance. I've already got someone waiting to get you in."

"Who fucking died and made you God?" Ryder spits, taking another step forward with his fist clenched so tightly at his side that his knuckles are white.

Rory doesn't move. His body language stays as calm as his icy, unimpressed expression. "Not God. Just king. This is *my* city. I don't need anyone to die for it to be so, but I can certainly arrange it."

I contain my gasp at his words because they don't feel as much like a threat as a promise. My eyes flicker over everyone, watching their reactions. There is no shock. No surprise. And certainly no cowering in alarm.

"Fuck you, Rory. We don't want or need your help." Ryder's face turns red and becomes contorted with anger. With his arms spread wide, he yells, "I asked Bastian to bring him here to help him and look where we're at." He seems to be barely hanging on.

I can relate. Those tangled, fragile threads are fraying by the second for both of us. When they finally break, the results will be the same. Devastation.

"Ryder." Dane puts a hand on his shoulder, attempting to calm him.

"No!" He flings Dane's hand off his body. "He doesn't give a fuck about Maddox." He waves his arms manically in Rory's direction. "He never gave a shit about him. He doesn't get to come here and issue orders like we're his little soldiers." He steps closer to Rory until they're nearly nose to nose. "I think," Ryder continues his rant, "you forget that they don't mean shit to us either. I'm no more afraid of getting my hands dirty than you are."

"Ryder," Hayes calls out with irritation. Moments ago, he was smirking, taking some sort of demented pleasure from the threats of violence. His mood seems to flip as quickly as a light switch. "Calm the fuck down, and accept the help."

"Ry, he's already got us a way inside without fighting the crowd. It would take me at least half an hour to track down the right people to get us in. He knows people here. We don't." This comes from a pleading Liam, who seems to be wary of the volatile man.

"What's it going to be, tough guy?" Rory asks as he shoves his hands into his pockets and rocks back on his heels. "You ready to accept my help, or do you need to keep measuring dicks? Mine is bigger by the way."

"If it gets us in faster, let him help," Dane says softly. Then even lower, but I hear it anyway, he adds, "You need to calm down, Ryder. We don't need any more problems right now."

Ryder's jaw flexes a couple of times, his fiery dark eyes still on Rory before he nods, turning away.

"Then, as I was saying: the bodyguard—"

"Henry," the man cuts Rory off. "I am former Sergeant Henry Weston. Not *the bodyguard*."

A smile that looks more threatening than friendly lifts Rory's lips. Suddenly, his icy automaton-like demeanor seems preferable. "You seem to be under the impression that I give a single fuck what your name is. As it's already been pointed out: I don't." He reaches behind him and beneath his suit jacket, retrieving a gun. I jump at the sound of his pulling the slide and engaging the bullet I know is waiting in the chamber for release. My eyes are wide as I take in the black metal he holds comfortably and efficiently. "But if I get interrupted one more goddamn time, I will shut all of you up. Permanently."

Ryder looks like he wants to challenge him again, but Hayes pulls him away before he can.

"*Henry* and Christian will drive you to the staff entrance."

"Uh, Rory," Tristan speaks up with a wince.

"Are you fucking kidding me?" He bites out as he spins around to face Tristan. "What?"

"Sorry. But I need to be the one to go with them. Delaney asked me to watch out for Quinn."

"Fine!" Rory grits through clenched teeth. "Christian and Drew will escort Liam to talk to the press. You'll give them whatever generic bullshit about respecting privacy, and then I'll make sure they leave."

It looks like everything is finally settled when Liam speaks up again. "Thanks for your help. Sorry for the disagreements. We're all worried about Maddox, but," his eyes shift to me full of contempt, "she's not going in there. It's my job to look after Maddox's interests. I'm not allowing his latest random fuck near him."

Tears sting my nose and eyes, but somehow, I manage to keep them contained. I want to argue, but I do understand their wariness. I keep reminding myself to empathize with them. They don't know me. They only have whatever they've seen in pictures or Maddox has told them, and I admit that knowing I work at a strip club wouldn't paint me in the best light for many. It's only natural to be suspicious.

Making them uncomfortable is the last thing I want, so I will keep my distance.

But I cannot and will not let them keep me from being as close to Maddox as possible.

I don't meet their eyes or acknowledge their words. I simply turn around with the intention of going through the front entrance. Even if I have to face the horde of—whatever they are because I refuse to call them journalists.

I barely take a step when my arm is gripped again. "Where do you think you're going?" Rory demands.

"They don't want me here," I tilt my head in the direction of the men, meeting Liam and Dane's suspecting eyes. They don't bat an eyelash at my statement. I suppose they wouldn't.

"You'd give up so easily?"

I tip my chin up and straighten my spine in a display of false confidence to the man wielding a gun only moments ago. "I will never give up on Maddox. I'll take my chances with the front entrance."

He gives me an approving nod but doesn't release my arm. "You're coming with us."

Liam begins to argue when the flash of a camera phone catches our attention. "Is it true Maddox Masters is dead?" the insensitive reporter calls out.

"Goddammit," Rory mutters as he begins to stalk toward the intruder. He speaks lowly as he yanks the phone from the man, tossing it to the ground and stomping on it.

More voices begin to draw near, and we turn to see a crowd heading for us.

"Get in the truck," Tristan demands. "I'll drive you to the morgue entrance since they're crowding the staff one."

Liam stands aside as Dane climbs in. I begin to back up, unwilling to argue with him when I can find a way in on my own when Ryder surprises me by grabbing my arm and shoving me in. "You come with us," he orders. Liam makes a noise in the back of his throat, garnering a hard glare from Ryder. "I said she comes with us." He climbs in beside me while Henry and Liam get into the car with Christian and Drew. "Drive," he barks, and Tristan pulls out, taking me closer to Maddox.

QUINN

A trail of tears

When we exit the morgue that played hell on my stomach, Rory is waiting for us inside, somehow dealing with the sleazy reporter and getting in without any trouble. The minute we're inside, the smell of disinfectant hits, my stomach turns violently in revolt after barely making it through the smell of death. At this point, I don't know if it's nerves and anxiety, the pregnancy, or the fact that I haven't been able to keep down more than saltines and a bit of soup for over a week.

As we pass the exam rooms, my knees grow weaker with each step until I'm forced to grab hold of something to steady myself.

"Are you all right, ma'am?" a nurse asks with a hand on my back as I bend at the waist. I know I won't throw up. There's nothing there. But the position is nearly involuntary.

I offer a weak nod. "I'm fine. Just a little dizzy."

Ryder and Rory, who are behind me, stop. Both scan me with their brows pinching. I can't tell if they're concerned or annoyed.

"She's pregnant," Ryder announces. My eyes squeeze, and my lips pull tight. He's only looking after me, but I don't want new getting out. "Maybe you should look her over."

I shake my head with determination, finding my fortitude through the ache in my chest. "That's not necessary. I just need to know Maddox is okay."

Ryder's brows fall further like he wants to argue, then finally nods, and he and Rory continue down the corridor, leaving me behind to get my equilibrium. I rejoin them when I finally feel like the floor isn't moving.

It doesn't take long to reach the private waiting room where Liam, Christian, and Drew have already arrived. I suppose Liam's announcement or whatever to the press didn't take long. I suppose I should've known since Rory met the rest of us at the rear.

As soon as I step into the room, Liam and Dane's eyes bore into me. I do my best not to let it bother me. But I have to admit, it's starting to.

Because I'm still feeling unsteady, I go to sit in one of the uncomfortable waiting room chairs. I choose a seat far enough to stay out of their way but close enough to hear what's being said. I already know I won't be told anything. Not without proper paperwork.

I listen as Ryder argues with them over the same issue. He's not family, so they don't want to share anything despite Ryder's insistence that he has legal authority. Ryder yells and shouts out threats ranging from legal action to bloodshed until another doctor approaches Rory. After they speak quietly for a moment, HIPPA laws become a thing of the past.

The doctor turns to Ryder and begins to speak. "As you know, Maddox was shot. There is no exit wound, so we must remove the bullet. To complicate matters, he went into cardiac arrest en route."

Tears well as I listen, terrified that I'm going to lose him.

"What the fuck?" Ryder asks. "Why the hell did he go into cardiac arrest?"

"He woke up and was highly agitated. It's standard procedure in cases like this to give them something to calm them down, but they didn't know he had several other drugs and alcohol in his system. The combination triggered the episode."

"Goddammit, Maddox," Ryder mutters as he drags his hand down his face.

"Under ideal circumstances, we would wait at least seventy-two hours before performing surgery, but he has bruising and swelling around his belly. I'm worried he's bleeding internally, so we need to get him in the OR now. The problem is he isn't awake to give us permission."

"Do it," Rory tells him. The doctor begins to argue, but Rory doesn't let him speak. "Bastian is on his way, and Ryder's paperwork should be here soon. Do what you have to and save him."

The information seems to send Ryder into a tailspin as he begins to pace the room like a caged animal. I understand his distress because I start to shake uncontrollably.

My mind spins, imagining the worst possible outcome. Lungs seizing, stomach flipping, heart racing. Panic consumes me. My eyes slam shut, and I grip the arm of the chair until I feel the plastic digging into my palms.

He's got to be okay. He's got to be okay.

I think the words over and over as my vision tunnels, the dark edges growing with each passing, strangled breath.

Isolation, desolation, desperation. The dark emotions take hold like the strangling hold of a vine. A sob escapes me as I gasp for air.

A sharp sting returns my oxygen and my vision. I rub my cheek absently as I stare into the green eyes of the only person I really know. And truthfully, I barely know Tristan. He's just the manager of the club where I danced.

"You okay now?" His eyes shine with a concern I don't expect.

I shake my head quickly because I'm not okay. I won't be okay until I know he is. "I love him." My voice sounds as choked as I feel.

"I know."

"No. You don't understand. It's more than that."

"Then tell me. Help me understand." He's trying to distract me, and I appreciate the gesture, but I could never explain to him how I feel about Maddox when there aren't words to describe it.

"You don't like him." It is a statement, not a question. On more than one occasion, I've noticed the looks he would give Maddox when he came to the club. "Why?"

He waves a hand as he stands. "It's not important."

"Please. If you want to distract me, then tell me."

"There's really nothing to tell." He shrugs his shoulders as he stares out the window. "I hurt the girl I love, and Masters was there to pick up the pieces."

I can't help but give a small smile because Maddox always tries to put the broken back together. "And you don't like him for that?"

He lets out a long sigh. "It's stupid. I realize that. I'm jealous. And she uses him or any other man to rub in my face as often as she can."

"Have you tried talking to her?"

He drops into the seat next to me with a chuckle. "I've tried a lot, but she won't have a conversation outside of work."

"How long ago was it?"

"Couple of years ago. I've tried so many times to talk to her that I'm exhausted, but whenever I see someone else's hands on her, I want to kill them. She's mine, and I don't like anyone touching what's mine. I'm being summoned. You gonna be okay?" He looks to Rory, who gestures for him.

"I could lie and say yes, but the truth is I won't be okay until I know he is," I tell him honestly.

"I get that. If this was…" he trails off, unwilling or unable to tell me the person's name, but I already know.

I've seen the way he glares daggers at anyone that touches Delaney. I've also seen the hurt in Delaney's eyes when she sees him flirting with another girl. It's an endless dance they're engaged in, and even though they may believe otherwise, they're not subtle.

"Go," I tell him. "Thanks for sitting with me."

He nods and walks off.

I lean back in the hard plastic chair with a heavy heart, avoiding the harsh stares being shot my way by the men huddled across the room. But I can still feel them burning me as if they were real flames on my skin.

My eyes are getting heavy. I'm exhausted. The night before last, I worked at the club and was up early the following day for work at the children's clinic.

Though our approaches differ, Maddox and I use music to help people. To heal people. While my parents and ex-husband never understood or approved of my career choice, Maddox thinks it's impressive. Music was my saving grace as a child, even though attempting to sing in front of people was one of my more humiliating moments.

I knew I would never be good enough to do what Maddox and his friends do, nor confident enough, but still, I wanted to share the gift. The way hearing a melody can soothe your soul, or a lyric can decimate your heart.

Maddox understood—understands—that. He knows the power of music. He loves what I do, though we disagreed once when he said what he did wasn't as important as what I did.

I won that argument when I told him how listening to Sons of Sin, hearing the beautiful way they played combined with his uniquely powerful voice and the meaningful lyrics helped me through some of my darkest days of depression and anxiety.

Music can save lives.

And if you listen closely enough, you might hear a cry for help.

We missed his cries.

Maddox lives his life striving for perfection. But Maddox strives for it because all he sees in himself is disappointment and failure. He believes he is the toxicity polluting the lives of everyone he loves. The one responsible for everything that goes wrong in their lives.

Guilt. He carries it everywhere. The weight has pulled him down so long that I wonder if he remembers how to breathe.

I stare out the window watching the storm outside. It has only gotten worse since we arrived. That ominous sense of Heaven and Hell at war has increased. Winds ravage the city as rain and hail beat down on every surface. I hope the worsening storm and the pressure in my chest aren't signs that Hell is winning.

Fight, Maddox. Please fight.

I lean my head back, thinking about Maddox and his music. His band. He loves it and them so much.

Sons of Sin. The world sees them as these dangerous, sexy rock gods. They think the name is suggestive of the way they live their lives. In a sense, they're right. But it's so much more than that.

I close my eyes and remember the night I asked Maddox about it.

QUINN

I must reveal I'm falling

We walked across the long pier, hand in hand, until we reached the end that stretched a few hundred feet into the water. We gazed as the setting sun's reflection shimmered across the water like something out of a fairytale. This was a fairytale for me. Maddox pulled me back against his chest and propped his chin on my head with a chuckle.

"What's so funny?" I attempted to turn to see his face, but he held me in place.

"Short girls are funny. They make great armrests. Good chin props, too, if you don't mind the ache in your knees from holding a squat."

"I'm not that short," I huffed, trying to elbow him in the ribs. It was a failed effort. And in his case, he wasn't wrong. At just a smidge over five foot four, he was nearly a foot taller than me.

"Nah, cher. You're just the right size. Especially on your knees."

I squirmed again to get free. He allowed it just enough to spin me around. When I went to swat his chest, he grabbed my hands, trapping them. With a mischievous smile and wicked waggle of his brows, he dropped his lips to mine, and I immediately forgot to be annoyed.

He wrapped my arms behind his head and deepened the kiss until I was melting into him. I would've been a puddle at his feet if he hadn't held me so tightly. The rest of the world faded away.

"You slay me, Canary." He pressed his lips to the top of my head with a heavy sigh.

I wish I could say it was a content sound, but I could feel his apprehension behind the sentiment knotting him. I pulled back and captured his sparkling gaze. Not that it was hard. His attention was always on me. I stared into those cerulean eyes, wanting so badly to tell him exactly how I felt but knowing he couldn't hear it yet.

"I don't want to slay you," I finally whispered. "I want to heal you. Like you've healed me."

"I know you do," he said, turning me back around and making my heart sink. It was his way of ending the conversation.

I couldn't push. I'd learned if I pushed, he'd walk away. Or start a fight.

I also couldn't dwell.

"It's so peaceful here." I changed the subject with a deep breath of the salty air, though the ache in my heart still squeezed.

"Usually, this place is packed with people fishing and crabbing off the edge. It's not this quiet most days. But it's always been one of my favorite places."

"I can understand why." I leaned into his chest, enjoying the feeling of his arms around me. Strong, protective, and unrelenting. Everything Maddox tried to be for everyone. I wished he would let me be that for him.

We stood there watching as the sun sank into the sea, casting a warm glow over the world. Over our little world. Because we spent most of our time in our own little bubble. But those were the moments I felt it most. Felt the love we shared like an electrical current flowing between us. Our hearts beat in unison. Our breathing mirrored the other. I inhaled, and he exhaled. Like our very existence was entwined in the other.

He propped his chin on my head again. As close to calm as he got, quietly singing one of his band's softer songs. I let the sound wash over me like the rain during a drought. His voice enveloped me in its soothing cadence and deep warmth. I felt every note in my bones.

"I could listen to you sing all day," I murmured.

"And I could listen to you all day," he hummed into my hair.

I smiled to myself. I was never able to sing in front of anyone. When I tried, nothing would come out of my mouth. But since that day I pushed through my vocal paralysis for him, he had me sing to him nearly every night. "And you don't have to share me with the world."

He mumbled something that sounded a little like "for now," but I stayed quiet, not wanting to confirm my suspicions and ruin the moment. Because I would never be able to sing for the world, and I didn't want to. That wasn't ever my dream. But more than once, he had expressed his desire for the *world to hear me.*

I turned around, wrapping my arms around him. "I don't mind sharing you with the world. It doesn't deserve to hear you, but it needs to."

His eyes grazed over me with... I'm not sure what it was; it was gone before I could decipher it. In its place was an unbelieving smirk. "You do know there are five of us, right? It's not just my words or music they hear. It's not even just my voice."

My cheeks heat with embarrassment. "I know it's not just you, but you... You're the only one I noticed."

"You're adorable when you're embarrassed," he teased with a laugh. "But I'm glad you never fawned over the other assholes. I don't want to kick their asses."

I twisted my fingers in the hem of his shirt as a light chuckle escaped me. "You'd never do that. You love them too much."

He tilted his head back and forth a second before he smiled. "I do love the jerks. They're my family. All of them. But I've put Dane on his ass a time or two. And Ryder and I... Well, we get a bit explosive on occasion. But for you? I'd kick all their asses."

I shook my head with a smile. A sad smile at what he said without saying. "I'd never let you do that."

He gripped my chin, tilting my head until I had no other place to look but him. So much said without a single word. He would burn the world down for me. Would do anything and everything to protect me.

He knew I'd do the same for him.

And that bothered him most.

The words were on the tip of my tongue. The ones he wouldn't say and couldn't hear. But they were there all the same.

I opened my mouth, ready to let them fall past my lips when an old fisherman patted him on the back. He recognized Maddox from when he came here with his family as a child.

Maddox shot me an apologetic look before he turned to the man. They chatted for several minutes. It gave me time to compose myself. To realize the consequences of saying those words at that moment.

We'd gotten close to those deep confessions on a few occasions. Confessions of falling. Promises that this between us was more. But they were always followed with vows of pain and heartbreak.

It wouldn't matter when I said them, the result would always be the same. He would lose his mind, believing the misguided voice in his head saying that he wasn't good for me.

But they would eventually come. It was impossible to feel and not declare just how much he meant to me. I wasn't going to last much longer. But that wasn't the time.

"Sorry about that." He grabbed my hand, leading me back up the pier.

"Don't be." I squeezed his hand reassuringly.

We strolled, taking our time and enjoying each other and the peacefulness around us. Like always, he seemed deep in thought. I had no idea where he always went, but I knew it was never good.

"So tell me, how did the band get its name?" I asked, hoping to distract him from whatever dark path his thoughts were on.

He casually shrugged his shoulders. "Same as any other, I guess. Just a bunch of guys, tossing out names until one stuck."

"Oh no, mister," I demanded with a hip bump. "I know you too well to believe it's just some arbitrary name."

When we reached the end of the pier, he pulled me to the small stretch of beach. "It really did start that way. We were all sitting in Dane's apartment, jamming away, when I mentioned Ryder and I got us our first gig at a club a friend of ours managed. We needed a name, so we started throwing out suggestions. Dane tossed the most, of course. Swear, sometimes it's like he never shuts up." He laughed as he sat on the ground, pulling me with him. He wrapped his arms around me, holding me close. He was always holding me close. Almost like he couldn't get close enough. "I remember wondering if he needed to get laid or had developed a fascination with monkeys."

His chest vibrated as he laughed, and I reveled in the beautiful sound while snuggling closer to him. It was seldom he genuinely laughed like this. Full of joy and just... peace. "Seriously, he threw out Love Monkey, Lust Monkey, Sex Monkey, Monkey Sex. It went on and on. Though, I didn't think it was too funny at the time. I just thought he was crazy."

"I bet you did," I giggled, enjoying this moment with him. "Well, obviously, you didn't go with any of his choices, so..."

I felt him smile against my hair, but I already regretted pushing him further because I could sense the moment of humor was over. He would play it off like it was nothing, but it was never nothing with Maddox.

"So, later that night, back at my place, Ryder and I were playing. We were always playing music back then. I sang a few bars of the song I'd been working on. Sins of the father passed on to the son. The sun would never shine on the one. In the darkness with the debt of his father, the son of sin will never matter to anyone."

My lungs seized, and my heart stopped beating, threatening to crumble, knowing that was exactly how he saw himself. I could hear the raw emotion in his voice. I knew he had demons, but in that moment, I realized they went far deeper than his addiction. I supposed it always did.

"When I finished, Ryder stopped playing and just stared at me. 'That's it,' he said. 'That's the name of the band.' The rest is history."

I spun around to face him, straddling his lap. My hands went to his chest, but he lifted them, placing them around his neck, then covered my mouth with his hand. "I know what you're going to say, but don't. That I'm not my father's mistakes or even mine. They don't define me. Or that I'm beautiful and whatever bullshit. I've heard it all before, cher."

When he dropped his hand, I pressed my lips to his for a second, pulling away when his fingers sunk into my hips. He groaned at the loss of contract, but I didn't want to lose my train of thought before I said what was on my mind. "I wasn't going to say any of that. It's all true, but it's not where I was going." His brow lifted with piqued interest. "I was going to say I get it. That feeling that not only are you being punished but also deserve it."

He gripped my face between his hands, his expression serious yet soft. "You deserve everything good, baby. You're not like me."

I placed my hands over his. "You don't know what I've done, Maddox, but it's not about comparing transgressions."

"There's no comparison, cher. I promise you that."

"Again, not the point," I laugh softly. "It's about what's in here." I tapped the side of my head. "I'm trying to believe and accept that I deserve to be happy. That I deserve you, but it's hard. So, yes, Maddox, I understand."

"The blind leading the blind," he murmured before slanting his mouth over mine.

It wasn't aggressive like usual. It was sweet and gentle but filled with so much passion and fire I was burning from the inside and out. Our tongues stroked seductively as his hands traveled under my shirt. Everywhere he touched scorched. It was like that every time. It never relented and never faded.

My fingers tangled in his hair, and my hips canted, feeling him grow against me. I moaned as his tongue plundered deeper, one hand gripping my breast as the other slid into the back of my shorts, gripping my butt.

"Tell me you want me, Canary," he demanded against my jaw as his lips and teeth trailed my jaw.

"I want you, Maddox. I need you. So much."

"Right fucking now, baby." He growled.

The sun had set. Darkness surrounded us. The Gulf lapping against the shore mimicked the sound of blood rushing in my ears.

Still, we weren't alone. There were still people not far from where we were. Families walking with their kids back to their cars, done for the evening. Fishermen carrying their gear back to their trucks, ready to go home with the day's catch. Teenagers lingered up the beach with bonfires and alcohol.

But I didn't care who heard us. Wasn't concerned with who might see us. I only knew I had this burning need that only he could slake.

On an inhale, he had my shirt and bra off. His tongue licked a path until his lips latched to my needy breast. He sucked and bit while his fingers pinched and pulled the other in painful exultation, leaving me begging for more.

My sex throbbed as urgency flamed. I ground myself against him, needing the delicious friction to provide some relief.

I arched my back until my hair swept the sandy ground in offering to him and his wickedly talented mouth. "More, Maddox," I pled breathlessly. "I need more."

He growled deep and low. He practically vibrated with his own desperate desires. "And I need to taste you." In a single swift movement, I was off his lap, my shorts tossed somewhere behind us, leaving me bare under the cloudless night sky. He grazed his nose through my slicked folds, something I would never get used to, inhaling deeply before removing his shirt and lying back on the ground. "Ride my face, cher. I need a fix, and you're the only thing that satisfies my cravings."

Heat rose within me. His mouth—his words—always confounded me. He could go from profound to absolutely filthy without missing a beat, and their desired effect was always immediate. Moisture ran down my thighs in anticipation as I began to lower myself over him.

I wasn't fast enough. I never was. He gripped my hips firmly, pulling me to satisfy his hunger. I didn't have a chance to think when his tongue plunged deeply. He devoured me like he was starving. Consumed my pleasure like he would never get another taste.

Insatiable. He often was just that.

The heat of his mouth mixed with the cool night air made my knees quiver. My breathing became more labored with each flick. My belly pulled taut as my release threatened to consume me with little more than a few swipes of his magical tongue.

I was embarrassingly close.

But he knew it too. He relished it. And often, he used it against me. Sometimes he would withhold them, tormenting me with the brink of pleasure before taking it away. Other times, making me come until I begged him to stop. He proved over and over, he alone was in charge of my pleasure, and no matter what his mood was, it was always my pleasure he sought.

He pressed a finger against my tight rear hole as his tongue continued to work me into a breathless frenzy. When that finger breached the tight entrance, I fell forward, my legs no longer able to hold me upright. The need to come was nearly unbearable. The aching, building pressure too much.

He added another finger, making me cry out from the painful invasion, but he was unceasing.

Tears streamed down my face as his fingers worked my ass, and his mouth ravaged my pussy. "Maddox, please," I pled, begging for relief.

Finally, he delivered mercy when he replaced his tongue with a finger, pressing just right as his lips wrapped around my clit. I screamed as my release rocked through me like lightning. Wave after wave of intense pleasure flooded me, and I flooded his mouth until I was limp and numb.

He pulled me from his mouth, sliding me over his pulsing erection but didn't immediately move. Instead, he wrapped his arms around me, brushing the remaining tears away before he took my mouth, feeding me my flavor.

I felt him twitch inside of me. His need shone on his face as he strained to maintain his control. But he still didn't move. "You okay?" he asked, brushing my sweat-soaked hair from my face.

My heart swelled. No matter how gentle or rough, he always showed his concern—his care.

I nodded, pressing my forehead against his. "It was... intense. It's always so intense."

"Mmm." His mouth moved across my shoulder, nipping across the sensitive flesh, and within seconds, I was burning again. I was as insatiable as he was.

But he still didn't move.

I needed him to move.

He nipped the tender skin where my neck and shoulder met, and I clenched around him, a physical demand for him to move, but he remained steadfast in whatever his mission was. A moan slipped my lips when he tweaked my nipple. Another involuntary pulse squeezed him, and he groaned. "You're killing me, Quinn."

Then it occurred to me what he was doing. He knew I was hypersensitive after such a long, hard orgasm. Too sensitive to come again so quickly. So he was waiting, not wanting his own release unless I was there with him.

I couldn't help but laugh, causing me to flutter around him again and his moans became growls. It wasn't often that it seemed Maddox was at my mercy, but it gave me a thrill when he was.

But I needed him as much as he needed me, so I put us both out of our misery and began to move over him.

Our mouths fused together as we rocked. I ran my hands over his hard, inked chest like it was the first time. Like I didn't have every divot and peak memorized. I knew the planes of his body better than I knew my own.

Hands caressed and explored. Tongues trailed fire, and mouths nipped, marking every inch.

He snaked an arm around me, taking control of my movements. He pulled me down as he thrust upward at a frantic pace. He knew what I wanted. It was always the same thing he needed.

An intense desire to be connected by our very souls. A need to merge ourselves into one, if only for a moment.

Each of those delicious barbells stroked my walls, and the bars at his tip pounded the deepest part of me as he increased his movement to the point that all I could do was hang on for the ride. His desperation seeped into me until I wasn't sure I could take anymore.

He pulled my legs around him, raised up on his knees, bouncing me on his length, plunging into my depths until I couldn't breathe. My fingers dug into his flesh as the waves crashing against the shore drowned out my cries. Completion washed over me just as the tide washed over the sand. He was the only man to take me to the highest peak and then dive with me over the edge.

It was a freefall we made together.

MADDOX

Knowing none of this is real

I kneel in the deluge, soaked utterly through as the storm continues around me. My chest heaves, and it hurts to breathe as I continue to stare where the tempest just swept her away. Tears mix with rain as I look up to the sky, to the God I've blamed, questioned, and cursed, begging him to bring her back.

"What are you doing, Maddox?"

Goosebumps skitter across my body. Chills run down my spine. If I had doubts this wasn't real, that voice just obliterated them.

"Maddox, look at me."

I shake my head. If I turn around, everything becomes true. If I turn around, it means I really have lost touch with reality.

But what if... What if it means...

"Am I dead?" I ask.

"No, my beautiful boy." My eyes snap shut, hearing her call me that. With great trepidation, I stand, turn around, and open my eyes.

Her warm smile brings fresh droplets to my eyes. I've missed her so fucking much.

I throw myself into her arms like I did when I was a boy and sob. "Momma." It's nothing more than a cracked whisper as I bury myself in her arms.

"Shh," she says, running her hand over my head. "I'm here, Madsy."

"No, you're not." I pull back as the river flows down my cheeks. "You died. You left me."

"I never left, Maddox. I've always been right here." She pats my chest over my heart. "I will always be right here."

"I'm tired, Momma. I'm tired of hurting all the time. Of always letting everyone down."

She pulls me into her body with a whimper. I look into her pale, translucent eyes, finding them glassy with emotion. "My sweet boy, you've carried so much for so long. I know it hurts, baby. That's life. We're not perfect. You were always going to mess up, and you will do so again. It's part of life and living. It's part of loving."

I shake my head. She doesn't understand. "I let everyone down, Momma. I can't do anything without fucking up. Everything hurts. And I always feel so alone. No matter how many people I have in my life, I feel alone. No matter how much I love and am loved, I'm never happy. And the pain never eases. I'm just tired. Tired of fighting. Tired of trying."

She pulls me away, and I realize for the first time that I'm not looking up. Her hair, eyes—everything is just like they always were. Age has not affected her, but I have changed. I'm not the little boy who clung to her any longer.

"I know it hurts, baby, but you can't give up. I didn't raise you to be a quitter."

I step back from her with a shudder of rage. My heart pounds as anger and resentment flood my veins. "You didn't raise me," I yell. "You left me. You left me all alone. No one raised me. I raised my fucking self. What does it matter anyway? This isn't even real. You're not here. I've just finally lost my goddamn mind!"

"Madsy," she whispers, "I didn't want to leave you. I didn't want to die. But I've always been with you. I've watched and guided you best I could. And just because this," she waves her arms around us, and I notice we're no longer outside in the storm. We are standing beside the piano she bought for me so long ago, "isn't real, doesn't make it untrue. You have people that love you. You have a girl that loves you."

"Quinn," I whisper.

"She loves you, Maddox. For everything you are and everything you're not. Are you going to put her through losing you?"

"I already lost her," I shake my head, remembering the gale that snatched her from my arms. But it's more than that. Something else teases the edges of my mind. Something I did.

"You haven't lost her, baby. Use your heart. Can't you feel her? She is right here, waiting on you to come back to her."

"What is this, Momma? Where are we? Where am I?"

"You know the answer to that. Now you need to decide. Are you going to give up or go back to her? To everyone that cares so deeply for you."

I lean against the piano with a heavy sigh. I've fought my entire life. Every damn breath I've taken has been a struggle. I'm so damn tired of fighting.

But her face appears. Those whiskey eyes that see into my soul. That sultry voice that delves into the darkest part of my heart.

"I don't know how to fight anymore," I admit. "I'm out of fight."

"You're fighting right now, Maddox. You're fighting to let go, but you've got a beautiful girl and a little boy that need you. It's not time for you to go. It's time for you to love."

The sounds of machines and beeping fill my ears, and blinding light pierces my eyes. I try to speak, but nothing comes out.

Hand flailing, I find the tube in my mouth. It's stopping me from speaking. I need to ask them—I need them to tell me where Quinn is.

"I need help in here," someone shouts.

I swat at their hands, fighting against them. I need to find her. I need Quinn.

Hands press down on me as I continue to struggle against them.

"More help, please," someone else calls.

"Calm down, Mr. Masters," a woman with green eyes tells me. "I need you to relax."

They don't understand. No one understands. I can't relax until I see her. Until I tell her.

Someone grabs my hand. My eyes go wide with panic as they bring the syringe to the IV. I try to argue and beg, but they don't understand me. Warmth floods my veins. It's a sensation I'm well acquainted with, but this isn't what I want. They've taken the choice from me as the drowsiness takes over.

My eyes grow heavy once more, and everything goes black.

QUINN

Blindsided

"Wake up." A deep voice booms, shaking me from the memory-turned-dream.

My eyes flutter open, focus on the man in front of me with his hard eyes and scowl, and reality comes crashing back.

"Maddox," I gasp, jumping to my feet.

"Is stable," Liam barks as he steps away from me. "He's out of surgery and in recovery, which means you can go now."

My mouth falls open, and my brows shoot to my forehead. "I can't leave. I'm *not* leaving him."

He looks at me like I'm the poison apple sent to destroy their lives. Never have I met a more suspicious or untrusting man, including Bastian. He crosses his arms over his chest as his jaw works in irritation. "You are not staying," he tells me before he grabs my arm, tugging me down the corridor.

I try to jerk away from him, but his grip is too firm. He's too strong.

My eyes dart around frantically, looking for Ryder or Rory but only finding Dane. For a moment, his expression gives away his shame but quickly hardens as he raises his chin.

Henry walks in, his eyes wide as he witnesses Liam dragging me away. "What's going on?" he asks Dane.

"Stay out of it," Dane tells him, dropping his eyes to the floor.

I stop struggling, hoping it gives Liam a false sense of confidence to loosen his grip. When it works, I pull free and begin shouting as hot tears fall down my cheeks. "I won't leave him."

He doesn't blink. There is no sympathy in his expression at all. "Save your crocodile tears, sweetheart. I'm immune."

He begins pulling me again, this time with a bruising grip. "That's not immunity," I cry. "That heartlessness. Why would you do this to your friend?"

"I'm doing this *for* my friend."

"He *needs* me."

He laughs a deeply bitter sound. "I know women like you. You look at Maddox and see money, power, and celebrity. When things get hard, you move on to the next big thing. The *last* thing Maddox needs is you."

His words hurt me, but what hurts more is wondering what has caused them. What happened to this large, imposing man to cause so much pain? And I can't stop the words from tumbling out. "Who hurt you?" The automatic doors slide open, and he shoves me out. His face is distorted with anger and outrage as he turns his back to go back to the waiting room. "You don't even know me," I yell. "I love him."

He stops walking. He rolls his shoulder and neck, trying to calm himself. He turns around, stalks back toward me, stopping just inside the doors. "Yeah? I bet you fed that line to your husband before you set your sights on Maddox." I gape, unable to believe he would say something so cruel. "Like I said, until something better comes along. But for argument's sake, say you do love him. If that's true, then let him go. He's got enough problems, and I won't watch you inevitably destroy him."

He turns once again, leaving me standing there in cold shock.

He's checked into me?

His knowledge of Scott makes that obvious, but he didn't dig deeply because he couldn't be more wrong. He has no idea what he's talking about.

I run back through the double doors, knowing it's pointless. But I have to try.

Security blocks my path, informing me I am not allowed back inside, then escort me back out of the building.

Unable and unwilling to leave, I slide down the brick exterior wall next to the doors. I pull my knees to my chest, cover them with my hoodie—Maddox's hoodie and bury my face. My chest squeezes, and my head pounds with each tear that falls.

I never meant to fall in love with Maddox. I didn't want my heart to get crushed again, but with each second he's in there fighting for his life and I'm out here, another piece crumbles.

Perhaps I'm naïve. I saw his demons that very first day. I might not have realized their extent, but they are apparent to anyone who looks at him.

But I didn't care about his demons. I fell for his soul; if the monsters come with it, I would love them too.

Just like he loved mine.

Liam's words about running when things get hard make me laugh. How much harder does it get than this? To be sitting outside, desperate to get to the man you love—a man fighting for his life in so many ways—with everyone he cares about fighting against you.

He's an addict. He's depressed. Others would run for so many reasons, but I'm right here. Doesn't that prove that I'm in this for the long haul?

Lightning flashes in the distance. The storm has finally calmed and moved on, but the rumbling of thunder and the strange clouds that linger offer a foreboding sense that the storm may have passed, but it is far from over.

The wind blows the rain under the covered canopy, chilling me to the bone. I should be in there with Maddox. Not out here, crying into my sleeves. I don't even know his prognosis.

With a shaky breath, I dry my tears on the wet sleeves of the hoodie. I need to get back in there. Even after all these months, I really don't know anyone. My first few months were spent trying to find myself. The next few were utterly absorbed in Maddox. I definitely don't have connections. Not really.

Except one.

I reach into my pocket, grab my phone, and press the number of the one person I know can help me. Verity may not be able to do anything herself, but she can call Bastian.

I'm such an idiot for not having his number myself.

I don't get her name tapped into my phone when I hear my name. Or at least his nickname for me.

"What are you doing out here, *riccia*?" I look up to see Bastian a few feet from me with another girl around my age.

When I first arrived, I stayed to myself, and he was definitely suspicious of me. Not to mention, Sebastian Delrie is not the type of man that concerns himself with getting to know someone. But somehow, despite all that, he's become my older brother.

So when I meet those strange heterochromia eyes, the dam bursts wide open as I launch myself into his arms. Not a care passes through me that the strange girl is witness to my vulnerability.

"Shh," he whispers as he runs his hand over my hair soothingly yet awkwardly because Bastian is not great at comforting anyone but Verity. "Why are you crying? And why aren't you inside?"

"*Figlio di puttana*, those assholes!" the girl answers. I turn my head to face her, meeting her vivid green eyes that flare with anger and outrage. She shakes her head with frustration, her long, dark hair brushing against her shoulders. "They made her leave, Bastian. If I find out that blue-eyed *diavolo* played a part in this, I will…"

"Slow your roll, *Striga*. I don't have time to clean up your mess today."

She scowls, her glare like daggers slicing through the space between us. "And after I came all this way to clean up this mess for you. Ouch."

"Don't kid yourself, sweetheart. You're here for the man you just referred to as the devil. Not me."

She doesn't respond to him or offer a reaction, but her body language says plenty as she strides through the doors as if she owns the place.

I look up to Bastian, not bothering to hide the plea in my eyes or voice. "I need in there, Bastian. I have to be with him. They told me he was out of surgery, and that was it."

"Why didn't you tell them?" he asks, his eyes hard and accusing.

I drop my head, wishing I had, but knowing it wouldn't have helped. "Because what proof do I have?"

He nods once, the jagged planes of his face etched in determined savagery. "I'll handle that."

He leads me back inside. The girl stands seething in front of security guards, gesturing around and yelling at them about gross incompetence. I almost feel sorry for the guards, who look absolutely mortified with hands raised in surrender. They look up from her to see Bastian and me approaching, and their faces turn ghostly.

"*L'uomo nero*," one of them whispers.

Bastian rolls his eyes with a growl. "These two are with me. I don't give a fuck who tells you otherwise. They come and go as they please. Understood?"

They stutter and stammer as we pass, visibly shaking in fright.

I look at Bastian curiously. "Why are they afraid of you?" I ask.

Bastian intimidated me when I first met him, but it was because he's so intense at times. Not necessarily broody, just assiduous. But these men are shaking in fear, not because of his fierce presence.

"Because they're smart," he grunts.

I pretend I don't know what he means. It's just better that way.

As we walk through the corridor, shouting echoes off the walls.

My nerves tic higher, worried the commotion means something is wrong with Maddox.

A hand grabs mine, and I turn to find a sweet, compassionate smile as she squeezes my hand. A vast contrast from the girl who looked like she would start tossing bodies only moments ago. "You must be Quinn. I apologize for not introducing myself when I first arrived. I'm Georgiana. You can call me Georgie."

I nod, and she laughs, probably at the confusion on my face. "Maddox enlisted my help to keep you anonymous in the press. I like to know who I'm working with, so I dug a bit deeper."

I feel like I should be bothered by her admission, but my attention is on the shouting coming from the waiting room that gets louder and louder as we get closer.

When we round the corner, it's much more than yelling. Ryder has someone pinned against the wall by his throat, his fist connecting with the person's face. The other men run to them, Hayes and Henry grab Ryder while Dane and Liam put themselves between Ryder and... Chris?

Why is Ryder beating up Maddox's brother?

Chris wipes the blood from his mouth with a hiss. His eyes narrow at all of them. "I said I want them out!"

A woman dressed in a pencil skirt and blouse looks at everyone apologetically. "I'm sorry, Mr. Jamison, but until the medical POA comes in, we must follow the next of kin's directions."

"It's coming," Ryder shouts. "I just haven't been able to get my attorney on the phone yet."

"I'm so—" the woman starts again but gets cut off by Chris.

"I want them out! All of them, including his little whore."

I flinch at the remark, but I'm not surprised by it. I've only met Chris once, but it didn't go well when I rejected his advances.

"This is bullshit," Ryder bellows as he struggles against Hayes and Henry's grip.

"I want the police called as well. I am pressing charges against your ass for assault."

"No, you're not," Bastian states, drawing attention to us.

All eyes land on the three of us. Liam's eyes linger on me with irritation while Chris's narrow on Bastian.

"Exactly, how do you think you can stop me, Delrie?" he challenges arrogantly.

Bastian offers him a sinister smirk. "I'm sure I can think of something. Besides, you and I haven't finished our chat from earlier."

"Go to hell," Chris spits. "I want this man removed also."

Bastian's grin widens. He stands straighter as he begins to stalk toward Chris. "Yeah, no one is removing me. But you see, Christopher, you do not now nor will you ever dictate what I do or don't do. As for next of kin, I'm pretty sure I qualify more than you."

"Fuck you. No claim you have is legal." He continues to run his mouth, but the slight tic in his cheek doesn't go unnoticed. He's afraid of Bastian too. "You can't prove shit. I'm the one with the same last name and parents. I'm the only one with the legal right to be here."

Bastian's jaw flexes. He steps into Chris, the tattoos on his neck contract as he rolls his head to the side. He runs his hand down the lapels of Chris's jacket, appearing to smooth out wrinkles caused by Ryder, but there is nothing gentle or soothing about Bastian's demeanor.

Part of me wants to scream at everyone for fighting. This isn't the time for testosterone-fueled ego trips or displays of power. We're here for Maddox, and everyone can't stop trying to prove who's in charge.

But Chris is demanding our removal. He wants the people Maddox loves most—his true family—sent away. And for what reason? Why would he want to do that to his brother, who is fighting for his life?

So I stay silent, watching the events unfold.

"Not that I've ever concerned myself with legalities, but since we're at a hospital, my relationship can be verified easily enough."

Chris's face turns red. Like he's on the verge of a tantrum. "That wouldn't mean shit, and you know it."

Bastian grips Chris's lapels and pulls him away from the wall just enough to slam him back into it with a sickening thud. "Let me tell you; I've been more of that brother to that kid in the last decade than you've been his entire fucking life. You don't give a shit about him, so do us all a favor and stop pretending you do. But since you want to be about what's *legal*, then until Ryder's paperwork comes in, there is only one person here with any say."

Bastian's eyes meet mine, and my stomach drops. It is not the time for this announcement. It should be something to celebrate, but I know it will not be well received. I shake my head slightly, a silent plea to stop. "They're gonna find out, Quinn," he tells me. "May as well be now. Should've been before *that stronzo* had you removed." His head jerks toward Liam with a growl.

"It's not the time," I whisper through my teeth.

"You did what?" Ryder demands, glaring at Liam.

"He's out of surgery. They said it went well. Dane and I agreed that we'd make her leave once we informed her."

Ryder's head jerks to Dane, who looks slightly ashamed. "Seriously, Dane? What in the bloody hell were you thinking?"

"We don't know her, Ry," he argues but holds his hands in front of him. "We can't trust someone we don't know."

"*We* may not know her," Hayes interjects. "However, Maddox trusts her, and this isn't about you."

"What I know is that Maddox doesn't have good judgment right now." Liam stares them all down with arms folded across his chest. "It's my job to protect him."

A ripple in the air, practically a physical force, surges as Ryder jerks free of Hayes and Henry. He stalks across the room with lethal determination. "I don't give a bloody goddamn fuck what his emotional or mental state is. No one knows people—can read a person like Maddox. But even if he couldn't, he doesn't chase ass. He's been pining after Zoey for over a damn decade, so the fact he kept her around should tell you something."

My cheeks heat. I know it's true. Maddox told me himself, but it stings a bit, considering the last thing Maddox said to me was that he would never love me because it would always be Zoey.

I know he didn't mean it. He was desperate to push me away. Desperate to run as fast and far as possible after learning I was pregnant. Hurt and in pain over learning his father died.

But it didn't mean it didn't hurt.

"Even Maddox is vulnerable to manipulation," Liam deadpans. "He's not God. And given this new knowledge, I'd say his judgment has always been questionable. Explains how a guy can be obsessed with a girl he can't have for so long."

Ryder is in Liam's face. Dane tries to slip between them, but Ryder pushes him out of the way. "*You* are walking a very fucking thin line, Liam. I suggest you shut your mouth before I shut it for you. I'm giving you a pass because you don't know Maddox like we do. You only know what he's allowed you to see." Ryder spins around to face Dane. "But *you*? You know better. You know him almost as well as I do. What the fuck were you thinking?"

"I was thinking that we don't know anything about this girl except she told Maddox he's pregnant, and now we're here," Dane yells, throwing his hands in the air.

"She's what?" Liam booms. "Are you fucking kidding me? *That* doesn't send up red flags? She needs to—"

"Do *not* finish that statement," Ryder growls. "If you want your teeth and job, you will stop now."

"Whatever," Chris says smugly. "That still doesn't give her any say."

"*Cazzo idiota,*" Bastian shakes his head. He lets go of Chris—roughly—and steps back. "They're married, you dumbasses. Which means that asshole," he nods toward Liam, "had no right to have her removed, and neither do you."

Everyone's expressions all change from anger to pure shock. Not one of them expected Bastian to say that. And I definitely didn't expect to tell anyone like this. The silence in the room is deafening. You could almost swear no one is breathing.

"They got married a few weeks ago in a secret ceremony," Bastian continues as he turns to face Ryder. "And before you wonder why he didn't tell you—"

"We didn't tell anyone," I finish for him. "Only his Dad, sister, and Justice of the Peace knew. And, of course, me because I know everything."

"This is fucking fantastic," Dane grunts. "*That* doesn't tell you something is off? He fucking married her without telling anyone."

"What. The. Fuck?" a voice breathes.

I turn to see two dark-haired men behind me. I've never met them, but I'd recognize them anywhere. Angel Martin and Jake Allen from the band.

"It's not legal," Liam declares with a smug grin. "She's already married."

"My divorce was finalized the day we got married," I say softly, knowing it's only giving Liam more ammunition for his vendetta against me.

"Proves my point," he growls. "Fame, power, and money."

"Quinn doesn't need those, *stronzo*. She's my wife's cousin. She has access to everything she needs. And I suggest you watch what you say about my family before you lose the ability to speak."

Everyone arguing about me like I'm not standing here has become too much. My head pounds furiously from the constant tension and my worsening anxiety.

All I want is Maddox. I need to see him. Hold him. Know he's okay. I won't be able to calm down until I feel his hand in mine. Until I feel the beat of his heart.

But these people are more worried about tossing their weight around. It's a power play to show who's in charge.

Ryder has said multiple times that he is Maddox's POA but hasn't been able to get his attorney to answer the phone. I don't doubt him. Knowing what I do about Maddox and his relationship, there isn't a doubt he has that authority.

While whatever pull Rory and Bastian seem to have may have gotten Maddox into surgery, hospital administration doesn't seem cooperative now.

The cat's out of the bag about me. I didn't have proof to validate my claim. My license hasn't been changed yet, and it's not like I carry a marriage license. But with Bastian here and Callie—the only other person who knew—on her way, I don't need it now.

Bastian is right. I'm the only one with say. But I'm not in the proper emotional or mental place to make decisions.

But still, I know what Maddox would want.

I run my hands over my face in exhaustion as they continue to clamor and fight. My fingers tangle in my hair; roots gripped in frustration until it all bubbles to the surface. There is nowhere else it can go but out.

"Stop it!" I yell, fingers still tangled in my hair. "Stop talking about me like I'm not standing right here. Stop arguing over all this stupid shit! Maddox has been fighting for his life—at least, I hope he's fighting—but all any of you can do is argue and throw around your damn weight. Just stop!" I drop my face into my hands as more tears fall. "I just want Maddox," I cry softly.

I'm pulled into a firm embrace. My fingers seek refuge in the soft fabric of his shirt. I look up, expecting to see Bastian, shocked when it's Ryder's hazel eyes I stare into.

"He'll be okay," he tells me. "If I have to go to hell and drag his ass back, he'll be okay."

I nod against his chest, praying with everything in me that he's right.

"Are you all right, darlin'?" a deep, beautiful timbre asks, warming me all over.

I turn from Ryder, looking into ocean blue eyes swimming with concern.

"Maddox?" I whisper even as I know my mind is playing tricks on me.

"No, *tesoro*, I'm Hayes, remember?"

I blink, then blink again to clear the fog from my eyes and head. I nod at him weakly. "Right. Hayes. I'm sorry."

My wobbly legs lose their strength, and my knees give out while I mentally prepare to kiss the floor.

"Whoa there, love," Ryder says as his arms wrap around my waist.

"Quinn, when's the last time you've eaten?" Georgie asks, rubbing my arm gently.

"It's been a bit," I admit.

"Why don't we head to the cafeteria? Maybe they'll have something," she suggests.

My throbbing head suggests that would be a good idea, but my stomach turns, the thought of food revolting.

My face must reveal my thoughts because an understanding smile pulls her lips. "Why don't you have a seat, Hayes and I will go and bring you something."

I give a weak nod of thanks and watch as they vanish down the corridor.

QUINN

Keep strong

I pull my knees to my chest and tug the hoodie over them, my favorite position when I'm stressed, hoping his scent will ease my hurting heart. I press my forehead to them, breathing deeply. Sadness rolls over me because his soothing smell has been replaced by the rain from earlier.

My eyes burn, and more tears want to fall, but there are none left. I've cried so many; they feel like sandpaper. Even my lips are cracked, and my nose is chapped.

With my cheek to my knees, I look around the room. All the guys are standing across the room, huddled together. If I had to guess, they're talking about me. It can't be a far stretch since all their eyes dart to me frequently. Dane and Liam's stares are always distrustful. Jake and Angel stare at me with amazement. They have all taken turns staring at me, but they don't look at me like I'm the devil. More like I'm an alien—a phenomenon they didn't know existed. Ryder and Bastian look at me like I might crumble at any moment.

I won't. I may cry. My heart might be breaking, but I won't. As long as Maddox is breathing, I won't give up.

I shut my eyes and imagine myself with him. I'm lying in bed, my back to his chest, his arms around me as we talk about life, read together, or listen to music. Or we sing to each other. Those moments were always peaceful.

"I'm sorry about Liam and Dane." Ryder's rough voice draws me from my thoughts.

"It's not your fault," I tell him, glancing up to see him standing over me with hands in his pockets. "And I do understand, I guess. They care about him, and it's because of all the reasons you said that they're worried. Maddox doesn't have girlfriends, much less marry one."

"Don't make excuses for them. I'm an asshole by nature, but they know better than to question Maddox. You might not believe this, but if he could see it, my reaction would be gentle by comparison."

"They're not excuses. It's just complicated. Everyone is on edge, making it difficult to think clearly."

He chuckles with a shake of his head as he takes a seat next to me. "You should know, the doctors removed the bullet. He did have internal bleeding from some nicked arteries that they were able to repair. He had some moderate blood loss. Bastian and Hayes have his blood type, but Maddox is AB negative, so he can take from all of us. We're all donating in case it's needed later. Henry got a phone call from home and had to leave, so he went ahead of us."

I sit up straight, absorbing every word like a sponge. "I'll donate too," I tell him firmly.

"Sorry, love, but you can't." He looks at me sympathetically, already seeing the objection in my eyes. "You can't give blood when you're pregnant."

My head falls back. For a split second, I forgot. "I just found out yesterday morning," I admit. "It's been a very long thirty-six hours."

"Maddox didn't react as you hoped, did he? When you told him?" The look on his face is a mixture of agitation and anger.

I shake my head and look away, so he doesn't see how the words still affect me. In my heart, I know Maddox didn't mean them, but it doesn't remove the sting. "He said things. Things I know he didn't mean—"

"I know what he said, love," he grits out. "You're right that he didn't mean them, but the problem is that Maddox *believes* he did, and I want to kick his ass for it. What I want to know is *how* it happened. He's always been so bloody terrified of having a kid that he *always* wraps up. No matter how high or drunk, he doesn't forget that."

Heat spread until even my hair feels hot. It's strange that after all these weeks with Maddox—the things he's done, places he's taken me—I'm still embarrassed when called out on it.

You wouldn't think so, given I take my clothes off for a room full of people, but that's different. I pretend there is no one else in the room and get lost in the music. Or I did before Maddox.

After Maddox? Well, he became the only man in the room. The only one I could see. And he made sure he was there every night after the first one. Even when I couldn't *see* him, I knew he was there. Could feel his eyes watching my every move. Could sense his presence as surely as I felt my own heartbeat.

"He never forgets," I admit to Ryder, "but one did break. We didn't stress because the likelihood of getting pregnant was nearly impossible. Carrying to term isn't great, either. I shouldn't have told any of you." I drop my head for a brief moment. "Maybe I shouldn't have told him."

A low growl erupts from his chest as he leans forward, resting his elbows on his knees. He exhales a frustrated yet exhausted breath as he stares at his folded hands. "Keeping it a secret is never the answer," he growls, then turns his attention to me. "Look, there are only two people in the world who mean more to me than Maddox. We've been through a lot of shit together. No one knows me better than him, and no one knows him better."

I take his hand in mine, albeit tentatively. He's hurting for his best friend, and I'm hurting for the man I love. I want him to know I understand.

"Maddox told me how close you two are," I whisper. "He loves you too."

He chuckles, but there's no humor in it. "Are you going to do what he said?"

I shake my head emphatically. "Absolutely not. I lost a baby once before, but even if I hadn't—even if this weren't a miracle, I still wouldn't because it's a part of him."

His eyes sweep over me, his dark eyes assessing. "Even if it means you lose him?"

"It won't," I tell him firmly. "Maddox didn't mean it."

"Don't be naïve, Quinn. He meant it. Or he thought he did, but he would never survive it if you went through with it either. I know he cares… No, I know he loves you. You wouldn't be here if I didn't believe that, no matter what Sebastian said. But you need to understand that loving Maddox isn't easy. I know this because loving me isn't easy either."

"Love isn't supposed to be easy," I tell him.

He grins a knowing smile at me. "No. It's not, is it? Everyone here thinks it's their job to protect him, but the only person Maddox has ever needed protection from was himself. Unfortunately, I've never been able to do that. We enable the fuck out of each other."

"I'm sure that's not true."

"Oh, love, it's true. Trust me."

"Is that why you two aren't —weren't… you know? Together?"

"Nope," he shakes his head. "We love each other, but we've never been in love. My heart has belonged to one girl for a long ass time, and his belonged to Zoey."

I try not to let his words affect me. I know what he means. Maddox does love Zoey. She owns a piece of him, just like Ryder does. But I'm not sure I'm successful in masking my insecurity.

"She never held his heart like that, Quinn. Yeah, he thought she did, but I knew. I think somewhere deep down, he knew too. But it was easier to use her as his excuse to avoid looking elsewhere." He shakes his head and slides out of his chair, squatting in front of me. His eyes grow stern. "Look, my point is that Maddox is our priority. All of us. That means no one is watching out for you. Means you have to look out for yourself." He shoves a stack of torn notebook pages into my hand. "You need to read this. See how Maddox's mind works, then decide if you can really be there for him. I already know it's too late, but I'd rather him hurt now, believing he pushed you away than later after he's finally stopped fighting it. I won't hold hard feelings if you read those and decide you can't handle it. But don't drag it out."

"What makes you think he pushed me away?" my voice breaks with the words.

"Because he called me that night. Told me he fucked up. Said a bunch of things that didn't make sense, so I knew something was wrong. But one thing was clear. He thought he broke your heart and thought it was for the best. But it also broke him."

I sniffle and nod. "I'll read them," I assure him, "but it won't change anything."

"I hope not," he tells me as he stands. He looks toward the nurse that calls them to give blood. He opens his mouth to say something else but seems to decide against it. Instead, he nods again and follows the others through the double doors, leaving me alone.

I stare at the folded papers. My hands start shaking, almost afraid of what I will find in them. Ryder's warning rings in my ears and tumbles in my mind. Will what's in these pages change how I feel? Do I really need to know what's in these letters to know how I feel?

The answer is as simple and easy as breathing.

Yes.

I need to know everything about him. Even those dark places he wants to keep hidden from everyone.

But nothing could change how I feel.

My feet tucked under me, I get comfortable as possible in the hard waiting room chair. As I unfold the pages, I take a deep breath and lose it with the first words.

His beautiful scrawl, which I notice is the same as the band's logo, fills the pages. Line after line of trauma and agony eviscerate my heart. My body shakes as I read of the abuse and manipulation he endured. Tears I thought were dried up fall for the son that felt lied to and abandoned. For the young man that sought vengeance from his tormenters. A friend that did everything to protect those he loved at the expense of himself. And for the man that carries the guilt of his sins on his overburdened shoulders.

The words begin to run from my fallen tears. As if the pages themselves weep in pain and bleed from the deep wounds caused.

When I get to the final page, my hand flies to my mouth, covering my sob. My fingers shake as I trace the words written to *me*. The words he never said, but I knew. That I felt in my soul.

I never loved anyone the way I love you.

My heart bursts with pain, hating that he's been so hurt. That he's felt so lost. But it exults at his declaration and glows from his words.

"Don't let that change how you see him." I look up to see Ryder standing over me once again. His arms crossed, and his lips set in a thin line, worried that it's done just that. "Maddox is not his trauma."

"He's more than that," I whisper. "Despite every reason to be angry and hate everything, he's still the most beautiful soul I've ever known."

The worried lines on his face soften with relief. I passed his test because I knew that's what this was. Just like I know, the test is far from over. Ryder wants more than my words. He gave me those pages to see if I would run.

I'm not running. I will never run from Maddox.

He drags his hand down his face with a hard exhale. I grab his other hand and meet his eyes. "He has so much light, but you can't appreciate the light without the darkness. Maddox is everything he was always meant to be. Light and dark. Love and pain."

He gives a satisfied nod, then turns away without another word.

QUINN

Battered, worn, and so afraid

I stare at my reflection as I splash cold water on my face after another round of vomiting. Dark circles reveal my exhaustion, while red-rimmed, puffy eyes give away the hours I've cried. My hair is a wreck, wild, unmanageable, and like a family of squirrels have made it their home. It's been a couple of hours since Maddox came out of surgery, and the waiting to see him is starting to get to me. I was anxious and scared before, but now it's so much worse. My stomach will not unknot. My anxiety is causing me to shake, and I'm freezing to death.

The saddest part of all? The outside isn't nearly as awful as the inside. I'm a wreck.

With a deep breath, I make my way out of the restroom and back toward the waiting room. Chatter fills the space, making me want to scream. I just want everyone to shut up.

I see why when I turn the corner. I must've been in the bathroom longer than I thought because the waiting room is filled to capacity. Jax and Zoey stand with Bastian and Rory. I recognize Zane and Tori talking to Dane, his girlfriend, and Liam. Angel and his wife are talking to Jake and another girl that looks a lot like Tori. If I remember correctly, she is Tori and Dane's sister, and Jake's wife.

Across the room, I see Ryder with a petite girl. He still looks irritated and angry but a little less tense with his arms around her as they talk to Hayes and Georgie.

Again, I'm reminded that I'm the stranger among these people. Among this extraordinary but united family who are all here for one purpose. To support Maddox.

I find the only empty corner in the room, sit, and curl my feet under me. My head falls back, and my eyes close in exhaustion. Sleep teases me, but I know I won't be able to, not with all the chatter and my nerves on edge.

The presence of people hovering over me has me peeking through my closed lids. The girl that was with Ryder stands above me with Georgie. "Hi," she says with a soft smile. "I'm Heaven, Ryder's girlfriend, and Maddox's friend. He told me you and Madsy got married?" Before I can say a word, she's bending over, hugging me. "I'm so glad he found you," her voice cracks with emotion. "He deserves love more than anyone I know." She brushes away a stray tear when she stands.

"I'm Quinn," I tell her softly. "Thank you for introducing yourself."

She looks around the room at everyone, then back to me. "I wish this was under different circumstances. I can't imagine what you're going through, but I won't let you go through it alone. Okay? If Maddox loves you, then I love you."

My nose burns with emotion.

"Me too," Georgie says as she joins us.

"Thank you both," I sniffle.

"I've known the guys in the band for a long time but only recently reunited. I know what it's like to feel like the odd one out." Heaven explains.

"She's not the odd one out," Georgiana scolds her before turning to me with the same fiery expression. "You're Maddox Master's wife and the only one with any right to be here. Everyone else can kiss your ass if they don't like it."

I give a soggy laugh that feels good. "You're right," I agree. "I know how it looks, but I'm not a doormat. This is just—"

"Complicated?" she offers.

"Very. They love him, and they don't know me. I understand where they're coming from."

"Still doesn't give them the right to act like jackasses." Heaven's brows fall between her eyes in frustration.

"Maybe not. I try to put myself in other people's shoes before I react. But they're not getting rid of me." That's a promise. They've tried once, and I let them when I should've said something. I won't make that mistake again.

The look she gives me is some odd combination of compassion and disgust. "Fuck them. They have no right to invalidate you. They need your approval, Quinn. Not the other way around. He's your husband; you need to remind them every chance you get."

"I agree," Heaven tells me. "You're far too accommodating. I don't know everything, but Ryder has told me enough. Liam and Dane are out of line, but I don't think they will back off until you show them you're not backing down."

"I'm not backing down," I insist. "But I have other things on my mind besides fighting with them." I throw my hands in the air and then drop my head into them when they fall. "I'm tired. I'm sick with worry. My nerves are shot. I just want to see Maddox. I don't have the energy to argue with assholes, and I don't have the headspace."

"You're an island in this room full of strong male personalities and biased opinions. You do know by Bastian and Ryder continuing to fight your battles for you, you're only solidifying all their assumptions about you, and things will worsen, right?" Georgie asks, slightly disappointed.

"I didn't ask them to do that. I don't want anyone fighting anything for me. But arguing gets nothing accomplished. I won't get into a screaming match."

"Why the fuck are you still here?" All our attention turns to Ryder, who is in Chris's face again, looking angry as ever.

"Because I have a right to be here," Chris taunts.

"Not anymore," Ryder yells. "I'm having you removed."

"Ryder, you can't remove him," Callie insists. I didn't even notice her come in. "We're Maddox's family."

Ryder turns to her as if she's next in his line of fire. Heaven slips in beside him, taking his hand. I watch as he inhales with eyes closed, then exhales. When he opens his eyes, they're still filled with wrath, but he seems calmer. "If it weren't for him, we wouldn't be here," Ryder tells Callie through clenched teeth.

"It was an accident." Her hands flail and wave with frustration. Her long blond hair bobs around her ears as she shakes her head, denying Ryder's words. "Chris would never intentionally hurt his own brother. He loves Maddox."

Ryder opens his mouth to say something, then closes it again, his jaw working from side to side as he chooses his words. "Fine, Callie. He can stay here for you since you choose to remain blind. But when we can go see Maddox, he doesn't. He's not allowed anywhere near Mads. Are we clear?"

Callie's eyes fill with tears as she nods her agreement, but Chris's smirk makes my skin crawl.

"Come on, baby," Heaven tells Ryder as she tugs on his hand. "Let's go get some fresh air."

Ryder shakes his head. "I want to be here when we get to see him."

"Someone will come get us," she tries to reassure him, but he's still shaking his head.

"I've got you covered, man," Hayes tells him, nodding toward the door.

With a sigh, Ryder relents and lets Heaven tug him out of the room.

"At least I'm not the only source of contention," I mumble, then wince at my callousness. I don't want all the fighting. I hate it. It wouldn't matter if it were directed at me, Chris, or anyone else.

"Do you think Ryder's hostility towards Chris is the same as Dane and Liam's irrational overreaction to you?" Georgiana asks. "I can't say I would be surprised. He's not known for his reasonable behavior."

"I don't know," I tell her honestly. "Chris is not my biggest fan, but I'm not a fan of his either. Regardless, this fighting is pointless."

"I agree, but these hotheads will continue to explode. Let's forget about the ongoing battle for biggest dick of the night and talk about something else."

I give her a grateful smile, appreciating that she's trying to distract me, but I don't want her to sit here with me when she could enjoy—well, at least, enjoy conversation with people she knows. I tell her as much.

"I much prefer your company. I don't know most of the people here well enough to call them friends."

"How long have you known them?"

"Hayes, a lifetime. The rest, a few years."

"There's a story there," I tease her, trying to take my mind off everything.

Her eyes fall to the dark-haired, blue-eye man that has given me déjà vu since I first saw him. A plethora of emotions crosses her face as she watches him. As if feeling her gaze, he turns his head in our direction. After a prolonged moment, he offers her a wink and a smirk. She frowns, turning her attention back to me, but his eyes remain on her, and the same emotions darken them.

"There's no story there. He's just a boy I once knew." She says the lie with ease. It would be believable if her eyes didn't give her away. But she obviously doesn't want to discuss it, and I'm not going to push. "Tell me about your epic whirlwind romance. When did you get married?"

My cheeks heat at the question, but not from embarrassment.

Meeting everyone and them finding out under these stressful circumstances hasn't been pleasant, but the day I married Maddox will always be a beautiful memory. Though more spontaneous than my first with even fewer people, it was so much... *more*.

"The whimsical look you just got." She smiles as she waves a finger around my face. "Yeah, I want that story."

Ryder and Heaven come back in. Heaven whispers something in his ear that makes him look my way. He gives her a nod and leans back against the wall a few feet from us as Heaven rejoins us.

"Sorry about that," she tells us.

"Don't be," I reach for her hand. "He has a right to his feelings."

"So what are we talking about?" she says, changing the subject.

"I was just about to find out how Quinn got the legendary Maddox Masters to say I do," Georgie smirks.

"Oh, I want that story."

I blush again with a smile. "There's not much to tell. It was very spur of the moment."

Georgie smiles, her eyes taking on a softness I haven't seen in her as she touches her chest. "I can relate, and I'm sure there is more. I must say, he has exquisite taste. Not that I expected anything less." She nods to my ring, a silent request to take my hand.

I oblige, slipping my hand into hers. She and Heaven ooh and aah over it as I chuckle, shaking my head. "He grabbed it from the closest jewelry store. Said it was the best he could do on short notice."

Georgie and Heaven share a look, then Georgie's eyes meet mine with a skeptical look. "Sweetheart, this set is custom-made. The band diamonds alone are 1.0 carat VVS2, at least. And you won't find a canary diamond of this size or quality in a chain jewelry store, ever."

I shake my head, laughter bubbling. "No. I was there when he went in the store. He didn't have time to have something made."

"Trust me," she says, reaching into her shirt. She pulls out a chain with a beautiful ring and some other trinket looped through. "I know a thing or two about custom jewelry."

"Quinn, I think Georgie is right," Heaven tells me. "And Maddox has the resources to get something like that done." She turns toward Ryder, waving him over. Squeezing the water bottle he's holding, he pushes off the wall and comes our way. He grabs her by the hand, pulls her to her feet, and sits, dragging her onto his lap.

"What's going on?" he asks, looking over us suspiciously.

"This," Georgie tells him, pulling my hand toward him.

"Nice rock," he nods. "Not surprising. Mads has the money to spend, and he doesn't half-ass shit."

"She thinks he got it from a local jewelry store," Heaven tells him.

His brows scrunch as he looks at the ring closer. He stands, pulling his phone from his pocket. "It's not from a local store," he declares. "And I have a feeling I know exactly where it did come from."

He walks off as he raises the phone to his ear. "He's calling his grandfather," Heaven explains.

"Quinn, your ring was designed specifically for you," Georgiana tells me.

"But that means..." I trail off as the pieces click.

"It wasn't as spontaneous for him as it was for you?"

I look at the ring on my hand and back to them. Shock makes its way through me. Maddox planned everything? I wonder how he would've reacted if I'd said no. "Did you say a canary diamond?"

"Three carats, square cut, fancy vivid canary diamond to be specific," Ryder tells us as he slips his phone back into his pocket. "With another two carats of FL quality white diamonds on platinum bands."

"He made them?" Heaven asks.

"He made them," Ryder nods. "Maddox called him almost two months ago."

Tears spring to my eyes. "He calls me Canary."

"All of these guys are nothing if not charming, cheesy, and hopelessly romantic at their core," Georgie tells me with a smile. "When you're questioning the validity of your marriage, look at this and remember, in his darkest days, you're his light, and this was his way of proving it. Don't let anyone tell you different."

I nod as my heart swells. I haven't said it out loud, but I've worried that Maddox jumped into this without any thought. That he regretted marrying me. Or he would eventually.

"Did you say two months ago?" I ask. He nods without saying anything.

62

He doesn't have to. That means Maddox started planning this not long after we met. Before things seemed serious, even to me.

A throat clearing grabs all of our attention. The doctor that took Maddox's case when we arrived stands there waiting for us all to gather.

"Come on," Georgie grabs my hand, pulling me with her as we follow Ryder and Heaven.

"How is he, Stephen?" Bastian grunts.

"He's stable at the moment. We'll be moving to a private room in a few minutes." He pauses for a second as he glances nervously at Bastian.

"Spit it out," Ryder hisses.

"When Maddox woke up after surgery, he was highly agitated again. He experienced another cardiac arrest while we were operating, so we've placed him in a medically induced coma because we need him to remain calm while he's recovering."

I try and fail to suppress my sobs. Georgie wraps an arm over my shoulders.

"Cut the bullshit, Stephen? Get to the point." Bastian growls. "You said he was stable earlier."

"He is stable, Bastian, but it's hard to give a proper prognosis right now. He was never gone more than a minute or two, but we can't assess any potential brain damage until he is fully conscious. Also, considering he'll be going through withdrawals, keeping him sedated is the best course of action." The man sighs with a hand dragging down his face. "Look, guys, he pulled through the surgery, but he's not out of the woods."

"What are we looking at?" Rory asks.

"There are a lot of possibilities, Rory. Best case is a full recovery, worst case, he never wakes up with a dozen other possibilities ranging from mild heart and/or brain damage to severe. I will say his years of drug abuse don't put the odds in his favor."

"There may be something else," Ryder says, gripping the back of his neck. "I don't know if it means anything or not, but..." He pauses, turns to me with a sad expression and an outstretched hand. "I need to show him the letters, Quinn."

I bite my lip as I reach into the hoodie pocket. I retrieve the pages reluctantly. I know Ryder is right. The doctors need to understand Maddox and his frame of mind. But I want to keep them too.

"What's this?" the doctor asks when Ryder hands them over.

"We've known for a long time that Maddox has issues," Bastian tells him.

"We've all tried to get him to get help at some point or the other," Dane quickly adds. "He's never been receptive."

"His issues may be worse than we thought," Bastian continues. "Apparently, he's been seeing things—people who aren't there for a long time." There are gasps among those in the room who weren't already aware.

"How long?" the doctor asks with a furrowed brow.

"Don't know, Stephen, but judging from what he's written, I'd have to guess most of his life."

"I'll take a look and pass them along to a psychiatrist."

"No!" Bastian barks, making the doctor flinch and me jump. "*You* read them and then pass along the *necessary* information. Those pages come back to one of us when you're done. Understood?"

"Yeah, Bastian. Understood. You can go up to see him soon. He'll be in ICU for the next few days."

As soon as he's out of the room, everyone starts arguing over who goes first. Everyone agrees it should be Ryder, but the consensus is split about Zoey, Dane, and Bastian going with him.

"Wouldn't you all agree his wife should see him first? Not the asshole who has been hell-bent on removing her or the bitch that fucked him then fucked with his head most of his life." The room goes deadly silent for a beat of a heart after Georgie's statement. Then all hell breaks loose.

Jax and Georgie are in each other's faces. Zoey is tugging on Jax, trying to calm him, while Hayes puts himself between them, trying to calm her. Georgie is irate. It's as if something has triggered her. Finally, Hayes physically carries her out of the room. Bastian and Rory are in Jax's face.

"That girl has been through every bit the hell Zoey has been through, and then some. She may be the queen of chaos and a pain in my ass, but she has a fucking right to be." Bastian yells.

Jax looks thoroughly chastised and remorseful, but everyone is still arguing.

"Are you okay?" a tiny voice asks me. I turn to face Zoey. Tears fill my eyes as I nod. "Are you and Maddox really married?"

"Yeah," I sniffle.

She gives me a bright smile and wraps me in a hug. "Of course, you should be the one to see him first, even if you weren't married. I saw how much he loves you."

"It doesn't matter," Liam declares. "Ryder is the one with the final say. It's up to him, not her, who goes first."

More arguments ensue. Bastian has Liam pinned against the wall. Rory tries to get him off while Zane stands in front of Dane.

"Enough," I yell. "Why the hell do you all keep fighting? You know Maddox wouldn't want this."

"She's right," Ryder says as he and Heaven step up behind me. Heaven grabs my hand while Zoey continues to hold the other. "I'm sick of this shit. No more arguments." He turns his gaze to Liam. "You're right. I have the final say, and I say his *wife* goes first. If she wants someone with her, she can ask. If you don't like it, there is the goddamn door."

They continue for a few more seconds, but I turn my attention to Heaven and Ryder. "Would one of you come with me?"

Ryder looks down at Heaven with a tilt of his chin. "You go with her." She opens her mouth to argue, but he cuts her off. "I'll trade places with you in a few minutes. I need to deal with them." He nods to everyone else in the room.

When he walks off, we turn toward the elevators to go see Maddox.

QUINN

Don't forget we're here to stay

When I walked into Maddox's room with my hand in Heaven's, I nearly collapsed. Seeing him lying there with tubes and wires everywhere almost killed me.

The surface reflected his heart and mind.

Heaven stayed with me for a while. We didn't talk. Simply sat on opposite sides, each holding his hands.

I'd decided that once I was in there with him, I wouldn't cry. I was determined to remain strong and lend him my strength. Even when my knees buckled, I didn't cry.

I sat at his side, took his hand while minding the IVs, kissed his cheek, and told him how much I loved him. Tears didn't fall even as I clutched the cross around my neck and begged God to let him be okay. I managed to stay strong as Heaven sobbed across from me, begging him not to leave when she'd just gotten him back.

But with each person that came into the room, it became harder and harder to maintain my composure.

I expected Ryder after Heaven, so I was surprised when Callie came in next. She told him how much she needed her big brother. She spoke of knowing how he went to approach some guy that tried to take advantage of her when she was a freshman in college and that she loved how protective he was of her. No matter how far apart they were. She begged him to get better and told him she'd lost too many people in her life and couldn't stand to lose another.

Zoey came in next, whispering how much he meant to her. "You finally found her," I heard her say. "You can't give up now."

After Zoey, came Tori with a slew of expletives and threats as tears fell down her cheeks. She promised to kick his ass if he didn't wake up because she needed her best friend.

Camilla and Josephine followed. They both told him he needed to wake up. That he was the glue that held everyone together. That they needed his wise words and insight but needed his heart more.

When Cara came in, I nearly crumbled. She sobbed heavily as she spoke, making the words hard to understand, but it was undeniable her heart was breaking as she whispered things like brother, protector, and friend.

When Verity walked in, sitting beside me, I fell apart. She didn't say a word. Simply wrapped her arms around me the best her expanding belly would allow and let me cry. She stroked my hair, softly whispering it would be okay.

Verity and I were always close growing up despite our age difference and the miles between us. We were more like sisters. When I discovered what her life had been like growing up, so many things I'd never understood finally made sense. Especially that we went several years without speaking. It made sense why she'd run away from her family and everything she knew. I was glad she'd somehow found herself here. I was also shocked to discover that we had a family connection here. For Verity, it wasn't like running away from home. It was finding it.

I'd struggled to find that same sense of peace when I arrived. I felt out of place and lost. But I'd felt that way for years before. Since the day my baby died in my arms. I would always be grateful for the few minutes I had with her, but my heart would never fully heal.

"I haven't spent a lot of time with Maddox," she said softly. "Touring all the time and living in New York didn't allow it. But I felt his spirit. He has darkness in him. Heavy and scary and just... not someplace you ever want to be. But despite that, he still manages to shine brighter than everyone in the room. And he always makes you feel seen. He made me feel seen." She looks down at her hands, turning red. "Maddox is the first person to do that besides Bastian. But Bastian is different. It's nice to feel seen by someone else, you know?"

I nodded. I did know. It had been a very long time since I'd felt seen by anyone. I'd been consumed with grief and anger for so long. But Maddox recognized it immediately.

The depression I slipped into after I lost my baby was some of the darkest days of my life. Even with therapy and medication, some days were still hard.

But when I met Maddox, it was like the stars aligned. Suddenly I could breathe. The sense of home washed over me long before I fully recognized that I was absolutely in love with him. Even before I found the courage to speak to him.

Unfortunately, just like Maddox, finding love—finding the other half of your heart and soul and spirit didn't magically make me all better. I still had dark days when everything felt hopeless. But he was there to pick me up on those days.

I wanted to do the same for him. But Maddox wouldn't share his burden and pain. He clung to it as if it were his duty to bear the weight of the world alone.

He was bound to break under pressure.

Verity left after kissing his cheek and telling him to get better so he could meet his future nephew.

A few minutes later, Hayes was standing across from me on Maddox's other side. His arms were crossed over his chest as he glared at Maddox through slitted, blue eyes burning with anger. Now that they were near each other, I could see similarities that had been haunting me for days. Both had blue eyes, dark hair, and tattoos. But it was the little arrogant smirk and glares like the one Hayes had right now that drew my attention. It was unnerving because no one else seemed to notice, so it made me feel a little crazy.

Perhaps I was projecting. I decided it was probably the exhaustion.

"Damn it, Maddox. Like I don't have enough shit in my life to deal with already," He chastises. "You're an asshole, in case I haven't made it clear. You have a room full of people... ah fuck it. Like you give a shit about any of them beyond, maybe four." He runs his hands through his hair, grips the back of his neck, and lets out a frustrated sigh. "If you weren't in this damn hospital bed, I'd put you in it. And when you wake, I might come back and do it yet."

He looked at me, caught between a scowl and a smirk. "Be sure to let him know when he wakes."

I nodded, he nodded, and then he was gone.

The door behind me didn't fully shut when Zane took the chair next to me. "You holding up, okay?" I nodded without looking at him. "I've been where you are. The circumstances were different, but that doesn't mean much when you watch someone, not knowing if they're fighting for their life or if they've given up."

"You mean Zoey?" I turned to face him, looking into his deep brown eyes. They relayed a lot about him. Zane Valen was an open book.

"He told you about that?"

"He told me a lot of things," I nodded.

He shook his head with a smile, his shaggy blond hair falling in his eyes. "People can say what they want about the guy, but he's not a liar and owns his fuckups."

"He owns a lot that aren't his, too," I muttered.

Zane leaned back in his chair, his hands linked behind his head. "Yeah. Took me a long time to realize it, but he does that. What he did when we were kids was messed up. More than messed up. But he owned up to it. He made up for it. Don't know many people like him."

"You know he thinks Bryan drugged Zoey, right?" I whispered as I divulged what Maddox told me weeks ago. Zane's brows snapped to his hairline, and his eyes widened. "He just learned Jewel was his mom. He was spiraling and wasted before getting to the party that night. He's convinced Bryan slipped her the drugs. He just took the blame." I dropped my head into my hands to cover my tears. "I'm afraid of what it will do to him when he realizes Bryan isn't real."

"It's going to fuck him up more," he told me, running a hand through his long hair. "Have you told Ryder or Bastian?" He blew out a heavy breath when I nodded. "I don't envy you, Quinn. Maddox, well, I was unreasonably harsh on him growing up. I thought he was an arrogant, cocky rich boy. My family had money but not Masters' money. I thought he was spoiled and entitled. He was, in a way, but over the years, I've learned he's a good guy with many issues. And all that money hasn't meant a damn thing to him. I owe him a lot. Hell, I owe him everything because of Zoey and Tori. I wish I'd given him more of a chance when we were younger."

I grabbed his hand, giving it a tiny squeeze. "We're all dumb when we're kids. We live, we learn, we grow up."

He gave me a warm smile and stood, patting Maddox on the ankle. "You gotta wake up, man. I'd hate to drag you back from the hereafter and kill you for breaking my girls' hearts." He offered me a final nod as he left the room.

Liam came in after Zane. He ignored me, but I didn't mind. I listened as he talked about meeting Maddox and learning to love the business again. "You're probably the most talented person I've had to pleasure to know, but you need to get better, man. Not just your body, but your head too."

His voice cracked as he spoke. He was struggling to maintain that hard-ass façade now that he was in the room. If I hadn't already known, I would've realized then that Liam truly admired and respected Maddox. "I still have a lot to learn about Maddox Masters, the man, and I can't do that if you're not here."

He sat there for a few more minutes without speaking. When he got up to leave, he still didn't look at me, but I was okay with that. I didn't need his approval, and he didn't need mine. I knew he loved Maddox and only wanted to protect his friend.

Jake and Angel were next. They both thanked him for working his ass off to get them where they were as a band but also having their backs while never being afraid of telling them to pull their heads out of their asses. They just wished he would have opened up to them more.

Dane came in next, and I held my breath. He hadn't kept his feelings about me a secret, but he wasn't as vocal as Liam.

He sat quietly for a few minutes as if he couldn't find the words he wanted to say. Then he lifted his eyes to meet mine. "I don't trust you," he told me.

I said nothing. What could I say? They were all entitled to their reservations and opinions. I would never deny them that. The way they continued to handle things might not have been the best, but under the circumstances, I was inclined to be understanding. Though my patience was wearing thin.

But there was no way I would change his mind with words. I wasn't sure actions would influence him either. It would take time. I would have to prove myself by staying.

Another few seconds passed in silence. He studied me with noticeable distrust and doubt. I think he was waiting for a response. A reaction to his declaration. I offered none, so he finally continued. "Ryder told me about that rock on your finger." He nodded to the hand wrapped around Maddox's. Then he noticed the tattoo circling Maddox's ring finger. There was no denying it was new, considering it was still healing. He brushed a hand over his face with a sigh. "I don't trust you because I don't know you, but Ryder is right. Mads wouldn't keep you around, much less marry you, so I'll respect his choice for now. But if you fuck him over, I will make your life hell." I shook my head with a chuckle that made his face turn red and his scowl deepened. I covered my mouth to hide my smile because he had no idea why I would find anything he said funny.

"You're right," I told him softly. I turned my attention from him to Maddox. I brushed a piece of hair off Maddox's forehead and gently stroked his face. "You don't know me. You haven't tried to know me either. But that's okay. I understand your mind has been on other things."

"Is this an act?" he asked through narrowed eyes. "This always understanding, quiet little mouse routine. Is it an act.?"

I thought for a second to consider the response that would satisfy him before finally deciding that there was no right answer. "I try to put myself in other people's shoes," I explained. "Understand the situation and emotions surrounding reactions and words. So no, it's not an act. But I'm not a mouse. I have thoughts and opinions that I'm not afraid to share, but I pick and choose what to share and when."

He leaned back in his chair, still studying me, then nodded. "You're right. I haven't tried to know you. So tell me about yourself. I'm all ears."

"You told me you'd make my life hell?" He nodded. "I've lived in hell. Nothing you could do could be worse than that. I was in such a deep depression for years. I just barely finished college because I couldn't get out of bed for days at a time. I pushed everyone away. And you know what? It would be so easy to let that darkness consume me right now. To wallow in the hopelessness of everything. But Maddox saw my pain and went beyond it to find me. He picked up my wrecked pieces, held them in his hand, and put me back together one piece at a time. He still has a lot of pieces to go, but they're all his. And I did the same for him. I wish I'd put enough back to heal him. I wish loving him were enough to exorcise his demons. But I'm not naïve enough to believe love is the magical cure-all. I know our love can't fix his mind. Just like it doesn't mean I can throw away my medication and stop therapy. It also doesn't make our love less than. It means we have to work a little harder than everyone else. So if you need to make my life hell, go ahead. I've been in those flames, and every day I wake up means I survived it, and I'm going to be by his side every day he survives it too."

He opened his mouth to say something, then snapped it shut with a nod. Leaning over Maddox, his mouth next to his ear, he whispered something, then left, and though I doubt anything I said made a difference to him, I felt better saying it all.

BASTIAN

How many lies?

Dane comes out of Maddox's room with a strange look on his face. Most of the time, I have no problem with the guy. But knowing he's played a part in the bullshit with Quinn has pissed me off.

I put the issues aside for the time being. I'll handle him later if I must, but now is my turn to go in since Ryder has been adamant about going last.

I get it. He's pissed off and afraid at the same time. I've been fighting the same emotions myself, and finding my composure hasn't been easy.

This has been one of the hardest things I've ever had to deal with. Fear isn't something I feel often, but I've been fucking terrified since I walked into that house and found Maddox.

But controlling my emotions is something I learned to do long ago. People think I'm a loose canon, but I control what I want. Just so happens that most of the time, I don't want. But since I got to the hospital, restraint is what's been needed.

But I feel that patience slipping as I open the door to Maddox's room.

With every step I take, my anger grows and builds. Everything is bubbling to the surface, and I'm not sure how much longer I can contain it.

I stand at the foot of his bed and slowly study his body. The sound of a ventilator grates on my nerves, reminding me how close he was to death. The sight of the chest tube has me clenching my fists.

"If you weren't already in that bed, I'd wrap my hands around your throat and squeeze until the light in your eyes went out, bring you back and do it me.

"Sebastian," Quinn hisses, reminding me she's in the room. Her brows furrow, and her mouth pulls down. "Don't say that to him. He might hear, you know? He doesn't need that right now."

I work my jaw side to side in irritation. Quinn reminds me so much of Verity. Same hair, same eyes, same dimples in their cheeks. They're both quiet too. But where Verity is reserved and shy, Quinn is simply waiting. Waiting for the right moment to say what she wants. Waiting until she has the right words.

But this time, the words and moment are wrong. "You're right," I tell her, leaning over until I'm in her space. "He needed it years ago."

She sucks in a breath, and tears well in her eyes. But she started this by inserting her two cents where it wasn't wanted or needed. Just because she's my wife's family doesn't mean she gets to speak to me like that. Anyone else would be collecting their teeth from the floor.

But she surprises me when she doesn't back down. Though I'm not sure why. I've been defending her all night, but she's also held her own a time or two. Blond curls fly wildly around her face as she refuses to accept what I've said. "He's had enough people riding his ass and placing unrealistic expectations on him long enough. You don't get to do it too."

The corner of my mouth twitches. I like her courage, even if it's being severely misplaced at the moment.

I grab a chair, spin it around, and straddle it while maintaining eye contact with her. "I never placed any unrealistic or unreasonable expectations on him. I've never ridden his ass. I've cleaned up his messes more times than I can count. Been there, even when he didn't know it, to make sure he didn't go down for some of the shit that could've sent him away for a long damn time. I also know all about the expectations that were placed on him. So don't tell me what he does or doesn't need."

"He didn't even know you were brothers until a few months ago."

And there it is. I've been waiting for someone to bring it up. I'm a bit shocked it's her, but it's out there. "I don't regret many things in my life, *riccia*, but that is one of them. I should've told him much sooner instead of him finding out like he did. And for the record, I'm not pissed he's here. I know he didn't put himself here, but you must face the facts. If whatever happened between him and Chris hadn't, he'd be in a morgue right now. Maddox didn't plan on coming back to any of us."

She looks down at the bed and sniffs as she tries to hold back her tears. I can't imagine what she's going through. If it were Verity, I'd be a wreck. River City would be ashes, consumed by my pain and anger. Quinn has impressed me with the way she's handled this so gracefully.

She's quiet for several seconds as she stroke his hand. I can barely look at him. It incites my anger more.

"Why didn't you tell him?" she finally asks, breaking the silence.

She's the first person to actually ask that question. I tried to explain it to him, but the stubborn, arrogant asshole wouldn't listen. I wasn't about to beg him to hear me out. After reading his letter, I think he knows why I didn't tell him sooner.

"I found out he was my brother the night shit went down with Zoey and Chris." I pause, wondering if Maddox told her about that night. I'd be lying if I said I wasn't surprised when she gave me a knowing nod. Maddox owned up to his mistakes. Never lied about the things he did. But he was the king of vague and frequently refused to talk about any of it. "Rory showed up at my dad's, wanting me to go with him to handle Maddox before Jax and Zane did something stupid. Soon as Pop's heard Maddox's name, he started acting cagey. Asking questions and fishing for information on some kid he didn't know wasn't like him, even if it did concern ones he did know. What really got my attention was a look he and Mom shared. As if they knew something no one else did. So I asked him what was going on. He avoided answering at first, but I wasn't letting it go. Finally, he told me that he was Maddox's father."

I stand up from the chair and walk to the window. Even now, the entire situation pisses me off. Knowing my dad fathered another, not one but two kids, while he was married to my mom was hard for me to swallow, but I eventually got over it because, for reasons I'm not sure I'll ever understand, my Mom forgave him.

I also hated that they were keeping it a secret. Maddox was my family. My blood. That meant something to me. But it seemed like the man that had taught me about the importance of family disagreed. At thirty-six, I understand the situation much better than I had at twenty-four, but it still left a bitter taste in my mouth.

I stare out the window, looking at my city—the city I've run alongside Rory for a while now and wonder, for the first time in a long time, what's the point? Dragging my hand down my face, I release a heavy sigh of frustration. Even before that night, I'd watched Maddox from a distance. It's something I've never told anyone except Verity. He was cocky and carried himself with an air of confidence anyone could see from a mile away. But when you watch from the shadows, you see things no one else does. I saw the heaviness he carried, and I didn't understand why this kid who seemed to have it all and access to more walked like he was holding so many burdens. I also saw his habits and thought it was such a waste because it was obvious the kid was smart. I figured he'd end up just another rich kid living on the streets because he couldn't keep his nose clean. But despite the load he carried and despite his vices, he was a good kid.

It wasn't like me to take an interest in someone that wasn't family or friend, much less a kid. I could've chalked it up to his connection with Zoey, but I knew that wasn't it. I *knew* we were somehow connected. When Pops told me he was my brother, it finally all made sense.

"Pops went to talk to Trey, and Rory and I went with him. My dad didn't want us to, but he also knew he couldn't stop us. They decided Maddox needed to go to rehab and then back to New York. I was pissed. The rehab thing I understood. The kid was going to die before he turned eighteen at the rate he was going. What I didn't understand was not telling him the truth or sending him away. Pops and Trey argued it was best for Maddox."

"You didn't agree."

"No, *riccia*, I didn't agree. They handled everything wrong. For a long time, I thought Pops was denying Maddox. That, where Maddox was concerned anyway, he was a deadbeat. I realized after a couple of years he thought he was protecting him. They all did. Over the years, I began to understand that Pops didn't want..." I have no idea how to finish that sentence. As far as I know, Quinn doesn't know much about me and my business. She doesn't know about *La Famiglia* or the role I play.

I turn around to face her, trying to find the words. She smiles. Something tells me she knows more than she lets on. I assumed she knows nothing because Verity didn't, but maybe Quinn knows more than I give her credit for, and she's smart enough to keep it to herself.

"Your dad wanted better things for Maddox," she finishes. The look in her eyes confirms my suspicion. She knows a lot more than she lets on.

"Yeah, he wanted better," I nod. "Maddox doesn't know this, but I fought for him to stay. Got into a fistfight with my dad. Beat Rory's ass. Had it not been for him, I probably would've killed Jax and Zane. They had every right to be angry, but they took it too far. And it wasn't really over what he did anyway. It was over Jax's jealousy and ego. He hated that Maddox and Zoey were so close, and he couldn't intimidate Maddox like he did the little bitches at his school. That's what really pissed me off.

"I should've told Maddox the truth, but after a while, I thought it would do more harm than good. Hindsight is a bitch, but the truth is, I knew he'd find out eventually, no matter how much I hoped he wouldn't, because how or when he found out, it was always going to be bad. Every time Maddox learns about another lie, he spirals."

"How did he find out? He never told me," she asks.

"Trey came to me several months ago with a proposal. Maddox's label was quietly putting out feelers about selling. He wanted to buy the label for Maddox but didn't have enough liquid capital at his disposal at that moment. It would have taken too long to get what he needed, and he didn't want to do it under his corporate umbrella because he didn't want Maddox to know it was him. He also didn't want it controlled by his board or his corporate red tape." I was doubtful about Trey's plan. I knew somehow it would bite us all in the ass, but Trey was adamant, and he wanted *my* help because he knew I would never say a word.

I tried like hell to talk Trey out of it. Maddox was barely talking to Trey as it was. I even tried to convince him that all his secrets would come out if he went through with it, but he believed he had a plan. I don't think Trey ever realized how resourceful Maddox could be. It's what made him such a pain in my ass.

Maddox had it in his head that Trey wanted to control him, and to an extent, he wasn't wrong. I guess that's why I went along with the insane plan because Trey wasn't trying to force Maddox into the model he intended for the first time in Maddox's life. He truly wanted to do it for Maddox.

I stand at the foot of his bed again, watching his chest rise and fall at a steady rhythm that does nothing to ease my uneasiness because I know machines are doing the work. "Maddox found out because he wanted to buy the company himself, but we'd already begun the process. He paid some people to dig; if I had to guess, he did a little on his own. Just not the legal variety. Didn't take long for him to realize it was his dad, but then he figured out I was attached too. He didn't understand why I would help his dad do anything. He confronted us both, and Trey just let it slip."

Maddox was enraged. I had to put myself between them to stop Maddox from doing something he would regret. He swung at me too, and I let him. He had a right to be angry. I knew it would take him a while to get over it.

I called Dane and Ryder so they would keep an eye on him, knowing Maddox's way of dealing with lies and betrayal was to self-medicate with anything he could get his hands on. I guess I should've expected the phone call a few days later that he'd overdosed, but I didn't. And I wasn't prepared for Ryder to ask for my help.

"You may realize by now, or maybe you don't, but I know you, Maddox," I tell him. "Nearly better than anyone. I've watched you for a long time, kid. Made it my job because it never seemed like anyone else would. Like it or not, you're my family, and that means something to me. You need to get better real soon, so I can kick your fucking ass."

I hear Quinn gasp again but ignore her as I exit the room, nodding to Ryder as I go.

QUINN

Never turn away

"Quinn, you haven't left this room in two days. You need rest and food," Heaven pleads for the third time in ten minutes.

"I eat what they bring him, and I rest just fine here." It's the same argument I've given everyone, including the nurses.

She shakes her head with a sigh. I can tell she is losing her patience with me, but how do they expect me to leave him? She grips me by the shoulders, turning me to face her. "Sweetheart, you are exhausted."

She's right. I am exhausted. My entire body is sore from sleeping in a chair with my head on Maddox's bed. And I need a shower. Verity brought me fresh clothes, so I cleaned up using the hospital supplies. It wasn't the same, but it was better than nothing.

I didn't want to leave him. What if he woke up while I was gone? Or what if something happened to him? The thought made me sick.

"I can't." I shake my head and wrap my arms around myself as panic sets in. "I'll just—"

"Go back to my place, eat, shower, and sleep. In a bed."

The deep, gruff voice makes me look over my shoulder. Bastian stands in the doorway with Ryder. "Only two people allowed at a time," I snap, a little irritated that he's telling me to leave Maddox.

"Then they can try to remove me. Now, get ready. We are leaving in twenty minutes." His tone rattles me just a bit. It's not soothing or gentle. He isn't asking me nicely. It's a command that he expects to be obeyed.

I turn away from them with defiant irritation. My teeth grind together, and I clutch Maddox's bed with a death grip.

But despite my irritation, sweat beads on my forehead as my heart start racing at an erratic pace. My breath feels trapped in my chest, and my vision begins to haze. All the what-ifs begin to spin in my mind like a merry-go-round.

"He won't wake up, Quinn," Ryder tells me as he walks around the room. He goes to the opposite side of the bed where he was a few days ago, except, thankfully, he's much calmer.

I don't know what I expected when he walked into Maddox's room for the first time. Maybe solemnness. Perhaps a few tears. That's not what happened. If I thought Bastian was harsh, then Ryder was absolute fury.

He yelled and screamed at Maddox's unconscious form for twenty minutes, calling him an asshole and a few other words until Dane and Angel finally came in to remove him. I had no doubt if Maddox had been awake and standing in front of him, there would've been bloodshed.

"They won't start weaning him down from the drugs they're giving him until later today. It may be another day or two before he wakes up," he continues. I can't help but wonder how he knew what I was thinking. Did I say it out loud? "If you get sick from staying with him, it will eat him alive. Not to mention he'll be pissed with all of us for not taking care of you. We're going to have enough to hash out without adding to it. Go. It doesn't need to be long, but you need real sleep and food. He would want you to take care of yourself and that baby."

I bite my lip as I place a hand on my flat stomach. Doubt creeps in as I replay Maddox's words to me, recalling the words in his letter. Would he care about our baby? Even Ryder said that Maddox believes he meant what he said.

"He would care, Quinn." Heaven takes my hand, squeezing lightly.

"Am I that transparent?" My eyes drop as I try to hide my embarrassment.

"No. But he told me once how he felt about kids of his own, so I can guess why you look doubtful. But Maddox feels the way he does because he's scared that a broken heart can be inherited somehow."

I know it's not that simple, but I understand what she's saying.

I sit for a few more minutes, mulling over their words. The only sounds in the room are from the monitor that tells me his heart is beating and the machine helping him breathe.

Deep down, I know they're right. It's been three days since I've slept for more than a few minutes. Or has it been four? I haven't eaten more than a couple of bites of food. Everything makes me queasy because of my lack of sleep, frayed nerves, and hormones.

I can feel the beginnings of—something coming on. I've had moments of uncontrollable shaking, and I'm absolutely freezing beyond the normal hospital chill. I know it's a lack of sleep coupled with stress and anxiety. My body is telling me that I need to rest. It's telling me I am getting sick.

And Maddox would blame himself.

"Quinn," Bastian's gruff voice breaks the silence. "You know I like you. I kind of like that asshole too." He nods toward Maddox's still form. "But Verity is making *herself* sick. The doctor is threatening bed rest if her blood pressure doesn't come down. My wife and son are my priority. We need him to bake for a few more weeks, and she needs all the rest she can get. So if I have to carry you out of here, I will. I won't hesitate, and I won't feel bad about it."

A dam of contrition breaks, flooding me to my very soul. I don't want Verity to stress. I'd never forgive myself if something happened to her or her baby.

Then a small smile forms on my lips. It's the exact same thing Ryder said about Maddox. And I don't want him to feel guilty over me.

"Okay," I finally relent. "But just for a little bit."

"I'll bring you back after you've slept." He looks pleased. Or, at the very least, less tense.

"Maddox won't be alone," Heaven tells me. "We'll take turns staying with him."

Slowly I stand, hesitation still pumping strong through me. I kiss Maddox on the cheek with promises to return soon, then follow Bastian.

Even though my heart is telling me to stay.

A shower, a tiny bit of food, and a few hours of sleep later, I stumble towards Bastian's entrance, following the sound of voices.

"What's going on?" I hear Bastian ask, his voice tight with annoyance and frustration.

"I overheard one of the dancers talking last night." I recognize Delaney's voice. I shouldn't eavesdrop, but curiosity beats morality. "Maddox was at the club a few blocks down the night he vanished. He was…" Her words fade, and my stomach drops. I clamp my hand over my mouth, so they don't hear me.

"Dammit," Bastian hisses.

"Her roommate works at the club. Apparently, things got rough. Said Maddox stopped her halfway through—"

"I get it, Delaney," Bastian cuts her off. I peek around the corner of the hallway. Bastian stands with tense shoulders and pulls his neck. Delaney's face is sad and full of sympathy.

"He changed his mind or something. Kept telling the girl that she wasn't the right one. That her eyes were wrong. The owner is pissed, and he and the dancer plan to blackmail Maddox and the band with the security footage."

"I'll take care of it," Bastian tells her. "Tell Tristan to take care of…"

"It was Krista," she tells him. I'm not surprised to hear her name. She's the gossiping sort. And the type to stir drama.

"Tell him to handle her. I don't want Quinn to know."

I know he means well, but that pisses me off. I don't need coddling. "Too late," I declare, stepping into view. "Quinn already knows."

They both look my way, Delaney with surprise and Bastian with aggravation. Though he has no right to be.

"Didn't anyone tell you that eavesdropping can get you killed?" he growls.

"Don't act like I've done something wrong, Bastian. I have a right to know."

He drags a hand down his face with a sigh. "Quinn, he didn't know what he was doing."

"That's supposed to matter? I still have a right to know." I throw my hands in the air with a huff. I don't know if it's days worth of tension and anxiety or the much-needed sleep that wasn't nearly enough that has given me loose lips and little patience, but I'm not in the mood for coddling today.

"If you say so," he grumbles as he turns back to Delaney. "I'll go to Lucky Gentlemen and handle Brendon and the other girl."

"I'm coming with you," I tell him.

"No." He nods at Delaney, who realizes without prompting that's her cue to leave. He walks to the table by the elevator that leads down to his garage, grabs a set of keys, and opens the elevator door.

"I'll follow you," I warn him with my arms crossed.

"You can try."

"I heard Delaney say the club's name. I'll go there on my own."

His nostrils flare as he huffs out a breath. "When the fuck did you get so ballsy?"

"When it involves someone I love, I've always been ballsy."

"Quinn, I don't know what's on that footage, but I don't think you need to see it."

"I'm a big girl, Bastian. I may have struggled with my emotions and feelings the last few years, but I'm not weak."

He jerks his head, indicating for me to come on. "Don't say I didn't warn you."

An hour later, my heart is in my throat as I walk with Bastian from his SUV to the club. The outside alone is already so different from Red. The exterior of Red is a brick front with a red neon sign. You find yourself in a bar when you walk inside from the street entrance. It's masculine and dark with vintage and antique touches and has a very upscale ambiance. There is a private entrance from both inside and out for the strip club side, and the dancer side is just as classy as the bar, even though it's strange that I think a strip club is classy.

Some of the girls call it a gentlemen's club, but not Bastian. And not Maddox. They said they weren't trying to make it sound pretty or regal. They called it exactly what it was. I like the other term better because the men allowed in there had to treat the girls with respect. Anything less was not tolerated.

I never cared what anyone called it or me. It was a means to an end. I had no idea it was even owned by Bastian and Rory when I started there. It mortified me initially, but in hindsight, it was probably a small mercy to be grateful for.

The club we are standing outside of is still in the more expensive and discreet part of the strip, but there is no mistaking what it is. Even though it isn't open yet, you can see the booths, poles, and the stage from the street windows. Every girl that works here would be blatantly on display for the customers and everyone passing by on the street.

Bastian opens the door, allowing me to enter first, and follows behind me. We're greeted by two large guys in suits with arms folded across their broad chests.

"We don't open until ten," one of them tells us.

Bastian grips me by the elbow, pulling me behind him. "Do we look like we're here for the show, chuckles?" Even without seeing his face, I can hear the smirk. "Get your boss now."

The men widen their stances, their eyes glaring harder. "Call his office and make an appointment," the man tells him without blinking.

To most people, they'd be intimidating. I know they're intimidating me, but Bastian is just as relaxed as he would be talking to the pizza guy.

When Bastian doesn't move, the man grabs him by the shirt with bared teeth. "I suggest you take your trick, turn around, and leave."

Instinctively, I take several steps back and to the side. This gut feeling that this guy just stepped into something he isn't ready for crawls over my skin.

I know I'm not supposed to know who or what Bastian is, but I do. Perhaps that should've scared me, but I knew he saved Verity from an awful life. I also saw how much he loved her. That was all that mattered.

My intuition proves accurate when Bastian slowly looks at the man's hands on him. A devilish smile crosses his face when he looks back at the man. "I'll give you one chance to let go of me and get Arceneaux, or you won't like what happens next. I'm hoping you choose to ignore me. I've got a lot of frustration I need to work out."

I watch as the man tightens his grip instead of loosening. Everything after happens fast and slow all at once.

Bastian's arms slip between the man's, breaking his hold. He grabs the man's arm, maneuvers behind him, and wrenches the limb until an audible snap and screams fill the air.

The other man steps behind Bastian, wrapping his arm around his neck. Bastian rolls his hips, somehow breaking the hold, and reverses their positions. Seconds later, the other man is on the ground as well, with Bastian hovering over him, knife in hand, tracing the tip over the man's cheek.

"Fucking hell, Sebastian!" a voice yells from across the room. "Stop, you psychopath."

A tall, blond man appears out of nowhere, though I imagine he came from another room. I would've noticed had I not been entranced by the violence in front of me.

"New guys?" Bastian asks, his eyes still focused on the man beneath him.

"They're hired security. Dammit, Bastian. The company probably won't send more now."

"I suggest the next time you hire people not from around here, you fill them in on who owns this place. I allow you to operate here, after all."

The man drags a hand down his face with a groan, muttering things like asshole and psycho when he finally notices me. He stands straighter, his eyes roving over me, making me shiver. "Who's this?" he asks, licking his lips.

"Not interested," I tell him, my mouth curling in disgust. "We're here about Maddox."

"Sorry, honey, I don't know any Maddox."

Bastian stands, puts his knife back from wherever he pulled it and dusts himself off. "Don't play dumb, Brenden. I don't have the time or the patience." He steps over the men, walking to the bar. He reaches over, grabs a bottle of something and a glass, then pours himself a drink. "You and one of your *employees* are planning to blackmail my brother and his band, which means you and I have a problem."

"Brother? What the hell are you... Wait." Brenden's eyes jump from Bastian to me and back. "Are you telling me that Maddox Masters is your brother?"

"Little known fact," Bastian tells him as he tosses back the drink. "And it's gonna stay that way, *stronzo. Comprendere?* I need to see the security footage."

His eyes widen as he puts his hands in front of him, palms out in surrender. "Yeah. Sure. Follow me."

We follow him up a flight of stares into a room that overlooks the entire club. Flicking several switches, the monitors come to life.

"You shouldn't be in here, Quinn," Bastian tells me as they cue up the footage.

"I'm staying," I tell him, sitting in the chair next to him.

"Why? Why would you do that to yourself?"

I'm not sure he would understand if I tried to explain it. I was cheated on unknowingly during the entirety of my relationship with my ex. It's a hard limit for me. But this isn't a normal situation. The desire—need to see for myself will determine what I do. I've already heard what happened. But if Maddox didn't know what he was doing, I need to know. I am unsure how I will feel or react until I see.

Call me weak. Call me stupid. I don't care. These are not normal circumstances. Sure, many men can claim that they didn't know what they were doing under the influence. But what Maddox was going through the other night wasn't just the effects of drugs and alcohol.

He growls when I don't answer. Arms crossed over his chest, he leans back in his chair. "Anyone else, I wouldn't give a shit. I'd probably cut their balls off for hurting you because when you hurt, so does Verity. But this is Maddox. You don't need to see him like that. He needs you, Quinn."

"Play the video, Bastian," I tell him. I'm quiet but firm. "I need to see."

He turns around, grumbling. The air in the room thickens when he presses play. We're both silent as we watch the scene play out before us.

Sandpaper scrapes my throat. The crumbling of my heart is nearly audible. Tears fall like rain down my cheeks.

And none of it for the reasons any other woman would break or crack.

My shattering heart is only for the demons I see on the screen.

We watch as he does line after line. Drinks straight from the bottle. Talks to someone that isn't there.

The girls on the stage don't even register for him. Not even when he tosses his head back, pulls his cock out, and begins to stroke himself while mumbling my name.

Not even when the curly, blond dancer settles herself between his legs.

Bile works its way up my throat at how gone he is. And not just because of the drugs. It's clear in his eyes. He was lost to his demons. Lost to the memories, burdens, and shame.

The moment he realized what was happening—the second clarity returned to him, with my name a whisper on his lips, a sob escapes me. The shame, guilt, and regret are so apparent I can feel them to my core.

Tears fall down his face and mine when he grabs the girl by the throat, incoherently mumbling that she's not his girl. That she's not his *Canary*. He shoves her roughly, and her head slams against the stage.

I would almost feel sorry for her if she wasn't conspiring to blackmail him.

He flips the leather sofa. Tosses the liquor bottles across the room. He screams and wails like an animal in pain. When the security guard walks in to grab him, Maddox quickly flips him and begins to pound his face until blood flies. The same happens to the next one until Maddox finally stops, stumbling out of the room and out of view of that camera.

I've seen enough, but Bastian watches the rest of the feed until Maddox exits the building. Hand dragging down his face, he sighs. He sits back in the chair, staring at nothing, hand covering his mouth, and lost in his thoughts.

"Quinn, that wasn't—"

"We don't tell him about this," I cut him off, knowing what he's about to say. Knowing that wasn't Maddox. Or rather, it was, but not the Maddox in control of his actions. I don't need him to tell me that. I know Maddox. I know the deepest parts of him. The most important. His heart and his soul.

Bastian's brows shoot to his hairline, obviously not expecting my response. "Excuse me?"

"We don't tell him. I want you to make all of this disappear. I know you can, so please, make it disappear."

Sebastian looks at me questioningly—doubtful. He starts to shake his head, and I grab his hands, not above begging. "Please, Sebastian. Make this disappear."

"And what if he remembers, Quinn? You want to lie to him? Haven't you learned by now that it's lies that tear him apart the most."

I close my eyes with a heavy breath. There is no doubt in my mind that Maddox would fall apart if he knew this. The destruction on the screen is nothing compared to the internal war he would fight. He'd push me away for good if he thought he'd betrayed me. "If he remembers, we tell him he hallucinated it. Fix it, Bastian. Make it, so he was never here. I don't care what you have to do, but please, make this go away for him."

After a second, he finally agrees. "Okay, *riccia*. I'll take care of it. He'll never find out."

I walk out of that room, relieved that I can protect Maddox from this but heartbroken that I have to protect him from it at all.

MADDOX

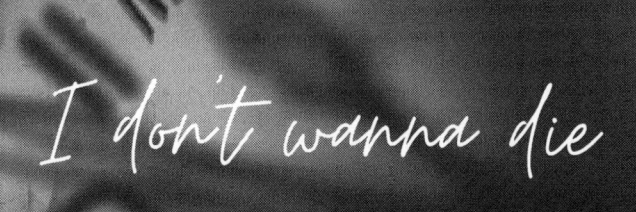

I don't wanna die

Carefully balancing two mugs of hot coffee, one regular and one decaf, I slip out the French doors of my house onto the back deck. I slide my feet into the Muck boots by the mat, then make my way to the slightly overgrown path that leads to the pasture.

The sun beats down on my head, and within seconds I'm drenched and regretting my choice of beverage. Concern builds in my gut, wondering if the heat is good for her. Not that it matters. This is our routine.

The moment the pasture comes into view, I lose my ability to think or move. I'm frozen, filled with awe at the beauty before me. It's a feeling that never gets old.

My heart stutters in my chest, squeezing tight, and breathing becomes a chore. Because she is breathtakingly, heart-stoppingly beautiful.

Her long curls flow gently down her back like spun gold. The bright blue dress she wears flutters around her knees, showing off tanned calves and shoulders. I beg my feet to move. To take me closer to this angel.

To my angel.

Her laughter fills the air like a song straight from the heavens as the dark-haired little boy chases the tiny terrier a few feet from her. Nyla, the Palomino Thoroughbred I bought with the house, gently nudges her as she brushes her golden coat.

Hands freezing mid-stroke, she turns slightly. A brilliant smile flashes when our eyes meet. Electricity flows through every inch of my body. Her shiver tells me she feels it too.

She mouths, "I love you," then turns back to the towering horse. My heart *cracks open.*

Because, goddammit, I love her too.

An urgency swarms inside my belly. The need to tell her is all-consuming. To let her know she's not alone in her feelings. Give her the words she has never asked for, but I know she wants to hear.

Determination measuring my steps, I make my way toward her. Sweat falls into my eyes and makes it hard to see, but my goal remains steadfast. My muddy boots pound the wet ground as I break into a run, the mugs in my hand long-forgotten.

Perspiration soaks my clothes and skin. My heart rolls like a drum. Fire fills my lungs as I struggle for air. My muscles scream for a reprieve. Exhaustion overwhelms me and threatens to slow me down, but she keeps me going through the pain.

Frustration bears down because it's taking too long to travel the short distance. I've been running for far too long for her to still be so far away.

Finally unable to go anymore, I stop. Hands propped on my thighs, I bend at the waist, fighting the urge to vomit. The barn is to my right, the custom studio is to my left, and straight ahead is my heart.

The exact same distance as before.

I freeze.

Her laughter drifts with the breeze as the small, black and white terrier runs from the tiny dark-haired boy. The horse bumps her with its nose as she strokes down its long mane.

When her hand pauses mid-stroke, alarms sound off in my mind. Terror reigns when she looks over her shoulder with a smile.

No. No. NO!

Not again.

My heart thunders in my chest as I drop to my knees. Another lucid dream torments me, showing me everything I want, but keeping it just out of reach.

Why can't I wake up?

I wonder again if I'm really dreaming. Wonder again if maybe I'm dead, and this is my hell.

Head buried in my hands, I fall forward into the dirt. Everything I've ever done—all the regret is nothing compared to this. The pure agony and pain are nothing like I've ever felt before.

Tears run down my cheeks as I look up and watch as she mouths, "I love you."

"I'm sorry," I cry out. "Quinn, I'm so fucking sorry."

"Nurse!" a voice cuts through. "We need help."

My eyes fly open. Dane and Ryder are on either side of me, holding me in place. I thrash against them, albeit weakly. White-hot pain pierces my chest and spreads down the side of my body. I open my mouth to beg them to let me go, but I can't. I fight harder against them, pleading with my eyes for them to understand.

"Maddox, calm down," Ryder barks out, his eyes wide with panic. "You're going to hurt yourself."

I can't calm down. I don't understand what the hell is going on. Where am I? Why can't I speak? Why does it hurt so badly?

"Fuck, we need the bloody nurse," Ryder yells. "Hit the call button."

"I can't reach it without letting go," Dane responds.

"Then let go."

Desperation fuels me, and when he releases his grip, my hand flies to my mouth. Panic takes over when I feel the tube taped to my face. I grip it and start to pull.

"Shit! *Shit!*" Ryder's panic is as apparent as my own.

"What's going on?" I hear Angel's voice. I search for him, hoping he'll help me. "Holy shit! He's awake."

"Stop stating the obvious and get some bloody help. Maddox, stop!" He demands. "Hurry before he hurts himself."

I continue to fight against them, ignoring the pain and their pleas. They'd fight, too, if they were in my position.

I don't know where I'm at. Or if Quinn is okay.

Another face appears in my line of sight. "Okay, Mr. Masters, we'll give you a little something to help you relax."

My eyes widen as I try to say no. I remember the other times I've awoken from these fucking dreams. Every time someone gave me something, it ended with me trapped in my mind.

"What? No!" Ryder calls out. "He just woke up."

"It won't knock him out," the nurse explains. "Only settle him."

I feel the instant the drug hits my veins. My agitation spikes momentarily as the fear that I'll fall asleep again consumes me.

Minutes pass. It feels like a lifetime, but eventually, my heart stops racing. Panic and anxiety lessen, though they still threaten the edges of my mind. And my mind stills enough for me to stop struggling and look around me.

No longer thrashing and fighting, I recognize the beeping of a heart monitor and the whirring of the ventilator. The stark white room, abrasive lighting, and the nurse standing beside me let me know I'm in a hospital.

But why?

"Glad you decided to come back, brother," Dane tells me with a relieved grin.

I look around and see Angel, who shares the same reassured expression as Dane. Ryder's face shows relief as well, but he's also pissed.

What I don't see is the face I want to see most. I don't see my whiskey eyes anywhere.

If I'm in a hospital, where is she? Is she okay? I search my memory, trying to remember. All I come up with is standing on Bastian's balcony, waiting for her.

The beeping of the machines escalates along with my heart. I jerk my gaze back to Ryder, praying he understands, despite knowing nothing about her.

"He wants to say something," Ryder tells them. At least he understands that much. "Can't you remove that tube now?"

"We have to wait on the doctor," the nurse replies apologetically.

Except, I don't have to wait on shit. I'll take the goddamn thing out myself.

Chaos erupts when I begin to pull the tape on my face. Ryder and Dane grab my hands as the nurse hits the call button. Her demands for assistance are met with the assurance that someone is coming.

Two more nurses run into the room. The syringe in one of their hands brings my hysteria back full force.

Once again, I try to say something. Razor blades would feel better, but pain doesn't deter me. If anything, it fuels me, and I continue to try to say something despite knowing it's impossible.

"What are you doing?" Dane commands when the nurse tries to go around him with the syringe.

"Giving him something to relax him," the male nurse answers, his eyes sparking with a challenge.

"You did that already," Ryder cuts in as he releases me. I grip his arm, our eyes lock, and I plead for him to understand what I want.

"That didn't work," the man barks. "This will."

Ryder's eyes stay on mine. His brows furrow as he nods. He understands, and I don't think I will ever be more grateful that he knows me so well.

"No," he tells the nurse, who's still glaring at Dane as if he's trying to intimidate him.

"That's not up to you. It's written in his orders."

"Do I look like I give a fuck what's written in his orders? He doesn't need that shit. He just wants the goddamn tube out so that he can say something."

Dane pushes the man back a step, angling himself in front of me more. "He's calm now, asshole." He waves a hand toward me. "He doesn't need that shit. See, he's stopped struggling."

I have stopped struggling, but I wouldn't say I'm calm. I also don't think this particular nurse is concerned. He appears to have a personal problem with us.

The nurse sneers at Dane. "I'll get security to handle this," he threatens.

"And I'll kick your bloody arse, then make sure you're out of a job before you pick yourself up off the floor." Ryder crosses his arms over his chest, his eyes flaring with tightly reined anger.

"I suggest you go find a doctor to remove the tube," Dane barks, then turns to the other nurse who came in with the asshole. "You get him a fucking pen and some paper."

The other two nurses leave the room, the original one the only one remaining. She hands me the paper and pen, then announces she will call my doctor before she leaves.

I grip the pen and paper with shaky hands. I'm surprised at how weak and tired they feel. Like the rest of me.

Despite the tremors, I write out a single word. A name.

Quinn.

I hold it up for them to see. Ryder glances at Dane with a strangely smug look before his brows pitch low, and he clenches his teeth. He's pissed. Maybe if I could remember what got me here, I would understand.

Although, for Ryder to be angry, I have an idea.

"She's fine." His tone carries a bite, and his eyes continue to flash anger. "She only leaves when we make her."

I breathe a sigh of relief. She's okay. *She's okay*. That's all I care about. Everything else is irrelevant.

Quickly I scribble—because that's all it really is—another word onto the paper.

Where?

"She's at Bastian's right now," Dane tells me. "Like Ryder said, she has to be forced to leave. Usually by Ryder or Bastian threatening to carry her out."

My heart squeezes with remorse. I hate that she's been too worried to leave on her own. That whatever happened has scared her that much. Which is what I want to know, so I write it on the paper.

"Are you serious?" Ryder snaps, making Dane and Angel flinch.

"Ryder now may not be the best—"

"Shut up, Dane. I'm not fucking happy with you either."

Dane groans, throwing his hands in the air.

I hold up my hands. I knew the tension in the room was thick, but it seems to be worse than I thought. I tap the words on the paper, asking again, the knot in my belly growing as I wonder what I've done now.

"Well, let's see. You found out you're gonna be a father about five minutes after you found out yours died, then snapped. You vanished and went on one hell of a fucking bender. Maybe I shouldn't be mad at you, but I am. I'm fucking pissed you *planned* to check out on me. And I want to kill Chris for putting you in that goddamn bed, but I guess I should be grateful since if it weren't for him, you'd be in the fucking morgue."

Wait? How did Chris put me here?

My brows furrow as I try to remember any of what he said. I won't deny any of it because it sounds like something I would do. But I can't...

"Need a refresher?" He reaches into his back pocket, pulls out a stack of papers, and tosses them on the bed. "Nice you decided to leave goodbye notes anyway."

"Shit, Ryder," Angel huffs, dragging a hand down his face as he turns around.

"You couldn't have waited?" Dane asks him. "Give him a day? A fucking hour?"

Ignoring them arguing, I pick up the papers and begin reading. My life, or most of it, there on the pages in my handwriting. All my greatest hits for everyone to see. The stuff I've worked hard to forget and bury has been laid out.

I flip through the pages to the letters he's talking about. Guilt slams into my chest as I read what I told each of them. My heart cracks when I read Quinn's.

I told her I love her.

In a fucking goodbye letter.

What the fuck is wrong with me?

I lean back against the pillows and slam my eyes shut. Everything I said and did crashes into me like a tidal wave.

But she's been here the entire time.

Then I remember...

Oh God, what did I do?

Again, panic builds in my chest as I remember the strip club. The girl...

There is no way Quinn will be able to get past that. Not after what she learned about her ex.

Now the dreams make sense. They were showing me everything I could've had and threw away.

MADDOX

Only you can make it right

    I walked into her room, stretching across her bed as if it were mine. The sound of the shower running had my dick throbbing against my zipper. I was tempted to go in there, but that was not why I came.

    The bathroom door opened, and she walked out. Wrapped in a towel and long hair dripping to her ass, she looked like seduction without even trying. The girl had no idea how fucking sexy she was.

    But she damn sure knew how to work that body.

    Eyes trailed over me, lingering on my mouth and lower. I smirked. Try as she might, she was not very good at hiding what she wanted.

    Her pink tongue darted out, running over her bottom lip. I cleared my throat loudly, trying not to laugh when she jumped, turning an enticing shade of scarlet. Red always was my favorite color.

    "Get dressed, cher," I instructed. "We got something to talk about."

    Still flushed from embarrassment and her shower, she turned toward the dresser, retrieving her clothes. I watched in agony as she slid the tiny pink shorts over her ass without panties and the thin tank over her head without a bra.

    She might have been embarrassed about getting caught ogling, but she wasn't above it.

    A slow, shy smile crossed her lips, but the sway of her ass contradicted her timidness. That's what she was. A tangled paradox that, in some ways, matched my own.

    She sat on the foot of the bed, legs crossed, and waited for me to speak again. Sometimes her quietness soothed me as much as her singing. She wasn't one for wasted words or idle chat, and though I sometimes sought those things to drown out the voices in my head, her stillness was almost like an anchor.

I often wondered where she found the strength because she struggled like I did. Maybe not in the same way or over the same things. But we both had demons and darkness that threatened to pull us under. My demons were winning.

I shook my head, clearing the dark thoughts. I needed to stay focused. Not get bogged down into the sludge.

"You still sure about what we talked about?" I asked her, wanting her to be positive about what she was asking.

She turned red again. It was cute.

I'd been honest with her about my previous sexual preferences, and she'd been curious. I had no expectations of her. She seemed far too sweet and innocent for that. Like she'd run away screaming at the thought. But the more I explained, the more interested she became. It ended well for both of us.

But she wanted me to take her to the Playpen, Bastian's other club. I wasn't sure it was a good idea, but I did anyway. All I did was walk her through, explaining things. She was squirming before the tour ended, and I reminded her that visit was only so she could see.

Her curiosity amplified, two days later, I handed her a list. "These are limits," I told her. "Hard limits are what you will not do. Soft limit means you're open to it, but you may change your mind later or have rules about it. Must limit is what you need to have, no matter what else is going on. These are what I'll do. If it's not on this list, don't bother asking. Now you need to decide what you're okay with and what limit it is for you."

To me, the list wasn't long. Contrary to popular belief, there were things I didn't do and had no desire to do. I wasn't into things like urophilia or degradation, and I wasn't about to start.

I liked pain, giving and receiving. I was always in charge. That was a must limit and a hard limit for me. Giving up control wasn't something I was willing to do for anyone.

I also like to watch and be watched. In the past, that included watching whoever I was with fuck someone else. I didn't care.

That wasn't happening with her. No one else was touching her.

After several minutes, she grabbed a pen and began writing. Almost immediately, she handed me the list. I looked at it and then back to her, very confused. She'd only written one word.

Cheating.

"That's my hard limit, Maddox. I know we haven't defined this yet, but that's the one thing that I won't tolerate at all. As long as we're doing... whatever it is we're doing, then you're only with me."

Her gaze dropped to her hands as they began to twist. Nervousness exuded from her. She was worried that would be the deal breaker.

Anyone else it would've been. I should've used it as my out. To end this between us before she got hurt.

Unfortunately, I wasn't ready to let go. I wasn't sure I would ever be. I fell hard and fast for the whiskey-eyed siren. Even if I couldn't admit it to anyone else, I couldn't lie to myself.

Without a word, I dragged her into my lap and kissed her forehead. "Don't fret, cher. There will only be you."

Shame and regret. The two constants in my life press down on me.

Followed by grief.

Grief over my father, sure. But it's the grief over the girl I've lost that threatens to swallow me whole.

It's inevitable after what I've done. Even if she can forgive the cruel words, overlook the vile things I've done in my past and everything else, there is no way she'll be able to accept what I let happen at that club.

Hands fisted in my hair, I release a muffled, strangled sound that annihilates my vocal cords. I can practically taste the copper.

Before, I wanted to die. Then, trapped inside nightmares that felt like hell, I wanted to live.

Now? Now I didn't know what I wanted. Because if dying meant I'd be tormented by thoughts and memories of her—of having her ripped away over and over... I wanted to die to end the pain, but that was the worst pain I'd ever experienced in my life. And it wasn't real.

But what would be the point of living without her? I'd still be in hell.

"What did you do, Maddox?" Ryder asks. He stares into my eyes, and I'm sure he sees all my sins.

Before I can answer, the door opens. Pulling a cart with equipment is a doctor, followed by the same nurse from earlier. "Glad you're awake, Maddox," he tells me. "I'm Stephen. We're going to unhook you from all the machines, but the IV has to stay for a while longer. It's the best way to give you the antibiotics."

Several painful minutes later, the nurse takes the cart as Dane hands me water. Swallowing is agony, but the cool liquid soothes the irritation.

The doctor—Stephen walks to the other side of my bed. He's young. Maybe late thirties or early forties. And acts like he knows me. "Am I supposed to know you?"

He shakes his head with a chuckle as he gets comfortable in the chair. "No. But we both know Bastian," he explains. I quirk a brow, waiting on him to elaborate further. "I've known Bastian for a long time. I guess you could say they've made me the doctor I am. They incentivize me to be a better doctor." A snort slips out of me. I regret it the minute it does, but it couldn't be helped. I can only imagine the kind of incentive Bastian gives him to ensure he has a high success rate. "Gotta say, you had me nervous. Especially with the two cardiac arrests."

That gets my attention. I glance at the guys in the room. They all have solemn looks at that piece of information, but they don't look surprised. I swing my gaze back to Stephen, my brows low. "Wait? So you're telling me I died? Twice."

"Scared the shit out of me," he nods as he pulls the bandage on my shoulder back. "But yeah. Once in the ambulance on the way here and once on the operating table. Bastian wouldn't have cared that I wasn't the one who administered the Ativan or that the fucking bullet moved when I went after it."

"Why the hell would they give benzos to someone with the shit I had in me?" The condescension is thick in my voice, but they're medical professionals. They should know better.

"They didn't know," he says as he has me sit to look at another bandage on my back. "You know you're lucky that bullet didn't do more damage. It made a pretty gnarly path before it stopped."

I still didn't understand that. Chris shot me? How did he know where I was?

But that was a question for later. I am still wondering how the first responders were so incompetent. "How could they not know? I had the shit everywhere." That much I remember clearly. I had enough heroin and coke to take out a horse and enough Jack to water an elephant. I was on a mission. A mission to stop feeling... everything.

Looking at my friends—my family—now, more shame threatens to drag me down. But I push it aside. The noise and the voices that tell me what a screw-up I am—that I can't even die properly— and how much I hurt people are ignored for the time being in search of answers.

"You were near the fireplace. All your shit was at the desk on the other side of the room. They didn't have time to look around since we all thought you were bleeding out." Dane's disgust for what I was doing is written on his face, from his narrowed blue eyes to his downturned mouth.

"They should have," Stephen tells us. "One of them should've asked questions."

"Maybe they did, and the other party conveniently *forgot* to give the answer," Ryder mutters.

Then something Dane said hits me. "What do you mean I was by the fireplace? There wasn't a fireplace in that hotel room."

They all share looks that make my skin crawl. Angel and Jake, who came in shortly after the doctor, both look at the ground. Dane squeezes his eyes shut. Ryder takes a ragged breath, then locks eyes on mine. "You weren't in a hotel room, Maddox. You were at your grandparents' house."

I shake my head. Over and over. "No. I was in a hotel. I remember driving for hours to get there. I was there for days. I would remember going back there."

"Fuck," Ryder hisses. He swipes a hand over his mouth, looks to the ceiling, and back to me. "Maddox, it wasn't days. It was hours. We found you around eleven the morning after your dad died."

"Maybe we need to slow down the questions," Stephen suggests as he takes my pulse, then clicks a button on the monitor. The tightening of the cuff around my arm tells me it's to check my blood pressure.

"No!" I yell, ignoring the squeezing around my arm and the tightening in my chest. "I couldn't have been there." I couldn't have been. I would know. I would remember. "I was at a hotel near the state line with Bryan."

Another pained look crosses all their faces, and they visibly flinch. My blood runs cold. Whatever is going on…

"Maddox," Ryder interrupts my thoughts, sounding completely exhausted. "Bryan isn't real."

I burst into laughter because this must be a joke. Not a funny one, but a joke nonetheless.

Except, the pain on their faces—the unease and stress written in the lines around their eyes that weren't there when I saw them last—tell another story.

But they're wrong. They know Bryan. They've seen him. I say as much.

"No, Mads," Dane says. "We haven't. Any of us."

"Yes. You. Have." My teeth grind together. Frustration and anger mix with panic that is building. "Jake, he was with us when we went after Cara. And he was there that night with Zoey. And the night Jewel died." I'm yelling at this point, even though it hurts like fucking hell because their faces are filled with so much pity it makes me sick.

"Madsy," Ryder starts, his voice cracking with emotion and eyes.

"NO! Don't *Madsy* me. He's real." He's got to be.

"No, mate, we haven't. We never heard the name until Quinn mentioned it except..." He drifts and looks at Dane. For backup, I suppose. And Dane looks just as uncomfortable.

In the nearly two decades I've known Ryder and the decade I've known Dane, neither of them has ever been uncomfortable around me or bashful to say what's on their minds. My stomach knots seeing it now.

"Except?" I grit out when they take too long to speak.

My patience is shot. My skin is crawling as I wait for them to say something.

And the *need* for something to make all this stop is strong.

"Maddox, the only time we've ever heard the name was when you used it as an alias." Dane finally says with a hard exhale.

My chest tightens. Everything around me begins to haze over. Buzzing fills my ears. My head erratically shakes from side to side. My whole body shakes. "Don't tell me that." My eyes sting and nose burns, but I push it down. I swallow around the huge lump in my throat. "Don't say that. Please."

My eyes jump to each of their faces. Remorse, sorrow, pity. Each of them has a mixture, and it makes me nauseous.

My fists tangle in the sheet. It hurts to even breathe.

I may have heard and seen things that weren't there, but I *always* knew they weren't there. My mind may have been twisted, but I was aware. I understood.

If Bryan isn't real... "He has to be real." My voice catches on the words. Struggles to get them out. "He's got to be."

Ryder reaches into his pocket and retrieves his phone. "Call him, Maddox. Look him up on social. Please, *please* prove us wrong."

My heart stutters, and my stomach lurches. If they want to be wrong...

I snatch the phone from his grasp. Staring at it, I try to recall the number. I've called and texted it dozens of times over the years. It's been the same number for as long as I can remember.

I punch in the number, hit the call button, then press speaker. Bile rises when the sound of a wrong number cuts in. "The number you have dialed has been disconnected," the automated voice says. I click end, unwilling to keep listening.

Silence fills the room. Sharp pain cuts through me. Absently, I swipe at the tears I didn't know I'd shed. My grip on the phone tightens until it's painful. My teeth clench until I hear a crack. Rage and pain rock my body until I'm vibrating.

The sound of the phone hitting the stone wall cuts through the silence. "GOD-FUCKING-DAMMIT!" I cry out, then lunge over the side of the bed, expelling all the water I drank.

"Mads, it's okay," Dane tells me. He's only trying to be supportive, but it makes me angrier.

"It's not fucking okay," I scream. "Do you know what it's like? Do you have any idea how it feels to know you're crazy? To know something is wrong with you? I've been aware for most of my damn life, but at least I knew. I knew what was real and what wasn't. Now you're all telling me that I knew nothing."

"This is good, Mads." Jake tries to reason. " You know he's not real now. We all know. You can get help now."

"Maddox, I wanted to talk to you about that," Stephen cuts in. "I wanted to give you some options for rehab and therapy. I would've preferred to wait a few days for this. You don't need to get so excited right now, but it's done and out there."

"Excited? You think I'm excited? I'm not excited. I'm fucking pissed. Why the fuck didn't you all just leave me there? Bleeding out would've been better than this shit."

"Maddox, shut up," Ryder hisses. "Just shut the fuck up, and listen."

"Maddox, you need rehab and a psychiatrist to help you," Stephen tells me.

"I don't need rehab. I had a goddamn slip. It fucking happens when addicts get bombshells dropped. As far as a psychiatrist, you've lost your minds if you think I'm talking to one of them."

"Maddox, based on the letter you wrote—"

I turn quickly to Ryder. "You showed him," I bellow. "Are you stupid?"

Ryder's eyes blaze with frustration and anger. His nostrils flare as he tries to control his temper. "Yeah, we fucking showed him. You need help, and if we have to lock you up for you to get it, then so fucking be it. I went to rehab. I went to a damn shrink. If I can do it, so can you."

"You didn't live through what I did," I grit.

"I lived through exactly what you lived through. He was manipulating us both, jackass. I figured it out when you beat the shit out of him. I never told you because I knew your masochistic, self-loathing ass would blame yourself."

I jerk back, unsure if I heard what I just think I did. "What do you mean—"

"He raped me too, Maddox," he spits out with so much venom the room should melt. "Just like he did you. And he blackmailed and manipulated me. Do you think I wanted to deal with another shrink?"

My head drops into my hands. *Everything* I thought I knew... I was supposed to be protecting him. Yes, it all started before we met, but I let it continue because I thought it would keep the sick fuck away from Ryder.

"Don't, Maddox. It's not your fault. And it's not mine. Do you know how hard it's been knowing all this time that I couldn't save you from that? But we were fucking kids. You know, this is why everyone says we are toxic to each other, right? Why they think we need to be on opposite sides of the planet? Because we do stupid shit together and for each other. Like drowning in bottles of booze and shoving enough white shit up our noses to create a snowstorm. But I had to go to rehab for Heaven and Tyler. I have to deal with this fucking anger that blinds me. And if you want Quinn and your kid, then you need to deal with your shit."

He storms out of the room like a whirlwind.

"I never said I wanted the kid," I yell at his back as he leaves.

"He's right, Maddox," Dane tells me, his eyes now just as flaming. "It's time to deal with *your* shit instead of taking on everyone else's."

"And *the kid* is yours, Maddox," Jake's eyes narrow. "*That* is something you better deal with soon."

"Don't fucking string her along until you decide, Maddox," Angel tells me.

They all walk out the door without looking back, leaving me alone with the doctor. "Got anything to add?" I snap.

"Look, I don't know you. For me, you're just a chart, and someone Bastian ordered me to save or else. All that aside, from what I've seen, you've got more people worried about you—that love you—than most people that come through here. You've had the waiting room full since you rolled in on that gurney. And you're girl, the couple of times I've seen her, has been a wreck and probably needs to be seen since she's pregnant but keeps insisting she's fine. You need help to figure out what's wrong so it can be fixed."

"You went to medical school. You should know my kind of problems can't be fixed."

"Maddox, depending on the problem, there are lots of options. Cures no, but it can be treated. You will always have the diagnosis just like you'll always be an addict. It's up to you to decide if those things define you. If they control you."

"I control me," I grit out, even though it's miles from the truth.

"Just think about it," he tells me, patting the bed.

He exits the room, leaving me alone with nothing but my thoughts.

Never a good place to be.

But maybe it's time I started listening too.

QUINN

Cast away regrets

I bolt upright in the bed. Intense pain squeezes my heart. Lungs burn as if I've been deprived of oxygen. Sweat coats my body. Even my hair drips.

Painful nausea swims in my belly. It quickly has me racing for the bathroom, barely making it in time.

Waves of urgency wash over me as his voice echoes in my mind. Hauntingly calling me. Pleading with me to hear his jagged cries.

Nearly tripping over my own feet, I rush back to the bedroom. Oversized sweats and a hoodie, all belonging to him, are tugged over my head and hips in a hurry. I don't care if it's the same thing I've worn all week. They smell like him.

Bare feet slapping the hardwood beneath me, I dash from the room, making my way through the massive converted warehouse, and up the stairs to Verity and Bastian's bedroom. I knock frantically on the door, turning the knob and pushing the door open when no one answers, without a care of what could await me.

The empty room sends a fresh wave of nausea through me as the smell of perfume and aftershave assault my senses. They're not here. I thought they would be here since Verity is on bed rest, but I suppose they had someplace to be.

Back down the stairs, I go to the table next to the antique and completely functional elevator. Dozens of keys stare back at me as I try to decide which one belongs to something I can actually drive. Finally, I grab the key fob with a symbol I recognize, knowing it belongs to something newer and not one of Bastian's vintage cars.

I step into the elevator and push the call button. The stupid thing moves at a snail's pace as it takes me to the huge garage but gives me a minute to try to call Bastian and Verity. I get their voicemail. The iron gate finally lifts, and I begin tapping the buttons on the key fob to find its owner.

Relief washes over me when the same blacked-out SUV Bastian let the others use lights up. Racing to the massive vehicle, I practically skid the last few feet, crashing into the side. I yank the door open, climb in, and press the engine button.

"No!" I exclaim furiously when the stupid thing doesn't start.

I push it again. And again. Until I slap the steering wheel with a scream. Then I see it. The fingerprint sensor.

"What the fuck, Bastian," I cry out.

I get out of the vehicle, slamming the door, the sound bouncing off the cement walls.

I push Verity's number again, then Bastian's, only to be sent to voicemail once again. Shoving thoughts that something might be wrong aside, I pull up my rideshare app. I can only afford to be concerned about one thing right now, and Maddox takes priority.

Not knowing the code to the garage, I use the stairs to go back into the main house, push my way through the door, then lock it behind me before taking off for the front entrance. Code tapped in, I step out the door, ensure the door locks behind me, then make my way down the metal steps of the building.

A silver sedan stops just as my feet hit the sidewalk. Dark hair and eyes greet me from the rolled-down window to verify who he's picking up.

At this point, I would've lied if he had said the wrong name.

Address absently rattled out as I climb into the car, the scent of alcohol and vomit nearly knock me back out. I try holding my breath as I settle into the back seat, but it still threatens to make me sick.

"Can we lower a window, please?" I ask when it becomes too much.

His apologetic brown eyes meet mine through the rearview mirror. He's just a college kid. Maybe even high school. "Sorry. A customer last night was pretty wasted. I've tried to clean it all morning, but the smell seems to have stuck."

"It's fine," I tell him softly as I all but hang my head out the window. "I just need to get to the hospital quickly."

"No problem," he smiles. "Should have you there in twenty."

Two hours later, I pull the hood tighter around my face and keep my head down as I slip through the throng of reporters surrounding the front entrance. They weren't there when I left. Bastian and Rory have been working tirelessly to ensure they stay away.

It makes my stomach hurt as I wonder what's changed.

The guard at the entrance gets a glimpse of me. He nods me through, and I start running, opting for the stairs instead of the elevator. I don't want to waste any more time.

I practically fall through the door of the fourth floor, nearly colliding with Dane, who jumps in surprise, sending his phone crashing to the floor. "Dammit, you just scared the shit out of me. Why haven't you answered your phone?"

Swiping at tears that have started to fall from fear that something is wrong, I pant, fighting to catch my breath. "I lost it," I answer his question. "Is Maddox okay? Please tell me he's okay."

Fingers I didn't realize I'd wrapped in the fabric of his shirt are pried away. "He's fine. Better than. He woke up. Ryder has been trying to call and text you."

Knees giving out, Dane catches me before I hit the ground as sobs wrack my body. "I've been in a car for two hours trying to get here. I think I dropped it before I got in the car. And I couldn't get Bastian's car to start. And they weren't there. And the bridge was backed up because of an accident."

"Whoa, whoa, whoa." He releases me after ensuring I won't collapse. "Calm down and back up. Start over with less snot on my shirt."

"Such a jackass," Angel grumbles when he walks up. "She can explain later. Let her go see him."

"Yeah. Fine." Dane brushes his hand through his hair, once again giving me a distrustful look. "He's asleep now, but he was asking for you."

"I know," I tell him as my heart hammers in my chest with nervous tension and excitement.

I'm down the corridor and nearly to Maddox's room when Dane's voice calls out, "What do you mean, you know?"

"I heard him," I whisper.

I don't know if he heard me or not. Waiting to find out isn't an option. I've done enough waiting.

I open the door slowly. The room is completely silent. Machines aren't breathing for him. Monitors aren't beeping.

I take a ragged breath and shake out my hands in an effort to alleviate my trepidation. I want to feel only relief, but fear is still there.

I know he was asking for me. I felt it. Heard it even in my sleep. But he's been awake for a little bit. What if he's reverted to pushing me away again? What if he still doesn't want our baby? What if he never does?

"You gonna stand there all day, love?" I gasp, not realizing Ryder is sitting in the corner of the room. "They gave him something to knock him out about half an hour ago when he started complaining of pain."

My eyes move over Maddox's sleeping form. Doubt and dread are shoved to the side. Shoulders straightening and chin up, I make a decision.

It doesn't matter what he does or says. How cruel and hurtful his words may be. Short of having me physically removed, he is not getting rid of me.

No matter how hard he fights me, I will fight *for* him that much harder. I am his, and he is mine.

I sit in the same chair I've sat in for days. His hand in mine, I stroke my thumb over the tattoo on his ring finger. "Why did they put him back to sleep?" I whisper, hoping Ryder can hear me.

"He was complaining about pain, but unless it's intolerable, they're not going to give him anything." I open my mouth to argue when he holds up a hand. "He's an addict. Giving him something will only make it harder for him long-term. They wouldn't give me anything if I were in that bed either."

"So we have to watch him suffer?" I slowly reach for him, gently brushing his hair out of his face. Every few minutes, his brows pull down, or he twitches, lost to his dreams.

"We've all watched him suffer for a long time, Quinn. This is mild in comparison. He's been through a lot." He turns around and walks to the window. Staring out at the city, he seems a million miles away as he continues to speak. "He and I have lived parallel lives. I think it's why we've been so dependent on each other all these years. Who else would you want to commiserate your pain than someone who's been through the same thing. Losing parents, never getting the emotional support from those remaining. That goddamn school shrink." He turns back around, his eyes looking haunted and tired. His hands scrub his face as if he could scrub the memories away. "Even what I went through with my sister and him with Zoey. What happened was very different, but I listened to Raina scream, completely helpless to do anything. For years after she died, I could still hear her screaming. Still can sometimes. He listened to Zoey scream every night for a year." With a sigh, he returns to the chair. He leans forward with his elbows on the bed and meets my eyes. "I hated her for what she put him through."

His admission shocks me. I suppose I understand it, but I still feel the need to remind him it wasn't her fault.

"I know that here." He taps his temple with two fingers. "But before that, Mads was trying hard to keep it together. I was the one in a long fucking spiral to rock bottom. To me she was selfish. Too blinded by her own pain to see she was slowly killing him. And Maddox's bloody savior complex meant he wouldn't stop her. It's his most toxic trait. I know you probably doubt about his feelings for you. It's obvious he's told you about Zoey—and me. But you need to understand something, he never felt that all-consuming love for us, and we never felt it for him. It was a love based on need. Don't think he loved Zoey from afar as a sacrifice. He used her as an excuse to avoid falling in love and getting hurt. The bloody git never understood that when love finds you, you can run and hide, but you won't get very fucking far."

He stands again, his restlessness making it hard for him to sit still. He and Maddox are so similar yet so completely different. Walking around the bed, he drops a hand to my shoulder, squeezing lightly. "Maddox isn't selfless, Quinn. Everyone puts him on that pedestal, but he's one of the most selfish bastards you'll ever know. His attempts to save everyone—to make sure their lives are happy and healthy are so he doesn't have to deal with his shit. He might need someone to force his hand. It won't be me because he's not afraid to lose me. He knows that no matter what he does, none of us are going anywhere."

I wrap my hand around Maddox's, gently rubbing my thumb across his knuckles. His entire body seems to relax to the touch. "I'm not going anywhere either," I whisper.

"You're in for the long haul, huh?"

"I'm in forever."

He nods and leaves the room. I'm left with my thoughts and worries. I'm in this forever, but the doubts tease the edge of my mind. Doubts that wonder if Maddox is in this 'til death does us part.

Reaching for the necklace around my neck, I trace the chain until my fingers find the cross pendant tucked underneath my shirt. Eyes close as I silently ask for strength and guidance. For direction.

Soon my silent requests turn into whispered pleas, no longer for myself but for him. For him to have strength and see his worth. Begging for his pain to stop.

For his demons to be exorcised.

"Don't waste your prayers on me, *cher*. God doesn't save those born in hell."

I lose my breath. The beat of my heart flutters like the wings of a butterfly just taking flight.

Hand over my heart, I wonder if it's beat at all these last five days.

I stare into those brilliant azure pools and barely contain my sob. "God helps everyone who asks for it."

He cups my face in his hand, swiping away the escaped tears. A tired, sad smile stretches his face before morphing into remorse and regret. "I'm so fucking sorry, Quinn," he murmurs. "I'm sorry I hurt you." He drops his hand, and his head falls back. "I'm sorry you were ever close enough to get hurt."

My stomach flips. Worry grows, and I steel myself for him to send me away.

Or try.

"I can't believe you're here after what I said. After learning how fucked up I am."

I grab his hand, kiss his palm, then slide my fingers into his. "I love you, Maddox. That doesn't just go away because you say things to hurt me. It doesn't change because you're not perfect."

He winces with a sharp breath. Tightness around his eyes and the flex in his jaw gives away his pain. Without a thought, I release his hand and reach for his face. My heart cracks when he grabs my wrist, halting my touch.

"I need to tell you something." His throat bobs when he meets my eyes. "You have to know. What I said the other night? I didn't mean. Not all of it anyway."

"Maddox, I—" I want to tell him it doesn't matter. That none of it matters except right here, right now. But he cuts me off.

"Let me finish, Canary. I'm not making excuses, but when Callie called me about..." He trails off and looks across the room. Shadows grow in his eyes, but he blinks them away and looks at me again. "One second, I was comforting her. Then we hung up, and everything got so damn loud. Dark. It felt like I was drowning. And then you were there. I should not have said that shit to you, but... I don't know." He shakes his head as he gets lost in the memories.

I want to tell him it's okay, but I don't. I don't because he said he shouldn't have said it, not that he didn't mean it.

Blue eyes drink my amber one. Regret and shame cloud his. My bottom lip slips between my teeth, biting down until copper floods my taste buds as I try to stop myself from saying something.

"It was like I was outside my body, watching. I could hear the words. Screamed at myself for being so stupid, but I couldn't stop it." He grabs my hand, squeezing it tight. Too tight. His panicked eyes search mine, pleading with me for... I don't know what. "I remember, but I swear I didn't mean to." He shakes his head, his frustration wearing on him. It's killing me to stay silent, but I know he won't listen until he says what he needs. "My perception of time was off. Way off. I thought I drove for hours. Thought I was trapped in a hotel with Bryan for days." The way he spits out the name, I know the others have told him about that. "I just wanted the noise to stop, Quinn. The pain. So I did what I do best. I bought enough coke and heroin to stop the pain and enough alcohol to drown myself. I fucked up, but I swear I didn't know what I was doing. I would never intentionally hurt you like that."

He's rambling. His words are drawn together in nothing but a rushed breath.

Thundering in my chest nearly drowns out his words. Knowing where this is going makes my heart hurt. What I saw on that screen two days ago has been playing on repeat in my mind.

But I needed to see for myself. The pain of it has been awful, but the knowledge that he wasn't aware of what he was doing—not fully anyway—makes it bearable.

I was hoping he wouldn't remember. But I've also been plagued with thoughts of him remembering but hiding it from me.

I should've known better.

Spine straightened, mental faculties in place, I prepare myself to lie. The one thing he asked me never to do.

Without meeting my eyes, he tells me what I already know without details. Not that I need them.

Fear begins to fester. Even without the details, he says enough to let me know that he remembers everything. Convincing him it wasn't real seems more impossible.

"I'm sorry, baby. So fucking sorry."

Swallowing around my nerves. I move to sit on the edge of the bed. Hands on each side of his head, I lie to his beautiful face.

MADDOX

The fault is mine

"Do you understand me, Maddox? Nothing happened. You watched a couple of girls dance, then left. Bastian and I saw the video." Those whiskey eyes look straight into my eyes and lie. She breaks my one rule. The only thing I've ever asked of her.

The one thing she asked of me, I shattered into a million pieces, and she breaks my rule because of it. To protect me. To save *me*.

Love presses down, squeezing my chest to the point of pain. It grows immeasurably.

I have no doubt she saw the videos. She doesn't know her pain radiates in those beautiful eyes. Has no idea the anguish I caused is etched on her face.

And yet, she still lies. Because she doesn't want me to feel guilty. She doesn't want me to hurt.

What do I say to that? How the hell do I react?

She draws her bottom lip between her teeth. Something she does when she's worried.

I pull it loose, running my thumb over the plump flesh.

Fuck, she's beautiful.

"You should run away, *cher*," I tell her, still staring at her full mouth. Fighting to keep thoughts that have no place in this moment at bay.

A tear she's been holding back slips down her cheek. She looks down at the rings on her finger, brushing a thumb over them. Panic seeps in when she takes them off.

I said she should run. Not that I would let her.

She holds them between her fingers, staring at them. Silence fills the air, giving me chills.

My heart hammers against my ribs. My stomach flips and rolls as waves of nausea ravage me. I can't take anymore when she absently swipes at the fallen tear.

"Put the rings back on, *cher.*" My tone is harsh, but all I feel is the hysterics building.

"Why did you marry me?" she asks without looking up.

Because the minute I saw her, I knew she was mine. She was made for me. Destiny plucked the stars from the sky and put them in her eyes. Fate molded her heart from the heavens. The Moirae spun her from the marrow of my bones, the blood of my heart, and the salt of my tears.

Jesus, I'm dramatic.

But it doesn't make it less true. She was put on this earth for me.

It seemed like a sick joke because I knew I would screw up. She deserved better.

I never denied—to myself—how I felt. Just knew it was doomed from the start.

That knowledge didn't stop me from calling Ryder's grandfather and asking him to make me a ring. A ring designed specifically for her by my hand.

Despite the burning, aching need I felt the second I saw her, I convinced myself I couldn't give her more than a good time. And perhaps heal a few of those jagged edges her life had caused.

I never thought I would give her the ring. I wasn't staying in River City, and she was just getting over her ex. She was still legally married.

But every day after I called Christopher—Ryder's grandfather—the need intensified.

It was delivered moments after the process server dropped off her divorce papers.

I never believed in signs before. Not the good kind, anyway. Life never offered them to me.

Yet, I latched onto that sign like it was the threads of fate weaving us together.

I always believed I was destined to ruin everything I touched. Fated to be the poison that destroyed all that I cared about. Love was never in the cards for me.

Until it was.

It feels just as doomed now as it did then. Fated to collide and destined to burn. But during my... coma, death, or whatever, I've realized that we may destroy everything in our path, but I'd rather burn alive in this love.

I don't just want her or need her. She is the reason I exist. The reason, no matter how hard I've tried to escape this life, fate had other plans.

She is the plan.

I don't know if it's my second, third, or final chance, but for her, I'm going to try. For her, I'll do more than survive. I'll live.

I take the rings from her and return them where they belong. "Come here, Canary."

She bites her bottom lip as she eyes the bed. I grab her hand, pulling her toward me as I slide over, grinding my teeth against the pain.

She slides in slowly. Rigid and tense, she attempts to make herself as small as possible.

Slipping my arm behind her, I grab her by the waist and pull her into my side. "I said come here," I say roughly. "I meant *here*. Beside me. Touching me."

Tucked into my side, she meets my eyes. So much apprehension fills the glistening amber depths. "I don't want to hurt you."

"Darlin', I don't remember a time I haven't been consumed by pain, but you have never been the cause." Fingers threaded together and her body pressed against mine soothes me. Finally, I can breathe again. After the non-stop nightmares, the guys telling me that she was okay did little to ease my mind. Even seeing her didn't help because I don't trust my eyes.

But feeling her? Relief finally comes.

"First, let me clarify," I say, brushing a thumb over her ring. "I said you should run. Not that I would let you."

"I'm not running," she whispers as those long, dark lashes flutter against her cheeks.

"I know. I'm the one who did that, and it fucking hurt like a bitch."

I ran under the guise of protecting her. Part of me wanted to protect her from this. The addiction. My fucked up head. My shattered, dark heart. She didn't deserve that. Didn't deserve to be saddled with me.

But I was also selfish. I was running because I was tired of the pain.

Except running from her hurt more than staying.

Deep down, I know this spiral was so severe because my heart couldn't handle being away from her.

"To answer your question—which you shouldn't fucking have, but that's on me—from the moment I saw you, I wanted you. I had to make you mine. Sure, I've fucked you when and where I wanted, but it was never about that with you. Outside the club that night, everything in me told me to walk away because I was consumed with the need to make you forget every pair of eyes that saw you on that stage but mine. That night on Bastian's balcony, I wanted them to see me taking you. Show them who you belonged to. Not because Bastian told me no, but to prove you were mine. I have *never* been jealous or possessive. I had no desire to get into a dick-measuring contest over a piece of ass. Except. With. You. From the moment our eyes locked, I knew my heart was never really broken. It was incomplete. You were holding all the missing pieces, and it had been waiting to find you. I married you because, despite everything I said about being bad for you, I wanted you tied to me in every possible way. Because I am the worst decision you have ever made, but, baby, you're the best I've made."

The words she wants still won't leave my lips. I would've done anything to say them to her in that infernal hell-loop of a dream.

Now I can't seem to force them out, and I have no idea why. Because I feel it. I feel it and so much more. Love isn't a strong enough adjective to explain what I feel for her.

She runs the fingers of the hand I'm not holding over the tattoo on my finger. A soft sigh escapes her as her body finally melts into mine. "I was already yours, Maddox. Tied and bound by my heart. My spirit recognized yours. Your soul spoke to mine. I never needed a piece of paper or a way-too-expensive ring."

A winded chuckle burst from my chest. I didn't want her to freak out, knowing I'd had the ring designed and paid for weeks before. So I pretended to run into that shop and buy a spur-of-the-moment ring. "You know about that, huh?" I kiss the side of her head with a grin. "I know you didn't need it, but I did."

I look down and see her fast asleep beside me. Within minutes, her soft snores lull me to sleep as well.

MADDOX

To every fool with an opinion

Lights flicking on wake me. I open my eyes to find the asshole male nurse from earlier doing something to my IV and Quinn sleeping peacefully at my side. Ryder and Liam walk into the room, with Bastian following close behind. They all look troubled, which doesn't bode well.

I gesture for them to be quiet, tilting my head towards Quinn's sleeping form.

"She needs to get out of the bed," the guy grunts. "It's against policy, and she could kink your IV."

My eyes swing to him, narrowed and tight. A growl bubbles in my chest. He's lost his damn mind if he thinks she's going anywhere, and I tell him as much.

"I'll get security if I have to," he threatens with a scowl on his face like he did earlier. But before, it was Ryder arguing with him. This time I'm perfectly capable of speaking for myself. It's obvious he has a problem with me, but now I have a problem with him.

"You must not like your job," I tell him, keeping my eyes firmly on his. "Because every time you open your mouth, you inch your way toward the unemployment line."

"Fucking rich, entitled bastard," he mutters as he replaces the saline bag.

Bastian starts toward him, his fists clenched and teeth bared. I shake my head, letting him know I've got this. He's watched out for me for a long time. Long before I even realized. We need to try words before we resort to blood. Or death. Bastian often chooses the latter.

Besides, I have never wanted or needed anyone to fight my battles for me.

"You fucked up, mate," Ryder practically hums as he plops into a chair, throwing his feet on my bed.

The guy swings his gaze toward Ryder, giving him the same disdainful sneer. His problem isn't just with me. It is with all of us in this room because we have money.

When I was younger, I never really flaunted my last name. Since I've accumulated fame and wealth based on my own talent, I still don't like to flaunt it, but I'd be lying if I said I'd never used it to my advantage. Occasions like this are moments where I do more than flaunt.

"Yep. That's me, The goddamn rich and entitled bastard with my name on this building and enough fucking influence to make sure you can't even get a job scrubbing toilets at Gas N Go. And you're lucky it's me instead of him." I nod my head toward Bastian, who is glaring holes into the man. "Or you wouldn't make it to the next *Fais do-do* I'm sure you are waiting for."

Bastian smirks and gives the man a smile that makes him shiver. Ryder burst out laughing. "Damn, mate. That accent got thicker with every word."

The nurse starts for the door, but I have one more thing to add. "Don't come back in here. If you do, I'll be making that call."

Ryder is still cackling like a hyena as the door closes behind the asshole. "Damn, you make me all warm and fuzzy when you get all assertive and authoritative."

"None of that shit," Bastian grumbles.

Ryder laughs some more.

But it's Liam I've noticed who hasn't said a word since he walked in. His eyes have been firmly locked on Quinn, and it's starting to piss me off. However, it's not taking much right now. Everything is pissing me off.

Stirring next to me draws my attention away from him. Whiskey eyes flutter. "I didn't mean to fall asleep." Her sweet, raspy voice sings to me.

"You're exhausted." I kiss the top of her head, breathing in the scent of lavender and jasmine.

"Which is why we have been making her leave," Ryder remarks as he leans back in the chair further.

"And where she was supposed to be when Verity and I got home," Bastian adds. "How the hell did you even get here?"

"Uber," Quinn shrugs.

"Don't do it again," Bastian tells her, and Ryder nods in agreement.

"I agree, Canary. Don't do that shit."

"I had to get to you. I heard you calling me. I know it was just a dream, but I heard you."

The last thing I remember before I woke up was calling for her. It's impossible, but for some reason, I believe she did hear me.

Her eyes swing around the room. The moment they meet Liam's, she tenses but challenges his arrogant glare with one of her own.

My eyes dart between them, noticing the tension I don't understand. Fire begins to bubble in my veins as anger grows at how Liam keeps looking at her. "Is there a problem I need to be made aware of?" I grind out between clenched teeth.

Liam stops glaring at Quinn and redirects his attention to me but doesn't say anything. After a second or two, he drops his gaze.

"We do have a problem," Ryder breaks the tension building in the room. Or rather, he replaces it with another kind. "News has leaked about Quinn."

"Dammit," I hiss.

The first time her pictured popped up on social media, I scrambled. I asked Christian and Georgie to help me get it down fast and put up code to block her picture and name.

I hated that she was seconds away from being national news. Especially given the pictures were taken when I had my fingers in her cunt in the alley behind the strip club. It wouldn't have been the first time that happened to me. I never cared before, either. Someone wanted to fuck me; who was I to deny them? Far as the other person went, I am Maddox Masters. It's *why* they wanted to fuck me.

Quinn wasn't like that. She wasn't like anyone else. She didn't expect it and didn't want it.

She has no inhibitions with me. Always open to anything, but I knew she didn't sign up to be plastered all over the internet or hounded by the paparazzi. Truthfully, I wasn't sure she could handle it. It's why I insisted on keeping her a secret.

"This isn't just a social media leak, Mads," Bastian tells me as he glares at Quinn. She flinches, knowing he's still angry she left his house without his knowledge. "Documents were leaked to RGD. None of us found out until they were everywhere. Prescott media is the only one not running the story."

"Goddammit," I yell, and Quinn jumps. "What the fuck documents? How the hell did this happen?"

The veins between Bastian's eyes begin to throb as he walks toward me. He stops when he looks at Quinn, but his jaw is still tight. I've pissed him off. If this were any other situation, I'd take pleasure that I've accomplished getting under his skin.

Who am I kidding? I still do.

"I've had my fucking hands full," he growls. "Trying to take care of my businesses, my overstressed, pregnant wife who was just put on bed rest, stopping *your* asshole friends from throwing your wife out like yesterday's trash. Not to mention stressing over your fucking stupid, masochistic, self-destructive dumbass, and I don't worry, Maddox. I don't fucking like it." His shoulders are at his ears. His chest heaves, and I'm surprised literal smoke isn't coming from his nose.

But one thing out of everything he just said stands out to me. "What the hell do you mean my friends were trying to toss Quinn out?" I ask as I look at Liam and Ryder.

"That's why there were so many people out front when I got here," Quinn mutters. "When I saw them, I thought..." she trails off and sniffles.

"Did they give you a hard time?" Ryder asks.

She shakes her head, offering a sheepish grin. "My weird need to smell like Maddox paid off. Nobody recognized the kid slipping by in the three sizes too big hoodie and sweats."

"That's convenient considering it's a bonafide shit show out there." Liam, without meaning to, just answered my question with his sarcastic tone.

Quinn's stomach growls loudly, giving me my opening to get her out of the room, so I can figure out what the actual fuck is going on.

"Why don't you go find something to eat?" I suggest when her stomach growls again.

"I'm not hungry," she lies, even though we can all hear that she is.

I press my lips to her temple and force a light chuckle. "You need to eat, baby. I'll be here when you get back."

"You've got more than just yourself to think of, Quinn," Ryder tells her.

A heavy sigh leaves me when he points out what I've been avoiding acknowledging. "He's right, Quinn. Go. I promise I'm not going anywhere."

She offers a half-hearted smile and attempts to ease off the bed as gingerly as she climbed on. Hand around her waist, I yank her back to me, biting back the shock of pain. "Stop with the cautiousness." I grip her face, probably harder than I should. This isn't the time to taste those sweet lips, but she needs a reminder.

There is nothing sweet and gentle about the way I claim her mouth. Not in the way I force her to open for me or the way I take her tongue between my teeth. For a moment, she tenses, then surrenders herself to me. Her hands fist the hospital gown as she moans softly. Her eyes are hazy and full of lust when I release her. "You can't break what's already broken, *cher*. Now go find food. Don't come back until you've both been fed."

She nods, climbs off the bed, and walks dazedly to the door, not hearing Bastian call out to her. He grabs her by the elbow and turns her around. Ryder snickers as she blinks and focuses on Bastian. "You dropped this by my front door." He slips her phone into her hand, not releasing her hand right away. "Do not go online."

Biting her lip, she nods, then leaves the room.

"Heaven is going with her," Ryder tells me, still grinning that cocky smile. "Thought it would be best considering the shaky legs you just gave her. Speaking of legs, seems like your third one still works properly."

I roll my eyes, ignoring him. Now that she's out of the room, I have questions. For one person in particular.

"Who wants to fill me in?" I bark with my glower firmly fixed on Liam. Between his stares and insinuation and what Bastian said earlier, we clearly have a problem. "You want to tell me why you keep glaring at my girl like she's done something wrong?"

"I just find it all very convenient." He straightens his spine, meeting my stern glare. Not backing down in the slightest. "A mysterious leak to the media about you. Your marriage."

"For fuck's sake, Liam," Ryder yells as he abruptly stands.

Liam throws his hands in the air and turns to face Ryder. "What? Why am I the damn bad guy here? I am trying to protect the band and Maddox. Why is that wrong?"

"Protect us from whom? My wife?" I spit as fury overtakes me.

"I cannot be the only one that finds all of this too damn coincidental. I mean, I know Dane agrees with me—"

"The fuck did you just say?" I blast. My head starts to throb. Ears ring and vision grows hazy. Wrath consumes me because he did *not* just say that to me. There is no way Dane would feel that way too.

"Maddox, I get this girl has you twisted, but come on. The pretty, young stripper? The rich, sex-god rock star? It's so fucking cliché that it's pathetic. And how fucking opportune that she gets herself knocked up by the guy that's seen more action than a revolving door at Grand Central. Let's not forget that less than a month ago, she was married to some other poor son of a bitch." His jaw clicks with irritation, but he has no idea. He doesn't know shit about her except what little bit he's dug up through whatever source. The surface, that's as far as he got.

Bastian grabs him by his shirt, slamming him against the wall. "Didn't give you a fucking right to make her leave the hospital. Or put your goddamn hands on her, *testa di cazzo*."

But Liam isn't a small guy, and he's not a pussy. He pushes Bastian off with a growl that only incites Bastian further. Before Bastian can pull whatever weapon he's reaching for beneath his leather jacket, Ryder is between them, shoving them both.

I yank the IV from my arm, ignoring the blood that spills onto the sheets. Biting back the grunt of pain, I sling my legs over the side of the bed. The fiery pain shooting through my body fuels me. It takes me a second to steady myself, but once I do, my steps are determined.

There is not a strong enough word to explain this volatile, incendiary rage that's burning through me. I'm not sure I've ever felt this kind of fury.

None of them notice that I'm no longer in bed until I'm standing next to them.

The radiating pain means nothing. The squeezing in my chest? The way it hurts to fucking breathe? None of it compares to this malice flowing through me.

"You are entitled to your thoughts and opinions," I tell him, my voice deep, gruff, and barely contained. They all turn to face me. "But who the actual fuck do you think you are to lay a fucking finger on her?"

My fists tangle in Liam's shirt just as Bastian had done only moments ago. I inhale deeply, trying to find my quickly slipping control.

"Mads, get back in the bed," Ryder says with a hand on my shoulder.

I shake him off, pull my fist back, and release. Liam's head snaps back, hitting the wall with an audible thud. But I'm not done. I push him into the wall and hit him again. And again. Blood pours from his nose and mouth. Ryder pulls me off of him, and he slides to the floor, pressing his thumb against his mouth.

"You don't fucking know her." My words come out fractured and ragged as I breathe through the pain searing my shoulder. "You don't know that her ex—the poor, unwitting son of a bitch as you called him—cheated on her the entire time they were together. Or that she came home to packed bags at the doorway when he knocked up his girlfriend."

The door squeaking interrupts my malediction. I look over my shoulder, and the irritation spikes again when Dane's face appears. "What's going on in here? We can hear you all the way to the waiting room."

Jake and Angel appear behind him, both looking equally concerned. "What the fuck, Maddox?" Angel's eyes narrow. "Why is Liam on the floor with blood pouring out of his face? And why are you out of bed?"

"Maddox, you're bleeding," Jake tells me. I look down, expecting to see it from where I pulled the IV out but find it over my chest instead.

"You've ripped your stitches," Bastian tells me.

I ignore him. I ignore the pain. I ignore it all. Pointing a finger at Liam, I say, "You are fucking fired." Turning, I face a gape-mouthed Dane. "And you can get the fuck out too. In fact, why don't you go find another band to play in."

"Mads, what the hell?" Dane jerks back in shock.

"Madsy, you need to calm down," Jake tells me. "Don't do something you'll regret."

"He's right, Mads," Ryder tells me. "You don't need to make decisions while you're pissed."

"Don't pretend you wouldn't do the same," I scoff.

"And you'd be there to pull me back."

"Not this fucking time," I hiss. "Get them both out of my sight."

QUINN

We're here to stay

Liam and Dane walk out of Maddox's room at the same time. Liam looks upset—and bloody—and Dane looks like someone just killed his puppy.

I look at Heaven, who seems equally confused and concerned. She shrugs her shoulders and follows me as I approach them. "What's wrong?" I ask them both as nerves begin to swarm.

Dane shakes his head sadly while Liam tosses me a look of contempt, but neither stop walking. Again I look at Heaven. Her brows pull low as she shakes her head. "No idea," she says.

We walk into Maddox's room. Bastian and Ryder are helping Maddox back to bed while Jake and Angel look upset. My heart throbs in my chest when I see the blood on his hospital gown and on the sheets of the bed. I practically sprint the eight feet from the door to his bedside. "What happened? Are you okay?"

"I'm fine, *cher*," he grinds out through clenched teeth as he tries to mask his pain.

"I'll get a nurse," Heaven announces.

"I don't understand. Why are you out of bed?" I look down and notice his IV just lying on the sheets. "You pulled out your IV? What's going on? Why did Dane and Liam leave?" I'm so confused. None of this makes sense. Everything seemed fine when I left. Except maybe for the daggers Liam kept...

Oh my God!

"Maddox, what did you do?" I look at Bastian and Ryder accusatorily. "What did you tell him?"

"The truth." Ryder crosses his arms over his chest and stares at me, daring me to lie.

"Why?" I yell, throwing my hands up. "He didn't need to know that."

Maddox glares at me. He grips his side in a hiss, but his narrowed eyes stay zoomed on me. "I did need to know, and you should've been the one to tell me, *cher*. I will not have you disrespected more than you have already been."

"Maddox, what. Did. You. Do?"

"What I had to," he yells, refusing to be straight with me.

"That's not an answer." I prop my hand on my hip and point accusingly at him, demanding answers.

He shifts in the bed, trying to get comfortable even though it's obvious he's in a lot of pain. The way he ignores, it reminds me of what Ryder said. He can handle the physical pain. Finally, with a huff, he answers. "I fired them. Okay? I mean it. I don't want them around you."

"Oh my God, Maddox. No." I gesture between the rest of them standing in the room, specifically at Ryder. "And you let him?"

"You think he could stop me, Canary?"

"It's a *band*. Isn't there supposed to be a vote or something?" I look at all of them, trying to figure out why they would let him do this. This is insanity.

"Fuck that," Maddox spits. "If they don't agree, *I'll* leave."

I look at all of them again, still wondering why they are placating him. They can't agree with this. I know they don't.

Well, if they won't stop this stupidity...

I spin on my heels and march out to the door, bumping into Heaven and the nurse when it opens. "Where are you going?" Maddox yells across the room like an asshole. "Get back here."

I ignore him. He's being unreasonable, and I won't be the cause of the band falling apart. I don't bother with the elevator—I'm still irritated with Bastian's ancient lift—and hit the stairs, hoping I'm not too late.

Just like hours ago, I'm taking four flights of stairs two steps at a time. When I reach the last step, I fling the door open and fall into Dane.

"Holy hell," he squeaks. "What is it with you and falling out of stairwells?"

I lean forward, grabbing my side as pain shoots through me from the exertion. Gripping Dane's arm for balance, I struggle to catch my breath. "I had to catch you," I wheeze. "Both of you."

"Do you forget you're pregnant?" He steadies me as I straighten.

"Only when I'm not making out with the toilet," I snap, and he flinches, grumbling about pregnant women and hormones.

"Not sure exerting yourself is the best thing," he says a little too calmly like he's suddenly navigating a land mine.

I bite back a retort that I am *not* hormonal. Then decide against it because maybe I am.

"What do you want?" Liam cuts in sharply. His eyes flare with resentment and anger. Can't say I blame him. Despite everything, he is out here because of me.

I wonder if this is how Yoko felt.

Though everyone should know Paul broke up The Beatles with his diva attitude. Not Yoko. The fact that the other three performed together on Ringo's album after the split speaks volumes.

I'm not going to be the reason Maddox loses his band. His family. He lives for the music, and these guys are his world.

No. Just no.

"You need to go back upstairs and fix this." I place a hand on my hip and tilt my chin. I hope it displays confidence, but I have a feeling it only appears that I'm looking up at them.

"He fired me. Why would I go up there?" he snaps.

"He's angry. Please, don't leave." I look at Dane, who's got that sad puppy look again. "You both know him. He'll get over it."

"I don't think he will, Quinn. Not this time." Dane tells me.

Grabbing both their hands, I try pulling them toward the elevator. They don't budge, and I get annoyed. "Please." I am begging at this point, but I know Maddox will regret it later. So will they. "Put your pride aside for just a minute. He's just emotional. You would be too if you were in his shoes."

The corner of Liam's eyes crinkle as a slow smirk pulls his lips. "Afraid he'll resent you?"

Irritation boils, and resentment builds. I'm making an effort to hold this found family together. Practically on my knees, begging these men not to give up. To put their issues with me aside as I am doing. I am here for Maddox, but for them too. They are family.

But this arrogant ass of a man has pushed my last button, and my palm connecting with his already bruised cheek relays my irritation at his near-constant implication that I have an ulterior motive. His smug smile is replaced with wide eyes, raised brows, and a gaping mouth. "I have let you berate me from the minute we met. You've treated me as nothing more than a gold-digging whore, and I. Am. Over. It. For the record, I am not worried about Maddox resenting me because you did this, you arrogant, condescending, motherfucking asshole. But he has enough regrets in his life. I just wanted to save him—and *you*—from one more."

I start to walk but stop, spinning—and instantly regretting it when the room keeps going—to face them for one final thing. "You know, I don't know who hurt you, but you are not the only person to have gone through something. You should stop acting like you are." I turn back around and go to the elevator.

Ignoring how my stomach clenches from the confrontation, I press the elevator button. When two large bodies step up next to me, I ignore them too, crossing my arms over my chest and tapping my toe impatiently.

We enter the elevator, and I grip my side in a hiss when the pain intensifies. I hope it's just from the exertion of the day, and it isn't a sign of a kidney stone. I've had those a few times, and they are not fun.

"You okay?" Liam asks.

My brows shoot up, and I mock scoff. "Don't tell me you're concerned."

"I'm not heartless," he mumbles, and I bite back a grin at the redness creeping into his cheeks.

"Don't strain yourself there," I tease, and he relaxes.

The elevator doors open, and we turn right to go to Maddox's room. We pass several other patient rooms before reaching his in the middle of the corridor.

I go in first; unsurprisingly, Maddox is pissed when I walk in. "Where the fuck did you go?"

I cringe because I knew it would set him off. Maddox wants what he wants when he wants it. His need for control borders on neurotic. Given what I know now, it makes sense to me. But finding that balance of what to allow hasn't been easy.

"Did you not hear us that everyone knows about you now? That means there could be reporters anywhere. Or belligerent fans. Or just some regular jackass looking for fifteen minutes of fame or a payday."

I feel the color drain from my cheeks. Those things didn't cross my mind.

Part of me thinks he's worrying too much, but I can't be sure. I don't know anything about that part of his life.

I take a breath, find my center, and steel my backbone. He may be right, but I would've still gone after Dane and Liam because I was doing it for *him*.

"I went to fix your mistake," I tell him firmly as I step aside and let Dane and Liam enter the room. "Before it was too late to take it all back."

"Fuck no!" he yells. "Not after how they treated you."

I'm not a doctor, but I know cardiac arrest—twice—only five days ago is a good reason he should not be getting so upset. So I do everything I can to keep my tone calm, even if my words must be blunt. "Maddox, I am a big girl. I can take care of myself. You don't need to defend me. And they had no business telling you like a couple of little tattling toddlers."

Bastian growls from his corner at the implication.

"So you expect me to sit back and let them treat you like shit?" He is irate and extremely dumbfounded that I would even consider such a thing.

I wouldn't. I know him too well, even in such a short time, to ever think he would allow that. But he can't and won't always be there to defend me. And I won't be the poor, pitiful little girl that runs to him in tears because his friends were mean to me.

But he's so angry he is shaking. And my heart is so full it's overflowing because I see how much he loves me in his anger. I can't imagine he'd allow someone to come between him and his family under any other circumstances. And that speaks volumes.

I also notice that he scratches absently at his arms. And though I know this is all because of me, I realize it's also being exacerbated by something else. Something I can't relate to, and he will struggle with along with everything else for the rest of his life. And my overflowing heart bleeds for him.

I walk across the room, climb onto the bed, and take his face in my hands. Our eyes meet, my heart stops, and he visibly calms. "I would never expect that of you. But I do expect you to remember these are your friends. Yes, their words hurt, but they wouldn't feel that way if they didn't love *you* and want to protect you as much as you do them. As much as you do me."

He closes his eyes with a deep inhale. They open on an exhale, and the stormy blue turns into those clear oceanic pools once again. "I can't handle the thought of anyone hurting you. Including me. And I know I've hurt you the most."

Dane steps up sheepishly. He tugs on the back of his neck, shoulders slumped, and meets mine and Maddox's eyes. "Look, Mads. When we got here, you were missing, and then the stripper—" Maddox growls, but it's not at the word as much as the sarcastic tone.

I grab Maddox's hand and slide closer to his side. "Let him finish."

He grits his teeth and rolls his eyes but nods tightly for Dane to continue.

Dane offers me a small, thankful smile. "Sorry. Then *Quinn* appeared out of nowhere, man. Eyes red and puffy from crying. Then announced she was pregnant. It just seemed off."

Liam huffs and steps beside Dane. "How many times have we seen this scenario? Musician meets stripper or groupie or whatever, they get pregnant, and the musician is trapped."

"And I'm not your average, green newbie with his first taste of the spotlight. Did you both forget that I've been chased, harassed, and hounded by women and men alike after their fifteen minutes of fame or some payday, my entire life?" Maddox grunts, his mouth pulling down in a frown as if the thought leaves a bad taste in his mouth. "I can spot that shit a mile away."

"We all can until we're blinded by ass and tits." Liam shrugs as if it's a well-known fact.

Maddox tenses and shifts in the bed. If I weren't wrapped around him, he'd be out of bed again. I only hope his last explosion didn't do more than tear his stitches. He doesn't seem to realize his body needs to heal.

"Not Maddox," Ryder chimes in. "You both know that."

"Except I didn't know as much as I thought I did." Dane looks at the ground, almost as if he's embarrassed he even had to make the comment.

My palm itches with the need to slap him. I understand where he's coming from, but he knows Maddox. Even I know him well enough to realize that no matter what mental or emotional demons he's fighting, he's aware. Frighteningly so.

But it's Maddox I'm worried about. I feel his entire body go rigid next to me. Can practically taste the guilt and concern he's emitting. "So now you're questioning my judgment," he whispers.

"His judgment is fine," Bastian's deep voice cuts through the air like a sudden clap of thunder. I almost forgot he was in the room. He steps out of the corner he is standing in, his eyes daring anyone to disagree. "If you read between the fucking lines of those damn letters or whatever the fuck they were, then you know, with very occasional exceptions, he's always been acutely aware. Even of the things that weren't real, he was fucking cognizant that it was in his fucking head. I'm no psychologist. Don't give a shit about that stuff either. But even I recognize how unique his situation is. *Nothing* about Maddox is typical."

"Gee, thanks," Maddox grumbles.

I grip his chin, turning his face to me. A war is brewing in those deep blue depths. The words of his friends and his brother are already digging deep inside of him. "You have never been, and you will never be typical. You aren't meant to be. That beautiful mind and even more stunning soul were meant for things most can't comprehend. You may not change the world, but you change every life you meet. Your mind? Your heart and soul? They're beyond all of us. Greater than us."

I watch my words bounce off of him like they were never said, and my heart sinks. He doesn't see it. Can't see himself through my eyes.

Jerking his head away, he turns back toward the men. "All of this is beside the point." He turns the conversation back to a place he feels in control. "I understand why you would have reservations. I can even understand your doubts about my competency because I've doubted it myself, which is why I've never told any of you about the shit that goes on up there." Liam and Dane start to speak, but Maddox holds up a hand. "What I don't understand is why you'd jump to conclusions about her. How you could take a single look at her and think what you did."

"She's a stripper," Liam says as if that explains everything.

Without meaning to, I flinch at the statement and instantly regret it when a ripple of anger flows through Maddox. I circle the inside of his wrist with my thumb in an attempt to soothe him. It seems to work, but it's hard to tell.

"First off," he growls, "I met her at Bastian's, where she was staying. You know, the place you assholes shipped me off to? I never asked the son of bitch to knock me out and bring me here." He flings a hand in Bastian's direction. "If it weren't for her, I wouldn't have stayed either." Bastian rolls his eyes, but I'm left in shock. I had no idea he was staying for me.

"Really?" I ask softly.

"Do you really think he could've kept me there if I didn't want to be there?" he asks me with a slight twitch of his lips.

I shake my head because if I have learned anything about Maddox, it's that he doesn't take orders or follow directions. Short of tying him up forever, nothing could've kept him in River City if he didn't want to be there. I'm not even confident that would've worked.

He kisses the side of my head. "Always you, Canary," he whispers so that only I can hear, then turns his attention back to them. "I doubt Quinn meant for me to find out what she did, considering she begged me not to tell Bastian and Verity." Bastian's brows pop up, and he grins at me. The urge to cover my face is overwhelming. I still feel silly that I didn't know he *owned* the club I was working. "There was nothing wrong with her doing whatever she needed to pay her medical and student debt, and you all should have your asses kicked for acting like there is. I mean, seriously? Since when do we discriminate against strippers?"

They open their mouths, then clamp them shut. Jaws tighten, and redness creeps up their necks and cheeks. They both look properly chastised and embarrassed. Dane drags a hand through his hair, looking like a scolded child. Suddenly I realize that Maddox may not be the oldest, but he plays the role of older brother well.

Dane looks at me with a sheepish grin. "You're right. Both of you." He turns his attention directly to me. "What you said before? I may not have a reason to trust you, but I didn't have one not to."

Liam huffs out a breath too. "Fuck," he mutters, then repeats it louder. His eyes grow hard then he turns away from us. The muscles in his shoulders momentarily tense before he turns back to us. "I'm sorry." His eyes jump between us as he nods. "I've been dealing with some personal shit, and I've been projecting."

I get off the bed, walk to them, and extend a hand. "I'm Quinn Toussaint—" Maddox clears his throat loudly. I look over my shoulder and meet his quirked, challenging brow. I roll my eyes while hiding my grin. "I'm Quinn *Masters*. Nice to meet you."

They both smirk, take my hand, and introduce themselves.

"There," I say, turning around to face Maddox. "All better."

"Not by a fucking long shot, darlin', but they can stay."

I roll my eyes, unimpressed and unsurprised. Maddox is stubborn. But at least his family is still intact.

I walk back to the bed, climb beside him, and kiss his cheek. Ryder gives me an approving nod and a smile.

"You're amazing," Maddox whispers in my ear. "And I'm fucking proud of you. Thank you for seeing what I couldn't, but it will be a long time before Liam and I are cool again."

I nod because I already know. He is a forgiving person when he wants to be. But forgiveness doesn't come easy for him. Giving or receiving. I am just glad this is one less regret he'll have.

MADDOX

Left in the Silence

Darkness surrounds me except for the light glow of the vitals monitor they refuse to turn off, but the darkness doesn't bother me. It's the silence that makes my skin crawl.

Silence allows the noise—the voices to come to life. That makes my thoughts run too fast. The quiet brings the real darkness.

Everyone left hours ago. Even Quinn, after arguing for nearly half an hour. But as the day progressed, I noticed she looked more and more exhausted. She's spent so much time stressing over me the last few days, and she's wiped.

She tried to hide it. Smiled through the conversation. Joined in when she felt she had something to add. She stayed by my side the entire time, except for when she excused herself to the bathroom.

But I could tell.

So when Bastian left after his second visit, I made her go too.

I've been lying awake since they left hours ago, replaying the conversations of the day. Truth be told, I'm exhausted too. It's information overload.

And I'm struggling. Nothing unusual there. I tried to hide it like always, but they are watching me now. Penetrating gazes when they thought I wasn't looking. Worried tones and nervous smiles were a constant reminder that I'd put them through hell.

They also confirmed what I knew. Soon as they found out just how damaged I am—just how damaged my mind is—their opinions of me changed. They can pretend all they want, but I saw the truth. They don't trust me. Don't trust my judgment.

Why would they? I'm the alcoholic junkie that hears and sees shit that isn't there.

Dark thoughts like that run rampant. Voices loudly scream until I'm gripping my hair in frustration.

You should've died.

They'd be better off without you.

Better to grieve for a short time than fear forever.

"Stop," I hiss to myself, clenching my teeth.

Because I know it's not true. If I learned anything from the hellish nightmares—and my own letters—it is that losing someone leaves permanent scars, and grief is lifelong.

It's taken me nearly thirty years to realize I don't want to inflict the pain I've suffered on the ones I love. I don't want my death to be a permanent stain on their souls or make them feel the crushing pain of missing someone. Especially when I can help it. I won't do that to Ryder, Dane, or any of them.

I can't do that to Quinn.

When I opened my eyes and saw those beautiful amber eyes pooled with tears and pain, everything in me was decimated. When I heard her prayers, begging for me to be okay—for me to survive because without me, she wouldn't, I lost my breath. Because they weren't the prayers of someone hoping their loved one survives a horrible accident. They were for the person who's living in hell on earth.

She was an angel praying for the devil. Telling a god I didn't believe in that she didn't want to live without me. And I felt the truth of her words to my core. Without a doubt, I knew she wasn't speaking figuratively. If anyone took those statements seriously, it was me.

I did that to her. It was my actions that hurt her. Everything I wanted to save her from was staring me in the face. She would be better if we never met, but fate, kismet, destiny, or whatever had other plans. Our paths collided, shattering us into a million pieces and merging us as one. There would be no after us. It was only us.

And for her, I want to live. I want to live, so she will.

But none of that takes away the pain. It's still real and excruciating. The voices still scream and demand I end it all. The heaviness in my chest is just as unrelenting as ever.

I need a fifth of Johnnie and a line of blow. And a hit of H to go with the blow.

I toss and turn, trying to let sleep take me. The stupid glowing green on the monitor has me contemplating unplugging the damn machine. The stupid plastic sound of the mattress every time I move makes me want to throw it out the window. If I could open it, that is.

I start to hum—to allow the music to drown out the silence. The melody in my head and the words on my lips. If anyone is listening outside the room, they'll probably become YouTube-rich tomorrow.

I close my eyes, picturing that tangled blond mass of curls and those whiskey eyes, imagining her sweet voice. It eases some of the craziness but not enough.

Finally, unable to stand it anymore, I grab my phone from the table, thankful Ryder brought me a new one since I have no clue where the old one is. I punch in the name and hit call.

It only rings once before her sweet little rasp fills my ears. "Maddox, are you okay?"

She doesn't sound like she's been asleep. She sounds hoarse and like she's been crying. "Why aren't you resting?"

"Can't sleep." Her soft voice hums through the lines. "What about you?"

"Same."

Seconds of silence pass, but just hearing her breathe makes a difference.

Then she cuts through the quiet with a plea that squeezes my chest. "Maddox, please don't leave me again."

The crack in her voice chips a piece of my soul. I close my eyes to fight against the stinging. "I don't want to, baby, but it's dark in here. I wish it weren't, but I can't make it stop."

"Give me some of it. Let me have it." Her sniffles cause my own tears to spill.

"Even if I could, baby, I wouldn't let you. I never want you to feel this way."

"I-I've felt it before. I can handle it."

"No, *cher*. This is all on me. I'm the only one that can deal with it."

"Then what can I do? What can I do to help you? Because you saved me, Maddox. You've saved me over and over since the day we met without meaning to. I want to be that for you. What can I do?" She gasps, her soft cries now full-blown sobs as her words come between ragged breaths.

"Just be you, baby, and don't give up on me."

"Never," she whispers softly.

"Sing to me, Canary."

She chuckles, takes a hiccupping breath, and begins to hum. "Mississippi in the middle of a dry spell."

Sleep finally takes me quicker than that molasses-setting sun.

MADDOX

I'm selfish

"No to rehab. No to a shrink." My voice is calm; a smile is plastered widely across my face. If I've perfected anything over the years, it's the mask of having it all together. *Mostly*. But on the inside, I want to scream and rip shit apart, even as Lincoln's slobbery fist tries to go in my mouth. "Nice of you to bring the kid, so I stay calm," I say, inflecting just enough sarcasm for my asshole friends to know I'm pissed.

Jake shrugs and laughs, knowing I'd be raising hell if this cute little dude with hair to match his mom's and eyes to match his dad's weren't sitting in my lap. "It wasn't for your benefit, but glad to be of service. Layla and Tori hijacked Cara, Heaven, and the kids to the zoo."

My stomach clenches. River City only has one zoo, and my memories aren't great. In fact, I haven't been to a zoo since I was eleven.

"Mads, I know you don't want to, and I get it, mate. But you need help." My dark thoughts are interrupted by Ryder. He has been begging since he got here. And I get his concern, but... Just no.

"I don't," I grit out. "I don't need rehab. I've done fine without it."

They're not going to change my mind. I've been down the rehab road. I don't do the sharing and hearing other people's stories is too hard. I swear I can feel everything they feel, and I know that should be a good thing, but it's not. Not to mention the fucking therapist in rehab called me an attention-seeking narcissist. I'm not saying they're wrong, but fucking hell, I was seventeen. Who says that shit to a kid? Especially the way they said it.

And I will never go to another shrink. I don't trust them. They have too much power to manipulate and abuse when you're already weak and vulnerable.

"Fine," Jake nods with a sigh. "But, Mads, you need a psychiatrist. You need to know what's going on so you can get the medicine and therapy you need. You said it yourself. You're hurting. The noise is too loud to fight some days. We've seen it. Always thought you were just hungover or detoxing, but you disappear for days into your room or bed or whatever."

"I'm a damn schizo, Jake." I'm nearly growling at this point. "And I've handled it fine for this long."

"First off, stop saying it like that. It's a disease that you can't help. *If* that's what's wrong with you. Not some derogatory term you get to toss around because you're pissed. Did you know my dad's dad had schizophrenia? My grandmother used to tell me stories. He was the best man she had ever met, but he couldn't control how his mind worked. Back then, they didn't have the medical knowledge they do now. But it didn't make him less of a person. Just like it doesn't make you less you."

Well, that makes me feel like shit, but I'm still not going to a shrink. Looking down at Linc, I mumble, "I said I'm dealing."

"Yeah, that's what you've done," Ryder snorts. His body language—arms crossed, jaw locked—tells me he's as annoyed as I am.

"Didn't see you complaining," I bite out, my moment of remorse gone in place of aggravation once again because why the hell don't they get it?

"Because misery loves fucking company, you bloody git. I had—*have* to deal with my shit for Heaven and Tyler. I can't expose them to this shit."

I lean back with a grunt and a sigh that makes Lincoln squeal with laughter. He's such a happy kid. Like Lyra. Jake's a good dad.

Ryder is a good dad.

I'm gonna be one...

I shove that thought away, not ready to unbox it just yet. "My issues are chemical, Ryder. Not just a build-up of years' worth of anger and resentment."

"Really, mate? You wanna talk about labels? Since you seem to think you're the only one with problems. Conduct disorder, ODD, chronic depression, generalized anxiety, ADHD, and my personal favorite, IED. That one sounds like me, right? Oh, and let's not forget I'm an alcoholic and an addict. Any of this sound familiar?"

Fuck.

I never would've guessed his issues went beyond years of abuse and resentment. Makes me feel like shit that I didn't look closer. "You got help,

Ry," I tell him.

"I *needed* help, asshole, and you do too. Why the hell are you so bloody daft? Or just fucking stubborn?"

"Because I can handle it," I yell. Lincoln starts to cry, and I feel like shit all over again. I pull him into my chest and rock him back and forth. "I'm in control, Ryder. I've always been in control. I ignore the voices. I can tell the difference between what's real and what isn't." I look down at Lincoln squirming against my chest, his cries becoming soft whimpers as his fingers begin to stroke my ear. I can't help but smile at him. He reminds me of Lyra when she was a baby.

This is real, I tell myself. I love this kid. I love all my friends' kids.

I rest my cheek on his soft head with a sigh. This is what I wanted for all of them. Just not for myself because I never wanted what I am to spill over onto another kid. I would never want this for anyone.

Yet here I am because the best-laid plans and all.

"There's one thing you're missing, Mads," Jake tells me, getting my attention back on the conversation I wish they'd fucking drop. "This isn't just about that. You're right. You've handled it. You kept it hidden from us—your damn family—so well that we didn't know how bad it was. But what you can't control is how you feel."

"I'm tired of finding you in your own blood and bile, Maddox. Twice in four months, you've OD'd," Ryder says as he struggles to contain his emotions.

"Once," I mutter. "Didn't get a chance to the second time."

"Seriously?" he snaps. "That's what you have to say about it? I *know* what you were trying to do, but for some reason, I don't understand, you didn't try to rush things."

"I needed to finish the letters," I tell him as shame creeps in.

"Well, thank God for small mercies, right? Guess I should be grateful that you decided to fill us in before you offed yourself for good." He drags a hand through his hair and walks to the window.

"I needed you to know it wasn't your fault, and there was nothing you could've done."

"Oh, well, why didn't you say so? Thank you, our sovereign king, for allowing us that knowledge."

"Ryder, you're being an ass. Give him a break." Jake tells him.

"No, I won't give him a fucking break. Like I said, twice in four months, you've OD'd. *Five* times in two years. I've cut you down from the damn rope. I've called nine-one-one while trying to keep you from bleeding out. You're suffering. I get it. But goddammit, Maddox, when are you going to learn that if you'd actually succeeded, we would've been left without you to suffer."

"I know," I run my hand over my face with a sigh. I never meant for him to always be the one to find me. Never meant for him to take care of me. Not when it was my job to take care of him. Of all of them. "I didn't see it that way before. All I could think about was making it stop. But it's different now." He casts me a doubtful look but doesn't say anything. Instead, he rolls his hand, gesturing for me to continue. "Asshole," I mutter. He responds by kissing the air. "I had... Fuck, it's so cliché, but it's true. I had an epiphany." I tell them about the dreams and what I am now silently referring to as my hell loop.

Ryder walks from the window and drops back into his vacated chair. He blows out a breath, then stares at me. "I'm glad you realized all of that, mate. Truly. But what happens next time you lose someone? The next time some bomb gets dropped? Anyone else's tragedy, and you're like a goddamn rock. You're there for all of us, keeping us together, being the strong voice of reason and the understanding heart we need. But every fucking time the heartbreak is yours, you lose it. And each time, you fall a little further than the time before. She won't cure your demons, Maddox. That's on you."

"I know," I say, but before I can continue, the door opens.

She walks into the room, and her eyes grow wide as she takes a look around the room they moved me to. "Holy shit," she whispers. "*This* is a hospital room? I've stayed in smaller hotel rooms."

I shake my head with a laugh. A breathless laugh because she takes it away.

She's wearing some mid-thigh, flowy dress thing that shows off those killer legs, all tanned and toned from dancing. Thin straps hold up the heart-shaped top that molds to her tits, giving the most teasing peek. Those curls that I love so damn much drape over her delicate shoulders like a golden waterfall. And those pouty lips are painted the sexiest shade of red that would look fantastic staining my dick.

"The perks of your name being on the building," Ryder spreads his arms, gesturing around the ridiculous room with a laugh.

When they moved me from ICU, I tried to argue that I didn't need this damn room. It's over the top and too stupid for words. I fully realize it's expected of me, but I genuinely hate this kind of privilege. To think, because of a condition of birth or by some fortune of luck, I deserve extravagance like this. Yes, it costs a small fortune, which is another thing itself, but still. Maybe the worst are those who think they deserve this because of how many zeroes are on their tax return.

Of course, given the amount I've spent on alcohol and drugs and every other extravagance I own, perhaps I should just shut up.

Quinn isn't wrong, though. The room *is* nicer than some hotel rooms. And I've seen my share of some seedier ones.

On one side of the room sits a queen-sized bed. In the middle sits a round coffee table with three armchairs. On the other end, there's a sofa and a couple more armchairs with another coffee table in the center. The damn bathroom, though hospital friendly, is customized with multiple jets in the luxury tile shower. There's even a small kitchen because the rich and famous are too good for hospital food.

On the other hand, that shit is why some people never leave the place, so maybe *that* particular convenience isn't so bad.

Quinn laughs at Ryder's theatrics, and I get a strange squeezing in my stomach. It only takes a second for me to evaluate and realize that I'm jealous that he's making her laugh. It's a ridiculous and pointless emotion. Ryder was, is, and always will be in love with Heaven. Even if he weren't, he'd never go after Quinn. So I quickly tamp it down, unwilling to give it more fuel.

But seriously, what the hell? I don't get jealous.

"I thought this kind of stuff was made up," she says as she walks across the room, carrying an overnight bag in one hand and a carryout bag in the other. She sets the overnight bag on the bed. "I thought you'd like your own clothes and some non-hospital food." She tells us. Her dress rides up as she bends over, setting the containers of food on the table.

The food smells amazing. But as wonderful as it smells, my watering mouth isn't because of the delicious aroma wafting from the containers. It's a hunger only for her.

Lincoln squirms in my lap, and I work to get my twitching dick under control because popping wood while holding a kid just seems wrong.

When Lincoln spots Quinn, he begins making grabby hands at her. She doesn't even ask who's kid he is or ask permission to take him. She just picks him up, squeezing him tightly to her chest. "And who is this cutie?" she finally asks when she sits on the sofa with him on her knee.

"That is Lincoln," Jake tells her.

Quinn's eyes are firmly locked on the wide-eyed, beaming infant as she begins to coo. "Hi, Lincoln. Aren't you just the cutest little thing?"

I can't take my eyes off her as she plays with him. He claps and laughs at everything she does. My heart and stomach do some kind of weird flip thing as I watch.

Watching her with Linc, there is no doubt in my mind that she was meant to be a mother. Something she lost and never thought she'd have again.

Something I know she's afraid she still won't have but hasn't said a thing. She hasn't even mentioned...

"Mathsy!" My favorite high-pitched squeal cuts through my thoughts as the toothless, blond princess barrels straight for me like a freight train.

Her wide, infectious smile grows with each step closer. I'm bracing myself for the inevitable pain I know she will unleash. One of her ferocious hugs is worth the pain, but I wouldn't have the heart to stop her, regardless.

"Whoa, princess." Jake grabs her just before she collides with me.

"Daddy, I want Mathsy," she yells as she kicks and flings her little body in one of her famous tantrums, and as usual, I have to fight off a grin. I always find her tantrums humorous, especially when Jake gets that panicked look on his face. He hates to see his little girl cry. Ever.

"Lyra, one more tantrum, and we will go back to Tori's, and you *will* take a nap." Cara takes her from Jake while giving him a murderous look. Not because he did anything, but because he didn't.

"I just want Mathsy." When that bottom lip begins to quiver, I'm done.

And I do exactly what I always do. "Cara, it's fine." I extend my arms, asking the five-year-old hellion out of her mom's arms. "Give her here."

"Ma—" Cara starts to argue, but I shake my head.

She purses her lips, wanting badly to argue, but she won't. Cara never argues with me.

And I know it's not cool to interfere, but I don't care. "Give her here," I repeat.

Cara rolls her eyes, sets Lyra in my lap, then sits next to Quinn. Lyra quickly wraps her arms around me and nuzzles my neck. "I misthed you, Mathsy." My throat clogs with emotions as I hug her back.

Tyler walks up to me with a fist bump, then stands next to Ryder. He nods his head at Lyra with an eye roll. "She's been a crybaby all day," he declares.

"Tyler! That's not nice," Heaven scolds while Ryder and I hide our grins. Lyra turns around in my arms and sticks her tongue out at Tyler, making him scowl.

"There's my sweet boy," Cara says as she leans over to take Linc from Quinn. "Come see momma."

My stomach and heart do that weird flip thing again when Lincoln shakes his head and buries his face in Quinn's shoulder.

"Well, okay then," Cara giggles.

Quinn smiles down at Lincoln, nuzzling him close, then flashes me a smile that decimates my heart. I don't return it. I'm too entranced watching her with him. The way they seemed to bond almost instantly. But when her smile falls and tension fills her eyes, I realize my expression might be relaying the wrong message, so I quickly flash her a smile of my own. Unfortunately, it's too late. Her mind is already working.

"Who is that?" Lyra whispers in my ear.

I look down into those curious blue eyes with a wink. "*That's* my girl," I whisper back with a kiss on her cheek.

"Your girl?" she scrunches her nose.

"Yep." I boop her nose.

She turns her attention back to Quinn. After a few seconds of observing her little brother in Quinn's arms, she climbs from my lap and goes to them. "I like your hair," she tells Quinn with a grin.

Quinn smiles as Lyra, never one to shy away from someone, climbs onto her lap next to her little brother.

"I like your hair too," Quinn tells her with a giggle.

Lyra has Quinn's full attention as she tells her about the animal she saw at the zoo, eating ice cream, and Tyler pushing her into a puddle. Tyler then goes to them and tells his side of things. He didn't push her. She tripped when trying to take a toy he won from the claw machine from him. Quinn laughs at them both as they argue back and forth.

And I can't look away.

Ryder clears his throat, getting my attention. He tilts his head toward them, then mouths, "Get your shit together."

A heavy sigh escapes as my eyes close.

"Well, we need to take the kids back. I'll be back later, though," he announces as he stands.

Minutes later, it's just Quinn and me. She curls up on the couch, smiling at me. I get up and go sit next to her. Gripping her waist, I pull her on top of me. Of course, my dick twitches at how close her hot little pussy is, but I push that aside for now. "You look tired," I comment, looking into her red eyes.

Pink tints her cheeks, and she drops her eyes. I love that about her. She's a fierce fighter one minute and utterly submissive to me the next. Never afraid to put me in my place when I need it but never one to cause conflict or drama. "I didn't sleep well," she admits, pulling that bottom lip between her teeth.

With a finger under her chin, I tilt her head to meet my eyes and tug at her lip with my thumb. "*Why* didn't you sleep, *cher*?"

Her eyes fall again, and she shakes her head. "It doesn't matter. You should be resting." It's clear whatever is bothering her—causing her to lose even more sleep—she doesn't want to tell me about it, which makes me want to know more.

I brush a few stray tendrils away from her face, then cup each side in my hands. "Look at me." When she does, I see all the anxiety and nervousness she's trying so desperately to hide from me. It pisses me off that I've done this—put her in a position where she feels like she needs to hide things from me. To protect me. Though my teeth grind, I swallow my irritation and focus on her. "Talk to me. Don't tiptoe around me because you're afraid of how I'll react. That's not what I want or need." Her bottom lips pulls between her teeth for a second time, and then she nods with a heavy exhale. "So, tell me why you didn't sleep. Were you worried about me? Because I promise, baby, I'm okay and not going anywhere."

"You're not okay," she whispers, her eyes filling with tears. "Stop pretending you are, and I'll stop tiptoeing."

I release her face and drag my hands over my own. My head falls back on the couch with a huff.

"I'm serious, Maddox," she tells me. "No matter what you are thinking or feeling. If you're having a good day or a bad day. You have to tell me."

"I'll *try*," I relent. "I promise, I'll try. Hiding and masking are all I've known for a long damn time. It won't be easy to break that habit."

"Okay."

"So tell me. Was I the reason you didn't sleep?"

"No," She smiles softly as her fingers tangle in the hem of my shirt. "Well, not entirely."

"Then tell me."

Her cheeks begin to flame, and those eyes well once again, but she puts on a smile despite her tears. "So-uh... Surprise, my parents know about us. They saw the news." She shrugs and bites her cheek. I can see it in her eyes. She's hurt and dejected, and everything in me wants to fly to Springfield and tell her parents to fuck off. But I manage, barely, to keep my composure. "I take it that didn't go well."

She smiles again, trying so hard to make it seem like they didn't decimate her, but her eyes give everything away. When the first tear falls, she leans forward, pressing her forehead to my uninjured shoulder to hide it, but all I need to see is the one for the desire to kick fucking ass to build. First, her parents for hurting her, and then my own for being the cause of it all.

"They were angry that I got married without telling them. Told me I was throwing my life away all over again after I just got it back. Though that was a very different perspective considering just a few weeks ago, they were telling me I needed to come home and get my life together. They never wanted me to come to River City, hate that I want to be a music therapist, and think that because I've been staying with Verity, I must need their help. The reason I started dancing is that I don't *want* their help. The only thing they think I've done right in years is divorce Scott, and that wasn't even my choice at first." She sniffles, trying so hard to sound strong when I know she wants to break.

"I'm sorry, *cher*," I whisper as I stroke her hair. "I know this is my fault. You weren't given a chance to tell them yourself because I fucked up."

She leans back, wiping the tears from her eyes. "It wouldn't have mattered, Maddox. All they see is that I've rushed into something on impulse. They think I'm a naïve little girl with stars in her eyes over the rock star that noticed her. That I'm impressionable because of what happened between Scott and me. They've been disappointed in me since I told them I was pregnant at seventeen. I'm not sure anything I do will ever change that."

"Maybe I could talk to them," I say, brushing another fallen tear off her cheek.

She shakes her head. "No. That wouldn't help. They think you are way out of my league and that you'll see it when the novelty wears off and toss me aside."

The fuck?

My fingers dig into her hips because none of that is true. "Now I *really* want to talk to them."

She shakes her head, takes a breath, and straightens her shoulders. "They don't have to like my choices, but they do have to accept them. And respect them. I know you. They can believe what they want, but they have no idea what kind of person you are. And besides, they are my choices, and I don't regret them. I don't regret you."

Pride builds and bursts. She is so much stronger than she ever realized, but she's grown by leaps and bounds in the last few months. I know she thinks I am the cause—that I restored her confidence, but it wasn't me. She's done it all herself.

But I still have to ask her. I have to be sure. Because the only thing I want in this world is for her to be happy, and I know a life with me won't be easy. She now realizes that too. "You sure about that, darlin'? I wouldn't blame you if you did. You didn't exactly have all the facts about me when I sucked you into my life."

She reaches up, stroking a finger down my jaw. A small but loving smile pulls her lips. "I know everything that matters, Maddox Masters. You can fool the world, but I see your heart, and it is beautiful. That's the only fact I ever cared about. I love you. I was lost and broken before you. You are all the pieces I didn't know were missing."

"Fuck, Canary," I whisper, gripping the back of her head and pulling her to me until our foreheads touch. "I knew my pieces were missing. I just never believed they would be found. Had no idea a whiskey-eyed girl with the voice of an angel was out there and made specifically for me." Closing my eyes, I take a breath. She is the sum of my missing parts. Every piece of her was made for me, and I almost threw it all away. Almost quit fighting. She may not be my cure, but she *is* my salvation. The angel with the broken wings was sent to save the devil from himself.

My heart hammers an erratic beat in my chest. Stomach so knotted it's painful. Lungs ache as I struggle to breathe. Irrational panic consumes that something will take her away the moment they leave my lips. But the need to tell her—to give her the words she never asked for, even after I put my ring on her finger and she took my last name. Because they are my utmost truth. They are the only thing I feel to my core. That I have felt from nearly the moment I laid eyes on her.

My fingers wrapped tightly in her hair, I open my eyes and stare into hers. Wanting her to see the truth. Needing her to know that I mean them with every fiber of my being. "I love you so fucking much, Quinn." Her warm breath caresses my face as she gasps. The pooled tears in those whiskey eyes slip down her cheeks. "I thought I knew what it was, you know? Thought I'd loved and been loved. Seen it in my friends' eyes. But I was so damn wrong. I think I loved you the moment our eyes met. I know I loved you when you stroked my hair and sang to me. And I could see it in your eyes too. It shone back at me like a reflection. It scared the goddamn shit out of me. Because this with us, baby? It's fierce and powerful and devastating. It has the power to create and destroy. And I was terrified it would destroy you. But god-fucking-dammit, Canary, I do love you."

Tears spill. Her hand clasps tightly over her mouth, muffling a sob. We stare at each other for a breath. Or maybe it's a lifetime. Then her lips crash into mine, making me hiss from the unexpected jarring. She jerks back, anxiety filling her eyes. "I'm sorry," she squeaks.

Gripping the back of her head, I pull her back to me. I swipe my tongue around the shell of her ear, then suck the lobe into my mouth. "Totally worth it, baby," I growl.

Then I devour her mouth. My tongue dives deep, tasting every inch of her mouth, inhaling and savoring her flavor. Cherries and mint make me groan as electricity flows and bleeds into the air. Our skin pebbles, and the hair on the back of my neck stands on end.

My hands begin to wander, but I cannot decide what I want to touch. The soft, silky skin of her shoulders. The supple, tantalizing flesh of her ass. Her smooth, taut thighs. I want to touch it all. All at once and right now.

My lips trail down her jaw, over her throat. I bite and nip, drawing delicious moans from her beautiful lips. I lave and suck my way to those silky shoulders as my fingers wander up her thighs until they dig into her ass, pressing her tightly against my fabric-covered steel erection. She so hot and wet as she grinds against me, chasing her pleasure.

With my teeth, I drag the top of her dress down, exposing those full, round globes. Her nipple point like diamonds, begging me to taste.

I flick slowly, teasingly at the peaked bud while looking up at her, watching her fall apart before we've done anything. I grin as I pull the tight nub between my teeth when her body begins shaking. Her hips rock against me as her heavy breathing fills the air.

She whimpers when I pull her from my lap. I run my hand between her thighs. Wetness coats her thighs. My mouth waters when I drag a finger through her dripping slit. A sound of desperation escapes me when I tear the thin, lacy thong from her body.

"Maddox," she breathes, "what if someone comes in?"

I grin at the thought. The idea of someone seeing her at my mercy. It's one of my favorite things to do. Show everyone that she belongs to me and that I am the only one that can make her body sing. "They can enjoy the fucking show," I tell her. She scowls at me, but she's not fooling anyone. "Don't pretend it doesn't turn you on," I tell her as I dip a finger inside. "That getting caught doesn't make your heart race. Or someone hearing you scream out my name doesn't make you scream louder. That you don't *love* when someone sees that *you own me*."

Her knees shake, and more of her delectable juices coat my fingers. "B-but this is a hospital." She is as convincing as a toddler who claims they want dinner before dessert.

"Then they should be well-versed in human anatomy, *cher*." Gripping her ass, I spin her around and force her to bend over the coffee table. I grab her dress, command her to hold it up, and spread her thighs wide. Her pussy, pink and swollen with need, beckons me to have a drink. And I willingly oblige.

I bury my face between her sexy thighs and inhale with a growl. Her salty, musky scent should be fucking bottled because that shit is more intoxicating than any drug out there. And addictive.

I run my tongue through her slick folds. Her flavor bursts, and my eyes roll back, making me drunk and dizzy with the need for more. Better than the finest whiskey.

I tease her entrance. Her whimpers of urgency are like a song floating in the air. I circle that dripping hole, again and again, drawing out her cries, loving the sound of her pleas until I succumb to my own weakness, needing every drop she has to offer, and sink my tongue as deeply into her wetness as I can go. Getting drunk on her.

Of all my addictions, she's the most potent. The one there will be no recovering from.

Pain tears at my scalp, and my throbbing cock weeps with the need to sink into her tight little body. Her thighs quake and quiver. Incoherent babbling tumbles. Hips gyrate when my nose presses into her clit. "Maddox," she keens, begging me for permission.

"Mmm. Not yet, darlin'," I tell her, then slip a finger deep inside, pressing against those sensitive inner nerves as I suck her clit into my mouth. I curl my finger, pressing against her innermost nerves coaxing her to euphoria but not ready to let her fall. I continue to stroke and suck until I hear her whimpers and moans become cries for release. "Come, *cher*."

She shatters, coating my lips and tongue. My hand is soaked as her screams of ecstasy fill the room. I grin widely, knowing it's only a matter of time before someone runs in to see who's being murdered.

Before her climax has ended, I have my dick freed, and I am pulling her onto me. Promised curses leave me as her tight as fuck heat swallows me. "Jesus fucking Christ," I grind and slam my eyes shut. The sensation is overwhelming, and spots dance as I adjust to the feel of her gripping my cock with nothing between us. Just her and me. No barriers.

Never—not a single time—have I fucked without a condom. For years, I doubled up until my dumbass realized I was accomplishing the opposite of my goal.

It never mattered how wasted I was. No amount of alcohol or drugs made me so out of it that my fears of getting some girl pregnant dissipated. Nothing made me stupid or uninhibited enough to abandon my rule.

I press my forehead against her shoulder with a chuckle because there's no need to worry about that now. And now that I've felt her, been inside her without it, I'm not sure I can ever go back.

She grinds against me, squeezing the life out of my cock. My spine tingles and dick twitches, making me groan. Fingers sinking deep into her hips, I halt her movements. "I need a second, Canary, or this will be the quickest eruption in history."

Her head falls back against my shoulder, and her hands grip her tits as she slides up and down on my shaft a few times, muttering my name.

I twist her head and take her mouth, plunging my tongue deep inside, sharing her intoxicating flavor. I take one of her hands and drape it behind my head. The other, I lead to where we are joined. Her fingers make a V shape as I pull out and thrust back inside her. "Feel that?" I whisper against her mouth. "Feel me taking you. The way you wrap around me. How wet you are. Feel it."

Her breathing becomes erratic as she begins to hurtle towards the precipice again. I take both her nipples between my fingers, tugging and pulling as I bite down on her shoulder. Her fingers stroking my cock as I dive in and out of her tight core soon have my balls tingling with fire.

Using her tits for leverage, I begin to thrust in earnest. Tilting my hips, pivoting my pelvis to hit her in all the right spots. Her head thrashes against my shoulder as she pleads for mercy.

Reaching down, I pull her fingers away from us and press them against her clit. I use her fingers to circle and massage that throbbing nub until her inner walls squeeze me like a vice.

But it's not enough.

Ignoring the burning pain—and hoping she doesn't notice the blood seeping through my shirt—I pull her off me and put her on her back on the sofa. I lift her hips, hooking her legs over my own, and slam into her with a growl. Her eyes roll back when I slowly pull back to the tip and repeat the same forceful thrust. Again and again. Until sweat drips from my face. Until my lungs burn from exertion. Until my entire body feels like it's on fire.

I give her every inch of me, demanding her body to accept me. Demanding she feel my love through my skin, sweat, blood, and tears.

She writhes beneath me, unable to go anywhere. Completely at my mercy as I punish her cunt and feed her need to feel the pleasure with the pain. Twisting and pivoting, she cries out each time I reach her oversensitive nerves.

Tears stream from the corner of her eyes. "Maddox," she gasps. "No more. I can't."

Arms braced on either side of her head, I look into her eyes. They're glossy and glassy with euphoria and exhaustion. "You can."

"No," she shakes her head. Her lashes flutter when I hit those nerves again. "Too much."

"It's never too much, baby," I tell her as I reach between us and roll her clit between my fingers.

Her back arches. Her mouth opens, but no sound escapes. Silent screams surround us.

The door to the room flies open just as I roar with my own release. My hips continue to slap her flesh as I unload deep inside her.

"Oh God," the nurse gasps. The sound of the door closing follows her hurried footsteps.

I look down at Quinn with a wide grin. Her face is contorted in total bliss. Her chest rises and falls as she fights to catch her breath.

And she takes my already staggered breath away. I've never seen anything more beautiful than her. Whether it's with red flushed cheeks and messy hair after I've fucked her into oblivion or when she's sitting with Lincoln and Lyra on her lap engrossed in children's games. Even when her heart is shattered and cracked. She never fails to stop my heart and leave me speechless.

I straighten her dress that I miraculously didn't destroy—I must be losing my touch—and slip behind her and let the sounds of her breathing wash over me until we're both fast asleep.

QUINN

One must decide

A knock at the door makes me jump. It only took a second for me to fall asleep in Maddox's arms after he brought me to orgasm three times. However, I must admit that the third time was nearly too much. I wasn't sure I'd survive it.

The doctor walks in as we sit up. We couldn't have been asleep more than fifteen minutes, but I swear it was the best sleep I've had since yesterday when I was curled into his side.

Maddox lifts me, pulling me into his lap, and I notice the blood on his shirt for the first time. I slap a hand over my mouth as remorse floods me for not seeing sooner. Tears fill my eyes, and I start to apologize, but he stops me before I can.

"Don't, Canary. Don't say you're sorry. It's not your fault, and you couldn't have stopped me short of refusing me altogether. Understand?"

I blink away the tears and nod. He's right. I couldn't have stopped him because I could never refuse him. It doesn't make me feel less responsible, but I shove it away best I can.

The doctor—Stephen—looks at Maddox and shakes his head with a laugh. "Twice in twenty-four hours, you have managed to tear your stitches open. You must like it here." Maddox only grunts, but my cheeks catch fire when Stephen's eyes dart between us with a knowing smirk. "You know, I shouldn't have to tell you that you just had major surgery. We didn't just remove a bullet. We had to hunt for it and repair a few small arteries. They told me your pain tolerance was high, but I'd think you would be too sore to move right now."

"I'm fine," Maddox waves, then strips off his shirt, revealing the small incisions in his shoulder, two just below his ribs, and there is another in his back. I have no idea why there are so many small holes. I assumed it was for the scope, but I really had no way of knowing. Judging by Stephen's intense gaze on that particular incision, he's still baffled that Maddox didn't have more damage. According to him, Maddox's insides should've been shredded.

Unconsciously, my fingers grip the cross around my neck.

"Well, I suppose it's too late to tell you no heavy lifting, strenuous activity, or sex for a few weeks since you've managed to get into a fight, *and* you're the talk of the floor right now since you apparently don't realize hospital doors have locks."

"Oh no," I whisper, throwing my hands over my face.

I remain hiding behind my hands as Stephen repairs the stitches below Maddox's ribs while mumbling something about it, at least, being a different one.

The thrill of getting caught is one thing, but *actually* getting caught is another. Not that we haven't had our share of exhibitionism, but that was at Bastian's other club, where people watch and want to be watched. At least not in a hospital room where his sixty-something nurse could see.

Of course, knowing what I do now—realizing how stupid I was to go along with any of it because of this press leak...

My heart begins to hammer against my chest as I wonder if any of *that* will appear in the news next. What if someone *did* catch us, and they've been waiting for the right moment to cash in?

My lungs tighten as I realize that my night job hasn't made its way into the press yet. My parents haven't heard about that. *Yet.*

"Whoa, baby," Maddox whispers against me. "Breathe. What's going on? Where did your head go?"

"M-my parents. They're going to find out about all of this. They're going to find out that I was working in Bastian's club."

His face hardens. "I'll handle that. I promise."

"You can't control the media, Maddox. I've been an idiot all this time because I thought that you were able to be yourself without the hassle. I convinced myself that all the pictures I've seen all these years must have been because you wanted to be seen. I should've known you were pulling the strings these last few weeks."

"Fuck," he hisses as my panic escalates. "Look, I swear it will be okay."

"You can't control everything. I know you'll try, but you can't." Tears start streaming down my face as my lips and nose begin to go numb. "My parents will never get over this. They won't."

He grips my face, his blue eyes searching my brown ones. "You're right," he sighs heavily as if the admission kills him. "I can't control everything, but I'll do what I can to keep that out. If I can't, then your parents can go through me. I'm not going to let them make you feel bad when you did nothing wrong."

I shake my head, and more tears spill over my lashes. "You don't understand. They'll want to know why I didn't just take money from them instead of *degrading myself*. That's how they are, Maddox. I've been nothing but a disappointment to them for years."

He brushes my hair from my face, softly kissing my lips. "I get it, baby. You know I get it better than anyone. But like you said earlier, they don't have to like it. They just have to accept it."

I take a deep breath and nod. I focus on what he said because it's the truth. I can't change what's done and haven't *done* anything wrong. I have nothing to be ashamed of, and it's time I stop acting as I have.

Stephen clears his throat. Embarrassment floods me that he witnessed my epic meltdown. Especially since I'm supposed to be here to support Maddox. Not the other way around. I apologize profusely, but he waves me off. "I've seen worse hormonal episodes than that." I accidentally flinch at the reminder that we are having a baby while he turns his attention to Maddox. "And I hate to tell you, but there's more where that came from. But anyway, I want to talk to you more about what we discussed this morning."

Maddox curses under his breath, and I'm curious why. "What did you talk about?" I ask him, but when he doesn't answer, I turn my attention to Stephen and repeat the question.

He gives Maddox a disapproving look, shakes his head, then turns to me. "Maddox needs professional help."

Eyes jerking nervously to Maddox, I hold my breath. I know firsthand how suggestions like this can go over for someone not ready to hear it. I haven't brought it up for this reason. But this is the doctor.

Before he notices my worried glance, I drop my eyes to my hands and bite my cheek to keep myself from saying something. This has to be his decision. If he does it so everyone will shut up and back off, it won't work. He has to make the choice himself.

Fingers press gently into my jaw. Blue eyes meet mine and express so much that it leaves me mesmerized. His eyes drop only for a split second to my hands—no, to my stomach, and my heart stops beating.

I haven't mentioned the baby since he woke up yesterday, and I've tried to hide the fact that the toilet is my new best friend. Partly out of concern, but also so it doesn't cause him stress. I have no idea how, but I fully planned on being with him and being a single parent—emotionally anyway. Naïve as it may be, I want them both. I want it all.

I try to tamp it down. To push away the fluttering of hope in my chest. Pressuring him to accept his child or to feel a certain way has never been on my agenda.

But hope bubbles despite the warning going off in my head. It refuses to subside, no matter how hard I try.

And when he meets my eyes, it rushes again. They don't leave mine when he says, "I'll see the shrink." He turns to Stephen with both hands out. "I don't know how well it will work, though. I can't stay here forever. I live in New York. My work takes me all over the world."

My nose burns and tears sting the backs of my eyes. This is a massive step for him; he doesn't need my blubbering to add extra pressure.

"I have a buddy in New York," Stephen tells us as he pulls out his phone. "I think your friend Cara uses him. You can talk about anything, and he will take it to his grave."

"Who knew the mafia kept shrinks on its payroll?" Maddox's voice drips with sarcasm and annoyance, but Stephen's eyes widen and jerk to me. Maddox winces, realizing what he just said, and shares the same nervous glance. His head tilts and eyes narrow when he realizes I'm not scandalized. "You knew?"

My shoulders lift and fall. "I didn't know, but I didn't *not* know. An educated guess, I suppose." When I don't say anything else, he raises a brow and waves a hand, ordering me to elaborate and making me laugh. "My mom would say things to my dad when she thought no one was listening about Uncle Vincenzo." A shudder ripples through me at the memory of some of those conversations. "She lost it when I told her I was coming to stay with Verity. Said she left all of that behind and did everything to shield me from it, and I was running straight into it. It seemed to make the most sense when I met Bastian and Rory."

"How did they make sense?" Maddox laughs. "They're anything but cliché."

My smile grows wide. "Aren't they, though? Gruff, alpha-male personas. A constant entourage of men that do what they ask without question. Too much money. And don't get me started on their hours of work. They work all hours and from anywhere."

"Baby, you just described the one percenters. You've watched too many movies."

Tilting my head, I consider his words. "Yeah. You're probably right since you fall there too, but I wasn't wrong."

He laughs again, kissing my temple. "No. You weren't wrong."

"All right, Maddox, I'll put in that call to my friend. Give him the rundown, and see how quickly he can see you. Have you thought any more about rehab?"

Maddox leans back into the couch and groans loudly. "Outpatient only," he grunts. "I can't stand those places. It's only been a day, and I'm already climbing the walls here."

"Yeah. I've noticed. Adam will address that as well." Stephen tells him, trying to hide his smile. I'm trying to hide mine too. I don't know what changed, but this is a far cry from the man they claimed was throwing stuff twenty-four hours ago.

Pride fills my heart. He's taking those first steps, no matter how reluctantly, and that budding hope explodes.

QUINN

Stand up and fight

"Now, Quinn, what about you?"

My head pops up, my brows reaching for the sky in surprise. "Me?" I squeak since I have no idea what he's talking about. "What about me?"

"Have *you* seen a doctor yet?" Stephen's tone suggests he already knows the answer and is daring me to lie.

Everyone knows I have only been here with him except when they force me to leave, so there is no point in lying. But I don't want to talk about this around Maddox. That niggle of hope turns to fear quickly at the thought of his rejection. Or the idea of it causing him anxiety. "I'm fine." I wave my hand as a brush-off. "I'll get to one soon. It's still early yet."

Stephen sighs, shaking his head. "Soon, Quinn," he tells me as he stands. "I'll come back as soon as I talk to Adam. I'll send you home tomorrow. You need to stay longer, but I have a funny suspicion you'll be plotting escape if I don't. Of course, this is only if you can refrain from ripping your stitches again."

"No promises," Maddox calls out as he drags me into his lap. When the door closes, he turns his attention to me, those Pacific blues blazing furiously. "Why haven't you seen a doctor?"

"It's fine. Really." I attempt to wave him off as I did Stephen and try to remove myself from his lap.

Of course, he holds me firmly in place, the fire in his eyes growing with each passing second. "Don't do that," he grits out angrily.

I feel heat rising to my neck and cheeks. "Do what?"

"This!" He gestures up and down to all of me, making me blush harder. "Don't brush it—or me—off like it doesn't matter. Like it's not a big deal. Stop skirting around it. The elephant is in the room, baby. It's too big to be ignored."

I close my eyes, unable to meet his fiery ones any longer. A heavy sigh escapes me as I try to choose my words carefully. "I—*we* were just enjoying the moment. And then you agreed to rehab and therapy. I know that's a big deal for you. Let's not ruin that. Okay?"

Those were definitely *not* the right words. The fire in his eyes grows tenfold. The muscles in his jaw flex over and over. I almost expect him to fling me from his lap. When he speaks, his voice is low and almost dangerous. "*Why the fuck would that ruin anything?*"

My breathing stutters, and my stomach flips. Nausea I've been ignoring since I got here demands to be heard. My late breakfast is about to make its reappearance in five, four...

I push off him quickly, racing for the toilet. This is the other reason I'm so tired. I spend more time wrapped around the toilet than I do sleeping. It's what sent me to the doctor in the first place.

My stomach is empty within seconds, and all I can do is painfully heave. Sweat coats my neck and forehead as my vision goes black.

"Fuck," I hear him hiss above me. He drops down, pulling my hair from my face.

"The bathroom is nicer than most hotels, too," I mutter, trying to defuse the tension. It doesn't work.

We stay like that for a bit—me hugging the toilet, him holding my hair back—in complete silence. Tension fills the air, and his anger is practically visible.

Several more minutes pass before we wordlessly move back into the room. I sit in a chair across from the sofa, more exhausted than before, with my knees pulled up to my chest.

He sits on the sofa. He leans back, props an ankle over a knee, sets his elbow on the sofa arm, and rests the backs of his fingers against his mouth. Those blue eyes bore holes into me with a jagged, pissed-off gaze. His mind turns and spins so quickly that I practically get dizzy just watching. Too many emotions flash through those oceanic pools to keep track. But I don't need to. I already know them all.

Breaking the silence, he leans forward, pulling my chair until it touches his knees, then places his hands on either side of me, caging me in.

"My feelings about..." he trails off, unable to say the words. "I haven't changed my mind."

The hope I felt earlier deflates, and I fight to keep the disappointment from showing in my eyes. "It's okay, Maddox," I say, reaching for his face.

He grabs my wrist before I can touch him with narrowed eyes and a set jaw. "I'm talking. You listen." He pauses for my response. Lips pressed tightly, I nod. His eyes close briefly as he blows out a heavy breath. "Quinn, you've got to understand I'm fucking terrified to pass this shit onto a kid. If this baby grows up feeling... If it feels half the shit, I do... I don't know if I can handle it. It will tear me apart."

Tears spring to my eyes. I feel like a terrible person, putting him through all of this. Hurting him is the last thing I want.

Am I being selfish? Is it unfair of me to go through with this pregnancy knowing what it's doing to him? Is it wrong of me to want it so badly when I know everything that could also go wrong? To get attached to something only for it to be ripped away again?

This baby has the potential to destroy us both for very different reasons.

Reading my expression, he tilts my head to look at him. "I haven't changed my mind, but I don't want you to hide your excitement. Or your fear. Not because you're afraid it will set me off or upset me. I know we haven't talked about it, but I already know you want it. I should never have told you to get rid of him."

The first droplet—or the first droplet of this particular session—slides slowly down my cheek. Anguish twists my heart, and dread knots my stomach. Doubt fills me. What am I doing to us? Is it really worth breaking our hearts to go through with this? To cling to a dream that might not come true. I open my mouth, ready to tell him he's right. There's too much risk involved for both of us. Too great a chance that it will decimate us both.

But before the words leave my lips, he warns me again. "I said, I talk, remember?" His tone leaves no room for argument, so I push the feelings aside and listen. "I know what you're thinking, and I want you to stop. You're not giving up this baby. Not for me and not out of worry. I also don't want you to neglect yourself or him. You will go to the doctor. You will do everything they say. *I* will *not* be your priority. You will be. He will be. Am I clear?"

I swipe away another tear. I hate that I've cried so much lately. Hate that I can't seem to control it no matter how hard I try. With a breath, I quell the flood for the moment. "I-I'm afraid to go," I admit. "Once I do, it becomes real."

"Baby, pretty sure the test the doctor gave you the other day made it real. Or the last hour in the bathroom. And I know that wasn't the first time, even though you've tried to hide it from me. It's why I begged you to go to the doctor in the first place, remember? I also know you were excited until I ruined it all."

"I was excited until all the what-ifs came rushing," I whisper. "But once I go to an OB—hear the heartbeat, see the sonogram—everything changes. I'll fall in love, and when I lose it—"

"Stop," he whispers as he presses his forehead to mine. "You won't lose him. My luck, you'll have twins or triplets." Unable to hold back anymore, the waterworks start. He pulls me into his lap as I sob and then bawl harder because I hate that I can't stop it. "Okay, okay. Bad joke. I'm sorry."

"It's not that," I wail uncontrollably. "I can't make it stop. I keep trying, and it just gets worse."

"You've been holding a lot back, *cher*. It's not hormones. Not completely, anyway. Thanks to my stupidity, you've been under a lot of stress. But I'm serious; you will see a doctor. *Soon.*"

"O-okay," I sniffle. It's on my lips to ask him to go with me because I do not want to do it alone. But I refrain. He just said he still wasn't okay with all of this. My urge to protect him will always be my priority despite his demands, so I won't push.

"So, you ready for New York?" he changes the subject, though I'm not sure if it's for him or me.

I look at him, giving him my biggest watery smile. "Yep. We can leave tomorrow. Nothing is keeping me here."

"What do you mean?" His brows fall, and I inwardly curse my slip.

I have been doing my best to avoid this conversation. Trying to prevent yet another thing he will blame himself over. But I can't lie now that I've screwed up.

We talked about this a few weeks ago. I am in the middle of my clinic hours to be a certified music therapist. Our plan was for me to finish out the month, then transfer to a hospital in New York—I didn't tell him that was easier said than done. But I lost my position after not showing up the last few days. I'm not angry. Music therapy is a competitive field with few open positions due to its relatively new practice. There are often far more applicants than positions available, so when I couldn't fill my hour due to being sick for a week—or at least I thought I was ill—then because of Maddox, they had to give my hours to someone else.

"So you see," I start, then explain to him the message I received this morning from my supervisor. "Nothing is keeping me here."

"Dammit," he spits out, and I already see the internal war starting.

"Don't do that," I toss his earlier words back at him. "This isn't your fault, and it's not a big deal."

"If you hadn't been with me for the last few days, it wouldn't be happening. So, tell me, how is it not my fault?"

"Because whether I was here with you or not, I've spent so much time in the bathroom being sick, I would never have made it to work anyway."

Of course, that's not the correct answer either, and I already see the guilt rising in his eyes. "Stop that," I snap. "That's not your fault either. I am just as fucking responsible as you are."

I can see he's not convinced, but the twitching of his lips provides some relief. "You're cute as fuck when you're assertive."

I roll my eyes. "I wasn't trying to be *cute*."

"Too bad," he laughs. "Okay, Canary. So tell me what the plan is now."

"When we get to New York, and I can stay out of the bathroom an entire day, then I'll apply for another position," I shrug because it's literally all I can do. What I don't tell him is that it could take months for a spot to become available or that I could be refused altogether. "But I'll have to find some sort of work. I still have a lot more student loans and medical bills to pay."

"No, you don't," he tells me. "I'll take care of that."

"Maddox, no. I'm not letting you pay *my* debt. It's my responsibility. I'll pay it." It annoys me that he would even suggest it. Because I did *not* marry him for his money.

"You can't stop me, *cher*. Nothing you do can stop me. And I don't need your permission. Wasn't asking either. But I will let you pay me back if it makes you feel better."

I chew the inside of my cheek, contemplating. He didn't have to say it for me to know that he would pay it off with or without my permission. At least he told me instead of doing it secretly. I already know there is no point in arguing, so I nod and agree. "If I can pay you back."

"So that's it? Nothing holding us back?"

"Yep," I smile brightly. "Where you go, I go. As long as we can come back after Verity has the baby."

"You're leaving?" a voice questions, breaking us free from our bubble.

We both look up and see Callie standing in the doorway. Maddox's head drops. "I live in New York, Callie. You know this."

"But we've been waiting on you to do... everything. His memorial. The will. The company." She steps farther into the room. Her bright eyes shine with unshed tears and frustration.

"Then don't wait on me," Maddox tells her plainly. "I never asked you to."

"Maddox, you have to be there. His directives explicitly state *you* must be present."

He throws his head back, staring at the ceiling as an irritated sound leaves his chest. "Then I guess you'll have to wait a little longer. I'm going back to New York to start therapy and all the other bullshit everyone wants me to do."

"You could do that here!" she argues, her face growing redder by the second.

"Why would I do that, Callie? Then I'd get through a few days or weeks here, go back home, and start over. I'm leaving tomorrow. Day after at the latest. End of story."

"You are a selfish asshole, Maddox. As usual." She spins on her heels, putting her back to us.

Awkwardly, I untangle myself from him and get to my feet. Maddox grabs my hand when I start for Callie. Warning and dread etch his face. Bending over, I kiss his cheek. "I'm a big girl," I remind him.

"This is between her and me," he tells me. "No need for you to get involved."

"If it concerns you, I'm already involved. Just like I know you're dying to tell my parents off." He smirks and releases me with a flourish of his hand, gesturing for me to have at it.

My heart breaks for Callie. She's lost her dad. Nearly lost her brother by the other brother's hand, and we still don't know the circumstances of those events. Only what Chris tells us. She's stressed and hurting.

And maybe Maddox is being selfish, but given how seldom he puts himself first, I think he's earned it. I realize that this is his MO. He doesn't deal with his problems; he runs and dives headfirst into someone else's. But that's not the case this time. He is dealing with his issues. He's just not ready to deal with that yet. So let him avoid it a bit longer while he works on himself.

But given the look in his eyes when she called him selfish—the grief that instantly struck, I know he's already starting to wallow. That's not what he needs right now. And I won't allow Callie to use it against him to force what she wants.

"Callie," I say calmly as possible as I place a hand on her shoulder. She turns around and faces me with anger and annoyance, pulling at her mouth. "You've all been through a lot, but Maddox not being ready to deal doesn't make him selfish. He needs time."

Her eyes flare and flash with anger. She steps to me with clenched fists and a tightened jaw. "All he has ever been is selfish!" she screams. "Only a selfish asshole would run when his family needs him. Or better still, try to fucking kill himself and leave his pregnant wife. How spineless can you be to act like everything is fine?"

"Hey!" Maddox bellows, standing to his feet. He's standing behind me in two long strides. I press my hands against his chest. Our eyes lock with unspoken words.

I've got this.

I know he wants to be my savior, but it's time he realizes he's got a protector too.

I turn back around to face her and grab her hand. "He's not running, Callie. He wants to be there for you and everyone else, but to do that, he's got to put himself first. Get healthy and learn how to properly deal with his feelings so he doesn't break again. He is in pain, and it seems like you've never bothered to notice that. That may be harsh, but it's the truth. All you've ever seen is your playboy, rock star brother. The one I *know* has always dropped everything when you've called.

"As for me? If you want to consider me spineless, then go right ahead. If loving him at his lowest point—through his mistakes and battles with his demons makes me weak, so be it. I'll gladly take the title and wear it with honor.

"But I think, for now, you should go until you've had time to calm down."

Her chin quivers as tears spill over her lashes, but she doesn't argue as she turns and leaves.

Maddox's head drops, pressing against the top of mine. "I'm always letting someone down."

I spin around and take his face in my hands. "No," I say firmly. "You don't get to feel bad, Maddox. She's angry and hurting, but she was out of line. You have got to stop carrying everyone's burdens. This pressure you've put on yourself to be perfect has been unrealistic and done more harm than good. And stop letting your family make you feel like you are a disappointment when you don't give them what they want."

He grins at me and runs a finger down my nose. "All right, darlin', but you must do the same thing with your family."

I bite my lip, feeling the flush of hypocrisy because he's right. I do allow my parents to make me feel like I constantly let them down.

I wrap my arms around his neck, reaching up on my tip toes. "Agreed," I say against his mouth as I gently kiss his lips.

His arms go around me, holding me in place as he kisses me back with far less gentleness. "Thank you, *cher*," he tells me as he pulls back.

"You're welcome," I giggle. "But for what?"

"For existing."

MADDOX

A cutting anguish

My knee bounces uncontrollably, and my eyes stay glued to the bathroom door. Quinn has spent nearly every second in there since take-off. I tried staying with her, but she said my tension made it worse. Which made me feel worse.

Rational or not, I feel like shit. Logic, unfortunately, doesn't override emotions. If it did, then maybe I wouldn't have nearly the fucking problems I do.

Reason tells me this is normal, considering she's pregnant. It also says it takes two to make a baby, and I definitely wasn't the only one there that night. So she's every bit as responsible for her current condition as I am.

Reason can kiss my ass because everything in me screams that I should've used my head when that goddamn condom broke. I should've taken it upon myself to get her the morning-after pill. If I had, she wouldn't be vomiting to the point of dehydration.

Let's not forget I'm the reason we're on a fucking plane right now. If I weren't the eternal fuck up with more issues than going to a show and realizing you're at the wrong venue, this wouldn't be happening.

It's only happened once, by the way.

"She's fine, Mads," Angel tells me for the tenth time.

"It's her new normal for the next few months," Dane chimes in like he's an expert when Cami is probably as far along as Quinn.

"You think I don't know that," I snap. "I know how it fucking works, jackass."

I drag a hand down my face and growl. Until yesterday at the hospital, it didn't even occur to me that she was still sick every day. I don't even know why considering it's the exact reason I was worried about her in the first place. Should've fucking known she was hiding it from me. Except for those few minutes yesterday, she hasn't even brought it up.

I lean forward, propping my elbows on my knees. Then I'm up again, pacing. The plush, black carpet probably won't be plush any longer once I finish walking a Maddox-sized path into it.

I stand by the bathroom door, a hand on either side of the frame, fighting my urge to open it. And to slam my fist through it. Mumbling curses, I start my trek over again, then plant my ass on the white leather sofa next to Jake, my eyes firmly fixed on that door.

"If this is how you are over morning sickness, how the hell will you handle her giving birth?" Jake asks.

I glare at him with a grunt. *Not helping motherfucker.* He holds his hands up in surrender and goes back to reading some book.

I am fully aware that I'm being a dick. All they've tried to do is encourage or support me, and they've taken my verbal abuse with... Well, maybe not a smile, but they haven't tried to swing at me yet.

I can't help it, though. Her pain is my pain. I hate every fucking minute that she suffers.

Because I was a dumbass.

That godforsaken door finally opens, and I'm on my feet, her face cupped between my hands before she can look up, with my teeth grinding at her pallor.

Her damn face is so ashen, it's nearly translucent except for the bright red circles on her cheeks. Her forehead is beaded with sweat and curls clinging to it. Usually bright, amber eyes look murky and muddy as she stares back at me. "Stop it," she grumbles. "I'm fine."

"Yeah, you look fucking fine," I bite out.

She sighs wearily. "Maddox, it's just motion sickness. Everyone gets it at some point."

Again, she tries to play off the real cause of this. I roll my head, attempting to loosen the tension in my neck and stop myself from biting her head off because I'm so tired of her trying to skirt around me. Dammit, it's not her job to protect *me*.

"Don't act like that's all this is," I manage to say with as much calm as I'm capable of right now.

"Let's go sit down," she says, shaking her head. At least this time, she's not denying it. Although, she's probably tired of arguing with me too. "We should be there soon, right?"

I allow her to drag me to the vacant seats near the bathroom. The jet is packed to capacity. It's not unusual for us since we usually travel together. We must look like some seriously co-dependent assholes. Of course, *I am* a seriously co-dependent asshole.

This is the first time Heaven, Tyler, and Heaven's brother, Matt, have been with us. Obviously, it's Quinn's first time too. Soon enough, Dane and Cami will be adding to our little chosen family.

And me too, I guess.

Our family has grown a lot over the last three years. The bad boys of rock and roll—the guys that partied from sundown to sun up with different women every night, were now in relationships and had kids. Suddenly, I'm not sure how I feel about that. Part of me thinks I'll miss it. The craziness and excitement of it all. But the truth is that craziness was only there because we were all trying to fill a void or escape the pain.

I lean back into the seat, and Quinn nuzzles into my side. In seconds, she's fast asleep. With an arm draped over her, I kiss the top of her head, then rest my head on hers, and close my eyes.

It's time to deal with the pain instead of running from it. I just don't know who I'll be on the other side.

"You have always thought too bloody loud."

I chuckle and open my eyes, unsurprised to see Ryder sitting across from us with a bottle of water in his hands. He's been biding his time while I lost my shit. He just knows sometimes you have to let me lose it a little.

"You should be in here with it." I tap the side of my head with a finger.

"I know what you're thinking, Madsy." He waves his hand up and down in front of me. "I had the same fucking thoughts a couple of months ago."

"What am I thinking, Ryder?" My brow quirked and head tilted, I issue the challenge. One I should know better than to impart because nobody understands me as he does.

We're a double-headed coin, him and me. Our lives strangely mirror each other in more ways than should be natural. In ways that shouldn't be allowed.

People have often questioned why I don't believe in God. My life is one reason. Ryder's is another. Hard to believe in some great, omniscient being that allows two kids to go through the shit we have. Harder still when you realize that some have been through worse.

Ryder believes. Not sure how in the hell he does, and the day he told me was one of the only times he truly shocked me. But it explained his anger. He wasn't just angry at the people in his life that should've loved and protected him. He was angry at his God for allowing it to happen in the first place, but it never changed his belief.

"You'll still be you, Maddox," he says, drawing me out of my musings. "Whatever labels they slap on you won't change who you are. You'll still have the whole *Beautiful Mind* thing going on. And your talent? Mate, you've had that since the day you took your first breath. None of that will go anywhere. But how you see yourself and the people around you will change."

I press my face into Quinn's hair, inhaling the sweet lavender scent. "I've always had noise in my head, Ry. Always too loud. Too fast. Just too much. Everything is too much. Like I wonder what the fuck I was thinking choosing this career because it's the epitome of too fast and too much."

"You chose it because you love it. Same as me. But yeah. I get all of that."

I nod because I know he does. "But until a few days ago, I thought the full-blown hallucinations were new."

He leans back in his seat and crosses an ankle over his knee as he studies me. Looking at me like he's trying to figure something out. "I think there's more to that, Mads. I'm no shrink, but something tells me the answer isn't as simple as you might believe. But none of it matters. Look around you, mate. What do you see?"

"That we need a bigger plane?" I joke.

He rolls his eyes and laughs. "It's getting there, but the reason we need bigger is because of you. You're the fucking glue, mate. You are why we are all together. Hell, you're why we have our women."

"I think you're giving me too much credit, Ry."

"Maybe," he shrugs, "but don't think I don't know why you bought the house on the lake. And stop pretending you didn't buy it the same day we ran into her. You aren't the only one that can check into shit. Just the only one that does. Most of the time."

"You knew where Heaven was the entire time, but I never pushed. Then we ran into her, and I saw it wasn't over for you. For either of you." It's the truth. Ryder never got over Heaven leaving, and my gut told me it wasn't the story his mother told him. The day we ran into Heaven at the label's building, her face told me she was far from over Ryder too. Then I bumped into Heaven and Tyler at a local store in her hometown. One look at Tyler was all it took for me to know they had both been manipulated.

"That's my point, Mads. You aren't *just* the talent or the brains. Any of us could do that. It might take a bit longer, sure, but without you, there would be no us. For any of us. You're the fucking heart, mate. And I don't mean the band. I mean this crazy, blended, fucked-up family we are. We *all* dropped everything to come to you. I know in your warped brain you believe you're the least of us. But you're not. You are so much stronger than any of us." He turns the water bottle to his lips, then scowls at the bottle like it offended him. He shakes it at me. "I hate this flavorless shit."

"How's that going?" I ask because I haven't forgotten he's going through his own shit, same as me. Yes, our situations and circumstances are different, but we're going through this shit at the same time.

Mirrored lives.

"One bloody goddamn second at a time," he tells me as he pushes his hand through his hair. "The urge is there. God, is it there, but I started this for them. Heaven deserves more than a drunken addict with anger issues, and Tyler deserves to have a dad that is present. Not one on the verge of explosion. But now I do it for me." We both look up at the sound system when the pilot comes on, telling us to buckle our seat belts. Ryder stands to return to his seat next to his girl and his son but pauses and looks at me. "Know why I'm doing it for me, Mads?" I shake my head because that's an answer I don't have and genuinely want. "Because before, when I looked in the mirror, I hated the person looking back at me, but now... I kind of like the git. Give all this a real shot. Maybe you'll finally start seeing yourself the way we all see you, and you'll like yourself too."

MADDOX

Let it go

Elevator doors slide open to the penthouse I've barely seen in two years. Pale hardwood and light, neutral colors welcome me back. However, the place I want to be is farther north and out of the city.

Soon.

I allow Quinn to step out first, then lead her through the corridor. I set our bags by the staircase while chastising myself for not leaving them on the elevator instead of carrying them upstairs.

I was essentially kidnapped and sent with nothing but the clothes on my back.

Oh, Maddox doesn't need anything. Besides, he's got money. He can buy something new.

Fuckers.

But they weren't wrong. Over the last several months, I acquired a few things. Not much. A few things to get me through my stay. Remaining in River City permanently was never in my plans.

Strange. The city I've always considered home is not where I want to live.

Quinn had two suitcases and an overnight bag. When I asked about the rest of her things, she simply offered a shrug. I'd wrongly assumed she had stuff in storage somewhere. She did admit a few items were at her parents' from before she was married, but after, she never had anything to call her own.

"He already had everything," she explained. "I just moved in, and that was that."

It pissed me off when she said it, but as I watch her walk across the living room to the floor-to-ceiling windows overlooking the city, softly touching furniture with interest as she passes, I realize I've done the same thing to her. I've brought her into my life that I established years ago.

Silently, to myself and her, I promise it will also be hers. And she can change anything she wants.

I lean against the doorframe, unable to take my eyes off her as she stares out over the city. She wraps her arms around herself, and her shoulders lift as her sigh fills the room. Apprehension takes over as I wonder what she thinks. Does she like my home? Will she be happy here? With me?

She turns around to face me as she leans against the glass. "This is a lot of space for one person."

I drop my head with a sheepish grin. "This was my *fuck you, Dad,* purchase when my trust kicked in after I finished college."

Her mouth falls open in shock. "How much was the trust?"

The heat of embarrassment starts racing up my neck. Looking back, what I did was insanely stupid. The amount of money I spent on this place just to stick it to my dad was not responsible in the slightest, but he always acted like I was like every other trust fund kid on the planet. Ready to blow through whatever I had and then come crawling back for more. What made it worse was that my dad didn't seem to care that I tossed half of my trust into buying this place. In hindsight, I think Dad probably saw this place as a sound investment. Or maybe he was hoping I'd come crawling back too, and he'd finally have me in the company. Though, I would've lived in this massive waste of space with no lights or water before I went to work for Masters Corp.

Dad realized he couldn't live my life for me long ago. But I was too stubborn to listen to him until it was too late. Now, we'd never make up for time lost.

I push those thoughts away when my stomach begins to turn. When I'll be ready to unbox those particular issues, I don't know, but it won't be today.

"I-uh... Let's just say it was enough." I tell her sheepishly.

"I'm sorry," she squeaks. "I shouldn't have asked that." Her hands cover her face as she tries to hide *her* embarrassment.

I close the space between us and pull her into my arms. "You can ask anything. No more secrets from me. Only reason I didn't say how much the trust was is that it's a little embarrassing for me. Which I know is stupid. Like the opposite of someone who has nothing trying to hide the fact, I pretend I haven't had everything handed to me."

"But you haven't," she argues. "You've worked hard to get where you are."

"True. I worked bars and non-paying gigs and whatever else to prove I wasn't some lazy, trust fund kid, but the fact is, I *was—am* a trust fund kid." I turn her around to look out over the city. "I can pretend all I want, but I've realized it's pointless. Whether I used that money or not, it was still there. If I so chose, I always had that safety net to use."

"There's nothing wrong with safety nets. We all need them sometimes."

"From here on out, baby, *I* am your safety net."

"And I'm yours," she says with a yawn.

"Come on," I say, kissing the top of her head. "Let's get you to bed."

She spins around, wobbles a bit, and looks at me with wide eyes. "But it's only six, and we just got here."

I wrap my arms around her waist with a chuckle. Her soft curves melt into me. So much smaller than I am, yet she molds to me as if she were made for me.

I sweep her hair off her shoulder and place a gentle kiss behind her ear, and marvel at the absolute adoration she has for me. Those whiskey eyes shine with love I know I don't deserve, but I'll do everything possible to try.

"We have time, Canary. You need to rest. That flight was hell on you. I'm just thankful it was a short one." I don't even want to think about how a cross-Atlantic flight would've been on her.

Without a chance to argue, I scoop her into my arms and carry her upstairs.

"Is that a pool?" she gasps as we walk past the window overlooking my infinity pool.

"Excessive?" I ask with a smirk. I put her on her feet so she can get a better look.

"Maybe a little bit, but it's beautiful. I can't wait to try it out."

"After you've rested, maybe we can go try it out," I say as I slip in behind her.

"I don't have a suit."

A rumble vibrates my chest, and my dick turns to stone at the images of her floating naked in my pool start filling my mind. "Even better," I mumble against her neck as I press my cock into her ass. "Less for me to take off." I smile against her silky flesh when it heats and prickles against my lips.

I tug her into my bedroom before my cock talks me into something other than sleep. Of course, I didn't consider the effects seeing her standing there would have on me.

That is until she noticeably tenses, and I'm cursing my stupidity. While I had my housekeeper come in and change the sheets, somehow, I forgot all about the swings and the benches.

I know it's not the furniture that bothers her. And she's more than aware of my past. But knowing they aren't here for decoration? That I've had others in this room? Yeah, that's different. "Do you want to sleep in another room?" I ask, cringing that I even had to.

She nibbles her bottom lip for a second. Then she straightens her shoulders, raises her chin, and shakes her head. "No. They don't matter."

"I'll get them removed tomorrow," I promise.

She turns to face me, her arms wrapped around my neck. "Maybe not removed. Just replaced."

I can't help but laugh. "My kinky little freak."

She shrugs with a wicked grin on her beautiful face. "You created a monster." On her tiptoes, she tugs my lip with her teeth as she rubs herself against my throbbing dick.

The control I show to turn her around with a slap on the ass and an order to sleep makes me proud—or dumb. She climbs onto the massive four-poster bed with a pout. I want to shove my cock between those pouty lips so badly it hurts, but within seconds she's out cold, and I know I was right about her needing rest.

Her massive curls splayed gently around her face, and her hands tucked under her cheek make her look so young. Hell, she is young, and I tend to forget that sometimes.

It's not fair that she's been through so much in her short life. Something we have in common. Living in that sense of hopelessness. But she was slowly pulling herself out.

Then I brought the darkness, and it swallowed her whole.

And somehow, she has fucking embraced it.

I don't deserve her, but thank fucking God she wants me anyway.

I go back downstairs to the kitchen and retrieve the ingredients I need to make dinner, along with a bottle of water. Moments like these are when I'm thankful for a fantastic housekeeper who stocked my fridge and pantry on short notice. Everything I need to make chicken noodle soup for Quinn is there and waiting. Not the shit out of a can that tastes like salt and garbage.

After I've chopped everything and put it into the pot, I go to the bags still sitting on the floor by the staircase, dig around until I find the pill bottles, and then go back to the kitchen.

The smell of butter, garlic, and onion fills the air, but all I notice are the bottles I've placed on the counter, taunting me. Stephen said he wouldn't diagnose me because he wasn't a psychiatrist. Not that I need one. I know what's wrong with me. I've read enough books to diagnose myself long ago. But his psychiatrist buddy told him to start me on whatever is in those bottles.

I sit on a stool, prop my arms on the counter, and rest my chin until I'm at eye level with them. Staring at them as if I'm waiting on them to do something. To give me answers to questions I'm too afraid to ask.

Finally, with an irritated growl, I empty the pills into my hand, toss them in my mouth, and swallow, barely refraining from throwing the shit across the room. The angel asleep in my bed is the only thing stopping me.

An hour later, I've finished cooking, and the silence is deafening. For only the second time since I woke up a few days ago, I'm alone.

I confuse even myself at times like these. Because sometimes it's too much, too fast, and it makes me feel like the world is closing in on me. My lungs will strain for oxygen that my brain has convinced me it's not getting.

But the silence makes my skin crawl. It's during the quietest times that all the other buzzing in my head is the loudest, and that's the shit I can't figure out how to turn off. At least, not without a bit of help of the chemical variety.

I walk through the penthouse, and it occurs to me that this place has *never* been so empty. It has always been packed with people in the seven years I've owned it. At the very least, the guys were here. Even when Zoey stayed with me, I usually had others here. Not like our paths needed to cross in this oversized place.

Quinn was right. It is too much for one person. Because it's also just dawned on me that I haven't been in half the rooms in this place. Out of nineteen, I've been in seven.

And now I find myself standing in front of the minibar in the game room.

It taunts too. With promises to stop the noise and ease some of this heaviness that's settled in my chest

I crack my neck a few times, shake out my trembling hands, and start clearing out bottles. Back in the kitchen, one by one, I pour a lifelong crutch down the drain. The clanking of the bottles each time I drop one in the trash makes me jump.

Hand raking through my hair, I blow out an uneven breath and go in search of the rest.

Eventually, I make it to my bedroom. Quinn is still sound asleep, so I move as silently as possible to the bathroom. I pull the bottles of Johnnie, Jack, and Jameson from the cabinets and watch the last of my liquor collection swirl in the basin, then take a big breath for what comes next.

If I were a wiser man, I would've had someone else do this for me. No, not smarter. If I weren't a goddamn masochistic fuck.

Opening the drawer to the right of the sink, I'm met with several plastic bags of my biggest albatross. My veins immediately start to burn, and my nose starts itching, begging me to feed the craving.

My skin crawls with need as I grab the bags and the paraphernalia, tossing the needles and syringes in the trash and flushing the bags.

I close my eyes and let the solace wash over me that I was able to do it. To rid myself of the shit I've clutched onto like a lifeline. Proud that temptation couldn't taunt me back into that dreary hovel of lies and false security.

Then I see it. Tucked in the back where I could leave it for an emergency. No one would ever notice. Then if things get really bad...

Shit.

I reach the back of the drawer and retrieve the torturous item from its hiding spot. Holding it between two fingers, I start to contemplate.

It might relieve some of this uneasiness in me. Maybe quiet the noise down a fraction. Stop the voices from screaming so loudly.

You know you can't do this.

What's the point in trying when all you're going to do is let everyone down?

You'll never be good enough.

You're a fuck up.

"Fuck it," I whisper.

It's all that's left. Everything else is floating in the sewers of New York. One line won't kill me. Hell, it won't do shit.

I open the bag, pour the contents on the marble, break it up, and arrange it into a nice, neat row with the credit card I pulled from my wallet.

Then I cut the line in half and make two rows. And a single row again.

"What am I doing?" I mumble. Grabbing the counter in a white-knuckle grip, I lift my head and face the man in the mirror. The ghosts and demons that haunt me swim through the blue abyss, but despite the darkness lurking, my eyes are clear. I wonder when the last time I looked at myself through clear eyes instead of hazy ones was.

I run my hand through my hair, gripping the roots tightly. "Fuck, fuck, fuck," I moan, then turn toward the door, worried I may have awoken Quinn.

Quinn.

"I did it for them." Ryder's voice tumbles around in my head.

I look at the counter disgustedly and rake the shit into the sink. After it's been disposed of, I grab a wipe from the cabinet and rid the counter of any remnants, not wanting it to touch a single molecule of Quinn's body.

I don't want this shit around her. To touch her. To affect her in any way.

I can do this for her.

I strip off my clothes, step into the shower, and let the water run over me as I wait for the need to pass while repeating to myself that I can do this. For her and *us*.

At least, I hope I can.

QUINN

Just look to the morning

Holding my breath, I watch him from the crack in the doorway. His struggle is palpable, and my heart cries out, desperate to reach out to him. But even without words, I know he wants to do this himself. He *needs* to do this himself.

My eyes close with relief when he brushes it into the sink.

His shoulders appear like one more straw, and he'll break as he pulls off his clothes to step into the shower.

When I hear the water start, I tiptoe in, remove my clothes, and step behind him. He's leaned forward, arms propped against the wall with his head resting against them. His shoulders are bunched, the muscles in his back strain under the invisible weight.

Stepping closer behind him, I gently—cautiously—trail my fingertips across his tight shoulders. The tension increases for a split second, and I hold my breath, waiting for him to freak out. But then he relaxes against my touch, letting me know I can continue. So I step even closer and trail my lips across his back as I wrap my arms around him from behind.

He shifts, looking over a shoulder at me, then turns around. A finger traces my jaw as I outline everything he feels about himself, etched permanently into his skin. He claims he doesn't believe in God, but the verse across his chest tells another story.

The weights and balances that hold the words *absolution* and *redemption* speak plainly of what he seeks, but *Guilty* marked just below shows why he believes he is beyond either.

Maddox doesn't *not* believe in God. He thinks God doesn't believe in him.

That he doesn't deserve love or happiness or forgiveness.

But I believe in him. I know this beautiful man deserves it all.

I fall to my knees and wrap my hand around his length, gently stroking—once, twice, three times. My tongue slips from between my lips, circling the swollen tip, dipping into that dripping slit before circling again. A groan tumbles from him when I draw him into my mouth, slowly at first, then to the back of my throat, making me wish I could take him all.

His hand grips my hair as I hum around him. I flatten my tongue against that throbbing vein as I trail up, then flick the jewelry on my way back down. My hand moves between my legs to alleviate my own building ache.

I look up at him and find him watching me through hooded eyes as water streams down his glistening, sculpted body. I can't stop the shiver as those dark blue eyes flame with desire as I worship him the way he deserves.

"Fuck, I love watching you suck me while you have your fingers in your cunt," he mumbles gruffly, then loudly groans when I cup his balls in my free hand and roll them between my fingers while flicking a finger over his guiche. "Fucking hell."

I groan around him. My fingers dip deeper into my pussy, seeking relief from the throbbing his words have caused.

His grip tightens in my hair, but he doesn't force anything. He's given me control. Something he has *never* done before, and I know he doesn't do easily, so I intend to make it worth it.

Hollowing my cheeks, I take him to the back of my throat, rolling my tongue around his head as I move up and down while I work myself into a panting frenzy. I repeat the motion and continue to flick my tongue over his shaft. When he begins to pulse in my mouth, I gently tug his guiche. He explodes down my throat with a groan, slamming his fist against the shower wall. I cry around him as his cum fills my throat and mine floods my hand.

But I don't let up. I continue to suck him until *he's* begging for *me* to stop. "Okay. Enough," he growls. He pulls me away when I don't immediately comply and drags me to my feet.

His mouth slams against mine as he devours my mouth. His tongue assaults mine with ferocity. If I thought the beast would be sated, I was poorly mistaken.

My legs go around his waist when he lifts me, and we make our way to the bedroom without breaking the kiss. Neither of us caring that we're leaving a puddle of water in our wake. I'm not even sure we turned off the shower.

He lays me on the bed and wastes no time licking and sucking every inch of my skin. I'm on fire, and the lingering moisture on my body turns to steam. When his mouth reaches my breast, I arch into him with whimpers and pleas for more.

He slips a finger inside me. "So wet," he growls against my skin. "Only for me, Canary."

"Yes," I moan, even though he wasn't asking.

His starving nips and licks continue to travel until he reaches my apex, and within seconds, only his name exits my mouth as I come undone.

The aftershocks of my orgasm don't subside before he slips inside. My body welcomes him home, and I cry out at our joining.

He grabs my hands, pushes them over my head, and entwines our fingers. His mouth meets mine once again, this time in a slow, languid kiss that brings tears to my eyes as he begins to move just as slowly inside me.

The weight from before is momentarily forgotten as he stares at me with nothing but worship in his eyes. "I love you, Canary," he says softly. "No matter what, never forget that."

My throat clogs, words lost somewhere between us, as tears spill down my cheeks.

"It was always meant to be you," he tells me, kissing the corner of my mouth. "You were made for me."

"Only you." My words break as I start to come once again. Back arching, I cry out at the unexpected liquid fire that explodes deep inside of me; whether, from the act or the emotion, I can't be sure. He groans against my mouth as I pulse and clench around him until he's falling too.

For several moments, we lie there, clinging to each other. Saying more with the beat of our hearts than words ever could.

"It's bullshit," Maddox yells, tossing his bottle of water across the room.

He's been unreasonable and... well, pissed since we left the psychiatrist. He handled what the doctor had to say about as well as someone getting a colonoscopy without anesthesia. "I don't understand why you think this is a bad thing," I say for probably the tenth time.

I want to walk around this counter so badly, wrap my arms around him, and tell him it's okay. But when he's like this, being touched agitates him more.

"I agreed to see a goddamn doctor. Isn't that enough? Why the hell do I need to see *another* one?" Hands are so tightly tangled in his hair that he's pulling out clumps. His face is red with anger, and the veins in his temples and neck throb faster with each passing second. I'm starting to worry about his heart. Though the doctors say there would be no long-lasting damage, it was only two weeks ago that he went into cardiac arrest.

I jump a foot and nearly fall over the bar stool when he puts his fist through the wall with another string of curses.

"Maddox," Ryder yells, making me jump again. "It's not the end of the bloody world."

When we returned from the doctor, all his friends were here waiting. At first, I wasn't sure if it was a good idea given his mood when we left, but I've since been grateful they're here. I know Maddox would never hurt me, but I don't believe inanimate objects are immune to his anger. I wouldn't have stood a chance at containing him if he decided to trash his home.

"How would you know, Ryder? Huh? Were you told, oh, it sounds like this, but we need to be sure, so you need to see *someone else* to be sure?"

I watch, feeling helpless. He might appear to be a spoiled asshole throwing a tantrum to an onlooker, but those closest to him know this is a big deal for him. He feels out of control, and he's terrified. He went to a doctor, seeking an answer, and got slammed with more questions. This is his worst nightmare. Not whatever diagnosis they slap him with, but that they won't be able to figure out what's wrong with him.

Guilt churns in my stomach, clenching and squeezing until I think I may be sick because I know this isn't just about *his* doctor's visit.

I had no idea he made the appointment, and I still don't understand how he got one so fast other than his last name and a lot of money. When he told me this morning, we argued for forty-five minutes because I didn't think it was a good idea to do both in one day. Much less back to back. When I finally caved on that, we argued because I told him he didn't have to go with me. Although, that wasn't as much of an argument. More like he raised hell because I said it in the first place. I simply don't want him to feel pressured, but he didn't see it that way.

Everything at my doctor went as I expected, but when she started to discuss the potential risks and complications due to my uterine deformity and history of loss and the medications I take for depression and anxiety, his anxiety escalated. When it took a good few minutes to find the baby's heartbeat, he stood in the corner with a hand covering his mouth to hide the fact his jaw was clenched like a vice.

We had lunch afterward. He was mostly quiet, except when he was telling me to eat. I wasn't hungry, but I didn't have the energy to argue with him.

By the end of his appointment, I felt hopeful. No matter which diagnosis he received, the medication they started him on was the right path because it treated several things, including the potential diagnosis they were considering for him. The doctor was simply hesitant to slap a label on him without speaking to his colleague first, who specialized in one of those areas.

Maddox had a very different opinion, which is why we're standing in his kitchen while he rants, raves, and throws things.

Like the glass bowl, he just grabbed off a shelf and launched across the room. It shatters, sending glittering shards exploding in all directions.

"Goddammit, Maddox! Stop!" Ryder bellows.

Dane says something too, but I don't hear because my attention is on the warmth I feel running down the back of my arm. I turn and look, finding several minor scratches and a tiny piece of glass lodged in the back of my upper arm. I never felt it.

Quietly, while they continue to argue, I head for the nearest bathroom. I search the space until I find a first-aid kit. Turning the water on, I begin cleaning it as best I can. No easy feat given the angle, and there is more glass than I initially thought.

"Quinn, where the hell did you go?" I hear Maddox bellow down the hallway.

I roll my eyes. I knew better than to walk away unnoticed. He's been strangely... clingy? No, that's not it. Apprehensive and unsettled are better adjectives. I'm not sure the cause, but whatever it is has made him wary of leaving me alone. Since we arrived in New York, he won't leave the penthouse unless I go along. Granted, it's only been a couple of days, but I can tell something is off.

"Fuck, this place is too—" His grumbles are cut short when his eyes lock with mine in the mirror, then cut to where I'm struggling to remove the glass.

I slipped away because I didn't want the others to be bothered or Maddox to lose it. They've all taken to treating me like crystal—fragile and breakable.

I also didn't want Maddox to feel guilty because this *is* actually his fault.

"I'm fine," I say before he has a chance to speak.

"The fuck you are." He's standing beside me, my arm in his hand, before I can argue. "Fuck, fuck, fuck. I'm so sorry, Quinn. *Dammit.*"

"You didn't do it on purpose," I tell him, pulling my arm away.

"Did you find her?" Dane's voice carries through the gallery.

"I wasn't lost," I mutter and roll my eyes again as Maddox answers him.

Picking up the tweezers, I return to my task—attempting to remove the tiny sliver of glass.

Maddox snatches the tweezers from me with a huff. "*I'll* do it."

Dane walks into the bathroom, eyes growing wide when he notices what we're doing. "Do you need a doctor?" he asks, then repeats the question to Maddox. "Does she need a doctor?"

"It's fine," I grit out, irritated that he asked Maddox like I'm not standing here.

"Got it," Maddox grunts, holding the tiny shard for us to see. I try to tug away from him again, but his grip stays firm.

"I need to clean it," I argue.

"*I'll do it*," he replies without looking at me. "I did it; I'll fix it."

He's retreating. Running behind his walls of guilt and self-deprecation. No one could be harder on him than he is on himself.

A few minutes later, I'm cleaned and bandaged. I start to leave the room until I notice he isn't behind me. Turning to face him, I lift a questioning brow.

"Give me a few, okay?" he breathes out.

"I'll give you five. That's all. Or I'm coming back."

I wander out of the bathroom in search of the others, unsurprised when I find them all in the music room, Ryder with a guitar across his knee and Dane twirling drumsticks between his fingers.

"You didn't seem surprised with his little outburst," Ryder comments when he sees me.

"I've seen a few of them," I shrug ambivalently as I walk to the piano and take a seat.

"He's worse when he feels out of control." I nod, acknowledging his statement, knowing it to be true. Maddox, even when spiraling, needs to feel like he's in control because he doesn't know how to process anything else. "I'm the one everyone calls explosive, but only because they see it more often. And because his is usually directed inward. Until there's no room left."

I turn and glance at the city skyline for a moment, collecting my thoughts. My fingers move unconsciously over the keys to the same melody Ryder is absently strumming on his guitar. "It's a symptom," I tell them.

He stops playing, but I don't. I turn my attention to him to find him leaning forward, elbows planted on his knees, and a keen look of interest lining his eyes. "You think you know what's wrong with him." It's not a question.

"I don't think it's one thing," I mutter as my fingers stroke the C, G, A minor, F major, and F6 chords for the verse. "I don't think it usually is, you know? And the longer it goes untreated, the harder it is to pinpoint. They thought I was suffering from grief and postpartum. And then, I refused to go back to the doctor for years, and it got worse until I reached my breaking point. I could see how much I'd affected everyone around me. I destroyed my marriage. Or so I thought," I mumble that last part. "Honestly, I just wanted to die. Wanted it to all be over with so I could see my baby again. But my mother and my brothers practically dragged me to the doctor. Long story short, I have dysthymia, panic disorder, and I had PTSD from losing my baby like I did."

"Makes sense," Dane says. "We want simple. Expect an easy answer. But since when is simple and easy ever the right answer?" He nods toward the piano when my fingers stroke the final G, F, and C. "Can you play anything else?"

"Not really." I shrug and turn around on the bench.

"Don't let her fool you," Maddox says from where he's been leaning against the doorframe, watching us quietly. "She can play that, and she can sing."

I duck my head to hide the flame of my cheeks. A tingle of fear creeps up my spine that he will ask me to sing. It took a bit, but I love singing for him. And he's managed to get me to karaoke a few times. But the thought of singing in front of Ryder and Dane makes me want to throw up.

Ryder smirks with a lifted brow. "I'm not surprised. Music is the language he understands. Of course, you'd speak it."

Maddox pushes from his spot and walks to the piano. He pulls me to my feet, sits on the bench, and then sits me on his lap. His face nuzzles in my neck while he whispers, 'I'm sorry' again. I shake my head subtly, telling him it's okay.

"I think we'd be more surprised if you couldn't," Dane laughs loudly as he starts tapping his sticks on the coffee table in front of him. "But judging from the lovely shade of green you turned, I'm guessing we won't be hearing it."

I blush furiously and hide my head in Maddox's shoulder, but breathe a sigh of relief. Maddox chuckles and whispers, "They'll hear you soon enough, Canary."

I shake my head, but there's no argument on my lips. Because I already know it's one I won't win.

MADDOX

What it is that's killing me

My knee bounces uncontrollably, and I chew on my thumbnail as anxiety tears through my body. Adam Lawrence sits across from me along with another doctor—the specialist. I didn't know psychiatry had specialists, but here we are.

The other doctor looks vaguely familiar, and I hope she isn't someone I fucked because that shit could get awkward. Though I usually remember, so maybe that's not it.

"Maddox, I filled Hunter in on what you told me last week, and she has reviewed your file, but I thought you could tell her everything in your own words." Adams prods me to speak up instead of glare.

Quinn's fingers tighten around mine. It eases a bit of the tension, but short of sucking my dick right now, there's not a lot of comfort to be found.

The point of this shit is to be honest, but there's only so much I can tell her. I stayed up most of the night, trying to figure out what to say to give her what she needs without stirring up a lot of shit that could potentially land my ass in jail.

"Maddox," Adam says, drawing me from my thoughts, "you can tell her everything."

The surprise on my face must be obvious because she laughs. "We have mutual friends and a certain... *family connection*."

"*Family* connections," I groan. "Are you trying to tell me that we're related? Or are you referring to another kind of family that I'm not technically part of?"

She laughs again. "You and I aren't related, but we do share relations. But to answer your question, the second, I'm Layla's cousin."

Hunter? Hunter?

Oh hell. I remember her. We only met once a few years ago when Ryder and I went to Rory's rooftop club after a show. She was there with Christian. That explains why she *knows* things. But I'm still not sure what I should and shouldn't tell her.

"Maddox, I promise nothing you say will *ever* leave this room." She tries once more to alleviate my concern.

Quinn squeezes my hand again as she looks at me with eyes of adoration.

After the way I exploded last week, I wouldn't have blamed her if she'd taken off right then. Fuck knows she doesn't deserve to be subjected to that shit.

But she didn't go anywhere. Didn't consider it. She's still right here, supporting me. So for her, I relent and tell them *everything*. Even things I didn't say in the last session.

When I finish, I hold my breath and wait for the gasps of shock at what I've done. For the defeated and sympathetic looks that say my case is hopeless. That they don't know what's wrong with me and don't have the answers I need. Or even for the fucking label that says I'm not quite right, and every doctor from now on will judge me by.

"Maddox, you've been through a lot," Hunter finally says, and it shocks me that her tone isn't sad or pitying. It's as neutral as if she said the sky was blue. "Adam tells me that you self-diagnosed yourself years ago."

I nod because it's true. You don't need doctors to give you the answers when you can study all the same books and journals they have.

"Can I ask why you latched onto what you did? Why you were so certain that was your problem?"

"Because it fit the most. The voices, the hallucinations. The way I kind of lose track of reality when I'm alone."

"That's because you dissociate. You always realize what's real and what's not, but when you're triggered, your mind shuts down, so to speak."

"I don't always know," I grumble. "Thought something—someone was real most of my life that wasn't."

"That plays a part too, and I think somewhere deep down in your subconscious, you knew Bryan wasn't real. You wouldn't have accepted the fact so easily if you didn't recognize it on some level. I think Bryan was a shield of sorts. The permission you needed to be less than perfect. To do things you knew you wouldn't normally do."

I scoff because this seriously sounds like bullshit to me, but I don't interrupt.

"That said," she continues, ignoring my blatant disbelief, "we aren't looking at one diagnosis. You are suffering from several issues that have gone untreated for so long that I'm honestly surprised you've lasted as long as you have without having a serious mental break."

"What do you call what happened to me a couple of weeks ago?" I snap venomously.

"I call that a warning. You're teetering on the edge. And the drug use and alcohol have only made things worse. How long have you been using drugs and alcohol?"

I rub the back of my head, suddenly feeling like a kid getting caught stealing or cheating on a test. "Off and on since I was thirteen," I admit. "I had a few years sober, though. And still had all the same problems."

She nods, understanding my train of thought. "The drugs didn't necessarily cause the problems, but they *did* escalate them. And the feelings of too much, too fast? The inability to focus unless it's something you truly enjoy?"

"Most of my life," I tell her honestly. "I don't remember a time when sitting still for more than five minutes was possible until my mom bought me a piano."

"How about the feelings of loneliness?"

"I-uh..." I trail off, unable to pinpoint exactly when it started. "I think it started shortly after my mom died."

"Which is when you were sent to boarding school and were abused by the school psychologist."

My teeth grind together at the mention of O'Dell, but I manage a nod.

She hums for a minute as she continues to go down her notes. "This is why I say not a single diagnosis. That would be easier to understand. I get that. But you have several things, both behavioral and mental, that have gone undiagnosed and untreated for a very long time. But I will say, *your professional diagnosis* is incorrect." I can't help but grin at her sarcasm. "That said, the medication we have you on will help. You should start seeing improvements within a few days if you aren't already. I know it's frustrating to take more than one medicine every day, but the combination will help balance you out. I will say that treating the ADHD at this time isn't in your best interest because the medication can trigger other issues."

"So that's it?" I question doubtfully. "Keep popping pills, and I'm all good."

Her brows twitch in annoyance. My smartass mouth is getting to her, and the asshole in me enjoys it because being here annoys me.

"Therapy, Maddox. Therapy is important. And you won't be *all good,* but you'll be better. Unfortunately, you know there's no cure for any of this. Only treatment to keep you asymptomatic for as long as possible. I won't lie and say you'll never have a relapse of symptoms from any of this, but the goal is to have fewer episodes and more time between each one."

She continues talking, going down the list of things she's determined is wrong with me as I drag my hand down my face, completely over it and exhausted from this whole conversation. I'm not sure if anything she's said has made me feel better or worse. It's not what I've thought all these years, so I guess there's that. But holy fuck, I feel like I've been tossed the alphabet of mental and behavioral disorders, starting at ADHD to DID to OCD to PTSD to a mood disorder with psychotic features all the way to zombie—which is how I've read this damn medicine makes some people feel—to God knows how many more between. I swear it seems like I have more disorders than they have names for. *And surprise, surprise*—they aren't curable.

"So we have a plan. How do you feel about it?" Adam asks, snapping me out of my moment of self-pity and depreciation.

"I feel like it's all bullshit and a waste of time." They wanted honesty, so I'm giving it to them. Then I bring the hand interlinked with mine to my lips. "But I'll give it a shot." I'm speaking to her, not the doctors sitting across from me.

"Do the exercises, take your meds, come to therapy, and *no* drugs or drinking," Hunter tells me. I salute with two fingers, making her roll her eyes, and I bite back a laugh at the sudden resemblance to Layla. "This is a marathon, Maddox. Not a sprint."

"Yep. Got it. Don't lose my shit when you take too long to get me results."

Adam blows out a breath. "Yeah, something like. I'll see you three times a week for a while so that sold-out tour I bought tickets for in September needs to be canceled."

I grunt and nod without telling him it was canceled a few days ago. I wasn't going on the road and leaving Quinn behind. At least not right now. Not until after she has this baby. "See you in a couple of days, doc," I grumble as I practically drag Quinn out of the office.

Her hand in mine, we walk through the brightly lit hallway of the posh office to the private entrance reserved for the doctors since the goddamn paparazzi are still heavy. So heavy, I've been using a driver.

"So, slight change of plans," I turn to her once we're moving. "I need to go to the label office and handle a few things. Then I'm taking you to dinner." I pause for a moment, second-guessing my plans as I recall she was up all night, hugging the toilet. "That is if you're up for it." I'm prepared to cancel everything since I don't want her out of my sight. All those damn dreams, or whatever they were, still have me fucked up. The thought of her anywhere away from me causes panic to churn violently, so I have refused to go anywhere without her or let her go anywhere without me.

"Of course, I'm up for it," she smiles so brightly it knocks the wind out of me. "But don't you want to talk about what the doctor said?"

"Nope. What they said doesn't change anything." For the first time, awareness washes over me at the truth of that statement. The labels change absolutely nothing. I'm still emotionally and mentally fucked up. Everything still hurts like hell. It's still inherited—partly anyway. I still have no expectations that anything they do will help because then I can't be disappointed if it doesn't work. "But maybe their plan will prove me wrong. I meant it when I said I'll try, *cher*."

"Okay," she whispers, and once again, I'm so fucking grateful for her. Because she doesn't push or force things on me. Her patience seems limitless, and I've come to one obvious conclusion. I may never deserve her, but no one will ever love her as I do.

QUINN

Like a song was sung

We walk through the record label's hallways, and I'm astounded at the number of gold and platinum albums mounted on the wall by so many famous names. Then I notice Sons of Sin at the end. I knew they were big, but I didn't realize how much success they had since they broke onto the scene. Has it been three years? More?

We come into the main lobby, and more awards are strategically placed like a museum display. Grammys and VMAs are adorned in glass cases throughout, and once again, I see Sons of Sin dominating as far as recent artists go. You'd think this label was nothing until they came along.

We continue walking, and I struggle to keep my jaw off the floor as we pass by artists I've listened to for years—even some from my parents' generation—all nodding their heads in acknowledgment of Maddox. A few stop with words of concern or sympathy and encouragement since what's been going on with him has been so public. A couple even congratulate him on getting married and say a few kind words to me. Of course, I awkwardly say thank you while trying to find a way to bury myself inside Maddox so they will stop looking at me. Because not all the looks are *not* friendly.

"Maddox, oh my God, dude," another person stops in front of us with his emphatic greeting. "You look fucking awesome for someone who was shot."

Maddox and I both cringe. The guy's statement is harmless and meant to be funny, but we're not quite there yet. Or at least I'm not. He shakes his shaggy brown head with a laugh and extends his hand to Maddox, who readily accepts it.

"Good to see you, Wyatt," Maddox smiles, then turns and introduces me.

Wyatt turns his dark brown eyes on me with a smirk. "Looks like the rumors are true that you went and got yourself hitched." His smirk turns to a genuine smile, and he winks at me.

"Yeah, they are emphatically true," Maddox tells him, pulling his hand out of mine and tossing his arm over my shoulder.

I offer the man my hand, but instead of shaking it, he brings me in for a tight hug. Maddox growls, pulling me back. "Take it easy, Roberts. She fucking pregnant."

People turn around and stare. A few start whispering.

I freeze. Blood drains from my face. That was something I wanted to keep quiet for as long as possible. Until just now, the only people that knew were immediate friends and family and a couple of doctors.

"*Shit,*" Maddox mutters, dragging his hand down his face. He turns his repentant blue eyes on me, his mouth pulled into a grimace. "Sorry, Canary. It just slipped out."

I don't say it's okay. I know he didn't mean to, and I'm also secretly thrilled he's concerned enough to slip. But I'm also worried about the backlash. So I just wrap my arms around him and bury my face against his chest.

"Holy shit! So that's why you got married?" His brown eyes rake over me, looking for the evidence. I, of course, flinch because it took him half a second to jump to the same conclusion everyone will.

Maddox shoves him, not hard, but hard enough to show his annoyance. "No, that's not why I got married, you jackass. Why would you even say that? Are you drunk or something?"

Another dark-haired, dark-eyed guy walks up. He claps Wyatt on the shoulder with a grin. "He's always drunk lately. Says it numbs his wrecked heart. So what did the big mouth say this time?"

Wyatt tosses his friend a scathing glare and shrugs his hand off his shoulder. "I am not *always* drunk," he mutters.

Maddox leans back on his heels, dragging a hand across his mouth. Understanding lights in his eyes. "It doesn't help, but it makes you think it does for a while," he tells them, then changes the subject without answering the guy's other question. "You guys cutting a new song?"

"Nah, man, not even close." He extends his hand to me with a smile. "I'm Dylan, by the way."

"What do you mean *not even close*?" Maddox's brows tug low with concern and confusion. Then he tilts his head down the corridor. "Better yet, follow me. I don't have much time before the guys get here. Talk while we walk."

He pulls me along behind him as Dylan and Wyatt follow along. We pass by several more people who stare at us with curiosity, along with several offices and rooms with closed doors and lights that say *recording* over them.

Dylan and Wyatt talk the entire way, and the tension in Maddox grows. It's the last thing he needs right now, and I want to tell the two men to shut up. But I manage to keep quiet. Just barely.

We enter a room with comfortable sofas and chairs and several guitars. Amps and drums are positioned behind a plexiglass wall, and a couple of microphones sit in the center of the room. Cords are strewn over the heavily carpeted floors, leading to a large console sitting off to the side.

I take a seat on one of the sofas and watch as Maddox begins moving and arranging things in the room while he talks to Wyatt and Dylan.

"So this buy-out and the new owner are why you're at a standstill?" he asks as he begins to unplug and plug in different things.

I can't help but watch in fascination as he does all of this so effortlessly. He barely glances at each cord or wire as he maneuvers and swaps out. I have no idea what he's doing, but whatever it is, he clearly knows.

I also notice that Dylan and Wyatt are watching him with equal looks of fascination and curiosity. They seem as clueless as I do as they cast each other questioning glances.

"Not everything," Dylan answers, then his curiosity gets the better of him. "Uh, Mads, you know that amp should face the other way, right? So the sound carries properly?"

Maddox looks over his shoulder with a smirk. "I like it this way." He winks at him and returns to what he's doing.

"Okay then," Dylan shrugs. "Yeah, well, anyway. Anyone on Sons' level is business as usual."

Maddox turns around with that same concerned look. "There's no one signed at our level right now."

Both the men lift a shoulder. "If you don't have a top 100 song, you're in limbo."

Maddox sits next to me with a guitar in his hand. My mouth falls open when he begins removing the perfectly intact strings. He deftly replaces each string with a new one as if it's second nature, barely even looking at the guitar as he speaks. "Because upper management thinks the new owners will trade you out for their artists." He twists the tuners, strumming different chords as he adjusts the sound, then sets the guitar aside. He leans forward with his fingers bridged in front of him while he thinks. "And now you don't have a drummer, and your rhythm guitar is MIA?"

"Knox is…" Dylan starts and trails off as he searches for his words. "Anytime we're not working, he disappears."

"Any idea why?" I ask, then immediately turn red because this isn't my conversation. "I'm sorry. I didn't mean to butt in."

Maddox chuckles and leans back, pulling me against him. "You're good, baby."

"What he said," Wyatt agrees. "But, nah, we don't know. We've tried asking a time or two. He just says it's personal."

"Corey just got a gig with another band. Can't blame him for taking a paying gig." Dylan lifts his shoulders in resigned defeat.

Maddox nods sharply, then stands. "I'll get everything straightened out. Just get your band together and new material ready."

"No offense, Mads, but not sure even you can influence *invisible* powers that be," Dylan tells him as he pushes off the piano he's leaning against, understanding the unspoken cue from Maddox that it's time to end the conversation.

Wyatt doesn't appear to be as quick on the uptake. Then again, he also looks like he's falling asleep where he stands. Maddox slaps a hand against the man's chest with a grunt. "Just do it, asshole. And get the fuck out of here. Flip the switch when you go."

When the door closes, Maddox begins to do something with the microphone. "You're going to record?" I ask

He doesn't answer me right away. Instead, he continues to adjust something and then goes to the console across the room. After he moves a few knobs, he returns to sit next to me, grabbing the guitar. His fingers move skillfully across the string as he plays a beautiful melody I haven't heard.

"That's gorgeous." I smile brightly at him. I love watching him play as much as I love hearing him sing. "When did you write it?"

"Been stuck in my head since the doctor's office. To answer your questions, Canary, *we* are going to record."

That feeling of panic swoops in no quicker than the words have left his sexy mouth. My head feels like it's on fire as I shake it back and forth. "Maddox, no."

He grips both sides of my head, brushing away fallen tears with his thumbs. "Breathe, darlin'," he whispers to me. "Do you know why I call you Canary?"

Closing my eyes, I breathe in his calming scent and let his touch soothe away the nerves barreling through me.

Peace. It's what we give each other when we can't find our own.

I open my eyes and stare into his, seeing nothing but patience and love. "Because you like to hear me sing."

"No, my little songstress. I *need* to hear you sing, and one day the fucking world will hear you, too. But today, it's only you and me. No one outside this room can hear us, and no one will come in as long as that light is on."

His eyes never leave mine; I couldn't take mine off of him if I tried. I could drown in them. If the eyes are the window to the soul, then his soul is more beautiful and precious than the rarest of gems. "Why is this so important to you?" I finally whisper.

"Because everything stops when you sing, baby, even if only for a minute. The noise, the clatter, all of it. I wouldn't need a single drug if I could always hear you sing." I follow his tongue as it runs over his bottom lip, and my spirit leaps when he brings those lips to mine. Electricity tingles throughout. It never gets old. His tongue slips into my mouth, and fire erupts. I push up onto my knees, needing more. Wanting him to quench the wildfire he's ignited. His arms snake around me, pulling me close, stoking the inferno. When his rough palms find the bare flesh of my backside, I'm practically a puddle of want and need.

Then he pulls back, both of us panting with lust-filled eyes. "As appealing as having you bent over anything here is, *cher*, our time is running out." I hear his words, but my lust-addled brain is not comprehending the meaning. He sees my confusion and laughs. "You have to reserve studio time. I reserved two hours, one of which is for a friend, and the guys will be here in…" He pauses and checks his watch. "Ten minutes. So, you gonna sing with me, Canary?"

I bite my lip but relent with a nod. He pulls a piece of paper from his back pocket and hands it to me. "I've marked the places where you sing."

"Okay," I nod.

His fingers move lightly over the strings, and his powerful voice begins. I look at the paper and gasp at what's written. He gives me a mischievous smirk and then starts singing.

"I saw you sitting in the dark, and you were crying

I asked what ya crying for

Said you were tired of believing

Couldn't do it anymore

So I took your hand, gave you a grin, and those whiskey eyes pulled me in."

Somehow I manage to come in with him on the chorus without sobbing and flow straight through to my verse.

"When I found you, you were broken in pieces on the floor

In your eyes, there was longing for something more

And even in your darkest hour you took my breath away

It's for you that I stayed

To see you smile

Watch you grow

To take your pain away

But you took mine instead

You were sitting on the floor, you were shaking

I knew your heart was torn

Said you were tired of hurting

Couldn't do it anymore

So I took your hand, sang you a song, and those ocean eyes called me home

I make it through the next chorus, but my voice is already breaking with emotion. I can't contain it. So much feeling courses through me. I have no idea how he found it, much less finished the lyrics and put music to it, but I'm at a loss that he's taken the little song I was working on and made this beautiful arrangement. At the bridge, as we each sing our line, I can't contain it anymore, and the words come out as fractured sobs.

You pulled me from the dark, helped me fight again

You gave me brand new hope, helped me live again

You are my whiskey eyes

You are my beautiful sin

He stops the recording before we sing the final chorus and brings me into his arms. I slap his chest in annoyance. "That was awful, asshole. I cried through half the song." His lips twitch as he fights a grin. I slap him again. "I'm serious." Then I start crying again. "How did you even find that? You said you wrote it at the doctor's office."

He can't contain his laughter any longer. "I did write it at the doctor's office. It fell out of your purse while we were in there."

"You did all of that *while* talking to the doctor?"

He shrugs like it's not a big deal, but he wrote that in an hour, and it took me two weeks to get my verse and the bridge. "You gave me something to work with. Soon as I read it, I had the music in my head. All I had to do was write a verse and a chorus that matched what you had. Wasn't hard since this is our story."

More tears fall, and he laughs again but holds me close and strokes my hair until my sobs become soft whimpers.

"Ready to try again?" he asks.

I look at him with disbelief. "Are you serious?" I hiccup. "I barely made it through the first time."

"But now the shock and surprise have worn off. You got this, baby."

"Why do I feel like this is a setup of some sort?"

I catch a glimmer in his eyes that's gone too quickly to be sure what I saw, but my eyes narrow suspiciously anyway. "For me?" he asks, and those blue eyes do me in.

And I get through the song before I burst into tears again. And again, he laughs at me. He cups my face and gently kisses my lips. When he pulls back, the fire in his eyes ignites my own. Sparks fly as electricity curls around us, and I'm climbing him like a tree, ready to lose all of my clothes when the door opens.

QUINN

Just pay no mind at all

Maddox sets me to my feet, cursing under his breath.

I glare at him accusatorily. "I thought you said no one would come in," I hiss.

"They aren't supposed to, but he sucks at following the rules," Maddox growls, knowing it's Ryder without looking.

"Don't stop on my account," Ryder smirks as he sits on the sofa. "Ya know, I don't mind watching. Can't say the same about the others."

The rest of the band walks in, and Maddox huffs as he drags a hand over his face in annoyance. "All I needed was fifteen minutes," he mutters. His eyes tease me. "Although I could've had you screaming in one."

"Shut up," I push him. "You could not."

He raises a brow at me, the corner of his mouth tilted upward, issuing a challenge.

My cheeks flame because he's right. He totally could.

"You wanted to see me, Maddox?" a girl with raven hair, tight, ripped jeans, and a fitted tank top asks from the doorway.

"Quinn, this is Heidi. Heidi, this is my wife, Quinn." Heidi gives me a tight-lipped nod.

Great. I've got another one assuming the worst of me.

"I asked Heidi to show you around while we lay a couple of tracks," he tells me.

"I can get Darren to drive me back to your place," I snap, irrationally annoyed at his hovering.

"Please. Just stay here." I instantly regret my momentary moodiness when I see the shadows of worry flicker in his eyes. Something is going on with him. *Something else.* It's been there since he woke up in the hospital. A fear of something I don't understand, and it's not fair for me to make it harder on him.

But we will have to talk about it sooner or later because I can't be glued to his side forever, or I'll start to feel like an interloper. The meddlesome, distrustful wife that can't leave her husband alone. That's not me, and I don't want anyone to think so. I've got enough negativity surrounding me as it is.

I lay my head against his chest and mutter an apology only he can hear. He kisses the top of my head as a response. Looking up, our eyes lock, and all is forgiven and forgotten. "I wouldn't mind a tour," I tell Heidi with a smile.

"Perfect," he says with a relieved exhale. "We won't be more than half an hour, and we'll get supper when we're done."

I nod and follow Heidi out of the room, closing the door behind us.

We walk down the hallway, and she gives me the history of the albums adorning the walls. She takes me into a recording room that apparently no one uses any longer, but the equipment is antique, and the last person who used it cut his final album there before he retired and then passed away several years later after a long battle with cancer.

She leads me back to the lobby and shows me each of the awards in the display case, telling me who won each one and why before taking me to what appears to be a break room. "You're not what I expected," Heidi tells me as we sit at a table with plates of fruit and cheese that she said were brought in earlier.

I cover my mouth and swallow my food, asking, "What did you expect?"

Her blue eyes rake me over with a shrug. "The cliché. Maddox isn't known for being picky. Just look at the tabloids. The blond bimbo stripper out for deep pockets and fifteen minutes of fame."

My cheeks flame. Indignant rage rushes through me on his behalf. The *tabloids* don't know a thing about Maddox. They only print gossip and bullshit that he doesn't bother to correct.

As far as her thoughts about me? I fit the stereotype. I'm blond. I was working as a stripper to pay off a mountain of debt. Maddox has seemingly whisked me away and solved all my problems.

But I'm sick of everyone making assumptions based on my appearance and the fact I worked at Bastian's club—oh yes, that became public knowledge yesterday. Or because I fell in love with Maddox Masters. And I'm tired of them portraying him as a reckless bad boy without regard for others.

I wipe my mouth and push my plate away. "I suppose I should be glad to disappoint you," I tell her as I stand and collect my mess.

"Look," she huffs, "I'm sorry if I offended you, but come on. You had to expect it, and you may as well get used to it because I'm not the only one that thinks it. That's *why* it's a stereotype. And Maddox has a reputation."

Maybe it's hormones, I can't say for certain, but my usual logic and understanding take a back seat to antipathy and resentment. "Maybe you're right about that, but perhaps if bitches and assholes let go of these so-called *stereotypes* and see the person, these things wouldn't happen. If people set aside judgment in favor of compassion and empathy, we wouldn't have so many misconceptions. But you are wrong about one thing. I don't have to *get used to* shit because that would mean I'm telling the world it's okay to judge what it knows nothing about. So fuck you and fuck your cliché."

She calls out to me as I storm off. Ignoring her, I head straight for the elevators. I stab the button for the garage floor and wait impatiently for the doors to close. Once they do, I let my tears of fury fall.

It must be the hormones because the last time I cried this much over stupid trivial things like this was... when I was pregnant before. The thought only makes me cry harder.

I register as the elevator begins its twenty-five-floor descent, that I have no idea what I will do once I get to the garage. I'm not even sure if Darren is still waiting or if Maddox has to summon him. Dammit, I probably won't even find the generic SUV in the garage full of identical blacked-out SUVs.

I furiously swipe the back of my hand across my face in an effort to remove the tears. I brought this on myself. Desperate to pay off hospital and college debt on my own—to prove I could do it—I took a job that has a multitude of negative stigmas attached to it. It's not fair. Most of the girls I worked with were good people just trying to earn a living. And some made more money in a night than they would in a month had they taken a "respectable" job.

But I've made my bed. I can't cry, lash out, or throw a fit every time someone says what everyone is thinking. What I can do is prove them all wrong with actions instead of words.

The elevator stops, and I drop my head, not wanting to be recognized or for anyone to see my blubbering. I don't want questions or sympathy because these aren't sad tears. Yes, I'm hurt, but I'm more angry than anything.

The door slides open, and a pair of electric blue peep-toes steps in. "Quinn?"

I squeeze my eyes shut, recognizing Cami's voice. I didn't want anyone to see me like this, especially anyone that would tell Maddox. Which I suppose I should've thought of before I stormed off.

I look up and meet her chocolate eyes with a watery smile. "Oh, honey, what's wrong?"

I shake my head and belt a laugh so fake that even I cringe. "It's nothing," I insist. "Could you *please* not tell Maddox you saw me crying?"

Her lips press together as she taps a finger on her chin. "On two conditions."

"Anything," I say with an unspoken plea that I don't regret it.

"Come home with me. Dane's fucking demon spawn has made my day a living hell, so I'm going home to indulge in ginger tea and push-pops. Then you can tell me all about who has upset you."

"Push-pops?" I laugh

"It's the only craving I have right now," she shrugs.

"I don't have any yet," I laugh again. "But I agree to your terms."

"Come on. We can commiserate the joys of being human incubators to overprotective assholes together.

MADDOX

Light the spark within

"That song, man," Angel shakes his head. "You know how annoying it is that you wrote that in the shrink's office?"

I lean back, exhaling the cigarette smoke from my lungs and crossing an ankle over my knee. I just finished showing them the other song that came to me while Quinn and I were in that office. One that I didn't show her. "Technically, I wrote two songs. But it's been a long time since I've come up with decent songs. Over a year, in fact," I point out.

"It's also the first time in five that you haven't been wasted," Dane tells me from behind his kit with a stern glare. A glare that takes in my relaxed posture and questions if I really am sober. It's irritating, but I suppose I can't blame him. If he'd seen me when we left the psychiatrist's office, he wouldn't be questioning a thing. Granted, I didn't lose it this time, but I was still tense.

"That's not true anyway," Ryder says as he sits next to me and lights a joint. He takes a couple of hits and offers it to me.

"Can't, man," I grumble. "They aren't sure if it would help or hurt me, so they've recommended I stay away from that too."

"Fuck, mate, that sucks. I was ecstatic when they suggested it to me." He shakes his head sadly and passes it to Angel. "Need me to put it out?"

"I think we both know weed has never been a problem for me," I laugh. "Just blow that shit this way, though. Maybe I can get a secondhand high."

He laughs loudly, accepting the joint back from Angel. "But anyway, what you said isn't true. You had loads of good shit from your lost hours."

Lost hours. I never can resist a hard eye roll whenever he calls my virtual psychotic break *lost hours*. I haven't decided if I lost too much or not enough. Part of me wishes I didn't remember any of it. The other part wishes I could remember what happened with Chris. All I have to go on is what he told the others. Never got a chance to ask myself because he didn't come around before I left. But something about his story doesn't ring true for me. Maybe it's Bastian and Ryder's suspicions wearing on me, but I just can't reconcile the story.

He claims he came to help me after he saw me losing it on the security cameras installed in the house a few years ago when the house was vandalized despite ten-foot brick walls and security guards at the gates. According to Chris, he walked in, and I had the gun in my hand. He fought me for the gun, and it went off.

But why can't I remember? Everything else has come back to me. Every last miserable fucking second, but not that.

"Where'd ya go, mate?" Ryder's brows draw down a bit in worry.

"Uh-nowhere," I blink the thoughts away. Ryder's brows pull deeper between his eyes. "Seriously, I'm good," I reassure him.

"Did you show Quinn the song?" Jake asks as he unplugs and stores his bass.

"Not yet," I tell them. "I have a plan that I will need all of your help on."

"Interesting," Dane says.

I stand up and go to the console. I move the mouse around until I get to the song she and I recorded earlier. "First, listen to this. Don't say anything until it finishes."

I hit play and watch them closely. When Quinn comes in on the chorus, Angel's eyes grow wide. Dane and Jake exchange disbelieving looks, then look at me with the same amazement. Ryder looks at me with a knowing grin. I've told him all about her talent and how she can calm me down with a few hummed lines. But the look on his face right now tells me I'm not blinded by love. She's every bit as amazing as I thought she was.

Their jaws drop when her solo voice comes in on her verse, and my chest feels like it's about to burst with pride. She is amazing.

I know I'm biased. Her voice spoke to the depths of my battered soul from the moment it cut through Bastian's kitchen as I sat on the floor in the middle of a panic attack. Pretty sure she could sound like a wounded cat, and it would've had the same effect on me.

But she doesn't sound like a wounded cat. She sounds like smoke and silk and honey and cinnamon. And if I don't know shit else, I know music.

The details aren't clear to me yet, but if I have anything to say about it, the world will hear her one day. One day soon. She doesn't need to be a star, have platinum albums, or have top ten hits. She needs to be heard. As much for herself as anything else.

Today was the first step in my unclear plan.

Ryder spins a finger in the air, ordering me to play it again. I click the track and watch as he leans forward. Elbows resting on his thighs and head dropped low, he tunes out everything around him. Focused on the music and her voice.

When it ends, he looks at me, his grin even wider. "You wrote that while discussing the woes of your fragile mind as well?"

I throw him a finger and laugh. "I did, actually, but on that one, I had help. Quinn already had her verse and the bridge."

"Did she now? So you two writing songs together then?"

"Not exactly. I found it and finished it. Brought her here and kind of tricked her into recording with me."

"That sounds more like you," Jake laughs as he leans against the wall with a sneakered foot crossed over the other.

"I get why you fell for her, mate. No way you were going to resist that voice."

I grab a pen off the console and chunk it at his head. "That's not why, asshole."

He laughs as he deftly dodges the projectile. "But it helped. Come on. You've told me yourself that she makes the noise stop."

"Definitely didn't hurt," Angel grins. "Music has always been the quickest way into your pants. You'd think you were the groupie."

"For fuck's sake. Yes. I'm in love with her talent, but it's because I'm in love with her. Now cut the shit and tell me what *y'all* think since you're not the lovesick puppy that thinks she walks on water." I don't know why I'm getting impatient to hear their thoughts when they are written all over their faces.

"It's been a long goddamn time since I heard a voice like that, mate. Almost as good as you."

"She's better," I smirk and let my bias show.

"Her pitch is perfect," Angel tells me as he turns up his bottle of water. "Got fantastic control too."

"And her range is sick, man. I don't know how you worked up a song so fast to showcase all that, but damn." Jake adds, shaking his head.

I look over to Dane, who's being unusually quiet. Considering his and Liam's initial reaction to her—which I am still not over—his silence is trying my patience. "Anything you want to add?" I snap.

Ryder shakes his head with a snort, knowing I'm already preparing to beat in his face.

"She's great, Mads. Really."

"But?" My jaw ticks, and fists clench as I wait.

"But I'm not sure what you're trying to accomplish here. That girl almost passed out the other day at the mention of singing."

I exhale and rake my hands through my hair. "You sure you don't have anything to add about her using me?" I grunt, even knowing I'm out of line.

"Aww, come on, Mads. I apologized for that. When are you going to let it go?" His blue eyes shine with remorse and apology that shouldn't be there because it's water under the bridge. I'm just being an ass.

I wave a hand and apologize. "I'm working on getting her over her fear," I admit. "When we met, she couldn't even hum if *anyone* was around. I'm making progress."

"Doesn't help if she can only sing in front of you, though," he tells me.

My teeth clench. He's not wrong, but I still don't want to hear it. "I've gotten her to karaoke a few times. Just trust me. I've got this."

"She doesn't strike me as the sort that wants the attention, so I'm not sure what your end game is, mate."

They all turn their attention to me. I chuckle with a shrug while admitting, "I have no fucking clue. But she needs to be heard."

"You know, you keep cranking out shit like this, you're gonna lose your bad boy rep," Angel grins widely.

"Please," I counter with a grin. "My balls are still firmly attached. You deposited yours in Josephine's purse that first day."

He throws his head back with a thundering laugh.

"So, changing the subject. What did the doctors tell you? Are you a total psycho or just a bit eccentric?" Ryder asks, his lips twitching at the corners at his dig.

I laugh for the first time since Adam and Hunter started tossing out diagnoses. "Somewhere between the two. Swear to fuck they tossed enough letters at me to write a book."

"I'll bet you'll win them some sort of medical award," Angel quips.

Jake thumps the back of his head with an eye roll. "So, it's not as bad as you thought?"

I shake my head, but it's not in admission or denial. It's in... I don't know. "It's not what I thought, but I haven't decided if it's better or worse. It seems more... daunting. Treatment is the same, though. Just like they said when they started me on it. Handful of pills every day." I lean against the deck and look at my feet, wondering why the thought of taking something every day bothers me so when I self-medicated for years.

"So it will feel like a regular day for you," Ryder smirks, trying to alleviate my irritation.

"Feel that way for you?" I return the taunt.

"Nah. I only get two pills with no fun side effects."

I flip him a finger and laugh.

"We are all proud of you," Dane says seriously as he stands up and walks around the drum set to sit in the chair across from Ryder. He leans back in the leather chair and props an elbow on the arm. "Both of you. My life wasn't the easiest. Hell, none of ours were, but the shit you two have gone through." He shakes his head and then looks directly at Ryder and me. "I know this hasn't been an easy step for either of you."

A torrent clogs my throat. I know Dane is the oldest in our group. Hell, I'm not even the second oldest. I'm stuck right in the middle of our band of sinners, but it's always felt like my job to take care of them. To make sure they were happy. But Dane has done the same. He has played big brother to all of us in a way. Hearing him say he's proud of me unleashes pride in myself.

I push off the console and rub my hands down my thighs as I roughly clear my throat. "Yeah, enough of this girly sharing shit," I mutter before I get sappy.

"Agreed," Ryder nods, his eyes swimming with affection as well. "I got a girl to knock up."

We put the instruments away, and I put everything I rearranged back into their original place, then we head for the door. When we open it, we're met with blue eyes, dark hair, and a cocky smirk to rival my own. "You ladies done sucking each other's dicks?"

He pushes off the wall and greets us with handshakes. Jake, Angel, and Dane say goodbye after shaking his hand. "I believe I owe you an ass-kicking," he tells me.

"You're welcome to try," I simper. "Don't let the pretty face fool ya."

He flips his hand at my hair. "Been missing you're weekly beauty appointments, I see. Your pretty boy highlights are nearly gone." He guffaws when I slap his hand away with a scowl. "But regarding the ass-kicking, I've been known to get... creative."

"All right," Ryder cuts in, "you two gonna bloody make out now?"

We all laugh, then reenter the room. Ryder and I show him the console and controls. Explain to him how the DAW software and audio interface work, then start for the door again. "You sure you don't need help?" Ryder questions.

"I don't need fancy layering. I just need the equipment and piano. Why waste time ordering the shit when I've family connections?" He waggles his brows at us.

I refuse to acknowledge his family connections comment, which only makes his grin grow wider while Ryder laughs loudly. I flip them both off, and their guffaws grow louder.

When they've finally gotten themselves under control, we say our goodbyes, and Ryder and I leave him to it.

We don't make it more than a couple of steps when Heidi turns the corner.

Without Quinn.

My pulse quickens, and my body grows tense with worry. *Where is she?*

Heidi spots us, cringes, and tries to turn around.

"Not so fast," I call out, barely containing a growl.

She stops with a hanging head, but before she turns to face me, she lifts her head and straightens her shoulders. When she turns, that famous temper flares in her eyes.

I've known Heidi for years. Ryder and I met her through Heaven when our music careers were just getting started. Then we came to the label around the same time, though she came as a backup vocalist and sound tech. She's tried to be more but hasn't succeeded in grasping that golden ring.

Since we first met, Heidi has always been sharp—quick wit and a wicked tongue have been her trademark. But the last couple of years, Ryder and I noticed she's also become bitter and angry. She hasn't even tried to reconnect with Heaven since she reentered our lives. However, it's not been for lack of trying on Heaven's part.

But I'm not worried about whatever is going on with her. I need to find out where Quinn is.

Her chin tips up, and she steps closer to me. "I'm not a babysitter. Your little child bride got offended and left. I tried to stop her, but she didn't listen, and I wasn't about to chase her down. So if you don't mind, I have a job to do."

She left!

My quickening heart starts racing in double time. My chest squeezes tightly with distress, and anger swirls in my gut.

She tries to walk away, but I catch her by the arm. "Your job was to show my wife around *without* upsetting her," I snap, getting angrier and more upset by the second.

Heidi jerks away with narrowed eyes. "Until you sign my paychecks, Maddox, you can fuck off." She spins on her heels and walks away.

Teeth clenched, I shift, ready to follow her when Ryder grabs me. "Unless you're ready to make some fast decisions and announcements, let her go."

Fuck.

He's right. I can't tell her that, that technically I do sign her paychecks. It just won't be official until my father's estate is handled. And I'm still not ready to deal with that.

I have more important things to worry about right now anyway. Namely, ensuring Quinn is okay.

And breathing.

I'm just grateful I've long since perfected the art of appearing to have my shit together. Or everyone here would be subject to my hyperventilation.

I pull my phone from my pocket while looking at Ryder. "I do have to figure shit out soon," I admit. "Talked to Dylan and Wyatt earlier. Some of the higher-ups have basically suspended production for everyone."

"What are you thinking?"

"I'll make a phone call and take care of that tomorrow. Right now, I need to find my wife before I have a stroke." I'm not exaggerating. The way my heart is racing and head is pounding, if I don't find her fast, it's only a matter of time.

"I'm sure she's fine," Ryder tells me. "And it's fucking weird to hear you say that."

Soon as my phone powers on, I see messages from her. My pulse slows—marginally—and I can breathe again. "She ran into Cami and went home with her." The text doesn't say anything about whatever happened with Heidi. And if she doesn't tell me later, she and I will be discussing her keeping this shit from me once again. She may not want me to defend her, but she's shit out of luck because my sole purpose in life has become protecting her and ensuring her happiness.

I tap out a message to her, telling her I'll be there soon. Then send a message to Dane to let me know how she seems once he gets there. Preferably with pictures, so I know she's really okay. Physically anyway.

I tuck my phone back into my pocket, and Ryder and I head for the elevators. "No stranger than hearing Tyler call you dad," I respond to his earlier statement.

We step in and push the garage level. "You know, you'll be called dad soon enough, Mads."

I force myself to appear relaxed, but he knows me too well. Between Quinn's absence and his remarks about me being a dad, I can't hide my anxiety from him. He doesn't acknowledge my irrational need to have Quinn close at all times and focuses on his statement. "You better get on board, mate, and not for Quinn. For that kid. Or this fucking cycle of feeling unwanted and never good enough will continue."

He gets off the elevator on his level, leaving me alone with his words.

MADDOX

Cast your sorrows in the wind

I rub her hair as I lie next to her on the cold slate of the bathroom. Her eyes are closed as her cheek presses against the floor. Sweat coats her forehead, making golden curls cling to her face. She's pale and tired and still the most beautiful thing I've ever seen.

We've been in here for two hours. I've contemplated another visit to the emergency room, but I know she would only argue. Since they learned she worked at Bastian's club, the tabloids have kicked into high gear, and after the first two ER visits, they began with speculation that we're on drugs—can't blame them on my part—and one suggested we were covering up an abusive relationship. All so far from the truth, but it's not something you want to see slapped on magazine covers at the grocery store.

The paparazzi haven't hounded me this much in years. I guess they were bored with the same ole' stories week in and week out about my alleged escapades. I mean, how many times can you show another woman or a drunken bender and still get sales?

I knew when they found out about Quinn, they'd have a field day. Lifelong bachelor secretly marries a girl he's only known for a few months isn't groundbreaking. But fuck if they don't eat that shit up. I hate that I couldn't stop it from getting out. At least on my own terms.

But this baby has been kept hush-hush. I won't let Quinn be subjected to more speculation, so I let the bogus stories go. Though I can see they stress Quinn out, she agrees she'd rather them print lies than draw attention to the baby.

But it's the reason I know she won't go back to the hospital unless it's absolutely necessary. Besides, she hasn't been sick in a while. She just isn't ready to start moving yet. Says the cold on her skin helps the nausea.

"I'm so sorry, baby," I tell her for the hundredth time while I push her soaked hair off her forehead. "So fucking sorry. If I'd... fucking dumbass. It was—"

Her fingers press against my lips. "Hush." Her voice is barely a whisper. I start to apologize again, and those amber fire flare with frustration. "Stop apologizing, Maddox."

"How can I?" I kiss her fingers softly. "You're fucking miserable, and it's my fault."

"First, it's *our* fault. Second, I love that I am miserable. I love every time I have to rush in here. Or when I can't move for hours." The tears in her eyes spill over when she blinks with a smile. "I thought I would never have this. I know it's not what you wanted, but it means everything to me."

Fuck! I wish I could get on board with this baby thing. Wish I didn't feel like no matter what, someone will get hurt, and I'm powerless to stop it.

"Maddox, why do you feel like it's your fault?" Adam asks as I sit across from him.

I toss him an exasperated look like I didn't just *tell* him why it's my fault. "Been that long since you fucked someone?" I snap with annoyance.

"I think I remember the mechanics." He hands me his phone.

I look at the wallpaper of a pretty brunette and an infant. Nodding, I hand it back to him with sincere congratulations.

I don't hate kids. I love kids. But this feeling I get in the pit of my stomach when I think about *my* kid...

"Thank you," he grins proudly. "Lots of years of trying. Lots of negative tests and several miscarriages too. Avery is our little miracle. But back to my question. Why is it your fault? I know you've heard it before, but I'll say it again. Quinn could just as easily have gotten the morning-after pill. She could've terminated the pregnancy. Still could. Seems like to me this is what she wants."

"There's no doubt this is what she wants. But if something happens, it's going to destroy her." I drop my head into my hands and grip my hair as that feeling of helplessness washes over me again. Followed by worthlessness because what good am I if I can't protect her from that pain? If I can't protect him before he's even here?

"Why does that affect your worth?"

I look up at him, not realizing I said any of that out loud. "Because it's my job. I need the people in my life to be happy."

"But why is it *your* job?"

"Because even if I'm not happy, at least they are, and that's what matters," I growl. I stand up, flipping the papers on the table between us away. "We're done here."

But he doesn't move. "Maddox, just because the world sees you as a god doesn't mean you are one. You take care of your friends and family, but their happiness is ultimately in their own hands. Just like *your happiness* is in your hands."

I go to the windows and stare out over the city. "That's hilarious, considering I've never been able to control that either."

"Which we are working on. You're taking the meds. You haven't missed an appointment with me in six weeks. So try this for me. Decide to find the good. In some situations, you won't, but most of the time, you can if you try. Don't let your mind go down that slippery slope. And in those moments where you feel helpless to stop someone's sadness or pain, remember that sometimes being there is what's most important."

As I look out over the bustling city, I think about how many times I've felt absolutely helpless to help my friends over the years. Dane when his grandfather died. Jake when Lyra's mom left him high and dry. And Ryder. When he lost Raina, his twin sister, I had no idea how to help him. Then all over again when Heaven left. I recall the times Cara would cry until she fell asleep after her mom died. And Zoey. Every fucking night for a year, she'd wake up screaming, and all I could do was hold her when she allowed and watch when she wouldn't.

I hated that they were hurting. Hated myself even more that I couldn't stop it.

Then I think about my dad after my mom died. He told me to stop crying. He was trying to comfort me in his own way. I close my eyes and see beyond the view of a little boy that was hurting to the father that didn't know what to do. To the father that felt... helpless.

That was the day I began trying so hard to make everyone happy. To ease everyone's pain. The day I shoved my own feelings aside, so I could be strong for everyone around me.

"*Fuck*," I whisper.

"What just happened, Maddox?"

I turn around and meet his dark eyes that sparkle with awareness. "It's just... Well, I've spent so long taking care of everyone else I never learned *how* to take care of me."

His smile grows until he notices I'm not as excited over this new revelation. "Why don't you look happy? This is a huge moment of self-awareness."

"Quinn's fucking pregnant," I tell him. His brows lift, and his mouth pulls to the side as if to say *congratulations, you figured it out.* My return expression is a scowl. "Assuming nothing goes wrong, how the hell am I supposed to teach that kid if I don't know myself? Between my fucked up DNA and my fucked up head, I'm doomed to *fuck* this kid up."

He begins laughing. Actual chortling that I would call unprofessional if we hadn't agreed to keep this as casual as possible. Especially after we opened the wounds of Murphy O'Dell wide. Some appointments, he even comes to me. Like today, because I wasn't leaving Quinn after she spent the morning in the bathroom, and she still wasn't up to leaving the bed.

"What the hell is so funny?" I bark.

"Maddox, I realize, for you, this is a serious thing, and we *will* work on it. But what you're feeling, every current parent has felt, and every future parent is feeling. It's perfectly normal. Kids don't come with instruction manuals. Even within the same family, each child can be vastly different from the others. The main thing they need is love and understanding."

"All the things my dad forgot. And my other dad forgot. Fuck my life," I mumble as I turn back around to the window.

"You're still carrying a lot of resentment for both of them," he states.

"I've been trying to let it go," I admit, and it's true, but it's been hard when I resent Paul for never being there and my dad for dying.

"Nothing is instant, Maddox." His phone buzzes in his pocket. He pulls it out, and his brows shoot up. "Damn, we've been talking for almost two hours."

"Bill me," I grunt.

"I'll do that," he laughs. "And remind yourself that you are not all-powerful. We do what we can—what's within our ability—if it falls outside that, it doesn't make us responsible. I know you want to protect Quinn. And even though you aren't ready to admit it, I know you want to protect your baby. But those things are beyond your ability. So focus on what's within your ability. Just like you did this morning. You were there with her through it all. That's what counts."

"I'll try," I promise. It's the only promise I can make.

"I'll see you on Monday."

"Wait," I turn around and walk to him. "I want to take Quinn to my house on the lake after her doctor's appointment on Monday. Think you can come to me next week?"

"Maddox, I like you and all, but I have other patients, and you still need three days a week. Not sure going two hours out of the city is wise. Especially since you're still refusing to leave Quinn most of the time. Which we will also discuss. *Soon.*"

"Work with me, Adam. You know how much I hate the fucking city right now." As much as I hate begging for anything, I will if it means we can get the fuck out of New York and get to the lake house. "We still can't eat a simple meal without the fucking vultures. I'm sure my lawyers would thank you for not having another lawsuit cross their desks." We've tried twice. Both times ended with my fist in a reporter's face for calling her a slut and a gold digger.

He runs a hand over his mouth and begins to nod. "Let's try this. You drive to see me twice a week, and we can try virtual appointments a few times. If they go well, then I'll consider cutting you back and doing them all virtually."

My head drops and shoulders sag with reprieve. "I can do twice a week," I agree.

"I can see the stress you've been under, but Maddox, you've got to start giving me more than you have. I thought opening up the O'Dell can of worms would've been the hardest for you, but you dig your heels in any time we approach your dad and Paul. Jewel. Your grandfather. Or get too deep into your impending fatherhood. You've barely scratched the surface on those issues. You're doing better than I could've hoped, but you've got to open up and deal with all of it so you can move forward."

The relief is short-lived, and I sigh. He's right. I'm just not ready yet. But if it will get me out of the city for a while, I'll do it.

QUINN

As we escape disorder

I stand in front of the full-length mirror in the massive closet. (Seriously, my childhood bedroom was smaller than this closet.) A mixture of fear and excitement surges through me as I stare at the tiny baby bump that seems like it appeared overnight.

With my shirt raised, I turn side to side, making sure I'm really seeing what I'm seeing. It's barely noticeable, but it's there.

"Your bags packed?" Maddox calls as he walks in from the bedroom. He freezes in the doorway and stares at the slight pudge I've been staring at for ten minutes.

Quickly, I drop my shirt as if I wasn't just examining myself and bend over to grab my bags from the floor. I don't want him to stress out, so pretending it didn't just happen seems like the better option. He's still struggling so much with all of it. Especially his guilt when I'm wrapped around the toilet.

Thankfully today, the nausea seems to be holding off. I'm hoping I've reached a point where it goes away entirely, but I'm not holding my breath.

"I've got them right here," I answer his question, hoping my voice doesn't give away my nerves.

His fingers wrap around mine, taking the bag from my hand, then he pulls me away. I stand with my back to him, head down, and breathing hard when he turns me to face him. "Show me." His voice is gruff, and his face is tight. When he's like this, I know he's barely keeping it together, but I'm never sure if it's from anger, fear, or both.

My hands tangle in my shirt, holding it down. My head bobs side to side, refusing his demand.

It's times like this I feel like a terrible person. I'm hiding my baby like I'm ashamed of it to protect Maddox. I'm treating this man I know is stronger than anyone like he's fragile. On top of that, I still feel like I've made a choice without considering his feelings. Because when it comes to this, we want different things.

Untangling my hands from my shirt, he places them at my side and lifts the hem.

When he places his hand over the small bump, I bite the inside of my cheek.

"I know Adam told you not to push or force this on me, but *I told you* not to hide. I don't want you hiding anything. Not your feelings, emotional or physical, and not your body. Do not push everything you feel aside to protect me. That very thing is part of what's wrong with me." He tips my head up, and the second our eyes meet, the river flows. He cups the side of my face, brushes a calloused finger over my cheek, and wipes the tears away. "I see you trying your best to hide it. You do everything to pretend you're not pregnant. To make me forget *this*," he lowers his hand to the bump again and sets his forehead to mine, "is happening. You don't talk about it. You change the subject when someone else does. All because you're afraid I'll shut down or fall apart, right?"

"I'm afraid of a lot of things." My voice cracks with the admission.

His lips cover mine for a brief moment. "I know, baby. I hate that I'm the cause of *any* of it."

"I-I'm just afraid you're going to hate me." The words come out breathless and jagged. "And I'm afraid you'll hate the baby."

He lifts me and plants me on the dressing table. A hand on each knee, he spreads my legs apart, steps between them, then cages me with his arms. "Let's get one thing fucking clear right now. I could never hate or resent *either* of you. This is all on me. It's a problem based on my fears and my issues. I'm fucking terrified my genetics will screw him up. Or that he'll grow up feeling like I did. But none of that is your fault or his. I do not want to take this experience from you."

I sniffle and wipe my face with the back of my hand. "That's the thing, Maddox. I want to experience this with you, not in spite of you."

"I know, *cher*. I'm trying. I swear on everything I'm trying."

Those cerulean eyes pierce my heart, brushing my spirit and searing my soul, pleading with me to understand and be patient. Begging *me* not to give up on him. To believe in him.

And I do.

He's proven time and time again how much I mean to him. Proven it with his time and his touch. Proven with words *and* actions.

He has held my hand for hours while I lay sick on the bathroom floor. Made it to every doctor's appointment even though his discomfort was obvious. Held my hand while he drove me to the emergency room at *his* command.

Which causes another fear to burn deep inside me. "I'm also afraid for you to *want* this," I whisper.

"Why would that scare you?" His brows pull down, and those bright blue eyes darken in confusion.

"I'm afraid you'll fall in love with it, and then my body will fail you both."

"Dammit, Canary." He wraps his arms around me, holding me tightly. "I'm afraid of that exact thing, except for you. And there is nothing I can do to protect either of you. I can't lose you, Quinn. And I'm so fucking terrified if something happens that I will."

I drop my head to his chest as one last tear falls. "We're a mess, Maddox."

His chest vibrates with a chuckle, and he kisses the top of my head. "We are. We're a fucking beautiful mess."

I stand at the window overlooking the back patio of Maddox's house in the Catskills, and a peaceful sigh escapes me.

Lush trees and beautiful, artfully arranged flowers grow in abundance over the perfectly landscaped area that only enhances the view of the mountains and the lake. The entire property is gorgeous, with a view for every desire. Rolling pastures with stunning horses galloping on one side, mountains, forests, and the lake on the other.

Even driving up the mile-long driveway was surreal as deer walked along as if they belonged here. I suppose they did. The house was beautiful and fit perfectly into the picturesque surroundings with its natural stone and glass exterior. The landscaping was impeccable, with ornamental trees leading to the covered entry.

The house is a bit smaller than the penthouse but still tops out at nearly eight thousand square feet. But somehow, despite its enormous size, it is… Perfect. This place feels like Maddox far more than the extravagant penthouse that sometimes seemed more like a modern art display than a home. He even openly admitted he had never been inside half the rooms there. *This* suits him with its clean, modern lines, neutral colors, and tons of natural light, balanced with natural stones and woods and soft furnishings throughout. Luxury and comfort. Stylishly beautiful yet warm and inviting.

This place feels like... Home.

Flutters have me pressing a palm to my stomach. They've been consistent enough for the last two weeks that I know it's the baby.

I see Maddox's reflection in the glass and drop my hand out of habit just as he steps behind me. He pushes my hair off my shoulder, kissing a slow trail from my ear to my collarbone that pebbles my flesh as his hands run down my arms. He entwines our fingers, lifting our joined hands, and placing them over my stomach.

"What did I tell you?" he growls seductively in my ear.

"Habit," I whisper, leaning back against him.

"One that you should never have felt the need to start." He buries his head in my hair, making a choked sound in the back of his throat. "I'm so fucking sorry, Canary. Sorry my goddamn bullshit has stopped you from being excited about him."

I turn around and wrap my arms around his neck. Easing up on my tiptoes, I press my lips to his. Words won't assuage his guilt, so I don't offer any. Instead, choosing to show my love.

"You keep saying *him*," I say when I pull back. Now that I think about it, I don't think he's ever said it or used any other gender-neutral pronouns. It's always been *him*. "Why?"

He lifts a shoulder, and his cheeks turn red. I don't think I've ever seen him blush. It's so endearing. "Just a feeling," he answers with a casual tone.

"It could be a girl, you know," I run my fingers under the collar of his t-shirt. The feeling of that small strip of skin makes my belly flutter. Ignoring the urge to rub my thighs together and biting back the hormone-induced sexual overdrive, I keep talking. "*She* could have dark hair, blue eyes, and..." I trail off when his hand moves under the hem of my shirt, softly stroking my ribcage.

It never matters how hard I try to ignore the sparks between us. He reads me like a book. Every line—every word memorized—engrained in his marrow.

Breathing deeply, I try very hard to focus. "Or she could look like me with wild, uncontrollable hair, brown eyes, and a slightly upturned nose."

His eyes darken. Lust and irritation fight for dominance as he growls deeply. "Fuck that. No girls." He hoists me up, my legs instinctively closing around his waist as he presses me against the glass. "We're trying to fix my crazy," he strips my dress over my head and tosses it behind him. "Girls will be fucking counterproductive."

He drops his head, circling a peaked nipple with his tongue as he shoves a hand between us. Pushing my thong to the side, he runs a finger through my drenched folds. My head falls against the glass with a thud. "Don't think we get a say," I pant.

He slips a finger inside and growls. "I get all the say," he grunts. "Always so fucking wet and ready for me. Feels so good, doesn't it."

He licks a path to my other needy breast with more growling, like a wild animal marking his territory. He nips and sucks the tight bud as his fingers move inside me, curling deliciously against my front wall.

His tongue skims my skin, his mouth devouring every inch he can reach. Teeth nip at my throbbing pulse as he drives me closer to the edge of insanity. "You love my fingers in your pussy, don't ya, *cher*," he rumbles against my neck, that accent suddenly much thicker than it was moments ago. "Love it when I'm strokin' your warm, wet cunt until it's drippin' down my hand."

My eyes close, and my chest heaves as I fight to breathe, though I'm not entirely sure I want to. His mouth returns to my oversensitive nipple, his tongue flicking for a brief second before his teeth latch on, making me cry out in beautiful agony. "Answer me, *cher*."

"I love it." My voice cracks when his thumb brushes my clit.

"Eyes on me, Canary. Unless you want me to stop."

My lids quickly fly open, meeting his dark ones, the blue a barely noticeable ring. "No! Please don't stop."

He adds more pressure to my clit, and his teeth dig harder onto my nipple. My eyes water as I struggle to keep them open and on him. He smirks, knowing damn well he's torturing me in the best way.

He brings his mouth to my ear. "Tell me somethin' you love," he breathes as he takes the lobe between his teeth.

"You."

The pressure on my clit leaves and the delicious friction of his fingers stroking my g-spot stops. "You know what I want, darlin'."

Desperation claws my very soul. "I l-love when you t-tie me down, spank me, then fuck me from behind. I l-love your c-cock pounding into my pussy until it hurts, your mouth on my tits until they're raw and aching, and your fingers in my ass, stretching me for you. I love feeling you everywhere."

"There's my kinky freak. Good girl," he hums as his fingers start working me in earnest, "Now come for me."

That's all it takes for my body to erupt in flames. Burned to ash.

But I'm rising from the ashes within seconds when his cock plunges in without warning. He thrust into me with abandon, his magical dick hitting that delicious spot all over again. I'm so sensitive that every thrust has tears springing to my eyes. In no time, I'm screaming his name all over again as a tidal wave of intense pleasure slams into me. I clench around him, and it intensifies the sensation. My entire body convulses in spasms of euphoria and insurmountable elation.

"Goddamn," he growls as his thrusts lose their rhythm. He swells and pulses inside of me as he continues to slam against that inner bundle of nerves, and another wave of rapture envelops every inch of my consciousness. "Holy... Fuck." His grip on my hips tightens with one final surge of his hips as he falls over the edge with me.

Finally, he stills, leaning his head against my chest with heaving breaths. "God fucking dammit, what was that? I thought your cunt was going to take my dick with it."

I try to laugh, but it comes out as breathless gasps. The action makes me clench around his length, still buried inside of me, and his cock twitches in response. We both groan loudly at the sensation. When he slips out of me and sets me to my feet, the loss of him is almost painful.

My limbs are like jelly, and I nearly collapse. He wraps an arm around me, keeping me steady. I drop my head to his chest with an exhausted sigh. "I need a nap now."

A deep rumble vibrates as he kisses the top of my head. "You go nap. I'll start supper."

"But it's my turn," I say with a loud yawn.

He laughs again. "I'm good doing a double shift. You go rest."

I nod and turn for the stairs. Before I've taken two steps, he grabs my wrist, pulling me back to him. Hands tangled in my hair, he forces my head back, and drops his lips to mine. I am dazed, once again, when he draws back. "I fucking love you, Canary."

He turns me back around with a swat on my ass.

After all that, I'll never understand how I made it to bed.

MADDOX

Hope is not gone

"Tyler!" Ryder yells for the fifth time. Tiny veins in his forehead throb. His patience was gone half an hour ago, but he hasn't lost his temper. Yet.

I chuckle as I turn the chicken on the grill.

Ryder finally has enough of the precocious kid and his inability to listen to his dad. He walks around the pool, picks Tyler up, and brings him back to the terrace where we are perched. He drops him into a chair with a huff. "If you can't bloody listen, then you can fucking sit down."

Tyler smirks at Ryder and holds out a hand. Ryder rolls his eyes with a grumble as he digs into his pocket and pulls out a couple of small bills. He drops the crash in Tyler's hand with another huff.

"What's that?" I ask as I sit in a vacant chair.

"Dad said fucking," Tyler grins, then drops his head and hands Ryder the money back with a pout. "Can I go inside?" he asks in a near whine.

"God, yes. Go inside. Find a video game and rot your brain. Just stop running everywhere," Ryder tells him, then quickly adds, "No jumping, diving, or anything aerial either."

Tyler leaps from the chair and takes off in a sprint. "Walk, Tyler," Ryder yells, dragging a hand down his face with a groan. "Damn, it's like he only knows one speed."

"Sounds familiar." I raise a brow while trying to hide my grin behind my water bottle. "Never thought I'd see the day you'd bribe a nine-year-old because you're scared of Cupcake."

"Ah, you know me better than that. I just try to keep her as trouble-free as possible. Less stress means longer remission." He drinks his own water, making a face. "God, I really miss whiskey. Not the effects. Just the taste."

I nod in agreement, but my attention is on the angel on the upper terrace, setting up for everyone's arrival.

"She's really popped this past month," Ryder points out. "You still struggling to deal with it?"

"Among other things." I nod with my eyes trained on her.

She's fucking glowing in the bright purple dress that barely reaches her thighs with her long curls pulled up into a massive, messy knot on top of her head. She's cute as fuck.

"Mads, I know you hate the meds and therapy, but you see the difference, right? Feel it, I mean?"

I've confided in Ryder about how much I really hate being told I *have* to take the medication. That stubborn, defiant part of me sees it as being told what to do. Like when everyone told me to stop drinking and snorting coke.

Therapy has proven to be easier than I thought it would be. Once I got past my suspicions anyway. But it's just as annoying since Adam still hasn't cut me back from three sessions a week like he promised. I guess the upside is that he allows most of my appointments to be virtual unless I'm in the city already.

"I see it," I admit begrudgingly. It has helped a lot. So much so that I've convinced myself a couple of times that I'm cured and don't need any of it. For about three days, I stopped taking the meds. When I mentioned it to Quinn, she lost it.

I don't think I'd ever seen her so angry and upset. She screamed and yelled that it wouldn't just hurt me if we went backward in my progress. That she needed me. All of me. And she didn't get that before.

She wasn't wrong. As much as I loved her, I was so consumed with my demons I was never going to be everything she needed. But I was shocked she lost her temper with me. She'd never done that before.

Then she started crying. She apologized for yelling and everything she said.

I couldn't help it. I burst into a fit of laughter at the switch that flipped so quickly. It was the wrong reaction. The switch quickly flipped again, returning to furious.

But I couldn't stop laughing. So tiny and cute waving her hands around like a feral cat with that wild mane flying manically around her face.

I smile at the memory from two days ago. Especially at how it ended with my dick inside her.

Ryder shakes his head with a laugh as I replay the story for him.

He turns his chair around to face me and rests his elbows on his knees. "Madsy, you've got to take the meds. You feel better because it's working. I hate it too, but we needed to make a lot of damn changes for them."

"Logically, I know that, Ry. I know every time the thought crosses my mind. But for a few days, there was this crazy, excited invincible feeling that I didn't need it." I shake my head and rub the back of my neck. I glance up and see his furrowed brows.

"You tell the doctor?"

"Planned on it tomorrow."

His eyes narrow, looking for the lie. Looking for what I might be hiding. He won't find either. "You slip up, Mads? Go get high? Don't bother denying that you want to. I *know*, mate. Feel it just like you."

"Not denying it. I wanted to. Fuck, I want to now. Every. Day."

He nods. "Me too."

"How's therapy going?" I ask. Because I'm not the only one that's had some revelations this year. The last nine months have been the most challenging of our lives.

"Been a lot of discussing Margret. She's always my favorite subject," he growls out his mother's name. "How about you?"

"Making progress."

"Yeah, mate, I call bullshit." He leans back in his chair, daring me to argue.

I jerk back, feeling like he just slapped me. I made progress by agreeing to go in the first place. And I've fucking kept at it. It pisses me off that he insinuates otherwise. "Fuck you," I spit out and stand from my chair to walk away before I punch him in *his* face.

"It's me, Maddox. Walking away only works for a little while."

I turn around, irritation and fury warring for space against rational logic. I lean over him, teeth bared, and grip the arms of his chair. But he doesn't take the bait. Doesn't waver in his firm and weirdly calm demeanor. "Wanna fight me?" he asks with a lifted brow.

A year ago, he would've pushed back and taken the first swing. And it would've ended messily.

I step back and run a hand through my hair. I inhale deeply, focusing on my breathing and slowing my heart, then exhale. "I want the drugs you're on."

"It's not the drugs, mate," he laughs. "Well, not *just* the drugs. I talk out my shit. I don't let it eat at me as I did before."

"You going soft on me, Ry?" The tease falls easily, even if I'm still struggling with my irritation. He's been by my side for seventeen years. We've fought and fucked and everything between the two. Our bond is solid. The love we have isn't written in the stars like what we feel for our girls, but nothing will ever break our friendship. No matter how big of a jackass we act.

"Maddox, you are not dealing with anything. I don't know what you talk to your shrink about, but you're still avoiding."

"We talk about my feelings, this crazy shit in my head. Talked about O'Dell some too."

"But not your dad, Paul, Bastian, or the baby."

"We've talked about the baby. I'm working on it," I defend.

"You still haven't settled your dad's estate. The label is still in limbo because of that. And because Bastian thinks if he does nothing, he'll force your hand. And then there's that," He nods toward Quinn, who's wiping sweat from her face. Talking about it a couple of times isn't dealing with it. You're afraid, Mads."

Immediately I grab my phone and text her

Me: Sit down, now. You're doing too much.

Canary: I'm fine. Besides, I'm almost done.

Me: Sit. Down.

I look up from my phone, meeting her eyes across the back patio with a quirked brow, and tilt my head, daring her to argue. She sticks her tongue out and sits.

"You going to acknowledge what I said? Or keep making googly eyes at her?" He asks with a grin.

"She's doing too much," I argue.

"So you do care."

"Of course, I fucking care, asshole. I love her."

He lights up a joint, takes a few hits, and waves the smoke away. "You know what I mean, *asshole*."

I know what he means. I don't *just care* about this baby. But he's right. I am afraid. Afraid of something happening. Of what it will mean for Quinn. Of what it will do to me if I really acknowledge it.

It's the same with my dad. I have barely talked to Callie since I left the hospital because she always wants to know when I'm coming back. His death sent me over the edge. I fell off the cliff at the speed of light, and the crash was hard.

When I woke up, I shoved it away—as far as possible—refusing to think or deal with it. What if I open that box and spiral again?

And then there's Chris. If this feeling in the pit of my stomach is true, I have no idea how I will handle that.

"It's okay to be afraid, Mads." He reads me well. "I'm fucking terrified every time I think about Heaven and the MS. But you've got to face it head-on. We've run too damn long from our problems, and it's gotten us nowhere. You're at a stalemate. Time to make a move. Your dad's stuff won't wait forever." He nods toward Quinn again. "And that baby is a reality."

"Not yet, it's not," I mutter, looking across the way to her.

"Why do you say that?" His brows snap downward as he blows out smoke.

"You know Quinn has health issues."

He nods. "When the hell are you going to get it through that thick skull? It's when we bury the shit—the good and the bad, that we hurt ourselves the most. Sorry to tell you, mate. The world doesn't run on King Maddox time anymore. The clock's run out. Time to handle your shit."

I look at Quinn, who's once again hopping around. I shake my head at her stubbornness, then bite back a laugh because I have no room to talk about obstinacy.

Ryder's right. I hate that he's right, but there it is.

Every time I've denied myself the excitement of the heartbeat or seeing that tiny, wiggling thing on the ultrasound, I've felt gutted. When I first saw that small bump, my heart raced with excitement that I quickly shut down, and it hurt like a motherfucker.

And every single damn time she's denied *her* excitement because of me, the pain multiplied times ten.

I stand up and tap his shoulder. "Thanks for always being there, Ry."

"You've always been there for me, Mads. You can't get rid of me. I'm your own special brand of herpes."

I burst out laughing at the ridiculous analogy. "Yeah, I'm holding you to that, you sick fuck."

"Takes one to know one, mate."

I start for the main terrace with intentions of showing her—and myself—exactly how I feel about our son, when time slows down. My heart stops beating, and it feels like my legs are stuck in sludge, even though I'm running full force.

She doesn't see the kids coming, and Tyler runs at full speed as he chases Lyra around the corner.

"Quinn, watch out," I yell.

She turns around just in time to sidestep the oncoming collision, but her foot gets tangled in the outdoor rug. She falls, catching herself with her hands, just as I jump over the chairs and skid the rest of the way to her.

My hands fly straight to her stomach. "Are you okay? Is he okay?" She looks at me with pained eyes, and my heart sinks. "Fuck, fuck, fuck. Okay, come on. I'll take you to the hospital."

She smiles weakly, then winces. "He's okay, but I think I sprained my wrist."

My shoulders sag, and I fall to my ass next to her. "I think you just took ten years off my life." I take her hand in my and examine her wrist. She winces when I try to move her fingers. "You said him," I whisper, examining the discoloration already forming.

"You were worried." She hisses when I touch the heel of her palm.

"I'm always worried. About both of you. And you are definitely going to the hospital. You've broken something." She groans and rolls her eyes.

"She okay?" Ryder asks, looking pissed and worried as he squats next to us.

Jake and Cara come flying out the back door with Heaven close behind. Jake grabs a crying Lyra while Tyler hangs his head.

"What happened?" Heaven asks.

"The kids running around the house," Ryder huffs because it's what he has been telling Tyler to stop all day.

"It's okay." Quinn waves them off with her good hand. "I'm fine. Mostly."

"It's not okay when he has been told *repeatedly* to stop." Heaven folds her arms over her chest and glares at her son.

I hear Ryder sigh. His impatience warring with his understanding. He knows where Tyler's restlessness comes from.

Quinn reaches over, grabbing him by the arm. "He's just a little boy," she whispers. "He'll learn."

Ryder blows out a breath and smiles at her with a nod, his anger dissipating. He stands, offering me a hand. After helping me stand, he walks to Tyler, whispers something in his ears, then kisses his head. Tyler throws his arms around Ryder with a sniffle.

I scoop Quinn off the ground and walk inside. "You all know this is your house too, so have fun. I'm taking her to the hospital for X-rays."

"Maddox, put me down." Quinn squirms in my arms, trying to get free. "My wrist is hurt. Not my legs."

I ignore her and grip her struggling body tighter. "Heaven, mind calling Delilah and letting her know we're on our way?"

"Absolutely," she replies, already dialing the number.

"Thanks." I nod and walk to the door with my pouting wife.

"Hey, Mads," Ryder calls out before we reach the door. "Happy 30th, mate."

MADDOX

Touch the light

"Breathe, Canary," I tell her as I kiss the top of her head. "He's fine. He hasn't stopped kicking since he started."

It's the truth, and right on time, his foot presses against her stomach. I'm glad I finally stopped fighting my love for my son and denying that I want him. I wanted him from the moment she told me she was pregnant. But unrelenting fear held me back from acknowledging it.

If I hadn't had that conversation with Ryder, his first kicks, which coincidently happened that same day, would've been met with anguish. Instead, it was a birthday I'll never forget.

That was six weeks ago. Now here were are at her twenty-eight-week appointment. The second appointment that I haven't walked in with dread. Wish I could say the same for Quinn.

"I know I'm being ridiculous." She twists the rings on her finger nervously. Since she hit the second trimester, every appointment has been like this, even though she tried to hide it. Her anxiety was too noticeable to hide, even if I didn't know all her little tells. At the twenty-four-week appointment, however, she was in near hysterics. It was so bad that the doctor insisted on giving her something to calm her down because it made her blood pressure go up.

Who could blame her since it was at that point that she lost her daughter. She went through that alone because her ex couldn't be bothered to pick up the phone—probably off somewhere fucking his girlfriend. No woman deserves to go through that alone, especially an eighteen-year-old girl. It's why, even in the beginning, when I was trying to pretend this wasn't happening, I was always right by her side. No matter how I felt or how much she insisted I didn't have to be, I was right there.

But since I finally pulled my head out of my ass, she stopped pretending these visits don't terrify her. That each time that sonogram machine or doppler is pulled out, she's holding her breath on the verge of a breakdown each second it takes to find him or hear him. She's stopped hiding her excitement and shows me all her fears.

But I still haven't gotten her to buy any baby items yet. When I asked about it, she broke down into sobs, telling me she was afraid if she started buying things, something would happen.

So I bought a few things myself. She doesn't know and won't find out until I have the nursery ready. But we still have time.

"You're not ridiculous, baby." I won't invalidate her fear when I'm scared shitless too. Afraid I'll fuck this kid up beyond measure. But absolutely terrified I won't get the chance.

She takes a deep breath and closes her eyes. Her fingers curl tightly around mine. "Okay. Distract me."

I catch a stray curl falling from the mountain piled on top of her head. I tuck it behind her ear, then draw my finger down the curve of her neck before sliding it under the strap of her dress. Goosebumps prickle her skin as I whisper in her ear, "What kind of distraction?"

She hums breathlessly when I pull my hand from her and slide it between her knees, stroking the flesh of her inner thigh. "You like my kind of distraction, don't you?" I say as I trace my tongue around the shell of her ear.

"Yes," she hisses, her legs falling open. Then she slams them shut, and her eyes fly open, shooting daggers at me. "No. None of that." She narrows her eyes and pulls her skirt back down. "Not here."

"Why not?" I laugh. "You enjoyed the other time."

She turns the color of cherries, and more daggers shoot from her eyes—figuratively, of course. "Right, up to Dr. Anders getting a look at my 'O' face."

"It was a thorough examination," I waggled my eyebrows. "Besides, darlin', she delivers babies. Pretty sure she appreciates us keeping her in business."

I drop my mouth to her neck, swirling my tongue around that throbbing artery that gives away her desire. She shakes her head and pushes me away. "Stop that. Distract me some *other* way."

"Fine," I laugh. "What did you have in mind?"

"Tell me why you think it's a boy."

I run my fingers through my hair with a nervous chuckle. That wasn't what I was expecting. I haven't told anyone because when everyone knows you hear and see things that aren't there, you don't give them more crazy.

"Why do you look so nervous?" She grabs my hand and brings it to her lips. "You can tell me anything."

I clear my throat and meet her sexy, whiskey eyes. "My-uh-my mom told me."

Her head tilts, and her brows fall in confusion. At least she didn't go straight to worried and panicked. "What do you mean?"

I blow out a breath. "Remember those dreams I told you I had?" I told her about the dreams when Heaven came by one afternoon for them to have lunch. I nearly had a fucking panic attack when she walked down the stairs with her purse on her arm, ready to go. Apparently, I hadn't been as low-key with my borderline obsession to have her with me at all times as I thought I had been because when I suggested going with them, Quinn promptly pulled me into a separate room and called me on it.

After several minutes of denial that nearly started an argument, the truth finally erupted from me like a shaken bottle of champagne. She cried when I told her about the dreams and my fear that they were somehow prophetic, then managed to get me to agree to talk to Adam about them. Then she told Heaven she couldn't go, choosing to stay with me until I could get a handle on this particular fear.

"I remember, but you never told me about a dream with your mom."

"It wasn't one of the ones that scared the shit out of me," I shrug. I step between her legs and run my hands down her arms. I clasp the cross pendant she always wears between my fingers. "She believed, you know? In God and Heaven and all that stuff." I release the charm with a sigh. "I was angry with her. Yelled at her for leaving me. Told her I was so fucking tired of letting everyone down, but she told me I had to hold on—to fight. She said I had to fight for my girl and my little boy. Said you both needed me."

I wipe the stream of tears off her cheeks and kiss her forehead.

"She was right. We do need you," she whispers, wrapping her arms around me.

"Now your turn," I say, ready to get the attention off me. "Tell me about the pendant."

Her fingers go to the small trinket. "After my little girl..." she pauses and takes a breath to steady her emotions. "My mom bought a matching set when I was pregnant. One for me and one for her. I buried hers with her, and

I keep this one. It makes me feel like she's with me."

Fuck. Again, not what I was expecting. I wrap my arms around her, holding her as close as I physically can, wishing I could bury her in my skin. "She's with you, baby," I murmur in her hair.

I take her face in my hand and tilt her head back. I stare into those whiskey eyes and see my life—everything that matters and everything I want to be reflected there. "And you have one thing very wrong. You don't need me or my shit. You're so damn strong it blows my mind. But I'm so fucking thankful you want me because I sure as hell need you." I press my forehead to her and place a hand on her belly. "I need both of you."

Right on cue, he kicks.

Quinn brushes her tears away when the door clicks and swings open. "How is the mommy-to-be today?"

"Better now," Quinn smiles at me.

After doing the usual appointment stuff, the doctor stands and shakes our hands. "I'll see you in two weeks." She smiles widely at Quinn. "Congratulations. You are officially in your third trimester."

Quinn laughs, full of relief.

"Wait, doc," I say when she starts to leave the room. "Can she still fly?"

Quinn's eyes snap to mine, full of questions. "Why would I need to fly?"

Dr. Anders looks between us with a grin. "For a little while longer," she answers. "But whatever you have planned, Mr. Masters, don't wait much longer."

I nod. "Just needed your approval to finalize."

I pull out my phone and quickly shoot off a text.

Me: Good to go.

A thumbs-up reply is nearly instant.

I tuck the phone back into my pocket and lead Quinn out of the office. Soon as the elevator closes, she spins around. I grab her by the shoulders when she starts to topple over. "Easy, baby," I laugh.

"Why do I need to fly?"

"Because it's faster than driving. " I turn her back around when the elevator doors open again.

"Seriously, Maddox, where are we going?" she asks as she slides into the backseat when we reach the car. I pull the seatbelt over her, click it into place, and shut the door without answering her question.

She looks ready to burst when I climb in on the other side. She's so excited, and it's absolutely adorable. "Tell me," she pleads.

"We're going to the beach for a few days. Just you and me. It will be a little cold, but I want to catch the last surf of the season. I'll catch a few waves, and you'll catch a few rays—as long as you wear sunscreen. I'll take you out on the boat, and we will fuck like rabbits the whole time. Oh, we'll meet up with some friends I've neglected for the last few months, too."

The call pulls slowly out of the garage to avoid injuring the swarms of media and reporters. Since news broke that she's pregnant, the shit storm has started anew. Honestly, it's worse than before, but we've been trying to take it in stride. I admit I'm jealous that the other guys don't have this problem.

Actually, Ryder does. Things have gotten pretty hairy for him since his mother's trial started a couple of weeks ago. He had to go back to London to testify, and since his mother's legal counsel thought it would be a great idea to smear his testimony by bringing up Heaven and Ryder's relationship, they're no longer a secret from the media. It was a stupid move to try to discredit Ryder when his testimony wouldn't be a deciding factor. But for his mom, it was about hurting him and Heaven.

If she hadn't been arrested there, I'd already promised her if she returned to the States, she wouldn't leave again. I had more than enough evidence to make sure they never let her out of jail. She scoffed at first. Claimed I had nothing against her. Maybe she was right.

"But I know people that can make it look damn convincing," I whispered in her ear that night. "I'm a Masters remember? Sky's the limit to what money can buy, and I hear you're running low in that department."

Since they returned from England, Heaven, Ryder, and the kids have moved into the house they had built on the lake ahead of schedule because the press were camping out around Heaven's house and diner.

"When do we leave?" Quinn asks and bounces with excitement. If I'd known a little trip to South Carolina was all it took to make her this happy, I would've done it by now.

"Day after tomorrow."

Several minutes later, we pull into a private garage where the rest of my family stands waiting. "What's going on?" Quinn asks.

"This, pretty girl, is an exclusive spa where you and the other girls will spend a few hours getting some well-deserved and overdue pampering.

Think of it as a reward for putting up with our sorry asses."

And it's the damn truth. The girls work tirelessly, dealing with our long hours recording. Josephine, Cami, and Cara have dealt with weeks and months on the road, both with us and away from us. When we aren't recording or touring, we're writing, doing interviews, and otherwise handling business. It's nonstop.

They take it all in stride, continuing on with their own careers and dreams—which Quinn will get back to once the baby is here if that's what she still wants. Now they're carrying our babies and raising our kids while navigating the constant chaos.

Not to mention a few of us—ahem, Ryder and me—have more issues than the Pentagon.

I look over my family and marvel at how much it has changed the last few years. Grown. We are all so different, yet still the same.

And I almost missed it because I couldn't see beyond the darkness. But the funny thing about the darkness—without it, you'd never notice the light.

"You girls do whatever girly shit it is you do," Dane tells them. "Get waxed, massaged, or whatever because we're taking you all out tonight."

"What's the occasion?" Josephine asks.

"That you think there has to be an occasion shows how much I've failed," Angel jokes, kissing the side of her head.

She laughs and wraps her arms around him. "I'll let you make it up to me later."

"So, are you guys going to tell us why tonight?" Cami asks as she rubs her belly.

I hide my smile behind my hand. She and Quinn are due days apart, but Cami looks like she could pop any day. And her mood swings have brought Dane from his house to mine on more than one occasion since they moved into their house on the lake too.

"We're going to put the final song on the new album while you guys are here," Ryder tells them. "The three songs drop tomorrow, and we are debuting them at a friend's club tonight."

Quinn looks at me with wide, excited eyes and a wider smile. "You're going to sing?"

Here it goes. She's going to freak out, but she can do this. "No, baby, *we* are going to sing." Her mouth falls open, and her face pales. I quickly put her face between my hands. "You can do it."

It's taken time, but we've gotten her to record with us. All of us. And she's been just what we needed on a couple of songs. What she doesn't know is that the duet we wrote is going on the album and is one of the songs we're releasing tomorrow.

And playing tonight.

"We'll all be up there with you," Jake assures her.

"And we'll be in the audience cheering you on," Heaven says as she takes Quinn's hand with a grin. Those two have become thick as thieves, and I couldn't be happier.

Quinn releases a shaky breath, tips her chin up, and nods. "Then let's go get me relaxed."

The lights drop, and Ryder starts strumming the first chords. An intricate intro to the song he wrote and our first debut of the night. I come in playing the exact chords two keys higher, and Dane begins a presto tempo on the drums. Angel and Jake come in on rhythm and bass as Ryder's deep, gritty voice breaks through. The song is fast and loud and all about letting anger control you.

When it ends, the crowd erupts. It takes a good few seconds for the room to settle, and I step up to the mic. With a deep breath, I look at the crowd of people. This is the first performance we've given since last year. First since mine and Ryder's lives took drastic turns that became public knowledge.

I was nervous about tonight. For most of my life, being in the tabloids has been a common thing. But the stories haven't changed in ten years. Until now. Now they've gotten a glimpse into the real me. And it's unnerving. "Damn, you guys are awesome," I say, and the cheers start again. "In case any of you were wondering who in the fuck these assholes that decided to take over the stage are, we're Sons of Sin, and what you just heard is one of three new releases we will be dropping tomorrow." More cheers and shouts of excitement make me grin widely.

God, I fucking love this shit.

"This next song is really different from anything we've ever done. Different tone and feel, but also because it's a duet with the sexy woman trying her best to hide behind me." I turn around and pull Quinn into me. She ducks her head into my shoulder with a smile. I can feel her shaking, and I'm a little worried she won't be able to do it. But when she finally looks up at me, I see determination in those amber eyes. I smile at her, kissing her temples, earning myself a mocking *aww* from my bandmates. "What can I say?" I tell the audience, who also *awws*, "I'm a man in love. Everyone, please give a warm welcome to Quinn, and be gentle with her. She's never sung live before. Oh, and by the way, none of this has been rehearsed. You guys get Sons of Sin completely raw and natural."

I begin strumming the first chords on rhythm and Ryder on lead. "You've got this," I mouth to her. She blows out a breath and nods.

We sing the song, and she is phenomenal. And I'm not the only one who thinks so if the boisterous cheers are anything to go by. Her cheeks are red and flushed with embarrassment and bashfulness. She quickly tries to run off stage since we told her she only had one song, but I grip her by the wrist, keeping her in place.

She looks at me with wide eyes full of questions. I just smile.

"My life has been on public display for as long as I can remember," I tell the audience, but I'm looking at her. "But only a handful of people got to know the real me. The jury is out on whether that's a blessing or a curse." Laughter erupts from the crowd while something soft hits me in the back of my head. I reach down, grab the towel, and then turn around to see Dane grinning. I shake my head and return to my very impromptu speech. I don't know why I'm saying all this, but now that I've started, I have to finish. "Truthfully, I hid a lot from those close to me too. On the outside, I played the part of Maddox Masters that you all know. On the inside, I felt lost. Swallowed and consumed by things I didn't want anyone to see because I was afraid of the labels, of people thinking less of me... Same old tired story I'm sure you've all heard a million times. I was afraid to deal with my demons. Then someone came into my life, and it took nearly dying for me to realize I had to keep fighting. That I have to hold on." I kiss her on the lips and whisper in her ear. "This is for you, baby." Then I tell the audience, "This one is called *I'm Holding On*."

I set my guitar down, turn to her, and sing.

All the lies, the alibies, all the secrets they disguised

They broke my heart, left battle scars, they tore my soul apart.

They didn't know I'd fall so far

But in your eyes, I see my reflection

The man I want to be

In your song, there's a promise

Just hold on, and I'll be free

From all the guilt, all the shame, all the pain that's haunting me

So, baby, I'm holding on

All the pain, the disdain, like poison in my veins

Torments my mind, these ties that bind, all the chains they confine

I didn't know I'd become so blind

But in your eyes, I see my reflection

The man I want to be

In your song, there's a promise

Just hold on, and I'll be free

From all the guilt, all the shame, all the pain that's haunting me

So, baby, I'm holding on

You see me through these broken memories

In my darkest depths, I hear your melody

Baby, I'm holding on

Cause in your eyes is where I want to be

In your song, you set me free

I'm holding on

Baby, I'm holding on.

Before the guys finish the outro, she's launched herself into my arms. Tears stream down her beautiful face as I hold her close. "I love you so much," she sobs.

"I love you more, baby," I reply. Then mold my lips to her. The crowd fades away because she's all I see.

QUINN

Through the suffering

After the show, we didn't waste time leaving the club. How could I when I was a sobbing mess? That song was... *Everything*. His story and promise emblazoned onto my heart with his lyrics and music.

But once we were back in the limo, my sobs were gone, and all I could think was how badly I wanted him. We came in each other's mouths before we reached the penthouse. Our clothes were gone before the private elevator doors opened. He tormented me for hours on nearly every surface before our final round in the bed, where I promptly passed out both wonderfully relaxed and deliciously sore, sated and utterly exhausted, next to him.

I reach for him in the still of the night and sit up when I realize that he is not here, but his side is cold. He's been up for a while.

A shiver wracks every inch of my body. Dread settles low in my belly. The baby rolls around like he feels it too.

I grab his t-shirt and a pair of shorts and search for him.

After searching the bathroom and the kitchen, instinct tells me to check his music room. When I reach the doorway, my heart stops. He's sitting at the piano, a glass of whiskey between his hands and the bottle on the lid as he stares out the window into the city's night sky.

"I haven't had any," he tells me without looking up. He digs in his pockets, pulls out a small plastic bag, and tosses it next to the whiskey bottle. "I haven't used this either."

"What happened?" I whisper.

The elevator door opens before he answers. In less than thirty seconds,

Ryder walks in, looking every bit as destroyed as Maddox. "Tell me it's not true."

Maddox sighs and drops his head. "It's true, Ry. He's gone. Bastian called me. I texted you as we were talking."

Ryder drags a hand over his face as he walks to the piano. His eyes quickly zoom in on the whiskey and drugs on the lid. His jaw clenches, and he grabs onto the piano with a white-knuckled grip. Temptation beckons him just as it is Maddox.

I go to them, pick up the bottle, and reach for the glass in Maddox's hand. His fingers wrap tightly around the glass, resisting me. I run my fingers through his hair. "This isn't the answer, baby," I whisper softly to him.

"Feels like it's the only answer," he sighs. "Knew things were too perfect lately."

He wraps an arm around me, pulling me close, but keeps the glass in his other hand. I continue to stroke his hair for several seconds; then, he hands me the filled-to-the-brim tumbler. I reach for the plastic baggie when he grabs my hand. "Flush the whole thing. I don't want you touching it."

I nod and go to the bathroom. I flush the drugs, pour the alcohol down the sink, and then make my way back to the music room.

"After all these years, we find out he's family, and now he's gone," Maddox says.

"He was working to get his wife and little girl back. Never seen anyone so fucking determined," Ryder says angrily.

"He was determined all right. Even when he seemed to give up, he was still fighting." Maddox replies sadly.

"That kid got his shit together before we did. How the fuck is this fair?"

"It's not. Not one bit." Maddox growls. I hear him push away from the table. The slap of his bare feet on the hardwood gives away his pacing. "But when the fuck has life ever been fair to any of us? He doesn't deserve this. His little girl sure as hell doesn't deserve this. I *wanted* to die. He was trying to live. I deserve it more than he does."

I fail to stifle a sob and bury my face in my hands at his declaration. At the guilt and self-loathing in his words and voice. He's come so far. Has what happened set him back? Does he once again believe his life is meaningless?

Big, warm hands pull mine away from my face. My head tips back, and I stare into the blue eyes storming with pain, regret, and sorrow. His hands on either side of my head and his thumbs brushing tears away, he places a gentle kiss on my forehead and pulls me into his solid body. "I didn't mean that how it sounded, Canary," he says against my flesh. "I just meant that... I don't even know what I meant."

"Don't leave me," I sob into his chest.

"I won't, Canary. Not by choice."

I wrap my arms around his torso, clinging tightly to him as we stand solemnly outside the imposing stone mausoleum. Tears run down my cheeks as family and friends say goodbye to a man I only met a couple of times, but he left a lasting impression on me with his bright blue eyes and larger-than-life demeanor. He was kind to me at a time I needed it.

Bastian and Rory stand off from the service, arms folded across their chest, dressed in head-to-toe black, looking solemn and intimidating all at once. While Ryder and Maddox have told me how they crossed paths with him years ago, I can't help but wonder how Rory and Bastian knew him.

I turn into Maddox, burying my face against him when the little girl starts crying for her daddy. Maddox's chest heaves as he fights back his own emotions, then kisses my head and pulls away to say a few words. Ryder grabs my arm, pulling me to the side opposite of Heaven.

The ceremony is beautiful but doesn't last long. I've only been to a couple of funerals in my life. The one for my daughter was the hardest, even if it was only my ex and our parents and siblings in attendance. Everyone has always conjured the same thought, though. *How is this comforting?* They say funerals aren't for the dead but for the living. But how do a few sad words spoken, songs sung, and a steel box provide closure?

Once the service is over, we go to Bastian and Rory for a few minutes while Maddox and Ryder wait to speak with the mother—the sister Maddox and Bastian never knew about. They wanted to see his wife. Bastian told us she wasn't coming. At first, I couldn't understand what could possibly keep her away when her little girl is here. Then Maddox explained about the son she lost, and my heart bled for her. To bury her son and husband at such a young age. I'm not sure I would survive.

"You heading back to New York after this?" Bastian asks.

"Actually, I'll be heading to RC," Maddox tells him as he squeezes my hand. "If I've learned anything from this, it's that I've got to deal with shit. That damn kid learned long before I did that you must deal with your past to have a future. He worked his ass off to prove he could be a good husband

and father. It's time I take a page from his book. Deal with my shit and put the past behind me."

Bastian grins, Ryder nods in agreement, and I swear I see Rory's mouth twitch.

"'Bout goddamn fucking time, *fratello*," Bastian says with that strange Italian-Cajun accent of his. "He'd be proud of you too," he nods toward the gravesite.

"You hanging around with..." Maddox nods to their sister.

"Nah. She doesn't need me reminding her of shit she doesn't want to think about. I've got *other* things to handle anyway." His multicolored eyes turn nearly black. "You should go talk to her, though. She can pass along that package."

Maddox and Ryder glance across the graveyard, spotting Maddox's sister, niece, and another dark-haired woman I can only assume is the wife's mother. They excuse themselves and go to them. Both hug her, then Maddox pulls something out of his jacket pocket and hands it to the dark-haired woman. Squatting next to the dark-haired little girl, he pulls out an identical object. The little girl takes his face in her hands and says something. Maddox looks like he's about to break when he shakes his head, then wraps his arms around her tiny body. When he releases her, she turns, wrapping her arms around his sister with her small shoulders shaking. Ryder and Maddox kiss the woman's cheek, then walk back to us.

"**Maddox!**" **Callie squeals**. She throws herself into his arms with an audible *oomph*, making him chuckle.

"I know I've given everyone the opposite impression, but I do like breathing, Cal," he jokes with a strained voice.

She releases him and steps back. Tears fill her eyes as she looks up at him. Her bottom lip quivers, and she drops her gaze to the ground. "I'm sorry, Madsy."

His brows scrunch, and his head tilts. Genuine confusion swirls in those blue eyes. "For what?"

"For everything I said at the hospital." Her cheeks glow with embarrassment. "I was out of line."

"You were upset, Cal. A lot happened. Dad. Me. Whatever the hell with Chris. You needed me, and I couldn't be there for you."

"It wasn't fair to put that on you." She ducks her head again. "And I shouldn't have said what I did to you, Quinn. You are exactly the kind of person my brother deserves. I wish I could be as strong as you."

Maddox throws one arm over her shoulder and uses the other to pull me into his side. "Enough of that shit. Let's get inside before the sky falls."

I am grateful. It isn't nearly as cold as New York, but I'm still freezing in the blustering winds.

We get inside and quickly remove our coats.

"Oh my God," Callie exclaims, reaching for my stomach. "Look how big you've gotten." My cheeks flame, but my smile is wide. "How far are you now?"

"Almost thirty weeks," I breathe out like an exaltation. For the last three months, I've held my breath, waiting for something to go wrong. When it didn't, it felt like a miracle. It's the same now. It feels like the greatest gift.

"Oh, not much longer now."

"Don't rush him," I laugh. "He still needs to bake a little longer."

"So you guys know it's a boy?"

I look at Maddox with a grin. "If you mean do we have medical confirmation, then no. I didn't want to know, but Maddox is convinced it's a boy."

"Come on. Let's get you guys settled."

Maddox looks around the entryway but doesn't make an attempt to move further into the house. He's looking at his past. The ghosts of yesterday don't seem so far away when you're staring at all the reminders. "Are you okay?" I ask, squeezing his hand.

He blinks a few times and looks down at me with a smile. "Just feels different, ya know? This was home for so long. Or I thought it was, but maybe…" He looks around for a minute, sighing, getting lost in the memories.

I gently tug his hand, bringing him back. "But what?"

"But I don't think this has been home for a long time." He looks a little sad as he says it. "I think I was clinging too tightly to what it was when Mom was alive. I didn't notice it stopped feeling like home years ago."

"It's cheesy, but it's true. Home is where your heart is," I tell him. "Springfield stopped being my home long before I left."

"And where is your home then, *cher*?" He looks down at me, his blue eyes looking mischievous instead of haunted.

"Where ever you are," I tell him honestly. "But I like the lake house better than the penthouse."

He laughs and drops a quick kiss on my mouth. "Me too, Canary. But it could be a pole shed in the swamp; as long as you're there, I'm home."

"Are you guys coming?" Callie calls out.

Maddox looks down at me and winks. "Go feed the boy. I'll be there in a bit."

I nod and walk across the marble foyer. Looking over my shoulder, I see him cut through the hallway that leads to his dad's office. Before I make it to the kitchen, I'm drawn to the windows overlooking the lake. It's no wonder Maddox was so drawn to the lake house in New York. It shares some similarities with this place. At least, as far as the outside goes.

The huge pergola where we got married stands tall. The wisteria and jasmine no longer bloom, but the vines still cling to the structure.

I close my eyes, remembering the day.

Everything seemed so spontaneous at the time, and I can't help but laugh at how, somehow, Maddox planned it all out. As I think back, I believe knowing his dad didn't have much longer was another reason for his decision. He hasn't said so, but it seems plausible when I consider we were married under that pergola with his dad and Callie as our only witnesses while his dad's justice of the peace friend performed the ceremony. We could have done it anywhere, but he wanted it there.

I didn't even wear white. The nicest thing I had at the time was that yellow sundress. It matched the ring perfectly.

A wave of dizziness washes over me for a moment, with some spots dancing in my vision. I hope it's not a migraine. I don't get them often, but they often start like this. After a few seconds, it mostly passes.

Eventually, I pull myself away and walk into the kitchen. My shoes clap against the finished brick floors, alerting Callie that I'm in the room. She turns with two bowls in her hand. The smell of gumbo fills the air, and suddenly, I'm ravenous.

"Hope it's good," she says as I sit on the stool at the center island.

I smile at her as I blow on the steaming stew. "I'm so hungry, I wouldn't care if it tasted like wood."

We eat in comfortable silence for a few minutes when Callie looks at me with a sheepish smile. "I meant what I said earlier," she says. "I really am sorry for everything I said last time we saw each other."

I reach across the counter and grab her hand with a smile. "Callie, it's in the past. Like I said then, and Maddox told you earlier, you had been through a lot in a short period of time."

She shakes her head, regret swimming in her eyes. "I shouldn't have said all that to him. You were right. Maddox has always looked out for everyone. He and Dad never saw eye to eye, but that never stopped him from being there for me. Or even Amalie before Jamie left with her. How is he, by the way? I wanted to go to the funeral but couldn't get away."

"He's okay. Better than actually. The last few months have been hard, but he's made much progress."

Her eyes glisten with unshed tears as she nods. "He looks better. Like he's not carrying this massive weight anymore."

"Just a mid-sized one, right?" I giggle.

"Right," she laughs. "It will never be in Maddox's nature not to care for everyone around him. But if he can stop feeling responsible for every bad thing that has happened…"

"He's getting there. He still feels a lot of guilt and regret, but he's learning to let it go. One thing at a time."

The conversation changes to how life has been, what her plans are for the future, and my plans to finish my internship. We clean the enormous kitchen, then she excuses herself, leaving me alone.

I wander around for a few minutes, trying to remember my way around the ridiculously large home. My fingers trail over a portrait sitting over the mantel of Maddox, Chris, and Callie as children. The picture of his mom always captures my attention. Her silvery blond hair—the same shade as Callie's—and eyes always grab me. They are nearly identical to Zoey's. Such a pale ice blue, they are almost white.

My favorite picture is of Maddox sitting at the piano, his feet dangling from the bench with a broad smile as his mom leans over the lid. She looked so proud of him. His dad told me this was the last picture she took with him.

After a few more minutes of wandering, I end up at his dad's office door. Maddox stands at the window looking out with his hands shoved in his pockets. Papers are scattered over the desk, and another box sits off in the corner.

"He kept journals," Maddox tells me without turning around.

"How did you know I was standing here?" I ask as I walk further into the room. I walk to the floor-to-ceiling bookshelves filled with titles I have no interest in. Book upon books about economics, marketing, sales patterns, and more business stuff.

"I always know when you close, darlin'." He turns around and watches me as I continue to peruse the shelves. When I come across a few works of fiction, I'm not surprised to find his father leaned more toward authors such as Vonnegut and Bradbury, but I am shocked to also see a few works by Authur C. Clarke and Robert Heinlein. Trey Masters never seemed the type to give much thought to science fiction. "You won't find Bronte on his shelves," Maddox tells me.

"I didn't expect to," I giggle. "What did you find in the journals?"

"I haven't looked at them. I'm not sure I want to."

I look at his rigid posture as he continues to lean against the window. His jaw is tight, and his shoulders are tense. "They might help you put things in perspective," I suggest.

"I don't need perspective, Canary. He told me everything he needed to before he died. What I needed was time to reconcile it all and find forgiveness." He blows out a harsh breath and walks around the desk. "He thought he was doing the right thing, and I will admit, I did not make it easy on him. We both fucked up our relationship."

"At least you got the chance to make amends."

He takes my hand, leads me to the oversized leather sofa, and pulls me onto his lap. "It just feels like we still had more to do, ya know? I needed more time. The reason I've waited so long to come back is that I wasn't ready to say goodbye forever. As long as I was in New York, I could pretend he was still here, waiting for me."

"He's here, Maddox." I rest my hand over his heart. "I know you had a rough relationship with him, but you loved him, and he loved you. He was proud of you."

He buries his head in my hair, and he lets go. His soft sobs shake me as he holds me tightly against his chest. "God, I spent years avoiding him, and now I'd do anything just to see him one more time."

"Shh. It's okay. You'll always have him. And you have those last moments to cherish forever. Focus on those, instead of all the regret."

"I fucking miss him so much. God, I miss him."

I don't say anything. I just hold him and let him finally give in to his grief.

QUINN

How many lies

"We are here for the reading of the last will and testament of William "Trey" Bryan Michael Masters, III," the middle-aged attorney says from behind his massive oak desk. I sit next to Maddox on an uncomfortable sofa, my hand in his, while Callie sits on his other side, wrapped around his arm.

This morning when they were finalizing plans to meet the attorney, I volunteered to stay behind, but they both insisted I be there. They would have understood if I had told them I had a massive headache to the point of nausea. But they needed me, so I remained quiet.

Chris was already there when we arrived, sitting in a sleek leather chair. It was the first time I'd seen him since the hospital. I wasn't sure when Maddox last remembered seeing him, and I knew he hadn't reached out because he was still struggling with the memory of what happened that day. He wanted to believe Chris's story, but something felt off to him. I couldn't blame him when he literally remembered everything that happened *but* that. He even admitted to me he knew I was lying about what happened at the strip club. Then started apologizing again while thanking me for not giving up on him.

It's taken a bit, but he finally realizes I am not going anywhere.

"As I'm sure you are all aware, Trey liked to do things his way. So a few weeks before he died, he made this video. Everything is in writing, of course, but you should all know this is completely binding. Should you try to contest, you won't win. Trey made sure it was ironclad, including affidavits by a team of psychiatrists and physicians."

"Of course he did," Maddox chuckles wistfully.

The attorney presses a button, and the bookcases across the room slide open, revealing a large television. The man presses play on his computer, and Maddox's dad appears on the screen. His face is sunken, and his eyes are sad, but the same indomitable presence that he exuded the few times I met him is just as strong.

"I won't get into bullshit formalities. I just signed plenty of papers that cover that." Instantly, I'm reminded of Maddox. That take no shit personality flows strongly in his veins from both sides of his parentage. "The first thing I want to say is that I love each of you. I'm sorry I wasn't a better father. I spent too many years working and not enough time paying attention to what you needed. I tried to mold you into who I wanted you to be—what I thought was best—instead of allowing you the freedom to choose. Especially you, Maddox. My biggest regret will always be pushing you away because you refused to bend to my will, but that is also one of the many reasons I am so very proud of you..." He trails off and shakes his head. I sniffle and squeeze Maddox's hand. When I sneak a glimpse of his profile, I see his tight-set jaw as he fights to control his emotions. He catches me staring and kisses the top of my head, reassuring me that he is okay.

"Maddox, I failed you the most, but you flew despite me. I only hope one day you'll see how goddamn special you are. All of you are special. You're the best part of me.

"Callie, you never wanted any part of this company, but you were so damned determined to make me proud that you immersed yourself with ease. Our East coast division has thrived because of you. You've given up a lot because of me. I want you to forget everything I told you and go after your dreams."

Callie burst into tears. Maddox pulls her to his side. She says a lot of unintelligible things about it being too late as Maddox tries to console her.

"Chris, apart from Maddox, I've probably let you down the most. You've always been driven and focused, submerging yourself entirely into the company, even knowing it could never be yours. I contemplated for a long time rewriting the company bylaws. But then I started watching you, and I realized your ambition and drive had turned to entitlement and greed.

"You learn what's important in life when you don't have much time left. It's one of fate's many cruel jokes because there is never enough time to set things right.

"But enough of that. I can't change the past. I can only prepare for the future. For your futures.

"I knew it would take Maddox a while to come around to this. Nothing less than I deserve. But starting from the time you watch this, Master Corporation is no more. I've negotiated terms and sold my majority shares to

Diamond Industries, stipulating that any current or future family members are offered an opportunity to prove themselves should they choose.

"Except for Chris. Chris, I know this isn't what you want to hear, but I believe you need to move on from Masters Corp. I want you to find success beyond business in this company. Blaze your own trail. Make your own path. But more than that, find happiness. Find it beyond spreadsheets and databases. Find it beyond the board meetings and hostile takeovers."

"What the hell?" Chris yells as he stands. His face is red, and his nostrils flare.

"Chris, sit down," Maddox tells him as if he's the older of the two when he's, in fact, nearly seven years younger.

Chris turns to face us. Maddox wastes no time launching himself between us, his entire body vibrating with tension and hostility. It makes me wonder if seeing Chris hasn't triggered a memory.

"This is your damn fault," he yells at Maddox. "Everyone's little fucking golden-boy prodigy. What a fucking joke. Just so you know, this isn't over. Not by a damn longshot."

He storms out of the room, leaving all of us stunned by his reaction. Well, except for Maddox. He's not stunned; he's pissed.

Fists opening and closing at his side, Maddox takes Chris's vacated chair. "Play the rest," he orders, rolling his hand in the air.

"Maddox, perhaps we should wait on—"

"I *said* play the fucking video."

The attorney nods, tugging his collar. Callie and I exchange, *oh shit,* looks and scoot closer to each other.

The tape goes on to divulge how Mr. Masters wanted his substantial wealth divided. Most of the cash assets will go to charity, some set aside for future grandchildren, and the rest divided equally among his four children.

"Amalie will receive her portion once she turns eighteen. Until then, Maddox will be the trustee, allowing a monthly stipend to Jamie for her care. All of my holdings and investments will also be divided equally between Amalie, Chris, and Callie, except L&D Records. That goes solely to Maddox. You can do with it what you want, son. I never bought it for myself or to control you. It was always meant for you.

"I love all of you. I've only ever wanted your happiness. Now go find it."

The video ends, and the attorney clears his throat. Maddox is stretched in the chair with a hand over his mouth. His brows are set low, and the muscle in his cheek tics. "Why did he want me to manage Amalie's trust?" Maddox finally asks. "Why not Chris or Callie?"

The attorney shrugs. "He said you were the only one who kept in touch regularly with Amalie and Jamie."

"I-uh..." Callie begins. We all turn our attention to her. Her cheeks blaze a bright cherry. "I may have had it out with Jamie a couple of years ago."

Maddox groans. "I don't want to know. That's for you to figure out. What about Chris?"

"Chris doesn't remember Amalie's name most days. He's never made an effort to get to know her."

Maddox nods as if that's all he needs to know. I suppose it is.

"So, that's the basics. You'll each receive documents detailing everything. Papers will need to be signed to transfer ownership. Maddox, you'll need to sign Amalie's trust as well. I can tell you that you will each receive eighty-five million in cash once the sale of Masters has been finalized, which will be midnight tonight."

Maddox waves him off. "I don't want or need any of that. Add it to whatever dad set up for future grandchildren."

The attorney nods. "I'll take care of it. He also retained ten percent of Masters Corp for each of you to divide."

"Anything else you need from us?"

"No, I'll have the papers ready to sign by end of day."

Maddox nods, then motions for us to leave.

We walk down the glass corridor to the private garage in silence. Callie climbs in the backseat of their dad's Range Rover while Maddox helps me into the front passenger seat. As has become the norm, we have to maneuver between people until we reach the main road.

Spots begin dancing in my vision like they did yesterday. My head is still pounding. I close my eyes and rest my head against the window.

"You okay?" Maddox asks, taking my hand in his.

"Mmm," I answer. "Just tired."

Once we are on the freeway, we begin to zip around cars. I grab the *oh shit* handle and place my free hand on my belly. Nausea builds. The nausea increase while Maddox drives like he's in a NASCAR race. It doesn't help that fast driving and heavy traffic have given me anxiety lately.

Maddox looks over at me and immediately slows down. "Shit, baby, I'm sorry."

"It's okay," I tell him with a wan smile.

"What's wrong? Is she okay?" Callie asks.

"She will be once we get there," he tells her, but his eyes dart back to me, his own worry showing. "She just gets car sick lately."

Half an hour later, we pull into the driveway, and Callie hops out. "Stay put," Maddox tells me, walking around the SUV to my side.

"I can do it myself," I grumble as he takes my hand and elbow.

"Baby, I've seen the effects gravity has on that little body and that belly the last couple of weeks. You've tripped on air. It's better if I help," he tells me as he opens my door. I huff and pout, but I can't argue because he's right. "Bastian is on his way over. I want to know why he didn't tell me about Dad's deal with Diamond." I can see the betrayal in his eyes.

I rub my thumb between his brows. "Don't be too hard on Bastian. I'm sure he had a good reason."

"There always is," he grumbles, then looks up at the sky. "Let's get you inside before the bottom falls out."

"You said that yesterday, and it never rained." As soon as the words leave my mouth, a loud clap of thunder sounds. "Okay, yeah. Inside."

We walk through the door, and a strange feeling comes over me. An uneasy eeriness as if someone else is here. I look around and see nothing out of the ordinary, so I force it away. But a shiver escapes anyway.

"You cold?" he asks.

"Maybe a little," I nod. "And my head is really throbbing." I finally admit.

"Go lie down on the couch. I'll go upstairs and get your pillow and blanket." He kisses my forehead and runs up the stairs.

I rub my hands over my arms to rid myself of the goosebumps that erupt. That eerie feeling won't go away.

When I step into the living room, the hair on my neck stands on end. I look around for the source of my unease, but I don't see anything. "Get it together, Quinn," I mutter to myself.

When I walk further into the room, an arm wraps tightly around my neck, and something hard digs into my ribs. I try to scream for Maddox, but it's barely audible because of the pressure against my throat.

"That fucking bastard has ruined everything—taken everything from me. Now, I'm going to take everything from him." Chris's voice echoes in my ears as terror doesn't just build but erupts in my chest like a volcano.

"Got your sweatshirt, too, Canary," Maddox's voice rings from the staircase.

I open my mouth to scream for him, but the words are lost once again. Chris spins, yanking me off my feet, further cutting off my airways. I slap and claw at his arm until I find my footing and gasp painfully to gather what little air I can.

Maddox walks into the room, his eyes instantly meeting mine, zeroing in on the tears streaming down my cheeks, then moves to Chris's arm wrapped around my neck and the gun in my side. His face drains of color, and those bright eyes shadow with fear and fury.

"What are you doing, Chris?" he asks. His voice is calm and relaxed. Even his body language shows absolute calm. But I see everything in those eyes.

"You're the genius 'round here, right?" Chris digs the gun deeper into my ribs, and I whimper with pain. Maddox's calm wavers, and he inches forward. "Don't try it, little brother," Chris taunts.

"Okay," Maddox says with his hands up in surrender. "Just put the gun down, let her go, and we can talk about this."

"You think I want to *talk* to you? Why the hell would I want to do that? You've been the bane of my existence since your crack-whore mother dropped your screaming ass off. Everything has always been to cater to you. I was so fucking glad when Trey *finally* shipped your ass off, but even that wasn't enough. Do you *know* how many times I had to listen to him go on about how smart, talented, and brilliant you were? It was exhausting as fuck to always pretend that I gave a shit. I was glad when I walked in on you fucking Tasha. Of course, it took her long enough to get you to do it. God knows we tried fucking long enough. I just needed a reason to drop the fucking act. And a reason to get Trey to send you back to New York. I just never expected in my wildest dreams for you to fuck up so epically."

Maddox's eyes widen. Even he can't hide his shock at his brother's deceit. But he quickly shakes it off. "Chris, dad talked about you too. Do you know how often he told me I should be more like you? That I should apply myself like you or focus on a realistic future instead of a pipe dream. He was proud of you."

"Yep, so proud that he decided he'd rather sell the company than let me have it. I deserve that company. But only a Masters by blood, right? Still, I knew I could convince the board to give it to me if you were out of the way. I just didn't know the bastard already sold it to McCabe and Delrie."

"Chris, I get it, but if you managed to kill me the day you shot me, then I wouldn't be here to get Sebastian to sell it back to you."

Oh my God. He does remember.

"Let Quinn go. I'll call Bastian and tell him to come over, and we can take care of this. I'll even back up your story about us fighting for the gun and it going off. Just please let her go."

"What makes you think they'll do that?" He asks, his grip finally loosening. My headache has gone from throbbing to unbearable. It feels like it's about to explode, and the room is spinning in a circle. But somehow, I manage to hide it all and remain still.

"They'll do it for me," Maddox assures him.

Chris releases me, pushing me away, then aims the gun at Maddox. "Call them."

I wobble on my feet, trying desperately to maintain my balance, but the room is spinning so fast.

"No need to call us." I hear the familiar voice and try to turn around. I feel the baby roll violently, followed by a sharp pain. I have the vague sensation of falling.

And everything goes black.

MADDOX

Into the fire

Time stands still. My legs push me forward before my mind catches up. I'm driven by pure instinct.

I barely comprehend that Chris has turned the gun on me as I launch myself across the room. Hardly register the gunfire sounding off around me or the sound of Callie's screams. If I've been hit, I don't feel it as adrenaline and terror fuel me.

The moment her already pale face turned translucent and her hand grasped her belly in a gasp of pain, my body went on autopilot.

I slide across the floor, unable to catch her before she hits the ground. Her head smacks the floor with a sickening thud and bounces. I pull her into my lap, brush her hair off her neck, and check her pulse. As I count the beats, my panic increases. I press my hand against her belly and beg him to move. He doesn't

"No, no, no, no," I cry out. "Bastian," I yell, not knowing if he's alive or dead after the gunfire.

He's beside me in seconds. I can see his concern despite his calm expression.

"Oh my God," Callie calls out.

"Calm down, Maddox," Bastian tells me as he taps out a number on his phone. "Chopper to the Masters' estate. Now." He hangs up without saying another word, only an expectation to be obeyed.

"We can't move her," I tell him.

He shakes his head. "It's faster than waiting on an ambulance, Mads."

He's trying to reassure me, but all I can do is shake my head.

I can't lose her. I can't lose either of them.

"Maddox," Bastian barks, and I snap my eyes to him. "Now is not the time to lose your shit."

I barely bite back my retort because he's right. But I am also not stupid, nor am I losing my shit. *Yet.*

But I can see this is bad. It's too soon, but I already know my little boy is about to make his entrance into this world. I just hope he doesn't break his momma's heart.

Or mine.

My heart stutters when her lashes flicker. Her pale brows pull together, and she clenches her teeth. Her hand moves to her stomach, then her head as she groans in pain. "Something is wrong." She grabs my hand, squeezing it tightly. Panic flashes in her dark eyes. "Maddox, something is wrong."

I brush her hair away from her face and wipe the tears from her eyes. "I know, baby. Help is coming. We're going to get you to the hospital."

"He can't come now," she begins to sob.

"Don't think we get a say in that, baby, but it will be okay," I promise her and hope I can keep it. "Babies are born early all the time. He'll be fine."

"Christian is here," Bastian calls out. "Can she walk?"

"She's not going to," I tell him as I stand with her in my arms.

Bastian's eyes shift to the spot, then to me. He sees the blood. I subtly shake my head, quietly letting him know that I haven't told her.

I walk quickly as I can, keeping my head lowered. I slide her across the seat, then climb in, placing her head on my lap.

"Ready?" Christian asks.

"Go," I yell.

I look down at her scared golden eyes. "It's gonna be okay, baby," I promise her again, then watch her eyes roll back as she starts seizing.

I pace around the waiting room like a lion in a cage. My breathing is heavy and irritated. The feelings I hate more than anything—the ones that often send me spiraling, course through my body like an electrical current.

Helpless and out of control.

But I can't spiral. Can't fall down that rabbit hole of darkness and despair as easy as it would be. I can't dive into the opposite end of that, the fury and rage that wants to erupt.

They need me to keep it together, so I keep holding on.

But I won't breathe again until I know they're okay.

"Any word?" Bastian asks as he walks into the waiting room.

"The only thing I know right now is something about pre-eclampsia and placental abruption. Ten days ago, her blood pressure was fine." I throw my hands in the air, but I'd much rather throw them into the wall. Or someone's face.

"Pre-eclampsia is what Verity had. She had a headache and was nauseous but didn't think anything of it until she passed out. She was about thirty weeks, so they put her on bed rest, made us keep her blood pressure checked, and started seeing her once a week. By thirty-six weeks, they induced her."

"Quinn had a headache when we returned from the lawyer's office. She was also nauseous on the way back, but we thought she was car sick." I drag a hand down my face and fall into a chair. "All the books say his odds are good. They all say she'll be okay. But this isn't how it was supposed to go."

"Maddox, given the odds were against Quinn from the start, I think there could've been a lot worse things that happened."

"This wouldn't be happening if I hadn't gone upstairs for her stuff. I would've gone into the room first. Or, at the very least, with her." I drop my head into my hands and sigh.

"Don't start blaming yourself. None of this is your fault."

I turn my head and stare into his hard-set eyes with outraged disbelief. "I *don't* fucking blame myself. I blame Chris. This is all on him, and I would have killed him if you hadn't. Without thinking twice."

Bastian mock sniffles and pretends to wipe tears. "You're all grown up."

"Asshole," I mutter with a grin.

"Proud of you, Mads. You've come a long way." He stands and pulls his phone out of his pocket. "I need to call my *principessa* and update her. She called Quinn's parents."

I shake my head with a growl. "They won't care. They haven't spoken to her since they learned about her working at your club. Can she call her brothers instead?"

He nods. "I already called Ryder for you. He said he would tell everyone else and that he'd see you in a few hours."

I give a nod of thanks as he walks away and look at my watch. We've been here for forty-five minutes. She's been in surgery for fifteen. It kills me that they wouldn't let me go with her.

This must be how Quinn felt when it was me behind those double doors. The anguish and agony she felt while fighting off my asshole family. I can almost see her in the corner chair of this very room, clutching that cross between her fingers, eyes closed in prayer.

Almost involuntarily, I leap from my seat. I race down the hallway, take a left, then a right, until I'm standing in front of the chapel. The *Amanda Nelson-Masters Memorial Chapel*.

I rake my fingers through my hair, down to my neck, and blow out a breath. Hand on the handle, I pull the door open and walk inside. Even though it's only a hospital chapel, I almost expect to burst into flames.

I linger in the back, staring at the large cross that stands tall and proud at the front. I almost turn around to leave when an older man places his hand on my shoulder. "Need some company?" I nod, and we walk to the front together.

"I've always wondered how the source of an execution could be held with such reverence," I quietly mutter as I lean forward.

"Because it's about the sacrifice and what that sacrifice meant. But if you don't believe, why come here?"

Looking straight ahead, I nod at my mother's name engraved on a plaque. "Because she did. And Quinn does." I turn and look into his dark eyes. "Why are *you* here?"

"Because you are my son, Maddox. It doesn't matter who raised you. You have always been mine. I have always been there, watching from a distance, just like Bastian. I wanted to be in your life, Maddox, but I didn't know how to do that and keep you out of my world." His eyes plead with me to understand. Plead for forgiveness.

A few months ago, I hated Paul Delrie. But a few months ago, I didn't know what I do now. I stopped hating him a while ago.

"I know you were there," I tell him. "When I was in the hospital? I know you came by that night after everyone left, and you thought I was asleep." That first night after Quinn sang me to sleep, I woke with the feeling of being watched. It took me a minute to spot him in the corner, but I saw him.

"After Bastian told me his suspicions about your brother, I wasn't leaving you alone." I can't help but chuckle. It's not funny, but my fucking life, man!

"I want a chance to get to know you better, Maddox. I've made a lot of mistakes with my kids. One daughter has vanished, another I never knew about, and now a grandson I'll never know."

"He looked a lot like me," I tell him. "Even had the same irreverent sense of humor. Hot-headed as hell too, and Bastian's thirst for violence. But he was a good friend. Long before *he* put together the family resemblance and figured everything out, he was my friend. His little girl looks a lot like him."

"I hope her mother will give me a chance to get to know her," he tells me sadly. "And I hope you'll do the same. I want to know you and my grandchild." He stands up and puts his hand on my shoulder. I look up at him. Emotions I am all too familiar with swirl in those nearly black pools.

"I will," I tell him sincerely.

He gives me a grateful smile. "You have my mother's eyes." He pats my shoulder. "I'll leave you to it then."

I don't know what else to say, so I nod.

When I'm alone, my eyes drift back to the cross. "Sacrifice, huh?" I rub my hands over my face as I stare, trying to find something resembling faith, but come up empty. "I never believed in you," I growl.

"You've seen my life. According to your book, you knew it would happen before I existed. Kind of makes it hard to put your faith in someone who takes a kid's mother away or lets a boy get raped over and over." I drop my head and close my eyes, pushing the memories aside.

"Logically, I know they'll be fine. Science and math say the odds are in their favor. But if my history is anything to go by, then the odds are stacked against *me*. So I need you to do me a favor. Consider it repayment for the shit I've been through. I'm not asking for a freebie or anything. I'm offering an exchange. A boy needs his mother. Not some shell of a man ruined from losing the love of his life. And Quinn needs her son. She's already lost one baby, yet she still believes in you. Don't take him from her. She'll see me in him and be happy."

I slide off the pew onto my knees and stretch my arms wide. "You're all about sacrifice. Take me. First time in my life, I don't want to die. I want to grow old with her, and I want to watch my son grow up. But I'll gladly die for them." I slam my fist into my chest as the tears begin to fall.

"Take me. You hear me? Take me, you son of a bitch." I fall back on my heels, bow my head, and let the sobs take over.

MADDOX

Breathe again

A hand on my shoulder startles me from my thoughts. I look up to see Bastian standing beside me. "Doctor is looking for you."

I wipe the tears away and leap to my feet. We walk back to the waiting room in silence. The room is packed. I swallow a lump in my throat when Callie launches herself at me. "What are y'all doing here?" I ask as I look at all the faces in the room.

"This is what family does for each other, Masters," Jax grunts with his arms folded over his chest.

"*And* as much as it *pains* us," Zane says with a wide grin, "you are family. That whole damn band of yours, too."

"Like it or not, you're stuck with us," Rory tells me.

"Thanks," I choke out while Tori and Verity hug me.

"Mr. Masters?" the doctor calls out.

I grab the back of my neck, trying to squeeze out the tension as I approach him. It takes everything in me not to bounce anxiously as he speaks.

"Everything went exactly as it should. We got the baby out quickly and began doing what we needed to get your wife's blood pressure in a safe range. We'll keep her in recovery for a bit longer, but you can go in and see her in a few minutes."

I close my eyes but don't give into the relief yet. "The baby?"

"Also, as well as expected. In fact, I believe your wife's due date may have been slightly off given he weighs slightly more than three and a half pounds."

My hands fly to my head as my lungs fill with air. I finally breathe again.

Then it hits me. The corner of my mouth twitches. "You said *he?*"

The doctor's eyes crinkle at the corners with a smile. "Yes, it's a boy. As I said, I think your wife's due date was off by a few days."

"She would've been thirty weeks day after tomorrow. We were going home for her appointment."

He nods. "Well within the margin of error. That said, he'll still need to be in the NICU for several weeks. He'll have a feeding tube and oxygen for a few weeks, and he'll be in an incubator. Assuming no further complications, I say his odds are spectacular." I drop my head and don't even bother stopping the tears this time. "You can go see him while you wait to see your wife. You can hold him as well. The nurse will take you there."

"Thank you," I tell him, my voice nothing more than a shaky crack.

"Congratulations, Mr. Masters." He shakes my hand and walks away.

I turn toward everyone and throw my hands in the air with a huge, watery smile. "It's a boy." They all cheer and holler. "They're probably in the air, but can you call Ryder and the guys and tell them?" I say to no one in particular.

I don't wait for them to answer. I follow the nurse to the NICU. Several minutes later, I've been prepped and led into a small, specialized nursery. I sit in the chair, and the nurse places the tiniest little human against my bare chest and a blanket over us.

I look down at him and feel like my heart might burst. Different than anything I've ever felt, I am consumed by unconditional, unquestionable devotion and love. He's so little that my entire hand engulfs his small body. I close my eyes and let the feel of his tiny heart beating against mine and listen to his soft breathing.

"I swear on everything I am, I will keep you safe," I whisper. "I'll never make you feel like anything is more important to me. You will always know love and acceptance. Even when you mess up, and believe me, you will, you will never feel like a disappointment. I promise I will be the best dad I can be."

He squirms a little bit but seems content. I think he might even recognize my voice as I continue to whisper promises to him. Then I begin to sing to him. I'm not even sure how much time passes when the nurse comes back in.

"When can his mom come to see him?" I ask as she settles him into the incubator.

"As soon as her doctor says it's okay," she tells me as she adjusts his tubes. "It's good for him to have as much skin-to-skin contact as he can tolerate. But for her as well."

I nod, hoping they don't make her wait too long.

I fight an internal battle. I don't want to leave him, and I want to see her. Eventually, I tear myself away and go to Quinn's room. When I walk in, my beautiful Canary is still sleeping peacefully. I pull a chair next to her bed, take her hand in mine, and softly kiss each of her fingers.

Her lashes flutter against her cheeks, and those gorgeous eyes stare back at me. "Hey there, pretty girl," I whisper as I brush her hair off her face. "How are you feeling?"

"Maddox?" Her voice is rough and groggy. Her eyes struggle to focus. She looks around us, and I know the moment awareness hits. Her hands grasp her stomach, and tears fill her eyes. "No," she whimpers, then covers her face with her hands. "*No.*"

I pull her hands from her face. My smile couldn't be any bigger. "He's beautiful, Canary. Black hair, blue eyes, and perfect."

More tears erupt. Tears of happiness and joy. I let her cry it out until the river runs dry. I kiss her palms and smooth her hair until the final shudder leaves her body, allowing her to bask in her elation and near heartbreak until she's wholly purged herself.

"You said he," she hiccups at the last tear falls. I nod and smile. "Your mom was right."

I bring her hand back to my mouth, kissing across her knuckles. "She was."

"When can I see him?" she whispers, looking like she'd fly out of the bed now if she could.

"Soon, baby, but they're going to watch you in here for a few more hours. In the meantime, we have a very important decision to make."

She blinks a few times, and I see a hint of fear return, so I quickly elaborate. "He needs a name, *cher*."

Her shoulders sag, and she exhales. Eyes falling to her lap, she bites that bottom lip. I fight my smile, pretending I don't know she's had his name picked out for weeks but was afraid talking about it would jinx us.

I found her journal on the counter one day. It was open, so I read it. Sue me.

"Asher Nathaniel. Asher means blessing, and Nathaniel means gift from God." It's clear how much she loves the name by how her eyes shine. "If you don't like it, I'll understand. It's not a big deal. It can be whatever you like. He's your son too."

Her rambling is adorable.

I press my fingers against her lips, unable to hold my laugh any longer. "Shut up, Canary. The name is perfect."

"Maddox, what happened to Chris?"

My jaw clenches. I'm going to need *lots* of therapy over him. Of all the betrayals in my life, that one had no reason except cruelty and jealousy. I looked up to Chris for most of my life, even though he ignored me. Felt guilt over a stupid teenage fuck up that I didn't have to feel guilty over. Now, if I could bring him back to kill him all over again except so much slower, I would.

Yep. Lots. Of. Therapy.

But hey! How's that for growth?

"Chris won't be a problem anymore, *cher*. I promise you that."

Her eyes swim with questions she won't ask. It wouldn't matter if she did. I pray she never remembers the gunfire. I wish I could take the entire memory from her.

She nods, but I can feel her fear. I make a mental note to make sure she also calls her therapist.

What a perfectly matched pair we are.

It will take time, but we'll move past this. One day, the only significance this day will hold will be the day our son was born.

Asher Nathaniel Masters.

QUINN

We will make a brand new start

2 months later

We pull into the driveway of the lake house, and a sense of calm washes over me. I look over at Maddox, who jerks his head toward the other cars and shrugs. "They're excited we're home."

"*I'm* excited we're home." I smile.

A loud coo from the back seat has us both laughing. "I think someone agrees." Maddox looks in the mirror at Asher, whose bright blue eyes take in everything. "Hope you're ready, little man. You are about to get all the love."

We climb out of the car, and Maddox walks around to my side. He opens my door for me, then goes to the backseat. He unstraps Asher, carefully removing him from his car seat. He hands our little miracle off to me with a kiss on his dark head. "Get him out of the cold, and I'll grab the bags."

I grin and bob my head in agreement, then cautiously walk to the door. It opens before I reach it, with Ryder standing on the other side. "'Bout bloody time," he tells me, taking Asher from me as soon as I cross the threshold. "How's my handsome godson?"

"Probably getting hungry," I admit as I pull off my coat.

Ryder laughs. "I'd say you're right if the way he's trying to swallow his fist is any indication." He throws his arm over my shoulder and begins leading me toward the living room. "Come on, love; everyone's waiting."

"Not even going to wait on me, asshole?" Maddox calls out.

I look over my shoulder and see him shake off the snowflakes as he sets the bags on the floor.

"Nope. You know the way." Ryder answers, still tugging me along. "You're not the star of the show anymore."

"Fucking asshole," Maddox chuckles, then fully laughs when Ryder flips him off with the hand draped over my shoulder.

When we reach the living room, a gasp gets caught in my throat. I expected everyone to be here. Maybe some food and balloons. But this?

A massive fir sits next to the piano, decorated with red glass balls and twinkling white lights. Atop the piano is several red ornamental presents with beautiful evergreen sprays and pinecones, all artfully arranged around three red and silver candles. Over every window and on the upstairs balcony are green garlands with bits of red holly and more twinkling lights.

"I think she likes it," Maddox says, pulling me away from Ryder.

"You knew about this?" I look at him with wide-eyed surprise.

"It was something they threw in after they did me a favor."

"What favor?"

"Show her, Mads," Dane grins like the Cheshire cat.

"Maybe we should get him settled first," I suggest, nodding at my baby boy.

"You will do no such thing," Heaven tells me as she continues to snuggle Asher, who she snatched from Ryder. Much to the other women's chagrin. "He's mine forever. You're never getting him back."

Maddox puts his hand on the small of my back but points at Heaven. "You got ten minutes, Cupcake. Then I want my boy back."

Heaven sticks her tongue out, then turns around to the other women. "You need to get that girl knocked up," Maddox mutters to Ryder. Ryder smirks. "Yeah?" Maddox's brows jump, and Ryder shrugs. "Congratulations, Ry."

"Don't say anything, okay?" he tells us. "She just took the test this morning."

I drag my fingers across my lips like a zipper. "Our lips are sealed," I whisper conspiratorily.

Maddox leads me up the stairs to the room next to ours. He opens the door, and the waterworks start instantly as my hands fly to my mouth.

Gray walls have black, grungy instruments painted on them. A soft, plush, red rug covers the dark hardwood. The white crib and glider contrast black dressers and changing tables. Over the crib is a mobile of albums that make me belt out a soggy laugh.

"What do you think?" he asks.

I turn to face him, throwing my arms around his neck. "I think it's gorgeous. And very you."

His brows pinch as anxiety darkens his eyes. "I don't expect him to play music. Or even like it. I just..."

I plant my lips on his. After half a second, his arms wrap around me, and he takes over the kiss, deepening it. Fueling the flames.

Before I completely lose all sense, I pull back. "Music is a huge part of who you are And who I am. It's okay to share that with him. I would be more surprised if he didn't love music."

A shrill cry rips through the air, and my breasts instantly ache from the sound. "He's certainly got the lungs for it," I laugh.

"Come on. Let's get down there before all the kids start crying."

We start for the stairs, but he stops and walks to the rails. I watch him as he watches the commotion below us. With my hand on his back, I ask, "Are you okay?"

He pulls me by my waist, placing me in front of him. I look down and smile. Everyone is smiling. Well, except for Cami, who we can hear yelling at Dane because their baby hasn't made its arrival yet. Tyler is off in the corner with Lyra, trying to teach her something on his guitar and rolling his eyes because she'd rather play with her dolls. Lincoln is trying to take the pacifier of Angel and Josephine's daughter, Tallulah. Asher is snuggly wrapped in Josephine's arms as she bats her lashes at Angel.

"No," we hear him tell her, making us both chuckle.

Liam is talking to a pretty girl a little younger than me in another corner. Actually, it looks like they're arguing. "That's Angel's sister," Maddox tells me when I ask. His blue eyes suddenly look conniving.

We stay there a few more minutes when he suddenly whispers, "I'm happy, *cher*."

I turn around in his arms. For most people, this is where I would say me too. But we aren't most couples, and he certainly isn't most people.

He brushes a fallen piece of hair from my face as his eyes soak me in. "It still hurts sometimes, and I have no idea how long this feeling will last, but I am truly happy."

"It will last as long as it lasts. And when it starts to fade, we will work to get it back. Together."

"Thank you for loving me, Canary."

"Easiest thing I've ever done."

Maddox

"You guys sure you don't want to stay here?" I ask everyone as they pack up to leave.

"We all decided you guys need time together as a family," Jake tells us as he lifts sleeping Lyra into his arms.

"You're all my family," I grumble.

Ryder laughs. "We most definitely are, mate, but I'm just behind you, Dane is on your other side, and the rest are staying at our places tonight. We'll be back first thing. Enjoy your girl and son in your home for the first time without any of us lurking."

I nod as they all walk out the door, then turn to the stairs with a content sigh.

Contentment. It's still a foreign feeling and sometimes fleeting, but I embrace every goddamn second it's there.

As I walk up the stairs, I hear her soft hums flowing through the air. Reaching Asher's nursery, I lean against the doorway and watch her as she feeds him. It's the most beautiful sight I've ever seen.

She looks up at me and smiles a smile that takes my breath away.

When she's setting him in his crib, I slip behind her and press my lips to her shoulder. "Time for bed," I tell her.

"Maybe he should sleep with us," she whispers as she strokes his soft, dark hair.

"Nope." I kiss her shoulder again, but she's tense beneath my touch. I barely repress a sigh. I saw this coming. There was no way she would leave him our first night home easily. Fortunately, I have plans to get her nice and relaxed.

"But your room—"

"Our room," I growl because it's been hell getting her to refer to anything as ours.

"*Our* room is sound-proofed."

The sigh I was repressing breaks through. She's not going to just walk away unless I make her. So I do. When we're out of the nursery, I take her face in my hands and look into those glassy eyes. "Baby, you know I have audio and video all over this place. Plus, we have the baby monitor. He *will* be fine."

A tear falls, and I quickly brush it away as I drop my lips to hers, slowly backing her up until we cross the threshold of our room. I kick the door shut behind me with a loud click. She pulls back, only just realizing my stealth maneuvers. This time when she looks up at me, her eyes are glassy for another reason.

The haze of lust swirls around us. Tangible and thick, its flames lick at our flesh. "Nine weeks, baby," I yank her top and bra off in a single move. "Told you a long time ago. You are my addiction now. One there is no rehab or recovery for. I'm a junkie in need of a fix."

I pick her up, toss her onto the bed, and tear the leggings from her body. Her swollen tits rise and fall with her heavy breaths. I crawl up her little body and grip her face. Pupils blown wide and filled with need, she licks her lips hungrily.

"Nine weeks, Canary. Do you know how it feels to be addicted to something? Have it right next to you, but you cannot touch it?" I wasn't laying a finger on her until the doctor assured me it was okay. I cup her pussy and circle her opening with a finger. "To be able to smell it but can't touch it? Remember how the flavor bursts on your tongue but can't taste it? Know all you have to do is reach out and taste, even when you shouldn't?"

She shakes her head, and those tantalizing curls tangle and splay seductively around her face. I remove my hand from her cunt, and a tiny whimper flees her lips. I grip her wrists, bring them over her head, and tie them to the length of rope attached to the headboard. I flip her over and pull her hips up. "You're my drug, baby. I will be forever addicted to every inch of you. Inside and out." I drag my tongue down her spine, watching her body's physical reaction to my touch. That full, round ass that I pray doesn't go anywhere beckons me. I can't resist bringing my palm down over the enticing globe and again on the other side.

"More," she begs.

My mouth quirks at my little freak. My hand comes down again and again as her screams fill the room. I gladly give her what she wants until that luscious ass is red and glowing from my hand, and her pussy is dripping down her thighs. The sight of my prints marring her beautiful flesh?

Fuck.

My cocks throbs painfully because *nine fucking weeks.* Actually, it's been sixty-eight days, but who the hell is counting? Not me. I would never know it's been over sixteen hundred hours since I've had her cunt milking the life out of my cock.

Dear God, I'm so fucked up.

But my cock will have to wait its turn because that delicious nectar begs me to taste. Gripping her raw, red ass, I spread her wide, brush my tongue over her puckered hole, chuckling when her body shudders, then indulge in the sultry nirvana that calls to me. A dying man drinking from the well of life, I thrust my tongue inside her, devouring that sweet cunt. I feast like it's my first and last meal until she explodes on my tongue while she screams out my name, and her body goes lax.

I crawl over her prone form, licking and sucking every inch of flesh from her ass to her neck before I take a forceful grip on her hair, pulling her head back until I have access to that beautiful mouth. I claim it with greedy passion, sharing her sweet flavor. "Don't get comfortable on me yet, darlin'. We're not done."

Her lashes flutter in a haze of euphoric aftershocks. Though common sense and consideration tell me to go slow, I don't. I impale her in one vicious stroke. She cries out. Her body lurches, instinctively running from the violent intrusion, but I hold her firmly in place as I relish the feeling of home.

Slowly I retreat, unable to take my eyes off where we are joined. At how well she takes me, then surge back to the hilt. I repeat the motion, again and again, watching as her pussy swallows my cock like a custom-made glove.

Her throaty, sexy as fuck moans consume me as her desire begins to grow once more. I plunge harder, deeper, faster, and her hips meet my tempo. I piston my hips ravenously, the sounds of our flesh and the moans of our desire and pleasure, a beautiful orchestra of lust and love, spurring each of our movements.

"Maddox," she cries out as she begins to spasm around me.

"That's it, baby." I reach for her throbbing clit, taking it between my fingers. "Come for me." And when I pinch and roll it between my fingers, she shatters and breaks. Her tight spasms and sweet cries trigger electricity in my belly and fire in my cock, and I free fall over the edge with a roar.

I reach up, release her wrist, and flip her over. Then I fall next to her, pulling her tightly into my side. The only sounds in the room are our heavy breathing as we both come down from our high.

Once I can breathe normally, I look down at her blissed-out face. Curls cling to her sweat-soaked skin. Rosy cheeks and hazy eyes reveal her afterglow. I lean over, taking her lips. She melts against me, and her soft sighs fill the air. "I love you, Canary. So fucking much."

Her fingers brush softly against my jaw, and her eyes fill with moisture. "I love you too," she whispers, the words catching her emotions.

The next few hours are spent wrapped in each other; our bodies merged as one again and again in an endless dance of rough, animalistic fucking and sweet, passionate lovemaking until the most seraphic sound cuts through, reminding us of the beautiful life we created together.

MADDOX

This is our destiny

One month later

"You've come a long way since you first came to me," Adam tells me with a smile.

I stretch my arms out wide. "I'm Maddox Masters. I'm nothing if not determined. Get it done right and fast. Do things perfectly."

"As long as you realize perfection isn't always attainable, right?" he counters with a grin.

"Eh..." I laugh. "Some things are easier to accept than others on that front."

I look around his office. It's been months since I've been here. All of our appointments were virtual while we were in River City. He's given the room a facelift. New, soft carpets cover the floors. The outdated wallpaper has been replaced with a fresh coat of tan paint. New bookshelves and a new desk bring the modern features back together. "Did a remodel?" I nod around the room.

"It was overdue. I meant to do it when I leased this space but never got around to it. How are you doing at home? With the baby and Quinn? Everything still okay?"

I smile widely as I think about the fact I'm running on four hours of sleep. "I'm used to no sleep. Years on the road prepared me. To be honest, I kind of like it."

"So the crying, round-the-clock feedings, and changings aren't getting to you? Causing stress?"

"No. But if it does, I'll call you."

I stand up as restlessness begins. My mind starts moving quickly, thinking about everything I need to do while I'm in the city. I walk to his window overlooking the city. "I'm not pretending everything is all right," I tell him. "I really am happy. Yes, life has been stressful the last few months, but Quinn is okay, I have my son, and I started working on getting to know Paul." I heave a heavy sigh. "I finally forgave my dad. It still fucking kills me that we didn't have time to repair our relationship, but I'm grateful I had those final weeks with him. I won't lie; talking about him is still hard. Still lots of regrets there."

"Understandable. What about Chris? How are you dealing with that?"

"You know how I'm dealing with that?" I growl. "I wish I could kill him again. And again. Quinn still has nightmares about all of that. I'm still so fucking pissed." I sigh, leaning my head back with my eyes closed. "But I'm trying to focus on the present. I can't change what he did or what happened. I can only decide how to move forward and move on."

"You quote me well," he laughs.

"Fuck you," I chuckle.

"Still taking the meds?"

"Every goddamn day. Yay me."

"You can't deny they help, Maddox. Especially after we adjusted the dosage. Not having so many superman days now."

"Those were always the days I liked," I joke.

"Yeah, they're usually the days most like, but the cost is high."

"Too fucking high." After a few seconds of silence, I turn around. "So we're going back on tour in the spring for six weeks. A lot fucking shorter than our last one, but our priorities have shifted. I'm not trying to avoid coming home anymore. I don't need to spend all my time hitting one city after another in a drunk, drug-fueled haze. But I admit that I'm nervous."

"About what?"

"The road. There's so much shit—temptation. I'm worried what will happen when it's constantly in reach."

He points to the chair I was sitting in, telling me to sit. With a huff, I oblige. "Are you worried about the drugs and alcohol or the women?"

"Not the women," I scoff. "Even with Quinn, they're always in an annoying abundance."

"But it will be different when she's not right there with you."

"No, it won't. I don't want anyone else. I would never do anything to jeopardize that."

"Then why are you worried about the drugs and alcohol? They're just as big a jeopardy. Why do you think they would be a problem?"

I shrug. "Because I *still want them* now," I tell him honestly.

"One day at a time, Maddox. Don't worry about that until it's time. Speaking of time."

"Yeah," I nod. "I have some business to take care of."

"Talk to you on Friday."

I walk out of the room, through the building, to the elevator. I climb into my SUV, annoyed to be chauffeured again but unable to deny the convenience when I'm in the city. We drive the short distance through ridiculous traffic to the label building. I spot the couple of the guys' cars and direct Darren to park next to them. My phone goes off in my pocket just as I'm getting out. Ryder pulls up next to us as I open the text.

My brows fall, and I wonder what kind of joke this is. "What's wrong?" Ryder asks.

I show him the number, and his eyes swirl with doubt and suspicion. I open it and the picture message loads, followed by a message to tell no one. "What the..."

"That son of a bitch." I mutter under my breath, irritated at yet another fucking secret but also filled with... hope.

"Think it's real?"

"Don't know, but you better believe I'm asking Bastian because he'll sure as hell know. Come on. Let's get in there and take care of business," I nod toward the door. "We've got women to get back to."

"First, I want to say thanks for joining us," I tell the room full of the label's artists and employees as I lean against the window with my hands in my pocket.

"No problem, Mads," Tyler King, the guitarist for Dirty Minds, calls out. I look around for their lead singer, not shocked that Blaze Erikson thought he was too good to come to a mandatory meeting with the people that signs his checks. "But weren't we supposed to meet the new owners today?"

"You're looking at them," I gesture between Ryder and me.

Whispered gasps echo through the room, which quickly turns to loud chattering. After a few minutes, Dane whistles loudly. "Shut the hell up so he can speak," he yells, then nods my way.

I shake my head with a grin.

After Asher was born, I didn't leave the hospital for a week. Eventually, though, at Quinn's encouragement—and Ryder dragging me—I finalized my part of my dad's estate with my signature. Signing my name on all those papers made everything feel so final. I don't know how I managed to get through it without breaking in the attorney's office, but the moment I was in the car, I cried. I shed tears over regret and time wasted, knowing that this was it. The only way to make amends with my dad was to forgive him and move on because he wasn't here anymore. That made me cry harder because, despite all our difference, he was still my dad. I loved him so much, and a part of me would also feel missing without him, just as I had with my mom. It would never matter if they were my biological parents. They were my parents all the same.

I also decided that I didn't want any more damn regrets or to look back at the wasted time I spent holding on to memories I couldn't change. So when I left the attorney's office, I went to see Paul. We talked more without the weight of a crisis looming over my head. I couldn't look at him like a dad. I had one of those. But I needed to know him, and he wanted to know me. And Asher needed a grandfather. Even if it happened to be Paul Delrie, ex-mafioso.

Then I had one last thing to settle. Bastian didn't want his part of the label. He only went in with dad because it was for me. He wanted me to take it off his hands, but I had a better idea. Or so I thought.

I approached the guys with an idea. We would divide the shares five ways. The band would own the label. That went down the toilet fast when Jake, Angel, and Dane turned me down. Said they weren't interested in the business side of the music and never had been. Then said it should be Ryder and me because this—all of it—was always our dream. We just let them tag along for the ride.

They were wrong about tagging along. Without them, there would be no us. But they weren't wrong about the dream. Even before the band, Ryder and I had countless discussions about making it big. On our own, with no help from our families. And though we may have funded a thing or two once we struck it big, we did exactly what we set out. We worked our asses off and made a name for ourselves. But even back then, our dreams were bigger than just a band. We wanted to build a label where we did things the way we wanted.

So Ryder bought Bastian out.

"Wait," Dylan says, "you're the new owners? It's been you all this time?"

"Not all this time," Ryder tells him. "We only recently took over."

We agreed no one needed to know the details. They only needed to know that we were the ones running the show now.

"As all of you know, I only recently got back into town with my wife and son. Then we had the holidays to get through, so we waited to make the big announcement. First to you guys, then later today to the press." I tell them all.

"Where does that leave all of us?" Heidi asks, barely making eye contact. I'm sure she's remembering her last comment to me about not signing her checks.

"Changes will be made that will benefit everyone, but they won't be made today. Today, it's business as usual." I answer her, then add."By the way, everyone, welcome to Sin Records."

They all murmur excitedly as they leave the room until everyone is gone except my band and Liam.

"Went well," Jake nods from his chair. "They all seemed genuinely pleased it's you guys."

"Still doesn't feel right without all of you," I tell them.

"He's right," Ryder agrees. "We do this shit together. Feels all out of whack, ya know."

"Dudes, when we're not recording or on the road, I got a tattoo shop I need to pretend I own. Jake is usually elbow-deep in grease in his grandfather's shop. You guys know he's going to help there as much as he can. At least until his uncle and grandfather decide to close the place." He jerks his thumb toward Angel with a smirk. "This fucker, I don't know."

Angel shakes his head and shrugs. "I don't want to play on the business end. Did enough back in LA to know it's not my thing. But I wouldn't mind working as a producer."

"Who knows? Maybe one day, when our superstar days are behind us, we'll all want to come in and work in some other area. But I'd still rather leave the hard shit to you guys. You're made for this. Both of you." Jake tells us.

"If you guys ever change your mind, a few pen strokes will—"

"Maddox," Dane laughs. "We're good. You and Ryder make this the most badass label on the planet. Just like you've done with the band."

"Fine." I huff, and Ryder grunts.

"On that note," Dane slaps a hand across Angel's chest. "I have a release party to plan. Needs to be extra special for Quinn."

I laugh. The full album dropped today. It was instantly number one. Quinn is officially a number one selling artist, even if it's just as a duet with me or as backup on other songs.

"I think maybe this is what he's secretly doing on the side," Ryder smirks. "First, the welcome home party that he had us decorate to the nines for Christmas. Now, this."

"Either that or he's trying to lure Quinn away from you," Angel adds.

"Not unless he likes swallowing around his asshole," I grunt.

"I am *not* a secret party planner, and I do not want Quinn," He scowls.

"Aw, look, you hurt his feelings," Jake says.

"Fuck all of you," Dane mutters.

"We already told you you're not our type," I cackle.

"What the hell? I never—" he yells as Jake pushes him out the door.

"I'm kinda hurt, Dane. You never even looked my way," Angel taunts as he follows behind them.

"I never..." Dane's voice trails off when the door clicks shut behind them, leaving us alone with Liam.

I level him with a hard gaze. "I know things haven't been great with us. Believe me when I tell you that I'm trying. If you haven't figured it out, I have a history of hanging on to the past."

He waves me off with a flip of his hand, then drags it through this long hair. "You have every right to be pissed. If I were in your shoes, I would've cut you off. I'm not making excuses, but I let the shit in my personal life influence how I treated Quinn. She didn't deserve it."

"Things better now?" Ryder asks, his brows pitched with curiosity.

"Yeah-uh-actually, not really. It's not important. Just bs with... Personal stuff."

"Your ex?" Ryder shoots me a sideways glance. "Casey? What's going on?"

"Like I said, not important." He's always so damn tight-lipped about his past, but I have no room to talk.

But... "Liam, I get secrets, man. We both do. But if you need to talk..." I let the sentence hang between us.

"Guess that's one thing that can't get reprogrammed, can it, man? Your need to save everyone."

I grin and shrug. "Not save. Just listen."

He nods. "I know, Maddox."

"Anyway, down to brass tax," Ryder says, always effectively changing the subject when we're dangling too close to feelings. "We want you to be our A&R VP."

"Holy shit," Liam mutters.

"Look, man, you've played a huge part in helping us these last few years. I know you don't have any interest in trying to cut your own album again or even a song, but you've got too much damn knowledge and talent, and it's wasted just being our manager."

He runs a hand over his two-day scruff, looking speechless. "You know I stayed on here, despite Davis and my ex because it helped me stay closer to Casey. Or at least I thought it would. I should've known they'd send me on the road with every band they had. I knew I was never going to move up. No way was Davis going to let that happen. Then you guys came along and changed everything. And now you're doing it again. Thank you. Both of you."

"There's a catch," Ryder tells him with a wicked gleam.

I have a smirk of my own when there's a tap on the door. *Right on time.* "We want you to personally work with our very first brand new artist."

He leans back with a wide grin. "Absolutely."

Ryder and I walk to the door, chuckling like Satan himself.

I open the door, and she steps inside with dark sparkling eyes of excitement. And possibly a bit of smugness.

"I believe you two know each other," I say with a straight face, then quickly step out of the room with Ryder. "We'll just leave you to it."

"Maddox! Ryder! Hell—" I shut the door, drowning him out.

Ryder and I burst into laughter as we make our way through the building. "We're going to hell for that, you know?" I grin widely.

"Add it to the list."

ACKNOWLEDGMENTS

There are too many to thank and not enough words to express the depth of gratitude I feel for each person that has walked with me through this insane journey. Readers, fans, and friends—you've all played a detrimental role in my career on both professional and personal levels. Words aren't enough.

Daria and Sionna, you two aren't my friends; you're my other half—or thirds. Maybe I could've done this without you, but I wouldn't want to. Your support goes beyond writing and books into personal. You've listened to me cry and laugh. Held my hand when I thought I couldn't do it anymore. And encourage me to strive for greatness and accept praise, no matter how reluctant I am to accept either. I love you girls more than you will ever know.

Anita, thank you so much for always being there. Even around the world, you light up my day, and your giant heart slays me. I can only hope that one day I can be as generous, thoughtful, and kind as you. Loves you big.

Crystal, you are one hell of a cheerleader. You bust your ass for me without much thanks. You step up when I think I'm going to lose my mind. I can't thank you enough for everything you do.

My beautiful Naughty Nerds, you make me laugh to the point of tears with our ridiculous conversations and pics that always seem to appear just when I need it the most. Thank you all for your unwavering support. And I apologize to those in the group that gets blasted by the ridiculousness, but you have to admit, you laughed too.

To every single reader that has taken the time to read the words, I've written. I can never repay the debt. I can only say thank you for loving these stories and living them with me.

A special thanks to Alter Bridge. Shed My Skin inspired Maddox and many more of their songs influenced the direction of this book, and will continue to influence book two. If you haven't had a chance to listen, go check out their songs in the playlist.

ABOUT THE AUTHOR

Louisiana-born and raised, Nola Marie loves spicy crawfish, rock music, high drama, and all the glitter. Full of brutal honesty and sarcasm, only the strongest survive in her presence. She is a true southern mom with the attitude and mouth to prove it and fiercely protective of those she deems worthy of her unwavering loyalty.

Evil to the bone, she rejuvenates her life forces with the blood of her characters and the tears of her readers. With books that shred your heart and burn your soul, it's no wonder she has been dubbed Mistress of Evil, and fans have given her the tagline: I live to break hearts...

Have you connected? Be sure to subscribe to my newsletter and join me on Facebook and Instagram.

Don't forget to join Nola's Naughty Nerds on Facebook where you can get recovery support from other readers.

OTHER BOOKS BY NOLA MARIE

River City Series

Welcome to Louisiana, where the weather isn't nearly as steamy as the romance. River City has it all. History, professional sports... organized crime. But the real draw are the men. Hot as hell, dominant, and unapologetic when it comes to protecting their women. These bad boys will have your panties melting with their style of no holds barred loving. Whether it's on the gridiron, in the city's underworld, or in the bedroom, the men of River City are all-in.

Violent Life

Zoey: Greek origin meaning life

Jax

That's what Zoey is for me. My life. The breath in my lungs and blood in my veins. It's been that way since the first day we met and will be that way forever. She ignites the fire within me, both for good and bad, and she calms the resulting inferno. She is on my mind and in my heart every time I throw the football or a punch. Zoey is the name etched on my soul.

Violent Night

Layla: Arabic or Hebrew origin meaning night

Rory

The night calls to me. I've lived in its shadows for so long, knowing that my crimes keep me from the light of real happiness. Then Layla comes back into my life. The elusive, seductive innocence that once stole my heart has grown into a maddening, vibrant seductress that fires my blackened soul. But I've grown too, and the night is now my playground. And I will never stop protecting what's mine. With Layla back in my life, the southern nights have never seemed hotter.

Violent Truth

Verity: Latin origin meaning truth

Sebastian

The truth has long been a bitter thing for me. Something I prefer to avoid. And when Verity appears like a shining beacon inside the dark club I own with my best friend, I do my very best to drive her away. But the truth is, I'm already addicted. The truth is, she can bring me to my knees. The truth, my ultimate truth, is Verity.

Violent Victory

Victoria: Latin origin meaning victory

Zane

I'm all about victory. On the football field, in business, and in fights. So, when Tori issues her own brand of challenge, I'm confident I'll win. Stubbornness is a family trait, after all. I hadn't anticipated that it might be a trait in her family too. But that doesn't matter. In the end, I know I'll win. Her heart, our happily ever after. I didn't consider that someone else might decide to enter our game. Now that they have, I'm kicking things into overdrive. Because Victoria is mine, and I'll be damned before anyone takes her from me.

Sons of Sin

Music isn't the only seduction with this band...

Sons of Sin is taking the world by storm. Hot, talented, and driven, nothing can stop the bad boys of the music world from reaching the top. Except their broken souls. Struggling against the demons of their pasts, each band member buries his pain in the age-old trinity, sex, drugs, and rock 'n' roll. Until love tears through their carefully constructed veneers like a bat out of Hell. Not one of these broken boys thinks their souls are worth saving. But will claiming their women fast-track the Sons of Sin straight through the Gates of Hell, or will true love grant them absolution?

Goodbye is a Second Chance

Angel

Anger and pride are my besetting sins. Both ignited by the same infuriating woman. I thought they'd be my companions for life, the only ones still with me longer than my bandmates. Then little Josie strolls back into the remnants of the world she burned on her way out the door ten years ago and sets me on fire once again. But this time, things are different. Sure, I might burn, but this time I'll make damn sure I don't burn alone.

Bed of Nails

Dane

If I had to own to one sin, my friends and family would likely say it's overprotectiveness. Maybe with a dash of righteous fury I have trouble controlling. I'm not apologizing for any of it though. When I see the people I love in danger, I react. And when it comes to a certain female best friend, I know my reactions are over the top. But so is the sheer lust I feel whenever Cami's near. Both are driven by my heart.

Shooting Star in the Rain

Jake

Years ago, lies kept me from shooting my shot with the girl of my dreams. But since those lies gave me my angel of a daughter, I was okay with it. Mostly. Now though, the girl of my dreams is back, except Cara's a woman now. Sexy and beautiful enough to set my soul afire. Broken enough to break my heart too. Lies and concealing the truth seem to be our currency now, but I'll be damned before I let any of it keep us apart again.

Break Me Down

Ryder

Anger consumed me, but it was Heaven who shattered me. Now, nothing but rage fills this empty shell I call a body. I do my best to control it. Drugs, alcohol. Sex. But the reprieve is all too brief. Then she comes back into my life. Secrets fly through the air like shards of glass, slicing what's left of my soul to ribbons. But Heaven is the most addictive drug of all.

Shed My Skin

Maddox

I'm the one who came up with our band's name. Because I am Sin. I have lived in Hell every day of my life. Every sin known to man, I've committed. Every vice mortals have ever used to forget their pain, I've tried. But I'm tired. My fight is nearly depleted. It's only for my friends, those I call family, that I've continued this long. They're happy now, and I have nothing left to give. Until Quinn, with her whiskey eyes and lullabies waltzes her way into my heart. For her, I can last just a little longer. Quinn is one more soul it will be my honor to heal.

Breathe Again

Maddox

My sins burned me to flames. I was ready to accept my punishment. But in my eleventh hour, I received a stay of execution. A reprieve. Another chance to atone for my crimes. The greatest of all was denying that this whiskey-eyed angel had changed me. She stayed despite my transgressions. Continued to fight for me when she had every reason to walk away. So for her, I will hold on and fight the demons that haunt me. She's not my cure, but she is my reason. My reason to breathe again.

COMING 2023

Wicked Games

Made in the USA
Columbia, SC
04 April 2024